*For those with a fire living beneath their skin. I hope you let it rise. I hope you let it burn.*

# RISE OF THE ASH KINGDOM

A SUN AND MOON TALE

ELIZABETH R. OLSON

https://www.elizabethrolson.com

Paperback ISBN 979-8-9912404-0-6

Hardback ISBN 979-8-9912404-1-3

eBook ISBN 979-8-9912404-2-0

Cover design by Stefanie Saw at SeventhStar Art. Editing by Heidi Shoham. Map by Virginia Allen. Author picture by Brandon Ross. Interior decorative elements by Belle O.

Printed in the United States of America

First Edition

Rise of the Ash Kingdom by Elizabeth R. Olson

ELYSIAN
ZERAH SEA
VALHALLA
Tynan's Chalet
Bramberg
Ice Palace
The Whispering Sands
THE GARDEN
Clive Steppe
Tamar
Ice Bridge
KALOPSIA
The Everwood
Palace
KASHMIR
The Pier
Cozbi's Temple
Bristol Gate
Palace
Market
EMPYREAN
GENESI
Palace
Fugberg Mountains
The Wildlands
MYSTIC ISLES

Pronunciation Guide

<u>Characters:</u>
Cozbi: Cause-bee
Darya: Dar-ya
Mavi: Ma-vee
Xosha: Zo-sha
Zafar: Za-far
Zima: Zee-ma

<u>Places:</u>
Elysian: E-lease-e-in
Empyrean: Em-peer-re-n
Genesi: Gin-nah-sea
Kalopsia: Ka-lop-see-a
Kashmir: Kash-mere
Valhalla: Val-hall-a

<u>Events:</u>
Solunar Saudade: (So-lunar Sow-dah-jee)

<u>Creatures:</u>
Najaonca: (Nah-yuh On-suh)

"Courage, dear heart."

— C.S. LEWIS, THE VOYAGE OF THE DAWN
TREADER

BEFORE

Controlling my anger was often like swallowing fire.

It waited, a constant swirl of warmth around the curves of my heart. Dormant, until not. Until someone nudged the inferno awake for no other reason than because they could. Because they knew I'd let them. The rush of flames would then detach from their anchor and leap for my esophagus. Until some invisible force reached out and tossed a blanket over the blaze, smothering it.

I'd like to call it self-control, but it was something else, something beyond me. And the truth was, I was scared of what that fire would burn to ash if it were ever allowed to surface.

This time, the invisible hand kept a firm grip over the waiting rage before the front door opened. Before the truck pulled into the driveway even. I could never fall asleep until after he got home, despite it being well past the sun's bedtime.

The door surged open and bounced off the ever-present dent in the wall. I silently thanked the mysterious tight grip that never gave my anger the chance to surface.

Had this not all been familiar, my brother and I would have thought someone was breaking in. We knew better by now.

A tall, lean shadow of a man awkwardly loomed in the doorframe, moonlight pooling in to expose his unstable footsteps, confirming what I already knew. No, we weren't being robbed. Dad was just home.

My brother's body tensed on his side of our layered pallet of blankets where we were meant to be sleeping. I was never sure if he tensed with nerves or a matching anger. Maybe it was a little of both. But his warning from years ago ran through my head each night this happened: *Do not make a sound. Do not call attention to yourself.*

Dad tripped and staggered down, and though I didn't see him hit the floor, I knew what one of his drunken stumbles in the house at two or three in the morning sounded like. He and everything within arm's reach went down with a sharp slurring of every curse word he knew. He crawled himself back up the wall, like the creature he was, and another loud tumble sounded as he crashed to the ground again, making even the bare walls rattle.

There was more cursing. Something about damning this whole place to hell before he picked up the closest thing within reach—a shoe this time—and chucked it across the house. The floor plan of our small one story, one bedroom house wasn't very large to begin with, but it was still an impressive throw for a drunk. The shoe flew from the entryway of the living room, past our homemade bed of blankets on the floor, and into the kitchen. It bounced off the back window and landed in the sink, making the dishes piled inside it clatter.

If my dad wasn't such a colossal disappointment, it would have been no surprise at all that he'd been a promising football player in high school and most of college. Until he wasn't. Until his too young girlfriend became pregnant, and the only way to make ends meet was for him to drop out. Until he blamed her for his shortcomings for the rest of his life.

He stumbled through the tiny living room, incoherent mumblings pouring from him every step of the way. Apparently, everything—the house, the kids, the girl that left him at the bar, we were all pieces of shit.

I closed my eyes tightly, pretending to sleep as he walked by us like we were nothing more than a rumpled heap of neglected laundry on the floor. Dad shuffled into the kitchen, only stopping when his knee hit a cabinet. He gripped the sink with both hands, holding himself up as his legs gave way underneath him. His head tossed back, a wolf in the night, and howled.

I willed my heart to beat softer in my chest, irrationally afraid he'd hear its thumping.

But he only flipped on the faucet and ducked his head to drink. When he finished, he eyed the shoe on top of the dishes, now wet and heavy, and examined it menacingly before tossing it out of his way. His laughter filled the house before the shoe landed, hitting Liam in the forehead. If there was any pain from it, my brother stifled it, refusing to move a muscle to avoid the attention. We'd grown quite good at that. Not that Dad would have noticed, as he laughed so hard he had to bend over and grip his knees for support. Hate bubbled in my chest.

Once he zigzagged his way into the one and only bedroom, and slammed the door shut behind him, the night returned to the sound of crickets chirping distantly beyond the windows. A dog barking from three houses down. A car backfiring from the street over. All the things that made up a normal functioning neighborhood. It was odd, insulting even, the way everything floated back to a peaceful night like that. Like we weren't even here.

"Are you okay?" I whispered.

Liam moved then, reaching under his pillow for his iPod. "It wasn't that hard of a throw. I'm fine," my brother lied.

I picked up the wet, gross sneaker that lay between us and set it off the covers as the light of Liam's iPod screen illuminated his face. Apart from the knot already surfacing above his left eyebrow, the light revealed features that were an equal mix of our parents. The sun-bleached hair and shining smile from our mother, but the chestnut eyes and athletic build from our dad's talented and wasted gene pool. My darker features were also an equal mix, only the polar opposite of Liam. I inherited my mother's bright eyes and my father's much darker hair color.

Liam shuffled through his playlist until he found a song he liked, slipped an earpiece into his ear, and then scooted closer so that he could hand me the other. Music. Our only way of escape from the things that filled this house. A sweet, somber male voice hummed in tone with a violin through the earpiece.

"Liam?" I whispered over the melody.

I searched for the words to express how grateful I was that he was my brother. He was old enough to leave this hell, but not quite old enough to support the both of us on his own.

So he stayed, he endured until he could leave with me. The right words never came, so I sighed instead and fell asleep to the sound of the sad string instrument and my brother's deep, sleepy, breathing.

It had always been this way between us. For as long as I could remember, it was Liam and I against the world—or against our drunken single parent, who at best ignored us on a sober day. There was something in that mixture of barley and wheat he loved more than anything in this world, but he lost himself in it. I gave up wondering why he bothered with it, knowing he couldn't handle himself like that. Gave up wondering whether he was like this because Mom left or if she had left because he was like this. It didn't matter.

The next day would be Liam's eighteenth birthday, his year of freedom. His year of escape. Except he wouldn't escape. He'd stay right here at this house of disappointments with me, for two more years until I reached the age of escape too. Two more years until Liam and I had agreed to combine our savings and leave together, start fresh—together. The same way we'd survived all these years since Mom left. Together.

"We should see a movie," I said the next afternoon, meeting Liam at the front steps as school let out for the day.

"A movie?" Such a normal thing for such normal kids. Except we weren't normal. What business did we have in a movie theater? But for a night, we could pretend.

I gave him a sweet little sister smile he couldn't argue with. His own half-smile was handsome. A flash of straight teeth and brightness—a rare sight. "Alright," he caved. "What are we going to see?"

"It's your birthday. You pick."

"Anything that involves an adventure."

I nodded in agreement. "An adventure it is."

We shared a large extra-buttery popcorn over a movie with plenty of action and no romance, much to Liam's liking. We decided to really go for it, this normal night of normal things, and got ice cream afterward. We joked, we laughed, we pretended. And for a glimpse that night, I saw the version of my brother he was meant to be. A carefree, popular seventeen—now eighteen-year-old—who would be off to college in a few months. I'd miss him, of course, but visit way too often. I imagined meeting his girlfriend, going to his football games. Playing the annoying little sister role as I tried and failed not to fall in love with his best friend and he lectured me about dating older guys.

It would never be that way for us though. We would never know that life. In a world like this, Liam didn't have plans for college. He wasn't on a sports team and I wasn't falling in love anytime soon.

Tomorrow, Liam would wake up, eighteen years and a day old, and everything would be just as it had always been. A repetitive cycle of hiding, surviving, and walking on eggshells with our heads down. And despite it all, it would be okay because at least we'd have each other.

But at some point during the night while I was fast asleep, something changed. Our plan was altered without confiding in the other and I woke up alone.

It was the last night I trusted again. And it was the last night I ever saw my brother.

# CHAPTER ONE

"Table eleven is all yours, Briar."

I blinked at the hostess's voice, so overwhelmed by the end of a double shift that my brain had checked out before my last table had.

My feet ached, exhaustion weighed on my eyelids, and my brain was numb from the amount of times the tip line had been left empty today.

"Oh—" I blinked, my own words barely registering. "That was actually supposed to be my last table of the night. Could you give it to someone else? Someone who is already closing maybe?"

Mattie waved me off, flipping open a kid's menu to color while there were no guests for her to greet.

I rubbed at my forehead, filtering through all the possible ways I could say no without actually saying no. "I'll be here all night if I take that table."

"They always tell me which sections to close for the night before they tell the servers." She scribbled away with a dark-green crayon that matched her eyes. "And no one's told me your section is done."

A spark flickered awake. I inhaled smoothly enough for Mattie not to notice. "I've been here for going on ten hours. I haven't eaten since I came in this morning." A lie. I hadn't eaten even then.

The kid's menu snapped shut and Mattie's sharp eyes met mine with only a third of the irritation bubbling inside me. "You know, they've been sitting there for like five minutes now, right? You could have gotten their drinks out to them by now instead of standing here talking to me."

The flames leapt for her. My nails grated into the wood of the hostess stand.

But then I did what I always do. I blinked. I unclenched my teeth. My fingers relaxed, and I swallowed the fire at the base of my throat, sending it back to its resting place. Wordlessly, I turned on my heel, reaching inside my apron for a pen and pad, and plastered on an unconvincing smile for my newest table.

My cheeks were still burning and my chest was only beginning to cool by the time I dragged myself up the flight of stairs to the second level of my apartment complex, the late night just beginning to nudge into a new day. When I walked through that door, everything that weighed me down throughout the day would be left at the doormat. I'd take a shower, letting the warm water rinse away what was left of the blush on my cheeks, along with the smell of steak and grilled chicken. I'd let it wash everything away, having trained myself a long time ago to leave even the most recent of pasts behind.

I shuffled through my keys but dropped them at a sudden bang that vibrated from the other end of the door. My body caved in on itself, readying for whatever strike was coming. But familiar laughter was the only thing that filtered through the thin walls.

My chest rose and fell too fast. I hated myself for it. Every single time I flinched from a sudden movement or sound, even if I was the only one around to witness it, I was ashamed of the way my body reacted. I leaned my head against the door, frustrated that all these years later, I was still the same scared little girl I'd always been.

*I'm safe here.* I thought. *It's safe here.*

Collecting myself, I stepped inside, setting my keys in the bowl beside the door, and ventured into the kitchen where my roommate and her friends were gathered, pizza and solo cups littering the counter. A trash can had fallen over and Leah was bending over to set it upright. A simple trash can. That was the perpetrator this time. Embarrassment flooded me again.

Leah's face lit up as I entered. "Briar!"

I smiled, hoping the dark circles under my eyes weren't truly as heavy as they felt. The others greeted me in unison, Viv handing me a slice of pizza and reminding me of the empty pit in my stomach. Forgetting about a shower, I bit into it. It tasted cheap and heavenly. Ian offered me a solo cup, already knowing my answer. His smile was warm and inviting. Hopeful even. I felt guilty as I shook my head as politely as possible.

"To this moment," Rhett belted out, a pepperoni and mushroom slice raised in the air just an inch away from Ian's face. Ian tried to bite a piece off the end and Rhett jerked it away.

"Let it live on forever!" Viv finished the mantra for him.

I stood a step outside of their circle, watching them lift their cups as their voices shouted as one, "And ever and ever!"

Viv and Rhett wrapped their arms around each other, Leah and Ian's knuckles conveniently brushed when reaching for a slice of pizza, and I quietly slid over to the sink, filling a solo cup with water to avoid looking so obviously out of place.

I didn't have to pretend long before Viv and Rhett wrapped themselves in whispered secrets too funny to share with the rest of us and Ian passed out on the living room floor. Leah could have pretended to be tired, but she wasn't the kind to leave an outsider out. We found ourselves sitting cross-legged on the balcony with a near-empty pizza box between us.

"So," I started, "how much longer do you think you can pretend you aren't falling in love with Ian?"

She grinned through a bite of pizza. "I'll say the same thing I say every time someone asks me that. I have no earthly idea what you're talking about."

Leah and Ian had been dancing the same dance since I'd met them, sharing quick glances, sending risky texts, and sometimes their fingertips got suspiciously close to touching in public, but that had been as far as either were willing to take it. I reached out with my leg and pushed the ajar sliding door closed. "No lying on the balcony. That was your rule, remember?"

Leah rolled her eyes but then squeezed them shut tightly and lifted her head to the stars. "God, he's so perfect."

"Then why not?"

"Because of the fact that he's so perfect! I need that man in my life, even if it's just as my friend. I don't want to mess this up." She glanced at his sleeping form through the glass door, a frustrated sort of longing blanketing her features.

I shook my head at their stubbornness.

"Oh, come on," Leah said. "You're one to talk. In the year we've been roommates, I've never once seen you bring someone home. If I have to admit my truth, so do you."

Usually, Leah respected the unspoken tension I wore like an oversized sweater, but every now and then she'd tap on the wall I'd built so high to see if I was ready to invite her in. Like all the other times, I didn't. "Relationships are complicated." I shrugged. "Who enjoys complicated things?" It wasn't a lie. Not really.

I reached for another slice of pizza, but Leah's hand moved faster, landing on my arm.

"I know you don't like to talk about it, whatever *it* is, but I wish you wouldn't hold so much in to deal with by yourself." The gleam of the moon reflected in her brown eyes, and my heart dropped at the boldness and honesty reflecting in her gaze. "I don't know all the reasons why, and I'm not asking you to tell me everything," she went on, "but I do hope one day you'll feel like you can. If not to me, then to someone. You deserve that. Someone given to you who you feel you can trust with those things. You deserve to be *happy*, Briar." She said the word happy like she knew I wasn't.

With my free hand, I fidgeted with the locket around my neck, the sudden attention making me uncomfortable. Her words, the truth and sincerity of them, hit a nerve I didn't know was there.

The locket had been my mother's. She used to say it reminded her of another life, another place. Of hope. I could never understand why she'd left something so meaningful behind. The day we came home from school to only one parent, Dad was in one of his drunken fits, crying violently and swearing as he stumbled, gathering up her clothes and belongings. We didn't understand what was happening, but something in me lunged for the locket on her bedside table, rescuing it before the rest of her things went up in a song of flames in the backyard. I wrapped it around my ankle, covering it with my pant leg so he would never see it and force me to get rid of it. It wasn't until I left too that I started wearing it around my neck like a normal person.

Leah gave my arm a loving squeeze before letting go.

Her words followed me even when I found myself restless in bed half an hour later. I shifted, fighting sleep for a reason I couldn't place.

I wanted to open up to Leah. I wanted to share with her why I chose not to drink, why I never made much of an effort to become a part of her friend group. But in all honesty, I didn't know how. How do I open my heart to someone when those who were supposed to love me the most had let me down time and time again? And if I did, if Leah knew how ugly the truth was, would she stay?

I already knew the answer to that. One thing was as certain as the rent's due date: everyone I cared about disappointed me. So if keeping Leah in the dark was what kept her around, that's where she would stay, just on the border of light.

My fingertips grazed the locket I never took off, and my eyes finally drifted closed. I was so exhausted that the dream came before my eyes closed all the way. I only dreamed in flashes, glimpses barely there long enough to stay. I dreamed of colors too rich to be real. Of greens so lush and vivid and flickers of a blue so blue it was almost green. Of the deepest purple that momentarily soothed every worry I'd ever owned. I dreamed of a place that couldn't be real. I dreamed of hope for the future. Of a home that didn't exist.

Bright light rudely pushed through the curtains, forcing me to participate in yet another mundane routine. Feeling as if I hadn't actually slept at all, I begrudgingly pushed myself out of bed and trudged over to the bathroom mirror.

After throwing some water on my face, I scooped my many long, mocha-colored locks into a loose ponytail and then took a second look. My ivory skin had some natural color in the cheeks already, so I rarely bothered with makeup, though I'd probably be prettier with it. The only thing that stood out about me were my eyes—sometimes blue, sometimes green. Sometimes the two colors combined, but the one thing that remained unchanged was the bright ring of yellow bursting from the center. My mother's eyes.

I slipped on a fresh set of clothes and poked my head out of my room. Rhett and Viv were still passed out; Viv's dark-brown skin relaxing on top of Rhett's much paler chest. Her dark space buns were still perfectly intact from last night, his tousled blond hair not so much. But Ian was gone from his place on the floor.

Leah's bedroom door opened then, her long golden hair falling carelessly down her shoulders and onto a white T-shirt that grazed just above her knees. I scanned her up and down, a delayed but wicked smile spreading as I recognized who had worn that shirt last.

*"Oh my God,"* I mouthed dramatically seconds before a shirtless Ian appeared at her side. He wore only his usual silver chain around his neck and a pair of jeans I could tell he'd just tugged on. He wrapped an arm around her middle, cedar brown hair nuzzling her neck as he leaned in to place a gentle kiss there.

"Smoothies?" she whispered, trying not to wake Viv and Rhett. I gave an approving nod and waited while she changed into her own clothes.

The smoothie café up the road from our apartment served as Leah's nutrient replenisher after she'd demolished them the night before. It didn't matter how hungover she was the next morning, it was our thing. It was her way of saying that even though I didn't go out with them, she still wanted to do things with me.

"Are you going to spill or not?" I asked on the way back to my pickup truck, smoothies in hand. All she'd told me on the short drive over was that after our talk last night, she'd made a last-minute decision before going to her room. She'd told me there was a kiss she hadn't planned. How her heart had raced with nerves, but then he'd placed his hand on the back of her head and deepened the kiss. How nothing had felt more right in her entire life. We arrived at the smoothie café before she could tell me what happened behind closed doors.

Leah's smile was the most content I'd ever seen. "Later. After my headache goes away. I need focus to give the details of last night the justice it deserves."

I hopped into the driver's seat. Leah went straight for the aux cord, and a few seconds later, Shania Twain's voice filled the air. Leah let out an echoing "Ow!" to "Man, I Feel Like a Woman." I stopped at the red light.

Leah reached for the radio volume and turned it down so that the twangy lyrics could hardly be heard. "I do love you, Bry," she said, relaxing back in her seat and taking a sip of smoothie.

I faltered at such foreign words. My mind tried to reject the statement, tried to convince myself I'd misheard, but as they settled in the air, I knew I'd heard them and knew that the words spoke true. As much as I tried to stay distant, Leah cared about me. And she would keep caring about me, all of me. If I could just be brave enough to put the words together. I vowed that by the end of the day I would.

I forced my next words out. "I think I might come out with you next time."

Surprise blossomed from the passenger seat. "Yeah?"

"Maybe just as the designated driver. So you won't have to get a cab or anything. And I don't think I have anything to wear but—"

"Briar," Leah interrupted and I whipped my head in her direction, worried my hesitance had ruined it. "I'd love that. We'd all love that."

My lips stretched into a smile I hadn't planned. Leah's own smile sparkled as she kicked a foot up on the dash, the sun spotlighting her. She lowered her voice, eyes closed in contentment. "To this moment."

It wasn't my mantra to complete, but Leah had once again tapped on the wall, and this time, I would crack open the door. Just a little bit.

"Let it live on forever," I added, feeling lighter for the first time in years. In all my life maybe.

The traffic light turned green, and I led the rest of the cars into traffic.

Leah raised her smoothie to the sun. "And ever and ever!"

I barely registered the massive eighteen-wheeler that came barreling toward us until a jolt unlike anything I'd ever experienced crashed into my side. I never placed if it was me or Leah who screamed, or both. There was a smash and then several cracks as metal and bone caved in.

Sense of direction vanished after the second time my truck flipped. A cloud of darkness washed in from the corners of my eyes and took over everything else. It flooded in, wiping out my vision until consciousness slipped away with the rest of my senses.

Distant sounds faded in the same way they'd gone out. My body lay rigid, secured to something sturdy. Where the roof of a hand-me-down vehicle had just hung over me, a clear blue sky loomed instead. A muffled voice sounded above my head, a male face fizzling into view soon after it, and even sooner was replaced with a bright light that stung my eyes. I flinched away, a shockwave of lightning shooting up my neck in response, but the pain simultaneously vanished as my eyes landed on a worse pain. The scream in my throat got stuck at the sight of Leah's body, unmoving and bent in an unnatural position on the asphalt.

My body buzzed with urgency as a sheet was thrown over her. Everything pixelated. The punctured Styrofoam cup and its splattered contents. The flashing red ambulance lights. The paramedic's voice. A broken scream escaped my lungs, and if my body hadn't been nearly numb, I would have sworn it shook the earth. I called out her name over and over and over again. I fought the darkness as it reappeared, screaming at it even as I realized I would lose again. I screamed as it crept closer, weighing heavier. I screamed until it became the victor.

CHAPTER TWO

Of all the dark places I'd known, this had to be the darkest. A horizon of endless, soundless night stretched on in every direction.

Goosebumps blossomed violently along my arms and up my spine. Something didn't feel right. My body didn't feel like my own, as if it were untethered, lost even. In a blink, a pang of deep guilt and regret thudded in my chest. It buried itself inside and narrowed in around my heart, constricting tighter with each beat. My hand went to my chest, trying to soothe the guilt...the unplaced hurt. Whatever pain was there, I'd never felt anything like it. It was physical and emotional and *deep*.

My fingertips shot to my face in a panic, the brush of skin on skin the only thing to let me know I was really physically here. I ran them along a set of cold full lips, a small nose, the slender frame of my face, and then the outline of two, catlike-shaped eyes. I was all there. I was here, not knowing where here even was.

I waited. For sound. For a speck of light in the vast pit of darkness. But apart from my own shaky breath, it was just...Nothing.

I took a small unsure step. Repeatedly, I willed my body

forward until I tripped over my own foot, my gasp echoing into the void. My hands hit an icy, hard ground with a cold *plop*.

Despite the ground being spotless of gravel or dirt—anything to indicate a soul had been here before me—my palms burned. I lifted one to my face to inspect the damage, faintly able to make out the shape of my hand as I flipped it back and forth.

And then, as if someone opened a door, a sliver of light suddenly appeared and trickled in through the spaces between each of my fingers. I flinched and squinted from the sudden contrast, slamming my hand back on the ground.

At first, the light shimmered like the sun dancing on water, and then it grew and grew until it slowly transformed into something bigger, clearer. An image displayed like a projector playing a film, the light unraveling to reveal a girl lying flat on a bed with tubes coming out of her nose and needles taped to her hand. Everything in the room was blaringly white in contrast to the dark surrounding me, except for the pale-blue gown she wore and...the bruises. They were everywhere, green and black dotting her arms, her face, any visible skin the bedsheets didn't cover.

I took an involuntary step toward her, wanting to help, and my own outstretched hand caught my attention, stopping me short. The back of my hand, now visible from the light, reflected not only the clear shape of it, but the colors. It was spotted with a deep, nasty green and outlined in black and blue. My eyes flicked back to the girl's face, hesitantly examining her features underneath the bruising. Mocha colored locks, full lips, small frame.

Truth slammed through me just as hard as the semi-truck had. "*No.*"

The unplaced guilt, now very much accounted for, was like a punch in the gut.

*Leah.*

Her badly beaten body angled all wrong, the sheet raised over her closed eyes and too still body.

I collapsed. Breathing became too hard as a hundred memories of the two of us flashed in the front of my mind. Her name on my tongue filled the expanse of the darkness I kneeled in. My throat burned with it, my sobs so intense I had to clutch my head to stay upright.

Leah was dead. That was it. Everyone had officially left me, and I was... I was...

I found myself again in the image, found the monitor next to me. The beeping line made jumps much too far from the last, but the movement was constant, and a small shred of hope flickered to life. The fact that I was here meant I was disconnected but not dead. Not yet.

My eyes landed on my bare chest in the image, my fingers shooting up to my own chest and landing on my locket. Only one of us still wore the golden oval. My forefinger ran over the vines engraved on it, contemplating what it all meant.

I almost missed it. The flicker at the corner of my eye. I turned slowly, half afraid of what else I would find in this lifeless cage.

A yard or two from where two versions of myself existed, a second image was born. Beginning as just a blurry flick of stark white, it wrestled with itself to take a form, until the ball of light finally unwound, revealing bright specks of white and yellow mixed in with a blue background. The colors danced amongst themselves, refusing to fully reveal itself the way the first image had. But there was something else too. The colors...they *sang*. I strained to hear their muffled words but couldn't make out what they were saying on the other side.

The lyrics were a mystery, one so easy to solve, and yet I couldn't unfurl them. But the message was clear. That voice wanted me desperately, like no one had ever wanted me before. I found myself leaning toward it. Those sounds, those beautiful voices, coaxed me to come closer, to find out more about them.

A nurse walked into the other image, and the click of a door handle opening sounded. I blinked, snapping out of the trance. The singing halted.

I don't know how long I sat there with my arms wrapped around my legs, just staring at myself in the hospital bed as nurses walked in and out throughout the day to check vitals and change bandages. It could have been hours. Eventually, I wasn't really watching anymore. My eyes were fixed there, but my mind had wandered somewhere else, somewhere much darker. Though I'd spent the entirety of my adult life trying to forget, I let the memory slip through. One I thought I'd forgotten completely.

*Each punch rained down heavier and swifter than the last swing. All I could do was cover my head with a purple-spotted arm, and he knew it. There was no use ever fighting back, and he knew that too. The red synthetic leather met my forearm with a repetitive clack.*

*"Briar, you've got to keep your arms up." Liam took my wrist, lifting it higher up, away from my face, and holding it there firmly. We made eye contact that I tried to break, but he gave my wrist a little shake until I met his serious gaze again. "It'll save your face from getting bruised."*

*I wanted to cry, and I hated myself for it. I never did though. Never once had a single tear escaped my eyes since Mom left. That part of me just went void, hollow, to match the absence of her. Physically, I felt everything, while my face remained a smooth stone. If anything, I was proud of that much. At least no one would ever know how much it all hurt.*

*I readjusted my arm and tensed my body, preparing for the next strike.*

*Liam threw another forceful punch, but it wasn't the best he could do. My arm faltered half an inch, but I kept it above my head. He threw a harder punch that I wasn't expecting. My arm caved, and his fist continued past, landing solidly on my cheek. My face flew to the side. The sting in my cheek had me biting the inside of it in frustration and a sad kind of anger.*

*Liam groaned, and it was all I could do to meet his exasperated stare.*

*I knew he meant well. Liam was the only true-hearted person I knew. He meant well. "How hard is it to keep your arms up?"*

*"I'm not strong, Liam." I waved my scrawny arm in front of him to display the lack of muscle there. "If you want to teach me how to protect myself, I need to have some sort of arm strength to begin with. I need a different kind of training."*

*He shook his head like I knew he would. He sighed and softened his tone. "Arms up, kid."*

Liam's face disappeared when the singing behind me started up again—soft and light and more beautiful than any song on Liam's iPod. My cheeks were stained with tears, my long-held record forgotten and broken. From the memory of my brother's betrayal or from the loss of the only real friend I'd ever known, I couldn't tell the difference.

"What do you want?" I glared at the colorful song behind me.

This time, the words trickled through clearly. *"Come,"* it called. *"Come home."*

I laughed at the word. Home. As if I'd ever known the true meaning of the word. I was dead, or damn near close to it, and *home* was calling to me, wherever that was.

The colors thrashed wildly, the singing intensified, and a sudden pull at my core lifted me to my feet.

Like I'd been instructed to, I took step after step until I was face-to-face with the mysterious colors. Close enough for salted air and vanilla musk to hit my nose, and in between the waves of song, birds—seagulls—squawked. A soft caress of...water crashing on top of each other. An even softer breeze kissed my cheeks and stroked my hair.

Those sounds, those beautiful voices, were a drug, coaxing me to reach out a hand.

My arm lifted, and the song grew brighter, hungrier. *"Yes, yes. Come. Come home."* My fingertips brushed over the image and sent the colors rippling around my touch. The singing steadily grew louder, delighted at my long-awaited arrival.

I was distantly aware that I was letting the song control me, but I was alert enough that I could fight it if I wanted to. But I didn't. Why should I? Everyone, *everyone*, had left me now. Even if my body were capable of attaching back to my soul, what was left for me now but an emptiness that had always been there, even with Leah. Even with her, it had never felt like home. There was nothing left for me back in that image but heartbreak, bitterness, and so much anger. And that beautiful song, the way it called to me... Whatever heaven or hell lay beyond had to be better than what I'd known so far. I dipped my fingers in.

It hissed, *"Finally."*

What happened next was too quick to comprehend. Startled, I drew back at the triumph in that voice, at the shift in tone, but a hand from the other side wrapped around my wrist and pulled me the rest of the way in.

# CHAPTER THREE

The song halted, and the Nothing was ripped away. My lungs filled with liquid that drowned out my scream as fear, regret, and the sea washed over me.

A pair of piercing, algae-colored eyes belonging to something not quite human stared back at me. She was dark-haired and naked from the waist up. Her nails sank into my skin, creating little crescent moons. I pulled away to no avail and met her glowing eyes again. A silent but clear message reflected back. She wasn't letting go.

In a panic for air, my foot kicked out, colliding with a rough, sea-storm-colored tail. The ends were as sharp as jagged swords.

She surged down, bringing me deeper, deeper to where the water's depth turned murky below us. I couldn't take a breath, couldn't scream, so I pleaded with my eyes instead. Her own stare remained dark and empty, her lips a hard but satisfied line.

A burning sensation pierced my other wrist, and I jerked to see a second figure, almost identical to the first but with much lighter hair, making her own mark in my flesh. A third creature claimed one of my ankles, helping the others pull me down, down, down.

Angry strawberry hair swayed around her face, momentarily revealing hunger-soaked eyes.

I wasn't much of a fighter, never had been, but I thrashed desperately. The harder I kicked, the deeper their nails disappeared into my skin and the lazier they swam, as if they were enjoying taunting their prey.

A blast of water hit us so forcefully the beasts were thrown off and away from me. I scrambled, kicking my legs with everything in them, but the half women didn't chase after me. They were retreating as frantically as I was. Their raven, sunshine, and copper hair disappeared into the darkness of the seafloor, not one of them looking back.

I scanned the ocean, finding a fourth creature with yellow hair longer than mine and a nautical blue tail that stretched far behind him. He gazed up at me and pointed toward the surface.

"*Go*," he mouthed.

I twisted my body, pumping my arms and legs, the need to stick around to communicate my thanks nonexistent.

Air. I needed air *now*.

Another torrent of water pushed into me, speeding my ascent. My vision blurred as the golden flecks of light sparkling at the surface neared. I kicked with the current, unable to hold my breath any longer, and inhaled just before my head broke the surface. I took the deepest gulp of crisp air I could manage and then choked violently, each cough both painful and relieving.

The waves carelessly bobbed as I panted in an endless sea, and when I finally caught my breath, I only had a moment to wonder at the artwork surrounding me. Gold-flecked light danced on top of the bluest water. The sun rested low in a tangerine sky, the combination of hues as if they'd been hand painted. And the *air*... It felt different. Lighter. Easier to breathe somehow.

My legs tangled in a sudden change of the current underneath me as it unnaturally shifted directions, toward the shore. Too quickly, the water keeping me afloat was replaced with a roughness along my palms. I was in the middle of the ocean and then I wasn't. Suddenly, I was sitting on a bed of rock and shells on the shore. I gazed back out into the sea and found a head sticking out of the water, lips barely poking out. The blond-haired merman watched me.

But the tug, the direction of the current hadn't been a push from him, but a pull from somewhere else. His eyes flicked behind me, his head barely tipping in acknowledgement before he dipped his head under the water and disappeared for good. And then I felt it. An unnatural presence at my back. I turned slowly.

A wall of silver armor collectively shifted in one movement, and slender spear-tipped rods pointed accusingly at me. I startled back and threw a hand in the air to cover my head.

"Wait!"

When flesh wasn't pierced with spearhead, I risked a look up. Through the wall of stationed protectors, a delicate face peeked through, and when she pushed through a gap, I was momentarily frozen by her presence.

She was the type that could be described for days. Everything about her was long, from her posture, to her fingertips, to legs that peeked out of a dress made of shells picked straight from the seafloor. Even her eyelashes, thick and full, were superior. Her other features were just as blessed. She was a goddess of sorts. I could tell that much by the importance that hummed off her fair skin.

A crown of opals, pearls, and assorted shells rested elegantly on her head. Her cotton-candy blue locks drifted in the cool breeze, and her eyes, just as piercingly blue as her hair, bore into mine with suspicion.

Her perfectly sculpted brows creased with concern, and when she spoke, even her voice held something higher in it. "What is your name." A command, not a question.

I didn't hesitate. "Briar."

"Your full name," she insisted.

I hated using my full name. I cringed as I let his last name force itself off my tongue. "Briar Clarke."

"Which realm do you dwell in? How did you find your way into my home without my knowing?"

"Realm?" My voice quivered.

"Did you come from over the desert?" Her tone was sharp as nails, but there was alarm behind it she couldn't cover. A fear almost.

"The desert," I repeated, scanning the beach in front of me. "I..." Confused by the questions, I let my voice trail off.

She took me in then, her cerulean eyes scanning me, and it was my soaked clothes that seemed to provide her with some new information. "What are you?"

In my core, I knew something was off. That no matter how preposterous the answer I felt she wanted would sound, it was exactly what she was looking for. I lowered my voice, unsure. "Human?"

Her features remained unchanged, but the rise and fall of her chest hitched. She examined me again, taking in my features with new interest.

"Human," she repeated slowly. "How?" But it wasn't a question directed at me, not really.

Defeat took over, and when I slumped with it, her ocean eyes softened. She lifted a hand, and gestured to her protectors or guards, whoever they were. They lowered their spears at the command. She walked around them, reaching a hand to me. I took it instinctively and just like that, her demeanor shifted into something else. Something softer. I let her help me out of the water.

"Somehow, little human, you've found yourself in Genesi. My realm," she said. "I'm guessing you don't know what that means." I shook my head, soaking in her every word, every minor and fascinating detail about her. "It means you're safe here."

Safe. An unfamiliar concept.

"How did you get here?" she asked again.

I looked out into the sea and explained a shortened version of my time in the Nothing. When I finished with my aided escape from the sea creatures, she turned to the guards. "Not a word of this leaves this beach."

Every head dipped in obedience.

"Come. The sun wishes to sleep and so should you."

This time, I paused. As if she sensed my hesitation, her brow lifted. "Or you can go back into the sea where it appears you came from?"

"No. I—" I shuddered at the thought of being left here for those things to come back for me. I may not know where I was, but I'd been lucky enough to run into someone who had guards. Loyal guards. She was protected. And to say it had been an exhausting day simply didn't cut it.

"You must be starving, and you're going to need some dry clothing. I can offer both," she said. "I have questions and I'm sure you do as well. We will ask each other in the morning." She smiled then, a small, unsure one, but for a reason I couldn't place, trust floated through me. She had a smile that brought comfort. One that felt like a mother's smile, reassuring me that everything was going to be okay.

"My home isn't far. Just around that bend of trees up ahead." She pointed to where the shoreline took a sudden turn and disappeared behind a forest.

We walked in silence, the waves crashing against the shore. My legs began to burn, but I seemed to be the only one struggling. The others eased through the sand even as the ground took a noticeable incline. She said we'd save our questions for the morning, but mine were piling high.

I glanced at the crown on her head. "Where am I? Where is Genesi exactly?" I ventured.

"Genesi is one of the six realms of Elysian. Genesi is not only my homeland, but my kingdom. My name is Darya." Pride welled in her voice. "Queen of Genesi, Mother of the Sea, and daughter of the late King Conway and Queen Kailani."

The information sank in so deep, the idea of stopping to curtsy wasn't even a passing thought. As more questions formed on my lips, the trees cleared to reveal a glittering palace overlooking the same sea I'd just emerged from. Its towering walls glistened in the lowering sun, sending little shimmers of light winking at us in greeting. Despite barely missing death at the hands of a gang of half-naked, gilled women, I suddenly felt the full weight of the truth. I truly was in another world. The singing image had taken me far, far away.

A collection of more guards stood at the gates, but they let us pass without a word, only bowing their heads as we approached. I gazed up in awe at the millions of shells and sea stones of every color that coated the sandy walls.

The guards trailing us departed, finding stations elsewhere. Only one remained a few steps behind us. Close enough to take me out just as quickly as the semi-truck had if I made a move on his queen. We crossed a short distance through a courtyard and to a set of wide sand-crested doors that opened for us without hands to do so.

I looked down at my soaked clothes, their sodden weight clinging to my skin, but when I passed through the threshold, they dried in a blink. I marveled at the transition and gaped up at Darya, who only smiled slyly, as if delighted to show off something so foreign to me and so normal to her.

"Magic." The word itself sounded lyrical as she spoke it. "My lady-in-waiting loves to frolic in the waters in between her duties. She rarely bothers to dry off before prancing inside. Without the help of a little magic, the rest of the palace staff would be annoyed with her quite often. More so than usual at least."

"Magic," I breathed, surveying all that surrounded us.

A grand open foyer made up the entire first floor, smelling of clean sheets and that fresh different air. In place of paneled windows, sheer drapes of blues and whites hung loosely from pillars, letting the ocean breeze drift in from outside. A wide staircase led to an upper level.

Darya turned to face me. "Are you hungry?"

As if on command, my stomach rumbled. I glared at it in betrayal, and Darya smiled in response. "Follow me."

Darya turned to the remaining guard and gave him a simple nod. He read the cue, finding post in a corner of the foyer, and only then did she lead me down a hall and to a large cluttered room. A round wooden table with four chairs around it sat in the middle of the room, and shelves stacked with food or ingredients lined every inch of wall space. Farther in, a set of swinging double doors led to what must have been the kitchen, judging from the smells lingering beyond it. This was just the pantry and where the kitchen staff might eat.

"Sit. Eat as much as you'd like, and don't worry about cleaning up. I'll be back in a moment to show you to a guest room." She turned to leave, and I examined the food stacked on the shelves, wondering if I was supposed to help myself to what I could find. But just as the last bit of blue hair wisped out of view, she flicked a wrist, and the bare tabletop before me was covered in bowls of grapes, bread, soup, and purple wine.

Too ravenous to wonder, I sat and ate until I couldn't fit anything else in my stomach. The soup was unlike any I had tasted before. It had squash and butternut flavors and tasted of autumn. The crostini bread dipped in it satisfied my taste buds more and more with every bite. I ignored the grapes and reached for more bread to dip in the orange soup, which was beginning to concern me. It should be gone by now, every last drop, but the bowl never emptied.

When I was done eating, I reached for the wine but stopped short. My fingers retreated in, and I reached for a clear decanter of water instead. I filled it to the brink of my glass and gulped sloppily, spilling some down my freshly dried front.

There was a movement I almost didn't catch by the door. Darya must be back for me. But when my eyes lifted, it wasn't Darya at all, and yet somehow it was. A small child not much older than eight or nine stood outside the frame. He peered at me and sank back an inch when our eyes met.

"Hello." I smiled, wiping the corner of my mouth. He smiled back and pushed the rest of the way into the room. "Are you hungry?" I asked. "There's plenty here."

He shook his head but sat in the chair across from me anyway. "What's your name?" he asked, his bright-blue eyes peering out from under full locks of brilliant-blue, many shades deeper than Darya's. But unlike Darya, even his eyebrows and lashes were blue.

"Briar," I answered. "What's yours?"

"Mavi."

"It's nice to meet you, Mavi."

He kicked his legs back and forth under the table and bit his lip, keeping those curious eyes on me. "Are you a monster?" He had to be Darya's younger brother. Apart from the shared looks, he was just as bold and straightforward. I couldn't help but give a friendly laugh.

"Me? No, I'm not a monster." My eyes grew wide, and I pointed accusingly at him. "Are *you*?"

"*Me?*" he asked in shock and then laughed back. "No." We laughed together.

"If you're not a monster, then what are you?" he asked.

I considered the question, remembering what Darya had

demanded of every witness of our introduction at the beach. "Just a visitor."

Mavi reached for a grape and leaned across the table, lowering his voice. "From where?"

I leaned in and whispered back, "From another land far, far away."

Mavi's eyes widened as if he couldn't believe he was having this conversation. "Whoa."

Just then, Darya walked in, and Mavi went sailing back in his seat.

"Mavi, didn't I send you to bed half an hour ago?"

"But, Mama, I'm not tired. Not at all."

I reined in my shock, taking in Darya once again. She didn't appear any older than me, and she definitely looked far too young to be a mother to a child this old. But I supposed that didn't necessarily mean anything.

"Off to bed, off to bed!" She clapped at him, and Mavi scrambled from the table, taking another grape and popping it into his mouth before heading for the doors.

As if cued, a palace nanny entered the pantry. She motioned for Mavi to come to her side, reaching out a forest green arm. Tendrils of brown bark and whirls of ivy wrapped around her body. I knew I was staring, knew it was obvious I was studying her, but I couldn't help it. At first glance, she wore pink flowers in her hair, but after a moment, I realized they *grew* there.

"Goodnight, Mama." He rolled his eyes when she bent to kiss him on the cheek, which he hastily wiped away while side-eyeing me sheepishly.

"Did you get enough to eat?" she asked me once he'd left the room.

I pushed up from the table. "I did, thank you."

Darya brought me to a room on the second level. She opened a door to reveal an unoccupied guest suite furnished with an inviting bed with a lilac comforter and matching sheer drapes hanging from the pillared balcony. The thick, soft carpeting was made to bury toes in. To a queen, it couldn't have been overwhelmingly extravagant, but I'd never seen a finer space.

"I will send for you in the morning. We will learn more about each other after you've gotten some rest. Is there anything at all you need before I leave you?" Darya asked.

"No, nothing," I replied. She had been so welcoming to me, a total stranger. If it hadn't been for her unexpected kindness, I may not be alive. "Darya," I called before she was out the door. "Thank you." Her smile was hesitant, and in that single second of reluctance, I could see that she was just as nervous about my being here as I was. But then she tipped her head a little in acknowledgment before closing the door behind her.

In just the time it had taken me to eat, the last remaining bit of sun had dipped under the water. The ocean waves lazily lapped against each other beyond the dancing curtains. I wanted to admire the view for a moment, but with the next crest, exhaustion rolled over me, and I headed straight for the bed, only stopping to kick off my battered shoes.

What a sin it was to let my dirty, possibly days old clothes touch such wealth. I felt for my phone in my back pocket, suddenly remembering I owned one. But my heart sank when it turned up empty. It was probably in pieces at an intersection.

With that, the image of Leah's body dashed through my memory without warning. I was paralyzed by the harsh truth. My brief friendship with Leah had been ripped away just as quickly as it had been offered. I clutched at my heart and squeezed my eyes shut, allowing a silent moment of grief. After several moments longer than I'd intended, I tugged the silk sheets up to my chin and welcomed unconsciousness, anything to take the image away. The breath of the sea kissed my cheek, and before I could finish another thought, I was asleep.

# CHAPTER FOUR

Apart from a dull ache in my arms, back, and legs—from what must have been the distant effects of a car accident a world away—I'd never woken so peacefully. Until I noticed the minor detail that there was an uninvited presence in the room with me. Standing at the foot of my bed was a stranger. She had the clearest, most youthful skin and brightest eyes. She was leaning down to set a tray of food on the ottoman when I caught sight of her. I shot upward, pressing myself into the headboard.

"Oh!" her small bird-like voice rang out. "I'm so sorry."

I only stared at her as she stared back at me. Her head tilted to one side, and she gazed at me as though I was a very curious thing. Eagerly, she plopped herself on the edge of the bed and leaned forward, her long, wavy blonde hair washing over her hands. "Darya says you are not of this world." Her eyes were bright and curious.

"No," I answered, still unsettled that she'd been in my room upon waking. "I'm not from here."

"This is very unusual. This has never happened anywhere that I've heard of," she said more to herself than she did to me, looking out the window as she spoke. She turned back to me. "Darya wants to see you." She reached for the tray again and set it on my lap. "Eat. Then come downstairs right after." Every word came out rushed, like her thoughts were too fast for her mouth. She scurried out of the room, and I gaped at the door as I processed the short, bizarre encounter.

Only the scents from the silver tray snapped me out of my puzzlement. Raspberry croissants, an assortment of wild berries, a small bowl filled with a mixture of nuts, and a tall glass of fresh juice. Now that my stomach didn't feel as though I hadn't eaten in days, I allowed myself to indulge in every bite, and just like last night, the food was fresher somehow. Bright sunlight spilled into my room and I admired the morning waves beyond the balcony as I chewed. Everything here—the food, the sky, the air—was richer.

When I finished, I started for the hallway with the empty tray, not a drop leftover. I was taken aback by the commotion that hadn't been present last night. Handmaidens and cooks scurried like mice in all directions, only identified by the trays of savory meals and laundry baskets they carried. Others walked about at a more leisurely pace, as if their only job was to enjoy the day. A few eyes met mine, but no one stopped to speak to me or lingered, apart from a blur of a staff member who stopped only long enough to wordlessly take the tray right out of my hands. I gaped like a foolish statue.

A small, blue-headed blob at the end of the stairs waved his arms. "Briar!" Mavi called, excitedly. "Down here!" He bounced on his heels as I made my way to him, trying not to bump into a laundry basket or a cart of food. He grabbed my hand and raced off, pulling me along. I couldn't help but laugh at this eager child as he pulled and tugged, urging me to hurry.

He rushed me outside and into a sandy courtyard where Darya was engaged in a deep conversation with someone noticeably attractive. He was taller than Darya, and his skin was so smooth it could have been made of marble. He wore no shirt, only loose white pants, the morning rays gleaming off a suntanned, muscled chest. Though Mavi displayed Darya's more dominant features, I immediately noticed the resemblance.

"Dad!" Mavi let go of my hand and ran up to him. His father scooped him up and onto his shoulders with ease.

Darya graced the morning with a gentle smile. "Remi, this is the girl."

Remi turned to me and surveyed me from top to bottom without attempting to hide it. It wasn't in a rude or uncomfortable manner, but in a way that suggested I truly was an odd sort of crea-ture that he was seeing for the first time.

"Briar." His teeth, just as white as his hair, flashed. "You know, the brambles that grow on the vine are prickly enough to draw blood, but the wild roses that grow on them are a sight worth the sting." He winked. Darya turned her eyes to the sky, and though she didn't see it, Remi's grin widened at that. "Will you be joining us for the festival?" he asked. "It seems you have perfect timing. It's the best night of the year."

Darya cut him a side glare. "That is yet to be decided. I hoped her and I might take a walk on the beach this morning and chat."

"I'll leave you to it then. It was a pleasure, Briar, and I do hope you'll be at the festival." He flashed another charming smile and set off with a giddy Mavi still on his shoulders.

"Shall we?" Darya motioned ahead.

The sand was perfectly warm under my feet and the soft roar of the ocean settled my mind as we walked farther down the beach. "Your husband seems fun." I broke the silence after we'd walked away from any listening ears.

Darya's head snapped up and her eyes met mine in what almost looked like embarrassment. "Who?"

"Well." I suddenly felt stupid. Had I misunderstood? Mavi

called her mama last night and referred to Remi as dad just now. "Remi?"

She snorted, a very unqueenly noise. "No."

The ocean waves sighed, filling the silence between us. She sighed with them at last, as if sensing my curiosity. "It's expected of me to marry and produce an heir. While I've always wanted a child...marriage—" She closed her eyes, either to think or gather patience. "A queen's court can be relentless about such topics. It's not that I refuse to marry, I just simply don't think it a top priority." That was something I could understand, and though she didn't need to elaborate, she continued, "I've known Remi since I was a child. He was a commander in my father's army. When the crown passed on to me, I made him a proposition, one that might save me from marriage. We agreed to have a child together with nothing beyond that. Once Genesi got its heir, the court backed off the idea of finding me a husband."

"And that works?"

She nodded. "Surprisingly, it works very well. Remi was the perfect match for such a proposal. There are no expectations over what we might be in the future. It's all about Mavi. We got a son out of it, and Genesi got its prince. Everyone is happy."

"That doesn't get hard?" I asked. "What if one of you wants to see other people?"

There was a beat of silence and then, "Sometimes I think Remi would like more, but we always find a way out of talking about it. If one wants to see another, we simply do. Though if he does, he's respectful about it, because I've never caught on to any of his... dealings."

The sun glinted off her skin and her eyes suddenly dropped to the locket I wore around my neck. Her brows furrowed, as if she hadn't noticed it before. "That is so quaint." She reached out to hold it between her fingers, but when she brushed it, she snatched her hand back, holding it as if she'd been badly burned. "I do not like how that feels."

I looked down at the locket, putting a hand to it.

"Where did you get that?"

It was only a simple oval locket with small vine-like designs carved over the surface. Once bright gold, it was now tarnished from years of wear. "It was my mother's."

She frowned at it. "It doesn't bother you?"

I shook my head in response.

"My magic does not like that necklace. There's something off about it."

"Your magic..." I looked around as if maybe I could see it in the air itself. The water reached out and tapped our toes. "Could it get me home?"

"Is that what you wish?"

I paused. Is that what I wanted? I had blamed the siren's song for luring me to the portal, but I could have snapped myself out of it if I wanted. But there had been no reason to. There had been nothing to stay for. "Shouldn't I?"

"Truthfully," Darya said a bit sadly, "this is not a world crafted for you. For many reasons at the moment."

I ignored the sinking feeling in my chest at that. "Then I suppose I should go back." Darya said nothing. "Right?"

She eyed the locket again suspiciously, as if it would attack her if she turned her back to it. "That really doesn't bother you?" When I shook my head again, she reluctantly peeled her gaze from it. "If circumstances were different, I'd say everything happens for a reason, and if you found yourself here, then you should stay. But circumstances in Elysian are very dark at the moment, and it is not safe, especially not for a human. I think you must go back, though I don't know how it can be done."

"Am I stuck here then?"

"No human has ever touched this ground. It goes against the

very creation of Elysian. If word gets out, and to the wrong one, not even Genesi can keep you safe for long. The only thing I know to do is to send you to the scholars. They may have answers."

At my lost expression, she explained, "They are far older than I, the oldest of the land perhaps. They keep records of Elysian's birth, its history, its secrets, of prophecies that have yet to be fulfilled. Their library is omniscient. I've heard they even house a book of no author, with pages that fill themselves as events come to pass. I've never held the book in my hands myself, but one queen said her future unfolded on the page as she turned it. If there is any explanation for your impossible arrival, you should also be able to learn how you could return in one of those books. I will send a dove out immediately. Until then, you are welcome to the room you slept in last night."

"And if word gets out before the scholars respond...how dangerous are we talking?"

Someone called Darya's name, an attendant of some sort with too many lists in his hands and a pencil tucked behind his ear. Darya clasped my hands. "Genesi is safe for now. You will come to the festival tonight, and I will answer the rest of your questions then."

"The festival—" I started to ask.

"Yes." She beamed. "Solunar Saudade. It's the longest day of the year. The sun forgets to sleep."

"The sun does what?"

"The sun will set, but she will not sleep. Instead, she stays up all night to meet with her twin flame. Sadly, they are granted only one night a year to be together, and though they sit too high to be heard, they spend the whole night catching up with one another. I'd love to listen in on that conversation, wouldn't you?"

I gave a confirming smile, though I had not one clue what she was going on about. She squeezed my hand before dropping it and turning our direction back to the palace. "There are still things left to do if there is to be a festival at all. Until then, I hope you'll be okay in your room. While my subjects are generally friendly, the ocean is another beast entirely, and your first introduction with her wasn't pleasant. You may be more comfortable inside until someone is free to accompany you again."

Following her lead away from the water, I glanced over my shoulder. I fought off a shiver as I caught a glimpse of the tip of a jagged sea-storm-colored tail diving under the waves.

## CHAPTER FIVE

How much, if any, of our conversation had the siren heard? And what danger had Darya been talking about? From the balcony outside my room, I fixed my gaze on the strange world below, mind spinning out of control until the wavy-haired visitor from this morning hopped—literally hopped—into the room.

"Darya says I am to take care of you for the duration of your stay." She clapped her hands in a blur of excitement, wearing a smile that showed all her teeth and deepened her dimples. She let me know her name was Blythe, but that I was to call her Bly, and nothing more, or else she would run from my room and never speak to me again.

She pranced between me and the wardrobe, holding up one dress after another until she seemed satisfied with one and tossed it on the bed. She began undressing me, despite my attempts to assure her that I could dress myself, but she insisted she would be insulted if I didn't let her do her job.

I was spun around and around until I was covered in a cottony dress. Then, she grabbed my arms and pushed thin cuffs shaped like garden vines over my biceps and placed a matching flower crown on top of my head. Bly fluffed out my hair and stepped away to give me a look over. Her brows furrowed.

"What's wrong?" I asked, looking down at the gown. "You don't like it?"

"I do, but—" She took a step forward, reaching for my locket. I took an instinctive step back, throwing a protective hand over the golden oval. She stopped short. "It doesn't exactly match," she explained, careful not to hurt my feelings. I shook my head in silent protest. My locket never came off. Never.

Bly simply shrugged and turned me toward the mirror. She bounced on her heels, all those teeth showing again. "Oh, Briar looks so beautiful!"

I did look different. In these clothes, I almost looked like someone special. Someone beautiful enough to belong here. The lavender dress had sleeves that dipped, exposing my shoulders. The fabric crisscrossed around the bust and hugged at my hips. The rest of it flowed down loosely to my feet.

The crown made of tiny purple flowers reminded me of the ones my mother and I tied together from the flowers in our back-yard. Except those weren't real flowers. They were weeds. I was happy with our homemade tiaras all the same and would pretend I was a princess. The vines around my upper arms and the purple flowers on my head sort of made me look like one now. I swatted the thought away.

"We must show Darya. She will be so pleased."

The halls were practically empty now, only a few others dressed in similar gowns rushed through the front doors. "We must hurry!" Bly picked up the speed, towing me down the stairs to catch up with the others. She was much faster than I was capable of moving, and when I tripped, she slowed, though she acted like it was difficult for her to slow down to my pace. We followed the others passed the small patch of beachy woods and toward the area where I washed up yesterday.

The sandy terrain stretched on uninterrupted for miles out of eyesight. No fishing piers, no boating docks, not a speck of pollution. Only white sand, patches of tall grass, and diverse-looking groups—of what I had now assumed were not people—spread all along the beach. Little bonfires sparked in front of each group. Wispy clouds and hushed conversations filled the ombre sky. The air smelled of woodsy smoke and salt.

Darya caught sight of us just as she was ending a conversation with a family of three. She took my hands in hers and stretched both our arms out to get a complete view of my outfit. "This dress was made for you, Briar. You look stunning."

I shrank at the unexpected compliment. Darya wore much simpler attire than she had the previous day, though the blues and whites of her straight gown, in addition to her natural features already, were far superior to anyone—*anything* on this beach. In comparison to her, I was plain and simple, completely unworthy of being called stunning.

My gaze caught on the family Darya had been speaking to. They were tall, abnormally tall, even the child, and their skin was cracked and uneven like tree bark. I scanned the beach, briefly studying each group. If this world wasn't built for humans, what exactly lived in Elysian?

Darya led us over to a bonfire where Remi and Mavi sat on a flannel blanket. They roasted fluffy white cubes that resembled marshmallows on wooden rods. Bly ran off then to join others at the water's edge. They splashed, and danced, and laughed joyously. Her sage cotton dress was drenched from the waist down in milliseconds. Darya laughed. "Such a free spirit."

"That's one way to put it," Remi replied, handing me a marshmallow. He was dressed exactly as he was from earlier that day, only this time he wore a matching white shirt halfway buttoned and carelessly untucked.

I turned the cube over in my hand, noting the pinkish tint and sugar coating. "Is this for S'mores?" I asked.

"What's that?" Mavi's eyes widened, looking frightened as he turned to his mother. "Mama, what's a S'more? Does it live in the mountains?"

But Darya only looked to me for an explanation.

"Oh no, no. A S'more is just a snack. You stick a roasted marshmallow and a piece of chocolate in between two graham crackers. Like a sandwich, except it's melty and delicious and it's eaten around a fire." Mavi looked intrigued. I took a small bite of mine, and something similar to jelly, only better, oozed from its center.

"You make your world sound exotic," Remi said and took a bite of his own toasted cube.

I almost snorted. "Trust me, it's not." But this. Everything here was amplified. The colors were brighter, the food richer, even the feel of my bedsheets was more luxurious than any thread found in my world.

My eyes landed on the bark-like-skinned family once more. Their features were blaringly obvious now.

Darya's eyes followed my gaze. "Trolls," she offered and then tilted her chin toward the water where Bly and her friends still splashed. "Naiads. They are river nymphs." She nodded toward separate groups on the beach, naming off species, some I'd read of in classical storybooks as a kid, and others I needed explained to me. A whole new reality unfolded before my eyes.

"What else is there? Is everything I was ever told was a fairy tale real?"

"I don't think I have a way of knowing every story you were ever told. So I'll say this," Darya began. "Everything that does not have a home in the human realms has a home here. Merfolk, the fae, jinn, fauns, shifters of every kind," Darya rattled on. "It's rare, but a few angels have slipped through the skies over time and settled here." I swallowed the urge to interrupt with more questions. "But it was with the Divines in which this world began."

"A unique creation from this world's Creator," Remi provided. "They have no set species. They simply are. And their power and strength are unmatched."

"And no humans?" I confirmed. "Not once?"

Darya smiled almost playfully. Remi lay on the blanket with a hand propping his head, and Mavi curled against him as if they were settling in for a bedtime story.

"Elysian." It rolled off her tongue like silk. "It is a place given to us by the Creator himself. It is a safe haven for His once-perfect creatures. In another world, there were creatures like you—humans—who demolished the innocence there. The humans were cursed as a punishment for their sins, but we—all His other creations who played no part in human transgressions—were given a second chance. Our world was plucked from yours and made into something new. Elysian is a fresh start and a paradise. It's a stretch of land and sea placed so far outside of human reach that no human can ever touch or destroy it," she paused, her and Remi giving me a thoughtful look.

"Until even we messed up our second chance." Darya sighed, melancholy filling the sound. "Trying once more, the Creator crafted again. Only instead of humans, he made five mighty Divine straight from the elements of Elysian to rule over us all. Each one of them were gifted differently, but overwhelmingly so by the land's sources, and were to rule over Elysian as one.

"He gave one the ability to control and manipulate any source of water. The next harnessed the wind, controlling its direction and bending it to his will. Another could light a spark of flame out of thin air. One could freeze water and manipulate it in its solid form. The last Divine could become one with the terrain and even shift mountains if she willed it."

I noted each in my head. Water, wind, fire, ice, earth.

"In the beginning, Elysian was one plot of land, and we lived in peace with each other. But just as in the human world, things like greed took over and changed the course of Elysian's purpose. The Divines became ego-driven and hungry for more. More land, more power. A war broke out. Some fought to protect what was theirs, while others fought to conquer what wasn't. It was a slaughter. The first and worst war our world has ever seen. It ended in a truce, and the maps were divided into regions, where our leaders ruled separately instead of together as intended. They drew border lines in the maps for the ocean region of Genesi, the mountains of Valhalla, the meadows of Empyrean, the icy land of Kashmir, and the desert of Kalopsia. And eventually came the sixth."

I recounted the founders in my head. "But there are only five elements. Five elements, five rulers."

Remi, who'd been gazing up at the faint stars a moment ago, watched us intently now. "Until there wasn't," he said. "Until there was the Garden, which now lies in the center of Elysian. When they agreed on divisions of land equal in size, it was so that no more argument could come of it later, but it backfired. Our Creator was angry about the war. Angry that we brought destruction and chaos into a second chance paradise, just the way His humans did. So we were punished as well. He created a new Divine. One far greater and of more power than all the others. One whose creation was made whole by each of the elements, instead of just one of them. Her magic is now tied to the land. She *is* the land. She is the Core of Elysian.

"While the Divines we now call the lesser rulers each possess a single drop of elemental magic, this Divine was gifted the land in its entirety, making her power undeniable. And He crowned her the High Queen, ruler of us all. A section in the middle of our maps, what is now called the Garden, was forcibly taken and given to the High Queen to dwell in, causing the equal parts of land we labeled for ourselves to shift."

"Another war didn't break out, did it?"

"No," Remi answered. "This is where the story gets interesting. From that day forward, if we ever try to rebel again, if we dismiss the High Queen's reign, we die. The magic woven in the soil of Elysian is the very same woven in her veins. She fuels the Garden, so if the Garden has no life, it cannot power the rest of us. Without our High Queen, our waters will be polluted, the lands will dry up, the crops will stop growing. Piece by piece the land will die, and soon after, all those in it."

I was in a trance by this point, fixated on their every word.

Remi settled his attention back on the sky, his voice coming back to his own. "It's a curse really. A slap in the face to the earlier Divines who started the war. Hundreds of thousands of creatures died in a pointless fight."

"Not all lesser rulers are true Divine today," Darya explained. "There have been rare cases where a Divine has passed on after a much-extended life span and without any offspring to inherit. When this happens, Elysian's magic will scour the lands to find a worthy soul. It will change them, their very genetic makeup, giving them a single drop of Divine energy, and with it, the title of that realm's newest king or queen."

"We've also bred with others so much by this point that our bloodlines have morphed all across the board," Remi put in. "But the Core of Elysian has always been daughters, never sons. And she has always been purely Divine. That much has never changed."

"Before my father was Divinely gifted, he was only a kelpie. My mother was a mermaid. Making me a little of a whole lot of things, but Divinely gifted no less."

"A mermaid," I repeated with wonder. "That's what attacked me in the water."

"We call those types of merfolk a more derogatory term," she corrected. "Those are—"

"Murderous male-eating water demons?" Remi teased.

"Sirens," Darya said, ignoring him. "The worst of their race. They may have been mermaids once but choose a darker path instead."

I looked to Remi, taking in his strong and sharp features.

"Draki," he provided. "Descendent of the dragon." His lips curved into a mischievous grin at my dumbfounded reaction. "It is said that the draki originally roamed the lands in their dragon form, but over time, we've come to dwell in a more civilized form and only manifest as dragons in a time of great distress or rage."

"Have you ever—" I didn't speak it aloud. Could he morph into an actual dragon?

"A long, long time ago. I'm out of practice now."

I tried to picture his perfectly sculpted face and body contorting into scales and talons and teeth.

Darya reached for my arm. "Briar, you look pale."

"I'm fine. It's just..." Unbelievable and impossible, I wanted to say. "It's a lot." I rubbed my forehead. "How old are you both?"

"I turned two hundred and three last month." Darya beamed.

"I've lost count," Remi said nonchalantly. "Somewhere in the four hundreds, I suppose."

I looked to Mavi, his eyes now closed and his breathing deep, and admired his sleeping form. I imagined all the potential power flowing through his body. Part mer, part dragon, but Divine blood mixed in his veins, nonetheless. I had a hard time imagining him as anything but this sweet, sleepy, blue-headed child.

"I knew he wouldn't make it." Remi's low laugh was a rumble, like distant thunder. The sun hung low on the water, the stars only faintly making an appearance, but the sky never transitioned beyond dusk. I took a deep breath of the fresh, somehow altered air, and suddenly missed it already.

"And the High Queen," I almost sighed. "rules over all this?"

Darya and Remi exchanged a glance, a silent conversation passing between them.

"She did." Darya seemed to struggle with her words. She was being careful, but why?

Remi was the one to finally answer, his voice dropping so only those on our blanket could hear. "Our High Queen was murdered." There was a breath of silence, an eeriness lingering in the air, like it too was listening. "No one knows by who or how the assassin got through the defenses of the Garden, but the High Queen and her king were found in their bedchamber, or what was left of them. Their skeletons were all that remained. Examiners found evidence of the use of a dagger. It had to have been poisoned with some kind of magic that could harm a Divine in the first place, let alone eliminate one's body."

I looked to Darya as all the pieces from the story clicked into place. "But the land... Its power is connected to the High Queen."

She nodded gravely, her voice lowering even more. "It is as Remi says. Elysian's Garden is barren. The land is dying." Hushed conversations around us dropped completely, as if no amount of distance or whispering could stop their inhuman ears from listening in on this. "Once flourishing forests are now fading. Kashmir's ice is melting, sending their wildlife fleeing to find cooler temperatures and leaving the subjects there hungry. Empyrean's meadows have all but wilted. It won't be long before the death of the land spreads farther."

For some reason, I looked to Mavi. My eyes welled and I swallowed hard, the emotion burning my throat.

The flashes of alarm I'd seen in Darya's eyes were visible now. And this time, I understood why. "The High Queen left behind two daughters at the time of her death. The youngest, Princess Zara, is said to be the successor. The High Queen's power is not always granted to the eldest, but to the worthiest of heart. The land itself decides whose power it will flow through. With Zara's budding gifts at such a young age, it was clear this sister had been chosen to be our future. She is so kind and gentle that many refer to her as the

Pale Queen. Unfortunately, she went missing a few days before her parents' deaths. No one has heard from or seen her since.

"The eldest, Princess Xosha, is her sister's opposite in every way. She was a troublesome child even then, though I can't imagine what losing everyone in your family would do to any child so young. When she grew up to delight in fear and punishment, she adopted a different name. We call her the Dark Queen, and it is she who sits falsely on the throne today. Instead of looking for her sister, she has taken control of the Garden. She's turned a blind eye to the dying land. She won't search for her sister, any tips on her whereabouts have been discouraged from being shared. She only cares about filling the role she feels she was entitled to since birth. She thinks she can force the land's hand, but it won't give."

"So, the missing successor... Is she..."

"The land isn't suicidal. If she were dead, it would have no other choice but to turn to the next in line." Darya's thoughts deepened. "But the Dark Queen's power still remains the same as the day she was born. The only ability she has is to turn dreams and enemies to ash at her feet. Until the gifts of the land have been transferred to the only surviving member of the royal family, we can assume the Pale Queen is still out there somewhere. And not only that, but when a High Queen dies, a redwood tree grows in the far north wing of the Garden. No additional redwoods have been added to the gravesite in the Garden, or anywhere else that we know of."

"Which makes no sense," Remi said. "Because the land *is* in fact dying. Unless the Dark Queen's heart is so rotten that Elysian is refusing her reign, but I can't believe that. There have been self-righteous rulers before this one. But if our Pale Queen is simply a lost queen, she'd still be tied to the land and our soil would continue to thrive. We are out of ideas about what exactly is happening."

I didn't dare voice that the answer seemed obvious. That maybe the land wasn't necessarily suicidal but tied to the laws of strict magic. That maybe the last remaining High Queen was, in fact, no longer living, leaving Elysian with no sand left in its hourglass. But surely Remi knew the laws of the land better than I did. I hadn't even known of its existence until yesterday. But if the Pale Queen were still out there, she had to know what was happening. And why would the rightful High Queen sit back and watch her kingdom crumple to ash? Even if she'd stayed away out of fear of her sister who'd grown so dark, surely she wouldn't let an entire world and the creatures in it die because she was afraid.

This was why Darya thought I should leave. I looked around, absorbing it all. I couldn't understand why I felt so attached already, but I did now understand why I had to leave and soon. Elysian wouldn't be standing for much longer.

"How long does Elysian have?"

"We've found ways to be resourceful. Genesi, thank the Creator, hasn't yet been touched by the curse. We'll collect and store as much as we can from the water until the curse reaches even the sea. We hope to have enough to buy ourselves and other kingdoms maybe a year."

"And then?" I asked.

The glisten in Darya's eyes was answer enough.

"Shhh, you're missing it." Remi pointed to the sky. The moon had made an appearance, creeping out from the ocean's horizon and gently floating over to the sun until they were side by side. The light from the sun's rays dimmed significantly. It was several minutes before anyone spoke.

"Remi," Darya broke the silence without taking her eyes off the pair, "tell her."

Remi whispered back, "Tell her what?"

"Tell her about how the moon loved the sun so much he died every night to let her breathe."

I thought I saw Remi roll his eyes, but he obeyed. "The moon and the sun are said to be twin flames, the deepest of soulmate connections there is. They complete each other. Where one is blanketed in a depthless darkness only the constellations can fathom, the other is so radiant not a soul can reach out and touch her. Where one is weak, the other is strong, where one basks in its rays, the other revels in its darkness. Since the dawn of creation, the moon and the sun have known of the curse that comes with their love for one another.

"Beyond their brief encounters at dawn and dusk, they can never truly be together, not physically. Their union defies the very laws of nature. But they did try once. The moon pushed through stars, and the sun viciously fought against gravity, her light growing dimmer and dimmer the closer she got to him. While the moon had nothing to lose, his twin flame grew weaker with her efforts. And it was the moon that ended her suffering. 'I will not ask you to abandon your blessing of light for my darkness.' Those were the last words the moon spoke to his sun for a long time. And as he spoke them, as he let go of his hold on her, the sun could feel her rays shining stronger again. She didn't feel so tired anymore. And it was clear what he had done. To let his true love breathe, he would die at the end of each and every day. He loved her so much that he gave her up.

"And so it's said, though it's silly, of course, that they do the impossible. The two conserve their energy so that for one night a year, the twin flames can fight forces that not even gravity and fate can come between. With their lights duller and the day longer than usual, they hold on for as long as they can until one has to let go. We all gather for Solunar Saudade to witness the impossible for ourselves." He gazed down at Mavi and smiled, clearly not taking the story seriously. But as my eyes lingered in the sky, the proof was right before us. The sun was dim enough that we could look straight at her, and faintly see every part of her wicking and flaring softly.

Water collected in the corners of my eyes and my throat tightened. "I don't know if that's beautiful or heartbreaking."

"I think it's a little of both," Darya mused.

A nearby splash drew my attention away from the star-crossed lovers above. On a formation of rocks settled partly on land sat three forms. It took me a single second to recognize their cutting features. The mermaids who had chosen a darker path—the sirens—were nestled on the rocks, razor-sharp tails lazily splashing in the water. Their eyes hunted me like a cat eyeing an injured bird.

The dark-haired siren, the one with the meanest face, rested slightly higher on the rocks than the others. She was the leader then. Her predator eyes shifted to my side, to where Darya was staring daggers at her. Their gazes held, but Darya didn't blink. The dark-haired siren broke first and angrily dove into the water, the other two following in after her.

"That may be a problem later," Remi commented.

"The heathens just may be." Darya's eyes still narrowed. "Our borders are monitored. If they make a move, I'll know it." There was authority in her voice and a story as well. One that would have to wait until another day. My head was so full of new information that even the thought of asking more questions made it heavy. But despite the fatigue of the past two days, I made myself look up. We watched the twin flames for hours, and eventually, no one spoke anymore at all. Though no one would say it aloud, not even Remi, we all strained to hear beyond the ocean's lapping, hoping we might listen in on whatever wonders the sun and her moon spoke of.

# CHAPTER SIX

I woke to a near-empty beach, though there were some left who were just stretching awake like me. The sky was bright, the sun back in her rightful place, and the moon nowhere to be seen.

Mavi still snoozed next to a sleeping Remi, their faces a near identical match at this angle. I lifted my head to see Darya sitting next to me with her legs folded underneath her. Her eyes were locked on the sea. She was still as stone, suspiciously perfect, and our conversation from last night sailed through my mind. Immortal. She was immortal and as close to perfect as one could get. Every being here was something I had thought to be imaginary, fairy tales spun as a means to make sense of my ordinary world. And yet here they all were in front of me with friends and families and lives of their own.

I sat up. "How long have you been up?"

"What kind of hostess would I be if I fell asleep at my own party?" She smiled at her own joke, but it didn't quite meet her eyes. She stood and reached for my hand, helping me off the blanket. "I want to show you something."

I followed Darya wordlessly back up the beach and inside the palace. Instead of winding up the stairs or to the hallway leading to the kitchens, she took me to the other side of the foyer where another hallway wrapped around the staircase. It opened on the other end to yet another open floorspace, this one much more impressive in size.

On one side sat a dining area, where Darya, Remi, and Mavi must have their meals as a family. The long oak table sat on the far wall next to an open, curtained pillar. Tealight candles and little glass jars of clustered blue azaleas, some with baby's breath in between and others with ivy, covered the tabletop.

Darya's throne rested in the center of the room, and behind it, the back wall opened to reveal a large terrace. The water's horizon sparkled beyond it from here.

"Darya," a deep voice came from behind.

We turned toward the archway from which we'd just entered to find an oddly familiar face approaching. I couldn't quite place him, but something about the way he looked at me told me he knew me too. Brilliant-blond hair flowed past his waist, and his skin was a few shades lighter than everyone else I'd run into here, as if the sun didn't touch him as often. "Wait here." Darya touched my arm lightly before excusing herself.

She strode over to the shirtless newcomer, and they turned their backs in conversation, but not before his blaringly blue eyes took in mine and gave a friendly nod. Their lips moved in a whisper, and it was clear whatever was being said was not meant for me to hear.

I turned toward the sound of the waves overlapping beyond and breathed in the salt-laced air as I waited. I eyed the throne, and unable to help myself, walked to it. It was almost an exact replica of Darya's crown. The arms were a cluster of white, blue, and pink shells with tight gold chains embedded throughout. I ran a hand over the top of it, feeling the rounded opals that expanded overhead.

Realizing what I was doing, I snapped my hand off the throne and glanced back at the archway. Darya remained in conversation with the visitor, their backs still turned and voices dropped.

A light breeze caressed a door on the opposite side of the room, bringing my attention to it for the first time. It was cracked open ever so slightly, the breeze gently swaying it open a fraction and then pulling it back again. I gave Darya a second glance and waited several more minutes before the breeze tapped on the door yet again, teasing me. I crossed the room, walking lazily as if I were only strolling around. I stopped by the door and peeked carefully through the crack. My eyes landed on shelves upon shelves of books.

I pushed the door the rest of the way open, letting it hit the wall a little too hard, and stepped inside, taking a breath full of the heavenly scent of dusty pages. From floor to ceiling, shelves lined the walls of the large room. A table stretched across the middle and took up most of the space there.

Excited, I reached out to examine the spine of a book. What did authors write about here? What tales did a fairy tale land tell? I reached for another and then another, until it became clear these books weren't the kind for leisure reading.

No, it wasn't stories these books told, but rather instructions. These were books for teaching things I had never dealt with. I turned to examine the massive table. There were no chairs around it. A map was painted on the indented surface, and game pieces were spread across what was beginning to look like a game board of some sort.

The map was so detailed it was hard to focus on one drawing for too long. Sections of territory were drawn, and within each main territory, the location of several major cities and landmarks were marked. The game pieces, I counted, were one to each territory drawn.

My eye went to the black figurine first. I picked him up from the top of the map and inspected him. Wings sprouted from his back and were folded in, his head bowed over a knee. He looked sad and defeated, even for an inanimate object. I fumbled him over in my fingers, trying to get a better look at his face, but the craftsmanship had left it undefined.

I put him down and picked up another, a brown one sitting over a white terrain. She stood tall and proud with a long sword clasped in her hands. She wore a hood, again hiding the details of her face. I set her down and moved across the board, examining each piece as I went.

On the opposite side, an ocean landscape was painted. I picked up the blue figure that lived there. She had long hair that flowed over her dress, and though her face also lacked character, the detailed crown of opals and pearls made me reconsider that this was a board game at all.

"It's beautiful, isn't it?"

I dropped the piece on the table. I'd been so engrossed in the map and its pieces that I hadn't heard Darya walk in the room.

"What is it?"

"Can't you see?" she asked, walking up to me and placing the fallen piece—her piece—upright. "It's Elysian." I inspected the map for a second time as she explained.

"Genesi." She pointed and then dragged her finger to a neighboring patch of dry land. "Kalopsia." She moved on. "Empyrean." A land that from the drawing appeared to be one big open meadow. "Kashmir." A barren land with pictures of elk and other furry creatures roaming the ice. "Valhalla." She pointed at the shaded area that lay at the top. In the center of it all was a thick cluster of trees encircling yet another territory. "And the Garden," she finished.

I'd been wrong both times. This wasn't a library or a game room at all. This was a strategy room. This was where Darya and her court held meetings and made decisions, a room I probably wasn't allowed in, though Darya didn't seem to mind my intrusion. It was all just so fascinating that I was having trouble containing myself.

"Sorry," I said abruptly. "I thought this might be a library. I didn't know this room was so important."

"This very map is what I wanted to show you. You should know where you'll be traveling and through what lands."

I placed my hands on the rim of the table and leaned closer, itching to know more. I pointed to the mass of trees that encircled the Garden. "What's this part?"

"That's the Everwood. It serves as a buffer between the High Queen and her realms. The forest, when prompted, will protect her from danger. It will give her days in advance, in most cases, to prepare for an incoming attack. If they get through the trees at all."

I reached for the figure in the sandy terrain neighboring Genesi. The viper standing tall bared fangs ready to strike. Darya gave an embarrassed laugh. "Don't worry, Kalopsia's realm isn't actually ruled over by a snake. Well, not in the literal sense, at least. This figurine is more of an inside joke."

I carefully sat the figure back in its home.

"Some call Kalopsia the Desert of Sin. Their Sand Queen, Cozbi, is the only full-blooded Divine left standing today. She is very old, very...controversial. When the lands shifted to make room for the Garden, her realm became the smallest. We don't speak about it in front of her. She's still quite bitter about it."

According to the map, what Darya said was true. While Kalopsia was still a long stretch of land, the desert held a drastically smaller portion of the map than all the others.

"In Empyrean there are two rulers." I looked over at the bottom of the map and found a figurine that contained two figures bonded together, their hands clasped over the same sword and crowns of flame resting on each of their heads. "Twins are extremely rare and of absolute equal power. Kenna and Keagan rule together. While their abilities of the flame may be identical, their personalities—" she gave a soft laugh. "—couldn't be more opposite. Kenna is the real force to reckon with. It is fae heritage that runs through their bloodline today." She moved on to the next realm. "Kashmir is under the rule of Zima, the ice gifted. She is an ice elf, a cousin of the fae. And then there's—"

"Your Majesty." The creature that had scurried Mavi off to bed the first night appeared at the door, reaching out a vined arm. "A dove just arrived."

Darya took the folded scroll and unwrapped the green ribbon from it. Her eyes scanned the message. "It's from the scholars." My eyes widened slightly. "They think they can help."

She placed a finger on a landmark that rested in the upper right-hand corner of the Everwood, just outside the border of Valhalla. "Clive Steeple. That is where the scholars live. You'll be crossing through the Kalopsian Desert and through the Everwood. No one goes through the Garden, so the journey could take you weeks."

I realized then she kept referring to just me and not us. A nervousness took hold over me as she read the question in my eyes and I read the answer before she gave it.

Darya frowned. "Briar, I can't go with you." Without meaning to, my shoulders sank. "The land may not respond to the Dark Queen, but she is still dangerous. When I first became aware of the threat she posed—when the body count rose to triple digits overnight, I had to do something to protect us. I had no choice but to close Genesi's borders and bring our trade to a halt. We're saving all we can in preparation for the worst, but until the land gives us no other choice, we can no longer send out shipments to neighboring lands, accept trade, or allow anyone from the outside in. Only those of Genesi citizenship can come and go as they please, as many have family in other parts of the world. Until the Dark Queen can be defeated, we've completely shut ourselves off from the rest of the world. Her power is... Why such a cold heart was gifted the ability to disintegrate things to ash, I do not understand, but it makes defeating her complex. I must remain here to keep the upper hand. I can stop her, I just need more time. I need a solid plan before I put myself in her path. Please understand."

"I do understand," I said, even though the nervous energy in my stomach didn't settle. There was more at stake here than my fate. There was a whole population here she had to think of. Her son. And she was taking the time out of all that to help someone she didn't know escape before it was too late.

"I wanted to get you to Clive Steeple quietly, but I'm afraid that's just gotten more complicated. Before the dove, a messenger from the sea brought news."

"The messenger," I said. "He looked so familiar."

"That was Zale, my Regent of the Sea. You recognized him as the one who saved you from drowning." Recognition dawned, his features matching the memory, all but the legs. "He is my eyes and ears of the waters when I cannot be there. He came to inform me that a siren left the sea last night and crossed the border. I fear she may have gone to the Dark Queen with news of your mysterious arrival."

"Where I come from, in the legends at least, mermaids aren't able to go from sea to land."

"Where you come from, they have it wrong," Darya replied. "It's painful the first few times, but a fairly easy transition."

"Why?" I asked. "What would she have to gain from traveling all that way just to gossip?"

"To defy me. My history with the sea is complicated. An old feud involving my mother. The sea is under my reign, but they like to think of it as their own territory. It's a mess down there, one I'll deal with after the threat on land has been handled."

She mused over the map, brows furrowed in concentration.

"With the waters on the siren's side, and if she is in fact on her way to the Garden as we speak, she could be there in half the time we can." She crossed her arms, examining Kalopsia for several moments as if she hated it. "I must protect my subjects first and foremost. If Genesi can't go with you, there is only one way to ensure your safety. I will send word to Cozbi and Kenna. If Cozbi will agree to give you safe passage through her desert, I'm sure Kenna will wait at the border to escort you through the Everwood and to Clive Steeple."

My skin prickled, my senses telling me even under the protection of a queen, my safety might still be questionable. "And Cozbi, the controversial one. You trust her?"

"No." Her answer was curt. "Kenna won't have to be bribed, but Cozbi will want something in return. And I just so happen to have something she wants." Her brows furrowed deeper than should be possible. "The desert's positioning isn't ideal. They do not have the natural resources others do and have always depended on the help of neighboring lands to thrive. And because Cozbi doesn't socialize well, trade with Kalopsia has never been something other kingdoms have sought. Kalopsia has nothing to offer us other than staying on civil terms. But now that Elysian is in peril, no one has cared to put up with more than they have to. No one has dealt in trade with Cozbi since the Dark Queen took the throne. Kalopsia was the first to fall, with so little flourishing there to begin with." There was a long pause before she continued. "Now more than ever, she needs an ally. I'll make her a deal she can't refuse."

"If you can't trust her, how do you know she'll keep her end?

"In Elysian, one's words can be bonded to another through a magic-laced deal. Once bound with magic, she will have no choice but to keep her promise, even if she doesn't want to. Her body would work against her if she tried to double-cross me. If she's willing to make the trade and bind it with magic, I trust that."

"Why are you doing this?" I asked. "Why go so far out of your way to help someone you don't know? Someone you owe nothing to."

Darya blinked at my question as if the answer were simple. "Because someone has to stand up for the innocent. Right now, I can hardly help my own subjects. When all this is said and done, if we all go down, at least I will have spared one soul from our cursed fate."

"And if I find a way out? Won't that be the answer for you all?"

Darya's face softened. "We have no home in yours I'm afraid. There are some things here you don't want finding their way out. The scholars know this. They will be discrete in their investigations." Darya looped her arm through mine and led me away from the map, the books, and the rest of my questions. "Cozbi being one of those things. Hopefully, she is feeling less troublesome than normal, and you will be on your way soon."

I was too distracted to focus on anything. I wandered onto the terrace behind the throne room and lounged in one of the wicker chairs, soaking in the sun. I kept my eyes closed, even through Bly's unending rambling. She never seemed to notice I wasn't listening. Eventually, I fell asleep, and when I opened my eyes again, Bly was gone.

I spent the next day on the beach with Mavi. If Darya had access to both legs and fins, I didn't want to be out here alone. At least with Mavi, if something happened he could run for help. But Mavi wasn't worried about such things. He said even if someone dared mess with the royal son, it was lucky for me that he was a brave, strong knight in training who would fend off any threat in my honor.

We collected seashells and traced our names in the sand. For a moment, I forgot everything—Leah, my family, the journey I was preparing to take without a friend by my side. For a moment, I enjoyed myself.

By the time the sun set and I beat Mavi in a race back to the palace, Darya had news. Both Cozbi and Kenna had agreed to give me safe passage through their lands as soon as I could make it there.

# CHAPTER SEVEN

The ride on horseback took a couple of hours. After a quick breakfast the next morning and an even quicker goodbye to Remi and Mavi, I was trudging through the beachy sand with Darya and an escort of soldiers, their spears freshly sharpened as they flanked us closely.

I rode Mavi's white dappled horse named Apple, and Darya filled the hours by teaching me about the creatures I might find throughout my journey. She described the strong minotaur and noble centaurs. She described creatures with top halves of muscled chests and sword-wielding arms and the lower body of a snake. Most interesting were the mutant wolves who hailed from deep within Empyrean. They'd been banished to a single area of woods there in previous years, but had recently made their way out into the rest of the world. She explained that Kalopsia was a melting pot, the most diverse land in the world, even though it was the smallest, where not one creature dwelled more than the other. She explained how all the lost tended to find their way to Kalopsia, that it would be intimidating at first, and that I should keep my head down. And most importantly, if anyone were to ask, I was a dryad, a forest nymph who lost her magic after an injury and was traveling to Clive Steeple in hopes of learning how to regain my gifts.

Ahead, the air rippled. Darya set her shoulders back, and our horses strode straight through the rippling effect with ease. I *felt* it as the magic reached out and touched me, deciding if I was a threat. Darya's ward.

The sun's heat intensified, and Darya slowed to a stop. A guard followed her lead, swinging off his horse and coming over to Apple to help me dismount.

Far in the distance, and beyond the heat waves, sat a populated city. My heart pounded in my chest.

"You must be cautious. The desert is not like Genesi," Darya said. "In Kalopsia, you are either a thief, a drunk, or a liar. Do not trust anyone. Get in and out as quickly as you can."

I lifted my chin, wanting to feel like Darya, wanting to *be* like her. She must have fears the same as everyone else, but she was willing to face them with her shoulders set back. But I found myself losing bravery the moment her eyes left mine.

I dropped my gaze to the sand. The soft, white sand that covered Genesi had turned to a darker, denser, hotter sand. I hadn't paid much mind when Bly dressed me this morning and offered me shoes for the first time since arriving in Genesi. Now, I stared down at the tan sandals wrapped around my ankles, wondering what else would be different here.

A collective pounding thudded ahead. A storm of sand trailed behind two sets of rapidly approaching hoofbeats. They came quickly, too quickly, and I took a step back when the dark horses came to a skidding halt far too close for comfort. Their riders said nothing, only stared down at us with storm-cloud eyes. Even their black horses looked angry, blowing out heavy puffs of air in our faces.

"I wish to speak with your queen," Darya spoke, seeming

unfazed by the nearness and fierceness of the riders looking down on her.

The two dark men—if they were men at all—didn't exchange a glance. They only stared as if we were very unwelcome guests. And then kept staring until it grew uncomfortable.

More hoofbeats sounded, and when I looked for them, I found two more sandstorms racing toward us from the city, but there was something else this time. The sand between the new horses rumbled as if something followed them underground. When they drew nearer, the rumbling lifted to the surface and transformed into the figure of a full-bodied being.

Particles of sand fell from the being's body to reveal more of the same tan colors. It was as if she were made of the sand she'd just risen from. There was so much of it woven throughout her brown, tousled locks it even coated the middle part of her hair, etched into her scalp. I fought the urge to scratch my head. No clothing covered her body, all her assets on display without so much as a hint of shame from her.

The Sand Queen gave Darya a curt nod that was hardly visible, and then her striking greenish-yellow eyes flicked to mine. Every nerve ending inside me told me not to look her in those eyes.

Her voice rang out, deep and authoritative. "This is the dryad you wrote about?"

"It is," Darya's voice was equally authoritative, different from the tone she'd used the past few days. "I trust she will be in good care with you and escorted on her journey quickly. Time is of the greatest essence."

"I trust your word is as good as my own?"

Darya's jaw tensed, but she stepped forward, reaching an arm out. "In exchange for Briar's safe passage through your desert, I grant your kingdom access to Genesi's border. Kalopsia may continue trading foods and goods with my waters as they have in the past."

I cut my head to Darya. She'd compromised the safety of her kingdom. *Why?*

"Only our waters," Darya added. "Once I return to Genesi, the wards will be rearranged to make an open path to the sea. Our towns will be kept inaccessible."

Cozbi's thin lips only stretched a fraction, and somehow, her features transformed into corruption. She clasped Darya's forearm, and the air swirled around their joined arms. The magic wound several times and then tightened like a knot before disappearing altogether. "You have my word, Darya. I look forward to getting her through my land as quickly as possible." Double meaning coated her wicked tongue.

Darya pulled me into an embrace that surprised me. A hug from a queen I'd known for all of a few days, but I returned the hug with meaning. "You will be fine," Darya said, and I wondered if she said it more for her comfort or mine. "Kenna will be waiting at the Empyrean border. She'll get you the rest of the way."

I gripped her tighter. "You've done more for me than I deserve. Thank you."

But when Darya released me, I found myself rooted to the spot. She mounted her horse, and a guard tied Apple's reins to his saddle. The air rippled as the border let them cross once again, and even then, I didn't move. I debated if I had time to change my mind before Darya and her soldiers were out of sight. If changing my mind were even an option.

An agitated impatience tingled at my back. The Sand Queen cleared her throat. Every instinct in my body screamed at me to run, but I took a deep breath, and turned to face Kalopsia.

Her thin, expressive eyebrows made her stare all the more

piercing, one arching to the sky. "Shall we go or would you rather wait for the stars to make an appearance?"

Cozbi had promised a safe and quick passage. She'd never promised to be nice to me.

Unlike the ride here, this trek was silent. The air grew thicker and dryer the closer to the city we got. Breathing became uncomfortable, though I dared not voice that I was beginning to struggle. No one offered a hand to pull me onto their saddle. No one spoke to me, or even gave me a downward glance. The riders sauntered atop their horses, and Cozbi glided through the sand, not lifting a foot from the ground and not seeming to care in the slightest if I fell behind. I quickened my pace, trying to keep close as we entered the brass city gates.

Darya was right. The city was a melting pot of mythical creatures, one that would have swallowed me whole if Cozbi let it. I tried to keep up as I took in a nightmarish minotaur and then a blue-skinned jinn. What looked like a seemingly human woman until she turned to reveal magnificent brown feathered wings and giant talons for feet. It was breathtaking, the differences between them all. I stopped in my tracks, gaze flitting from one body to the next. I didn't realize I had been smiling until it abruptly melted into a frown when Cozbi's grasp squeezed my upper arm, and she snatched me close to her face.

"Don't waste my time, child," she spat. "I can't very well get you out of my sight as promised if you're standing around waiting to be trampled." She released my arm as if disgusted she had touched me in the first place.

I scampered along, clutching my arm, and followed Cozbi into the shade of a temple-like building stretching high before us.

Inside, the noise and the thick of the heat softened. The light faded, and a green-patterned tapestry lined the walls. A towering statue on the back wall took over everything else in my line of sight. It was great, mean, and beautiful, and I instantly recognized it for what it was—a statue of *her*. And there on the floor—heads bowed and palms laid flat on the ground at her feet. Heat and confusion flooded my cheeks as I tried to work out why I was so furious. Who did Cozbi think she was, the High Queen herself? I scoffed and turned to face her. I didn't know what I wanted to say, but I hoped the emotion showed enough on my face to tell her exactly that. But as I readied for whatever silent message I was about to send, my mouth closed just as quickly as it had opened.

Cozbi assessed my clothing with disdain, but it wasn't her judging stare that stole my breath. It was the force approaching from behind her and his captivating green-eyed gaze.

The newcomer came to Cozbi's side, then took three additional smooth steps so that he stood directly in front of me.

Long, wavy black hair curtained his face and brushed his shoulders. The stubble on his chin was just starting to grow out from his last shave. His nose was wide and strong, if a nose could even be strong. I remembered to take more breaths in and out as I took in the rest of him. A scar began above his brow and ended just below his eye. I wanted to know how it got there. I wanted to know everything about him. I wanted to know how I immediately knew he was going to be a problem.

He scanned my face, my body, and then trailed his eyes back to mine. And then he smiled in a way that made me want to call him a bastard, even though he hadn't said one word yet.

"Zafar," Cozbi's voice boomed. "You are to deal with this now."

I lifted a hand to fidget with my locket, but he caught it in his, like it belonged to him. His lips brushed over the back of it, sending shivers up my arm. He rose from his partial bow, penetrating green eyes boring into my soul. He was enjoying this. "It would be my absolute pleasure."

At that, I instantly regretted leaving the beach.

"Shall I escort her to a chamber?" Zafar asked his queen, his eyes never leaving mine.

"She will stay in the city."

Zafar whipped his head to her. "The city? Did we not promise Darya she would not be harmed here? Surely the city isn't the best option, my queen."

That sharp eyebrow of hers rose higher than should be possible. "You expect a foreigner to sleep in my temple?"

His silence was her answer. No, this wasn't the beach at all. I couldn't trust my safety to anyone here. I was going to have to look out for myself, something I was used to by now anyway.

"Figure it out, Zafar. I am not to be bothered with it." Turning her back on us, she waved a hand, brushing us off, and I swore a speck or two of sand flew from her fingers.

Zafar looked puzzled with himself as he looked to a nearby guard standing watch by the entrance for help. The guard only shrugged in return.

I took his moment of distraction to scan him the same way he had me. His clothes were less like individual pieces and more like one piece of fabric wrapped around his entire body. Layers of brown linens hung loosely from him, yet tightly enough to sculpt his body and the muscles that made him. When my eyes found his again, he was watching me, obviously pleased I'd taken a moment to inspect him.

He raked a hand through his hair and rested it behind his head. "Right. The Sand Queen's personal guard...to be assigned with babysitting."

I shrank into myself, feeling like I often did, an inconvenience. "I swear I won't be any trouble."

The green in his eyes thrashed like fire. "What fun would you be to me then?"

I swallowed, and he scanned me up and down again with growing interest. "Fascinating," he said more to himself than to me. I waited for an explanation, but his gaze only traveled to different realms of my body. For some reason, my dormant flame woke from slumber. My chest warmed.

"What is?"

"A human."

The beat of my heart tripped and my whole body went still as stone. His devilish grin was all play.

"A friend from Genesi beat you here and gave up Darya's little lie."

I wasn't breathing anymore, my skin hotter than the desert itself.

"Relax." His voice was sultry and maddening. "Your secret is safe with Cozbi, human. Darya's bargain ensures that." He rolled his eyes, as if that weren't any fun at all, but my chest rose with a relieved breath. Only my eyes followed while he circled me. "I've never seen one before. I wasn't sure what I expected to see, but—" he was at my back now, "—it wasn't quite this."

I hated every second of this. Of him looking at me like I was a plaything he'd just bought with the tags still attached. "And what do you see?" I breathed.

He considered my question, stopping in his tracks at my side. "Glass. Beautiful, easily broken glass." I snapped my body in his direction and gave him a sharp look. A flash of surprise and enticement lit his face. He was ready to play. "Or perhaps a flower. Delicate. Still beautiful." I said nothing. "What is your name?" he asked.

I gritted my teeth. "Briar."

His jet-black hair tipped back with his head as he barked out a laugh. "That is perfect. A flower indeed." I wanted to punch him in the face, if I were capable of such a thing. "Come on, Flower," he added through another laugh. "Let me show you where you will be staying."

"Staying?" I didn't want to spend one night here that wasn't on horseback. But he strode toward the temple entrance, annoying confidence in every stride. I jogged to catch up with him. "I was hoping to be on my way."

"That takes planning, Flower. Cozbi tells me nothing until the last possible minute. My whole week will have to be rearranged for this." As he walked out into the open, a path cleared for us on the crowded streets. Maybe it was the sword slung over his back, or the muscles begging to rip their way through his shirt. "Once we do leave, we can make it through the desert in two or three days."

We weaved through the crowd as an endless stream of beautiful and terrifying creatures hurried off to their destinations, not seeming to care about much other than avoiding Zafar's broad shoulders.

"And then how long from Empyrean to Clive Steeple?"

"Days? Weeks? Who knows. They don't call it the Everwood for nothing."

"Why do they call it the Everwood?" I had to raise my voice now to be heard.

"Because if you don't know your way around, the woods seem to go on forever," he shouted back. Someone bumped against my shoulder, the force of it turning me in the other direction. My other shoulder was hit immediately after and I stumbled back, the second hit taking me by greater surprise. When I looked for Zafar again, he was gone.

I whirled around, looking for him. I stood on my toes, trying to see over the crowd. I pushed my way through the swamp of bodies, a clear path no longer present.

I unconvincingly told the rising panic in my chest to calm down and scanned the crowd for any sign of someone pushing their way back to me.

"Move it!" a voice barked, and I was bumped into by a bulky, green-skinned creature. I stumbled to the side, momentarily becoming a ping-pong ball in a sea of angry faces, until I landed roughly in the dirt.

Stunned by how quickly the situation had escalated, I didn't have time to push myself off the ground before a collective beat of thuds hit the dirt from nearby. Sand trembled at my fingertips.

The sea of bodies scattered, revealing something that resembled a horse, except three times the size of one. A long, thick mane fell from its neck and giant tusks protruded from the sides of its long face. Suddenly, it didn't look like anything closely related to a horse at all. And it was headed straight for me, refusing to slow on my behalf.

Someone shouted, but my body didn't respond, couldn't respond. I could only stare at the horse who was a few strides away now. Another shout. I snapped to and jolted off the ground, but only got halfway up before a body collided with my side, throwing me out of death's path. Giant hoofs raced by.

I would have coughed from the amount of dust inhaled had the breath not been knocked out of me. Fingers gripped my shoulders, digging into me to the point of pain. Fiery green eyes blazed through a canopy of jet-black hair.

Zafar.

We breathed on the ground together as the traffic around us returned to normal, as if nothing had just occurred. As if creatures were trampled and forgotten every day.

Zafar finally stood and reached down a strong arm in offering. He hoisted me off the ground, but the moment his hand left mine, his eyes turned from wild and confused to downright angry. I waited for him to start yelling or to throw insults, but then he blinked, and his teasing grin returned.

He shook his head. "I knew you'd be trouble. Do you think you can make it a few more minutes without getting lost?"

Still stunned and slightly whiplashed, more so by his back-and-forth reactions, I only nodded. Maybe I couldn't look out for myself here. Maybe I should stay very close to my personal guard.

Had there not been so much traffic in the way, it would have taken seconds to walk from Cozbi's shrine to the row of doors carved into a stretch of sand dune.

Zafar approached one of the doors and gave it two sharp knocks. A face appeared in the cutout, and a set of dark eyes skipped over Zafar and landed directly on mine. Zafar cleared his throat, an order to draw the doorkeeper's attention back on him. The door swung open in response.

It was dark inside, the air cool and slightly damp. I fought a shudder walking past the doorkeeper and stayed at Zafar's heels. He turned his face ever so slightly, revealing a sly grin.

We walked down a short flight of steps and came out at a narrow hallway lined with doors on each side. Mounted torches were the only source of light as the underground apartments went deeper and deeper. He stopped at a door with the number thirty-three etched above it, opened it, and gestured with his arm for me to enter.

The room was windowless. There was nothing but a small mattress pushed in a corner of the room, a bare, cold fireplace in the center, a chair too dusty to sit on in the other corner, and a rack for hanging clothes on its opposite side.

"This is where the personal guards and some of the temple staff live. There's a room at the end of the hall you can use to relieve yourself. There's no lock on the door, so I suggest you use it during our working hours when this place is mostly empty." He paused, giving himself another too obvious moment to scan my body. "I'm in room thirty-eight if you need me. On the opposite side of the hall and farther down."

"I won't need you." I responded without thinking and then froze. Did I really just say that?

Zafar grinned, as if waiting for the opportunity to tease me. He crossed his arms. "We'll see about that the next time you find yourself nearly trampled by a war horse."

Silence filled the air between us, and his eyes were expectant, waiting for a retort that wouldn't come. He huffed out a breath, disappointed, and turned to leave. "Wait," I said a little louder than I meant to. "What am I supposed to do until we leave?"

"You stay here, and you don't make yourself known. Trust me, you don't want to find yourself out there alone, human or dryad. Food will be brought to your door twice a day, and if you need to... wash up or anything, you'll let me know, and I'll escort you to the washrooms."

"So I'm not allowed to leave?"

He raised both hands and stepped to the side, making the path to the door clear. "You want to leave? Be my guest." More silence. "Don't leave this room," he advised again, sensing my unspoken response. And then he was gone, having shut the door behind him.

I sat on the edge of the hard mattress, exasperated. This definitely wasn't Genesi. I missed my last guest room, missed the way I buried my toes in the plush carpeting each morning, missed the silk sheets on my freshly washed skin and the heavy comforter. I picked at the thin rag that lay at the foot of the mattress now and shivered.

I went to the fireplace to find books inside of it in place of logs. Angrily, I swept my hand across the ashy pile inside. My hand met with a book whose cover had only been singed before the last fire had been put out. I plucked it from the pile, shaking and dusting off what I could. Taking it back to the mattress, I wiped the leftover soot on the so-called blanket and then opened it to the first page.

It didn't take long before I was heavily lost inside the story, hovering over the open pages with my elbows resting on crossed knees and knuckles on my cheeks. It was about a siren princess and a pirate prince whose families were at war with each other, and of course, they fell in love. Or at least, that's where the story was headed. Romance novels were so delightfully predictable. I'd only made it to the thirty-second page, just as the two sworn enemies met unexpectedly for the first time, when the door swung open and Zafar abruptly entered the room. I jumped, slamming the book closed as if I had something to hide.

Someone else accompanied him, but I pointed my stare at Zafar. "Jesus, could you knock?"

Zafar lifted an arrogant eyebrow. "The name is Zafar, not Jesus. Pay attention." His eyes dropped to the book in my lap. "Sorry to interrupt your sex novel. I'll knock next time."

I scowled.

"I came to introduce you to Keyon." He motioned behind to the newcomer. He was handsome with a young face and tawny skin. His hair was cut close to the scalp. He half bowed, hands clasped behind his back. "Keyon works within the personal guard. He'll be stationed outside your door when I can't be here." I was taken aback, though I tried to hide it. Keyon didn't look much older than a teenager, let alone a trained guard.

"And how long will I be here?" I asked again, growing more anxious each time Zafar indicated I'd be here for a while.

"At least a few days. A pack of wulvers were spotted crossing the same route we'll be taking. We're on good terms with them as a realm, but if we want to keep you out of center stage, it's best to avoid them. And I do believe we promised Darya your *safe* passage through the desert. If we leave now, we'll run into them head-on."

I didn't respond. While I didn't feel a rush to get back to where I belonged, no part of me wanted to stay in Kalopsia longer than necessary. I hoped Empyrean would be softer.

Zafar sighed and put his hand on the other guard's shoulder. "Keyon, my friend, good luck with this one. I'll take over tomorrow." Before I could protest, he was gone. Keyon stood there in the middle of the room, hands still hooked behind his back. Though his face was hard and trained, his tensed shoulders gave him away. He was uncomfortable.

"Can I get you anything?" When he spoke, it was strained, as if he were foreign and trying to speak a language he didn't know that well. But there was kindness in his eyes.

Still rattled, I only shook my head, not trusting that a bite in my tone wouldn't be present if I spoke. He bowed again and wordlessly left the room, stationing himself on the opposite side of the closed door. No one had to be stationed outside my door when I was in Genesi. It was as if they were keeping me from something here.

Darya's warning came back to me. *In Kalopsia, you are either a thief, a drunk, or a liar. Do not trust anyone. Get in and out as quickly as you can.*

I recalled the way no one but Zafar had bothered to help me out of a near-death situation. How anytime someone's gaze lingered on me in the city, it made me want to cover up. Maybe Zafar wasn't keeping me from anything. Maybe he was keeping things here away from me.

CHAPTER EIGHT

I finished the book by the next afternoon, having cried twice by the end of it. I checked the fireplace for more books I might have missed but came up with nothing. I debated reading it for a second time. There was nothing like reading a book for the first time, no matter how much you adored it. But I feared if I read it again, it wouldn't quite be the same, and I wanted to hold the memory of how the story made me feel in my heart forever. Just when I was about to give in, a series of taps sounded on the door.

"Come in," I tried to respond cheerfully, wanting to try a new approach with this rugged personal guard. But it was Keyon who entered, a meal tray in hand that smelled of roasted tomatoes and melted cheese over some sort of fish. I reached out, accepting the tray. "Thank you."

Keyon's face was like marble, and if it weren't for him concentrating so hard on my words, like he was trying to decipher them, barely a muscle would shift out of place. "Um." I stopped, not knowing how to ask. "I need a shower."

Keyon's eyebrow twitched. He stared, as if processing that small sentence like a computer. An old, slow one in need of an update.

"A wash." I tried again, pretending to scrub at my skin with an imaginary bar of soap.

Keyon's head nodded slowly before he turned on his heel and left without a word. I sighed, looking down at the promising scents of a decent meal. I picked up the plate, examining it for anything that looked poisonous. It looked fine. It *smelled* heavenly, and after deciding that dying of poison would be better than dying of starvation, I took a small bite. I closed my eyes, delight settling on my tongue. The dish was just as enjoyable as the meals served to me in Genesi. It was hard to give Kalopsia credit for anything, but it was good to know that if I were to stay in this dusty, sand-covered, secluded room, at least I would be well-fed.

I brought the book over to my lap, opened it once again, and flattened the pages on my knee so I could read between bites. I made it four pages in before the door opened abruptly.

My head snapped up to find Zafar in the doorway, an expectant look plastered on his face.

"Well?" That was all I got from him.

"Well, what?"

"Keyon said you needed a wash?"

"Yes?"

"You've been here a day."

I could feel the muscles of my face matching some of the looks Keyon had given me. "Yes."

"We're permitted two washes in the private washing stalls a week. You want to use one of your two now?"

"*Two* showers a week?" I set the fork down, baffled.

Zafar only looked at me as if I were naive. "This isn't Genesi, Flower. Kalopsia thrives in few ways, water supply not being one of them."

I looked Zafar over. He was rugged, yes. Dirty...maybe, but it was a look that suited him. I swallowed my shock and pressed on. "Okay, well... I would like to wash now."

He allowed a breath of silence, enough time for me to change my mind before he said, "The desert is a sandy place, in case you haven't noticed. You will not be permitted a third wash if you don't time them wisely."

"Hopefully, I won't be here long enough to have to use my weeks' worth."

"The water will be cold by the time we get there at this time of day," he warned again.

I stood, setting the plate on the bed and tucking the book into my chest. "Better hurry then."

Zafar frowned, taking in my clothes. "Your dress is...bright."

I was all of a sudden aware that I was still wearing the same baby-blue dress I had arrived in. My cheeks stained with blush. "I wasn't sent with anything to change into."

"It's not the typical style of the desert. You stand out. Not something you particularly want to do in a place like this."

I tapped the cover of the book in my hands, not knowing what he expected me to do about it. Zafar stepped up to me, and when his stride didn't slow, I found myself leaning back. He stopped in front of my toes, the green in his eyes brightening as they drank mine in. He took the book from my grasp, his calloused fingers brushing against my smooth ones. He glanced at the cover without even really looking at it, flipped the pages open long enough to scan one line, and then tossed it over his shoulder carelessly. It landed hard enough to dent the corner. Zafar's hands slid into invisible pockets, and his lips curved into a delighted, mocking grin.

My usual spark of outrage was too overwhelmed with shock to make an appearance. I stared at the book, thinking, if only to keep my jaw off the floor. Was he baiting me? Did he really want a reaction out of me so badly? I breathed in as deeply and unnoticeably as I could, collecting myself, before meeting Zafar's excited, gleaming eyes.

I wordlessly slid around his solid build and to the door. I paused when I made it to the hallway alone, looking over my shoulder to find Zafar staring at the disrespected book, his lips slanted.

"Are you coming?" I asked, stealing his attention back. "I don't know the way."

I couldn't read the emotion on his face when he approached this time, but I did note the way he regained composure I hadn't seen him lose as he sauntered by and ahead of me. "Stay close this time, would you?"

The washing stalls, like everything in this city, were not far from the sandpit apartments, but took far too long to get to with all the traffic. There were so many creatures in such a tightly compressed area.

I stayed on Zafar's heels, keeping my eyes only on him until we reached a break in the crowd and came before a large solid structure. It was a giant ugly block of concrete with no craftsmanship to decorate it. It was all business here, all of Kalopsia's money having gone to Cozbi's overdone, unneeded shrine. I followed Zafar inside, refusing to let him get too many steps ahead of me. But what I found inside had me freezing in place and almost turning on my heel. Row by row, shower stalls lined the small space, separated only by wood railings. There were no doors or coverings at the front. Nothing to hide the two naked bodies standing inside separate stalls, all assets on full display for anyone walking in. My gasp tumbled out, and my eyes shot to the wet stone floor.

"Out," Zafar demanded.

A gruff voice responded, "Piss off Zafar, we just got in here."

A shower head turned off, and a series of grumbles emitted

from a second male as his form leaned for what I assumed to be a towel and his clothes. It took him seconds to dress and exit the showering building, while the other male, the one who had spoken, remained under the water stream.

Zafar's voice was level. "You have three seconds to reach for that nozzle before I reach it for you."

"I *said* I just got in, so piss—"

Zafar's form left my side three words into the sentence, though I didn't dare look away from my own feet to see what happened next. All I heard was the water shut off, followed by a thud and a loud grunt.

"Fucking Kingdoms, alright!"

A few seconds later, a pair of wet footsteps passed by me much too close and too slow for comfort. Close enough that my gaze couldn't help but trail up to his blocky shins. I made it up to his kneecaps before realizing where I was headed and sent my stare back to my own feet.

"Never seen one before have you, sweetheart?"

"Keep moving," Zafar's voice interjected. The male obeyed, though an amused laugh trailed out the door with him.

Rattled, I stood there staring at my toes and feeling like the child I'd just made myself look to be.

"You won't have long. Maybe ten minutes before the next group of males come in for their scheduled showers."

I lifted my gaze, looking around helplessly at the open showers. "Males?"

"This showering stall is reserved for the temple staff, which yes, are all male."

"There's not a separate showering stall somewhere I could use?"

"Private showers are for private homes. The temple staff aren't granted private housing. Relax. I'll stand guard at the door."

I shifted on a foot. Zafar's lips curved into mischief. "As tempting as it may be, I won't peek. I promise."

Something about standing naked at Zafar's back, even if he offered a magical oath with it, didn't sound reassuring at all. He must have read the worry on my face, because his eyes rolled to the ceiling. "Go to the second row where you can't be seen."

I examined the second row, considering it.

"Nine minutes now, I believe."

At his reminder, I walked around to the second row, finding that once I was in a stall, only my head would be visible if someone were to walk in before Zafar could send them away. I stripped out of my dress and hung it over the bar outside my stall. There was a towel I could tell had been used maybe only hours before. I forced myself to ignore the thought, coming to terms with the fact that one of Kalopsia's shining traits wasn't comfort and hospitality. I flipped on the nozzle and stepped into the thin, hard stream. The water barely hit enough surface area to wash what I needed in such a short amount of time.

My eyes flicked to Zafar, making sure his back was still to me, even if I was mostly hidden.

"I can hear your stillness. I'm not joking about the small time frame here."

"Forgive me if the setup isn't exactly ideal." I eyed the small bar of soap, used God knows how many times before me, and held in a gag.

"Would conversation help?

I stared accusingly at the soap. "Maybe," I said after a beat.

"Tell me about yourself then, Flower. What should one know about the infamous and rare human."

I finally picked up the soap and held it under the water long enough to hopefully wash away the leftover filth from the last renter. When I allowed it to touch my skin, it smelled of dust. Certainly not the blend of coconut and brown sugar I was used to.

"I don't like talking about myself."

"Work with me here."

"Why don't you tell me about yourself? I'm a much better listener than I am a talker."

"What do you want to know?"

Everything.

"Why is everyone here afraid of you?"

Zafar didn't sound surprised even though he said, "Are they?"

My tone was flat in response and I squinted at him even though he couldn't see it. "You don't seem like the modest type, Zafar. Why pretend now?"

His laugh came out a very immodest rumble. "Do you know what the name Zafar means?" There was the perfect mixture of pride and taunting in that question.

"No."

"It means victory." He paused, as if wanting the statement to sink in and leave its mark. "When I came here, I had to prove myself just to stay fed and alive. I did just that. Well enough to grab the attention of someone very important. I've lived up to the meaning of my name."

"When you came here?"

"I don't originally hail from Kalopsia."

"Really?" I asked, taken aback. Though I'd seen so little of Elysian, Zafar even looked like the desert, with his already deeper complexion tanned even darker by the sun's relentless rays. As though the desert were a part of him rather than the other way around. "Of all places, why come to Kalopsia?"

There was enough of a hesitation that I could sense he was debating giving me the honest answer or one coated in a half truth. "I have a skill only the desert would appreciate." A half-truth then. "And specifically, Cozbi. When things didn't work out back home, Kalopsia seemed the only logical place to go." The place where all the lost went, Darya had stated.

"Kalopsia doesn't seem very appealing to me."

"It has its perks."

"Oh yeah? A part from the thieves, trampling war horses, and the never-ending sunburn?"

"Don't forget the drought."

"I rest my case."

Zafar blew out an amused huff. "It's the desert. You learn to adapt. We work around the drought. We thieve before we can be thieved from. You build your reputation around here, because that is what your survival is based upon."

"But why? You could live so much more comfortably elsewhere."

"Nothing is comfortable right now, Flower. You could go to the ends of Elysian and still find its creatures near starving."

"Right," I replied a bit sadly. "Because of the dying land."

Zafar almost looked over his shoulder but caught himself. "How do you—"

"Darya filled me in," I offered.

He hummed in what sounded like doubt. "Yes. The dying land. And the real kicker is that we found a way to barely survive, only for one single creature to screw even that up. Now, we're fucked all over again."

I rummaged through my mind, searching for this missing information I must have forgotten from Darya's story, but came up with nothing.

Zafar must have read my hesitance and said, "It's complicated."

I ran my face under the water and then said, "We have at least five minutes left and the walk back."

"Well," he started. "The death of the land is the death of all things bound to nature. At first, the realm's elements stopped existing altogether, leaving us without rain and harvest. It's only by the existence of the lesser rulers that Elysian has held on this long without a High Queen. A history too long and complex to explain in four minutes."

"Darya explained enough. There are five of them, each with an elemental gift, but the High Queen powers the land. Without her, the rest don't really matter."

"Well...yes," Zafar said, a bit surprised, as if it were impossible and impressive I'd summed up a great history in a matter of seconds.

"So you were saying?"

"Before the High Queen, it was the lesser rulers who held Elysian's life source together. Post High Queen, their gifted roles are essentially irrelevant. They simply stick around because our High Queens after them have allowed them to do so. They have power and authority over their assigned regions, but they aren't truly needed. Or they weren't before all this shit happened with the missing heir. Anyway, one would think that without a High Queen, the lesser rulers who once weren't lesser rulers, would come back into play, but that's not what happened. We are cursed."

I didn't interrupt Zafar to let him know I knew all of this already. I wanted to hear the story from his point of view, and also desperately needed the distraction from what my bare feet might be touching on this ground.

"But even still, together, the remaining elemental gifts from each region have allowed us to stretch on the life just a few years longer than what we originally had. We were barely holding on, but we were holding on, nonetheless. Until one of those rulers idiotically got himself into trouble with the Dark Queen. I'm guessing Darya filled you in about her too."

"She did," I said, envisioning Darya's map. "Which of the rulers are you talking about?"

"Valhalla's *king*." He sneered. "He and his element have been magic bound in a cell for almost a year now. It only took the land two days to recognize things were off all over again, and now it's dying quicker than ever. It's as if it's making up for the time we gained back."

"The wind-gifted one," I said in response, as if this was the only thing of importance. I wasn't sure why I cared to clarify, but I had to. "Who is he? Darya never got around to talking about him when she explained the lands to me."

"The Valhallan king?" Zafar asked, confusion filling his tone. As if, yes, me picking up on that detail out of everything he'd just said was questionable. "A ruthless devil. A selfish prick not worth remembering. Because of him, things have gone from one extreme to the next, too fast for us to keep up with. His winds cause chaos, but it was a chaos we needed. The rainstorms haven't been seen in a year. Crops aren't growing anymore, and no one will trade their stock with us. Soon the air will become thick and dry. Yes, more so than it already is. I bet we suffocate before the food supply runs out."

I turned the water off at that moment, and Zafar turned in my direction. Our eyes met, and everything stilled. My breath was heavy, caught between his stare and the sudden realization that if I didn't get out of here *fast*, I was going down with Elysian.

Approaching voices drifted in from outside. I raced for the towel while Zafar walked into the outside light. I hardly dried off before flinging the dress over my head and letting it slip down my body. I slid my feet back into the sandals, old sand sticking to my toes and heels. When I made it to the entrance, a group of seven very disgruntled looking males waited impatiently in front of a stoned-faced Zafar. All seven pairs of eyes landed on the bright-blue dress clinging to my body.

Zafar took my arm immediately, pushing past the gathered group. He walked us briskly back to the sandpit apartments without another word, only urgency in his steps. I let him hold my arm the whole way, let him force me away quickly from the eyes I still felt burning into my back. It was always outside that I was most thankful for his unapologetic roughness.

By the time I was back in my underground room, my feet were

already covered in dirt, and the bottom of my dress was stained brown. Flecks of sand coated my freshly washed skin.

"I hate this place," I mumbled to myself.

"You get used to it."

I shook my head, examining my arms and brushing them off. "I will never understand how anyone can live here."

Zafar laughed, and my eyes shot up at the sound of it. It said everything without him having to say a word.

"What?" I asked eventually.

"You don't have to tell me anything about yourself. Enough of the truth comes out naturally."

I made a face I couldn't help. "What does that mean?"

"You're judgmental."

My face screwed up even more, taken aback. "I am not."

Zafar shrugged, somehow making me feel the urge to defend myself more.

"Just because I don't thrive off two showers a week or enjoy sand sticking to me like glue, doesn't mean I'm judging those that do. I can want a different way of life without either of those ways being wrong."

Zafar looked me over as if I were a puzzle to be solved. A newly discovered specimen to be studied and then written about. And then he did the most infuriating thing of all. He smiled. Unkindly. "Do you ever relax?"

The flame quietly living inside me sparked awake. My mouth twisted, and I tilted my head just the slightest of a fraction as I debated how to react. I allowed myself every awkward second of silence just to cool that spark. A retort would do no good, neither would the fight in me I knew I'd never act on. I turned my back to him silently and bent to take my sandals off.

"Why is it always the beautiful ones that are the most uptight?"

My back snapped into a straight line. I stared at the wall in front of me, the word *uptight* leaving me in a trance. My heart raced with a fury I didn't understand. I carefully turned to face him.

"It never fails," he went on before I could come up with a response. "The more attractive, the bigger the head."

My jaw slackened. Never, not once in my life had I believed myself to be better than anyone. If anything, it was the opposite.

"I'm not uptight." My voice was all screwed up, wound as if it were in fact in a tight ball.

Zafar's lips slanted in a way that confirmed it. His posture slackened, and his expression went nonchalant. "Loosen up some. Life isn't that serious."

"I'm not uptight," I said again. "I'm scared." The confession startled me. All my life, I knew I was scared, but it was the first time I'd said the word aloud.

His eyebrows bunched. "Of what?"

"Darya warned me about this place. She told me not to trust *anyone.*"

Zafar laughed, but it was a humorless sound. "And you know Darya well enough to take her word as gospel?" When I didn't respond, he pressed on, his voice suddenly angry. Offended even. "Heed this warning from a stranger who doesn't care enough for you to lie to you. Maybe don't take warnings from those you've just met. And maybe have a mind of your own to question those misguided warnings."

Zafar's attention went to the half-eaten meal from before my wasted shower. "Another piece of advice? Only recently has Kalopsia seen good food. We can thank you for that, I suppose, and the deal that came with you. It was only a few days ago that the fish would have arrived stale and unseasoned. It would be wise to not let such privileged meals grow cold." And with that, Zafar was out the door, letting it shut behind him a little too loudly.

A knot formed in my throat. "I do have a mind of my own," I barely managed to say to the closed door. I plopped down on the hard mattress, begrudgingly taking his advice and finishing the last few bites of food. But the taste was ruined, and my body felt somehow dirtier than it had before.

I turned Zafar's parting words over in my head as I chewed. He thought I was uptight. He saw the way I responded to his teasing over and over again and had concluded I was no fun to be around.

And he was right, I didn't know Darya. She'd taken me in, and though her reasoning had sounded purehearted enough, I didn't really know anything about her. My heart sank, and I felt so, so stupid. But I didn't know what reason she had to lie to me about Kalopsia either. From what I'd seen, it was a place you should—a place you *had* to watch your back in.

I lay back on the mattress, clasping my fingers together on top of my stomach. *Uptight.*

I was guarded and scared of the world. Scared of letting anyone truly get to know me. Never had I imagined that coming across as being too good for anyone. The word replayed over and over in my head until it turned into the word *flower*. He'd viewed me as something delicate and weak from the moment he'd laid eyes on me. Before I'd even opened my mouth. And that was the way it always went. It was the reason I always got stepped on. Trampled like an inconvenient weed. Because I lacked the confidence Zafar strutted around with so effortlessly.

My knuckles squeezed against each other while the flame refused to weaken. At least it kept me warm in place of the bare logs in my room.

I loosened my fingers and the scowl on my face. Tomorrow, I would try to evolve. Even if it only lasted for as long as I was in Elysian. I could do better. There was still time to change this world's view of me before I returned to my own.

If it was a challenge Zafar wanted, it was a challenge he would get.

# CHAPTER NINE

"Eat." Zafar set a plate of food next to me on the bed. Another sandwich of some sort—roast beef by the smell of it.

His voice had returned to normal, but the way he spoke to me in commands, the way his eyes absorbed me... It ignited any hard feelings I had from the day before.

"Not hungry."

"Perfect," he replied, sounding unbothered. "Then we can head to the market now."

I let my eyes do the asking, not ready to use more words than I had to. Not ready to dive into this new Briar I'd promised myself to be only twelve hours before.

"No time to explain. If we waste much time standing around the market will be too packed to get anything done."

I gave in and asked questions as we walked. Zafar ignored them all. And by the time we made it through the crowded streets and into an even more congested area, all I cared about was staying close enough to him to be seen as something to stay away from. But there were too many bodies and not enough room to fit us all. Not even the sword strapped across his back was enough encouragement to grant us some personal space.

Zafar came to a stop in an area that held pop-up tents and carts, each one barely inches apart from the other. Some displayed golden trinkets and odd gadgets, while others held folded garments.

Merchants aimlessly called out, making known what they sold, and why it was exactly what you were missing in your life. Some patrons stopped occasionally to admire products, others roamed by without flinching, as if they'd been trained to do so. Many of them wore pieces of fabric over their mouths and noses to shield them from the dust and debris in the air. But all of them walked around, shouting over one another, looking completely unaffected by the commotion of it all. If this wasn't the kind of traffic Zafar was worried about running into, I wanted to cooperate and get done whatever needed to be done so we could leave.

Zafar's alluring voice hardly sounded over the noise. "That dress will turn to rags by the time you reach Clive Steeple. You'll need clothes for your journey."

Before I could ask why he cared at all about my upkeep, Zafar instructed me to lead the way, and when I found something I liked, he'd take care of the rest. That was enough to send my anxiety through the roof without the bustling of the market square. I stared out into the intimidating crowd, unsure.

"Flower," came Zafar's rough, sensual voice from behind my shoulder. He'd dropped his tone to one that was gooey and enticing, like a hot cookie right out of the oven. Everything about it seemed like a great idea, but if you weren't careful, it would burn your tongue. "Not to rush you or anything, but this isn't even the market's busiest hour. I suggest you move."

"I don't have any money."

He held up a hand. "I told you I've got it. The Sand Queen pays enough."

I was sweating with nerves that had nothing to do with the heat. I didn't like Zafar. And even if I did, I couldn't bring myself to let him spend money on me. "I don't like that. You paying for my things. I'd feel guilty."

"There's no reason to feel guilty for accepting something I'm offering you. Have you never had someone do something nice for you?" He had no idea. When I didn't answer, he rolled his eyes, took my shoulders, and turned me toward the endless line of pop-up carts. "Go, Flower."

"Stop calling me that," I bit out.

"No." I could sense the curve of his smile behind my ear. "Now, if you don't walk up to one of these stands and pick a pair of damn harems, or earrings, or one of those flowy gowns you females look so ravishing in, I will pick something for you. In which case, you may wind up in something that barely covers you at all." The skin at my neck crawled. He released my shoulders and pushed at the curve of my back. "Go."

It was a nightmare, but I forced myself to stop at a random stand and pointed at a pair of loose, thin pants, and then at another stand where I asked to look at a lightweight top, something I imagined would keep me cool and covered from the sun on our ride. Almost everything in the market was the color of bronze, the fashion not differing nearly as much as its creatures did.

Zafar took out a heavy pouch and traded some kind of currency both times. I'd never seen someone who looked so dangerous doing something so nice.

When I assured him the two items were enough to get me through my time here, he blew out an impatient breath and dragged me by the arm from table to table. We moved like that for half an hour. He'd point to something, have a merchant hold it up to me, and either give a dissatisfied shake of his head or an accepting nod. Each approved item was slung over my arm as coins were tossed.

I looked at my covered arms. "This is too much," I panicked. "We have to take some of this back."

He pinched the bridge of his nose. "Would you really offend me so?"

I snapped my eyes up, the instinct to be cold to him harder after he'd done something nice for me. "That's not what I'm trying to do at all."

He tapped my chin. "Relax."

Zafar took some of the clothes from me, lightening the load on my arm, and leaving me speechless as we maneuvered our way through the crowd. Keeping up with Zafar's personalities gave me whiplash.

A broad shoulder collided with mine, almost knocking me down, but instead, only the clothes tumbled to the sand.

"Watch it, bitch." The thickly accented voice led me to an impatient, bearded face glaring down at me. A face that quickly changed expressions when a long blade rested against his neck. Zafar's sword. His dirt-brown eyes traveled to Zafar's scar, and some kind of recognition settled in them.

"How odd. I know I couldn't have heard you correctly, but I could have sworn these old ears of mine heard you call this beautiful maiden... Was it a bitch?"

The bearded stranger's eyes flicked back to mine. In his hand, he gripped a chain that trailed behind him. The opposite end attached to a golden clasp wrapped around the neck of another. Matching chains circled each of her wrists.

Chocolate hair clung to her arms, thick with sweat. Round, honey-soaked eyes filled with sorrow and defeat. As if the chains weren't enough, a silver band clasped tightly around her upper arm, leaving the skin there reddened and raised.

Her handler's scratchy voice barely tore my gaze from hers. "Maiden? I would have guessed concubine." The blade pressed inward, and a hint of red trickled down his neck.

"Careful," Zafar warned.

Whoever he was, he knew of Zafar well enough not to challenge him further. "I...apologize," he grunted out.

"How smart of you." Zafar lifted the blade, and the handler straightened, rubbing his neck and eyeing the nervous crowd. Zafar didn't bend down to help me gather the fallen clothes until the handler finally carried on his way through the crowd, pulling on the chain as he went. Only then did he return the sword to his back and kneel to pick up the fallen clothes.

"I can't take you anywhere."

My heart raced, eyes still locked on the retreating pair. "Why was she chained?"

"She's a slave. Just purchased from the looks of it," he responded mindlessly, focused on patting out the clothes as best he could.

"She had something on her arm." I rubbed my upper arm, imagining the pain the silver band caused.

"The mark of a slave. One day, if she's ever freed, it will be removed."

I tore my gaze from her disappearing back. "It was too tight."

His disinterested tone matched his face. "She's property."

"How can she be freed?"

"Well, someone would have to pay a great deal in the first place to take ownership and then remove the band themselves. Secondly, they'd have to care enough. That's not likely to happen. Kalopsia's economy is dependent on our slaves."

"How much?"

He raised a brow, the scarred one. "How much?"

"How much?" I repeated.

"An awfully bold question for someone who has no form of currency to buy her own clothing." He tapped my chin again. "This is how things are, Briar. It's not for you to worry over."

Briar. He used my name this time. But as we made our way back, I couldn't stop the image from deepening in my mind.

"What makes someone's life less valuable than the next to make them someone's property?"

"Probably where she's from. A lot of aged-out orphans from the scummier cities in Kalopsia have nowhere else to go but to a slave master's hands. It's better than dying in the desert."

"Is it? She isn't actually *living*," I pushed. "And that was a rhetorical question, by the way. The correct answer should be obvious."

Zafar whirled as we approached the sandpit apartments. "Lower your voice," he hissed. "You don't want to be overheard saying something like that and it being reported back to the Sand Queen. That's a great way to get kicked out of here. Or worse, you might find a chain wrapped around your own neck."

The speed at which he'd turned on me had shocked me and reminded me that he wasn't human. We weren't on the same level. I balled my fists at his sharp stare and lifted my chin. I wasn't ready for the fire inside me to reach the surface just yet, but at least this time I wouldn't shrink back the way I usually did. The way I *always* did.

The fact that Zafar was bringing out that side of me, a side I'd never let out my entire life, scared me.

His face barely softened when he finally took a step back. His hand came out, closing over the wrist of a passing attendant. The far too young worker stopped short, recognition coming over him. Zafar handed him the pile of clothes. "Wash these. They are to be returned to unit three, room thirty-three by sunset."

The attendant dipped a knee in response. The flame in my chest leapt, more awake than it'd ever been. It shot up my throat, made its way to the top, and nearly escaped. The hand that usually reached out for it caught it just in time.

"Is he a slave too, or is he here of his own free will?" I couldn't help it.

Zafar halted in his tracks and slowly turned to face me. "Remember when you said you wouldn't be any trouble?"

Defiance swelled in my chest. Followed by a strange satisfaction.

"Yes, he's here voluntarily and receiving pay, if that's what you're asking."

I followed him wordlessly to my room, the tension thick even underground.

Zafar fell back at my door, waiting for me to let myself in so he could be done with me already. I matched his stare and then reached for the door, turning my back to him.

Zafar closed his hand over mine, his grip rough as he spun me around. My breath hitched. My back pressed into the door, and our noses were too close to touching. His other arm rested on the door just above my head, caging me in.

"For the record, I like troublesome things." Zafar looked at me with that *thing* in his eyes that sent the green thrashing like a dancing fire. "I crave them."

His chest brushed mine with a heavy inhale. My body reacted instantly to his touch, but not in the way I expected. It hummed with desire and confusion. One side of his mouth tugged upward in a silent dare.

I should stop him. Whatever he was doing, I should stop it. But one of the last conversations I'd had with Leah played in the background of my mind. Something about being happy. Something about not fighting things exactly like this.

And suddenly, I knew. Though I couldn't understand how, I knew if we went in that room together, there was definitely going to be some trouble.

His gaze dropped to my lips, and he leaned in. Panic disguised as playfulness took over and I twisted the doorknob and leaned back, following the door as I let it open wide. Zafar fell forward, and instead of colliding with my face, he halfway tripped inside.

In the middle of the empty room, he turned so slowly toward the door where I remained, his expression shifting from shock to delight. I gave him a taunting smirk. I'd been taking notes from his games, and it was his move now.

"You're going to pay for that." He stalked toward me, but then something caught my attention.

The chair that usually sat empty in the corner was occupied. The snap of my head caught Zafar's attention too, but I made eye contact with the visitor before he did.

A hooded figure sat casually with a leg thrown over the arm of the chair, toying with a short, slender dagger. The shadow cast by the hood only revealed a feral grin. A long, blonde braid spilled out from under the hood and trailed along her arm. A polished nail flicked the tip of the knife seductively.

Fight or flight alarm bells went off in my head. Flight. It was always flight.

Fast as lightning and silent as a viper, she was out of the chair, her knife coming down on me in one swift motion. I pressed against the door, turning my head and closing my eyes just as Zafar's longer, heavier sword clashed with her smaller blade a few inches from my nose.

Zafar glared at the hooded figure.

A smooth, confident voice came from the hood. "I was so hoping I'd catch you alone, but what fun it'll be to kill two birds with one stone."

She took a step back, readjusting, and then came down on him. There was a flurry of silver clashing against silver.

I turned to run for help, to shout into the hall that someone was attacking a guard, but she was fast, faster than Zafar. There was a grunt and a tumble, and the next moment, she ran, kicked off the door, and landed between me and the only way out. Air sailed past my neck as I instinctively stepped back, barely avoiding the blade.

She followed every retreating step I took, my speed surprising me, some part deep within me wanting to stay alive.

Zafar rose, but she was inhumanly quick. She pulled a second dragger from somewhere on her thigh and threw it in his direction without ever taking her green eyes off mine. The dagger met with his shoulder, and he staggered back, cursing. She kicked my foot out from under me, and my back thudded against the floor.

The sand-crested ceiling was my view for only a moment before her face hovered over me. Victory shined in her eyes, but...instead of taking the killing blow while Zafar was down, she just stood there. And smiled. She stood there until Zafar grabbed her by the braid, yanking her head back with brutal strength, exposing her neck, and rested his sword there.

"I wasn't expecting to see you again so quickly," he said.

"It's a pity I have to go so soon then." Her elbow shot out to a very sensitive place, and both Zafar and his sword went down. The blonde-haired beast took off for the door, and she was gone before either of us could recover.

I shot to Zafar, hauling him up by his uninjured arm.

"That bitch."

"Who was *that*?"

"*That*—" he took a steadying breath and examined his shoulder, "—was embarrassing, first of all." Blood soaked through his shirt. "That is called the Assassin."

"And she came to kill *me*?" I pointed to myself as if to clarify.

"Well, she certainly wasn't popping by for a visit, was she?"

I thought of the slaver I'd bumped into earlier. The threat Zafar had posed to him. The slave owner didn't seem like the type to let public disrespect slide. "You don't think the slaver from the market..."

"Hasn't anyone told you this place is ruthless?"

I'd been told plenty. He gazed at the doorway as if he debated trying to catch up with the Assassin.

"There's only one way to find out."

I gave him a questioning look. "Do you know her or something?"

"Or something, yeah. She's tried to kill me a few times." Zafar ripped a piece of his shirt from the bottom and held it with his teeth as he wrapped it tightly around his shoulder. "I'm going to ask around. See if I can get a location on her. I also intend to find out how the fuck she got in here in the first place."

"So she's tried to kill you a few times and your response is to run toward her?"

"I'm still alive, aren't I?" He opened his arms wide to showcase that he was in fact alive, flinching slightly at his new wound. "It's more of a never-ending game between the two of us. She wouldn't dare actually kill me. Then she'd have nothing to do in her free time. Besides, I'm curious now what the Assassin could want from you of all creatures."

So was I, but I wasn't willing to go straight into the den of the lioness that was hunting me to find out. He stared at the door again, deep in thought. "I'll send Keyon to guard your door. Get some sleep."

"Wait—"

But he didn't wait. He left, not checking to make sure I was unharmed or shook up.

It all happened so fast. One minute we were dangerously close to crossing a line. The next, he was on his way to go clean a knife wound.

I closed the door behind him and stood with my back to it. I'd been in Kalopsia for less than a week, and I'd already been silently undressed by any pair of eyes that found me, threatened multiple times, and almost murdered by a paid assassin.

The desert was *not* like the ocean at all. The desert sucked.

## CHAPTER TEN

I tried to sleep to pass the time. There was nothing else I could do in this place. But even that didn't work. I couldn't see if the sun was awake or asleep in this windowless room, but my body knew. It wasn't time to sleep, and my brain was going to remind me of that as it dwelled on questions I'd never get the answers to. The slave from the market—How had her arm not become infected? How was it that even though Genesi and Kalopsia shared a border, they operated as if on different continents entirely? And most concerning, what had gotten into me? I'd told myself I would give Zafar exactly what he wanted, but even still, I hadn't expected for it to feel so *good*.

I welcomed the questions swirling in my mind. Anything to wipe away thoughts of Leah and all the other broken things I'd left behind. But no matter how hard I tried to think of anything but Leah, tears fell for her anyway.

I didn't even get a chance to say goodbye at her funeral. I made that decision when I decided not to return to my image. My tears ran hot. None of it was fair. Leah had so much to live for. She had a family. She had friends. It should have been me that died.

I squeezed my eyes closed and forced myself to think of the best memory I owned.

Instead of a memory hidden deep from the good parts of my childhood, the little of my mother I remembered, my thoughts drifted to a night with Leah and her friends.

I'd just moved in, and her friends had helped me move my things all day. We were exhausted by the end of the night. Someone ordered pizza, and the crisp October breeze was too good to pass up. The stars were countless. We piled on the balcony, which was entirely too small for the five of us, but we made it work. We stargazed for what felt like hours, almost completely still and quiet.

"Do you really think we're the only ones out here?" The question had come from Rhett. His curly blond hair was the brightest thing in the night. Viv's ever-present space buns rested on his shoulder, and a blanket was pulled up to her chin. She'd been the first to fall asleep.

"Black holes, man. Of course, we aren't the only ones," Ian responded.

My heart panged when the memory flickered by of Leah's head resting on my legs. We were so cramped on the balcony that she had to kick her feet up on the railing. Ian sat beside me, his arm draped over a knee and fingertips just barely grazing Leah's raised leg, as if no one would notice.

There was something special about the stars that night. About everything. The way they twinkled more than ever before. It was as if they were alive that night.

Looking back, Leah's friends had welcomed me from the start. They'd accepted me because Leah accepted me, and that was all it took for them. I had been the one standing in my own way, too afraid of another betrayal to step inside their circle. I had to remember us all like that, on that night specifically. It was all I had left to hold on to.

I pushed my thoughts and myself off the mattress and went over to the rack of clothing. I pulled on one of the new harem pants and paired them with a sand-colored tunic. The fabric was thin but layered, making it suitable for the strong winds and harsh sand it kicked up. I had to get out of here. Someone had to take me on a supervised walk or *something* to distract my mind.

My door opened abruptly, and I scowled at Zafar as I snapped the last hidden button in place.

His eyes immediately found my fingers and lingered there before he spoke. "I know where she is."

"Where who is?"

"Nilsa."

My brow arched on its own accord.

"The Assassin," he clarified. "Yes, believe it or not, the psychopath has a name."

"Yes, well, that's typically what happens when a child is born, isn't it? I would hope no one would actually name their child Assassin. Are you going to come in?" I pointed at the doorway that he was still only halfway standing in.

He stepped the rest of the way into the room. "We're going to go pay her a visit."

I paused. "*We're* not going anywhere."

His smile was sin itself. "Come on, Flower. Not that delicate, are you?"

"Are you joking? She just tried to slit my throat." My hand went to my neck, still feeling the wind that had sailed past it with her missed strike. "Wait, how did you find her so fast?"

Zafar lifted a hand, and I noticed the brown square note he held. "She left a note on my door. Telling *us* to come pay her a visit where she lives."

"That doesn't make any sense."

He rolled his eyes. "You're so challenging. I love it."

My cheeks heated. "I'm not trying to be challenging."

"Well, that's a pity. You're so good at it."

They heated more as his eyes roamed over me. "The clothes look good. I have exceptional taste." It was my turn to roll my eyes. "It means she doesn't plan to attack. It means she wants to talk."

"I don't understand," I said, slipping on a pair of boots tall enough to keep the sand out. I dreaded how sweaty they would make my feet once I got out in the heat. There was literally no benefit to living in this place, and I couldn't fathom why anyone would choose it over any of the other regions. "She was just here, and it didn't seem like she wanted to just talk."

"Nilsa likes dramatics. Nothing can ever be so simple with her. This was just her favorite way of getting my attention."

"That makes even less sense."

He walked up to the rack of clothing, shuffled through the way too many clothes he'd bought, and tossed me a hooded cloak. "Put this on."

I obeyed, slipping the cloak around my shoulders and tying it around the neck.

An everlasting thirst darkened his eyes, and he stalked up to me. By some miracle, when his face stopped in front of mine, I was able to keep my feet planted firmly on the floor beneath me. Was he going to try to kiss me again? He reached both hands to my face. Oh God, he was. My heart tripped over itself, and then his hands were behind my neck, gently raising the hood over my head. His faint smile was as gentle as the touch, but his eyes burned, the green flickering like emerald flames.

The difference in that touch from when he'd grabbed my wrist yesterday made me wonder how much kindness there might be in him. How much of all the taunting and play was really him, and how much of it was a way of surviving in the Desert of Sin?

My body made a decision before my brain could catch up. I grabbed his wrist before he released the hood. His eyes lit up, but he didn't move a muscle.

"How did you get that scar?" I asked. "In a battle?"

His voice was low and rough. "You could say that."

"I've seen the way things look at you here. As if they know who you are just by the way you walk. Who did you piss off enough that they left a permanent mark on even an immortal?"

"Sometimes we run into blades that are just as angry as their wielder's heart."

I tilted my head to get a better look at the blemish. My body still worked on its own accord when I took my free hand and rubbed my thumb over it. Zafar stilled as though shellshocked by the brazen act, but I did it anyway. I hadn't noticed how deep it ran until I was touching it.

"Does it hurt?" I asked.

The air was heavy and still while he watched me study him. When he spoke again, his voice came out hushed, like he was reliving a distant, unpleasant memory. "Only when it rains."

His green flamed eyes went still, face slack. There was no teasing and no games now. I held his stare, held this most brief moment of what might be as close to the real Zafar I'd get to witness.

I traced the scar again, running my thumb along the very tip, over his eye, and down to where it ended just below his bottom lashes. "It's sort of beautiful in a way." The words were out before I could stop them, but this time my cheeks didn't heat. I released his wrist, and it fell to his side slowly, as if even his hand were speechless.

After a moment of heavy silence, he blinked. "We should go before she moves on."

I almost forgot what he was talking about and why he'd come to my room in the first place. Something in me told me I should say no. That I should tell him I was going to see the scholars right now, and that I didn't care about the Assassin.

But suddenly, I didn't feel such a rush to leave.

The Pits. That's where we were headed. The slum of the desert, Zafar had said, where the lowest of the low lived. The drunks, thieves, and liars Darya had warned me about. No part of me wanted to go if this was to be the ugly side of the desert, and yet I still allowed Zafar to help me onto a horse.

We rode side by side in silence for twenty minutes. I could feel his eyes land on me and then flick away every few minutes. After the fourth time, I broke the silence.

"Something you want to say?"

"No."

"You keep looking over here."

His teeth finally reappeared in the grin that on day one had seemed so dangerous. After only a few days of short interactions with him, I was coming to learn those annoying grins were harmless, nothing more than a facade.

"Can't I admire how good you look in my clothes?"

I returned the smile and the challenge as well. "I thought they were my clothes?"

He laughed so suddenly it startled the horses. He reached down to pat his on the neck. "For now," he replied, coolly.

"For now," I repeated.

He whipped his head toward me in surprise, fiery eyes ablaze. I had surprised myself too, though I wouldn't let him see it. Elysian didn't know who I was, so why not pretend for a while? And I liked the part I was playing. A Briar that wasn't afraid to speak up for what she wanted. And what I wanted right now was him. I wanted Zafar.

Abruptly, the sand dipped into a plane, and a city rested inside a crater below us, an actual pit.

"We're here."

A mixture of booze, sweat, and urine hit my nose. "Great."

Our horses descended the slope that leveled out in the narrow streets of the pit. Windows were covered by worn, tattered sheets. Drunkards swayed out of dive bars and pickpockets strategically waited to stumble into their path. Street dwellers in secondhand clothing eyed my shoes as we passed, but they hid their stare at the gleam of Zafar's sword hilt. We didn't stop at any of the hitching posts, and I didn't have to ask why. I got the feeling if we stopped and tied them up, we might not come back to horses at all.

Zafar veered off the busier main street and into a narrow alley lined with beggars with tin cups at their feet. Some reached their hands out to ask for spare coins, while others didn't look up at all, as if they had completely given up hope. Zafar didn't so much as blink in their direction.

We rounded a series of bends that led to an empty alleyway, most of the noises and scents weakening this deep into the maze of alleys. Zafar's every tug on the reins told me he knew exactly where he was going. That he'd been to the lioness's den more than once. For what, I didn't want to know.

I followed Zafar's lead when he stopped his horse and swung out of the saddle. We let the horses rest at a water trough within eyesight.

I glanced over my shoulder with each step. "I can't believe I let you talk me into coming with you."

"Just stay behind me and don't speak."

Windows lined the cracked walls on each side, a ledge outside each window. And each ledge, barely big enough for a row of potted plants, was empty, all except for one that had a lone figure sitting cross-legged far above our heads. She was dressed in the same clothes from yesterday, and a golden braid snaked out of the Assassin's hood.

Zafar let his feet shuffle heavily, making his footsteps noisier than they needed to be to make our presence known. As if he didn't want to spook her like one of the horses.

She didn't acknowledge us at first, only tilted her head to the sky to take a giant swig from a tall, green bottle. She swallowed and inspected something she held in her other hand, though it was too small to make out what it was from here.

"I hope we aren't disturbing your...whatever this is."

Her green eyes were sharper than his. "No, no. Of course not. I invited you, silly. It's been ages since we've last caught up." She eyed the toy in her hand, careful to keep us from catching a glimpse of it.

"A little early for a drink, isn't it?"

The Assassin, who had wanted me dead earlier in the day, didn't so much as flick her gaze to me now. "I'm celebrating. I've landed myself in quite a bit of coinage."

"Ah," Zafar said, playing along. "Have you now? That's surprising, considering how picky you are when it comes to accepting job offers. Usually, you have more class than to come for someone who has done no harm. You must be getting desperate these days."

This time, she slid her eyes to mine with a sly grin. She put down both hands and gave us her full attention. "What, no small talk first? You used to be more fun, Zafar."

"I'm not in the mood for games today, Nilsa." Her features fell in annoyance, her eyes cutting a killing blow at the use of her real name. She opened her mouth, but Zafar cut her off. "You wanted to talk, so let's talk. What do you want with Briar?"

"Oh, is that her name?" She assessed me with new eyes. "She doesn't look like she has thorns."

I obeyed Zafar's command not to speak.

"Who hired you?" he demanded.

"The Dark Queen," she cooed.

It was the answer neither of us had expected. "What the fuck does the Dark Queen want with Briar? She's no one." My heart sank at that, even though I knew what he meant. I *was* no one here.

A queen shouldn't be giving me a second thought or even a seventh.

The Assassin shrugged and took another sip from the bottle. "Ask her yourself. I just carry out orders."

"You know what I can't figure out?"

She lazily smiled, and I wondered just how much she'd had to drink already, but something told me she could handle her alcohol better than that.

"I can't figure out why Briar is still here, to be honest. There's not a doubt in my mind that you would have taken us both out if you really wanted to." He paused, thinking it all over. "But you didn't want to, did you?"

"Ah, so he's truly not as big of a dumbass as he looks."

He ignored the insult. "You let her go on purpose."

"Warmer," she teased.

"Why?"

The Assassin—Nilsa—inspected every inch of my body before answering, glaring with something that wasn't quite annoyance, but close enough to it. Her next line was directed only to me. "If I wanted you dead, you'd be dead, girl. Do you know that?"

Zafar pressed on. "Why did the Dark Queen hire you to kill Briar?"

"I don't ask questions. I was given half the payment up front to accept the job. The second half would have been paid once I delivered her body to the Garden's gates."

Zafar was growing impatient. "But you didn't deliver, Nilsa. Why is Briar alive right now?"

"Because you're right," she shot back, suddenly too acute to have been drunk a few moments ago. "Why? Why does the Dark Queen want her, a mere human, dead?"

That shut Zafar up. My muscles tightened, and there was a heavy silence as those words settled in the air.

"So the truth is out then," Zafar finally admitted.

Nilsa held back a laugh. "You think it was at all believable that the Dark Queen cared about a little forest fairy?"

"How?" was all he asked.

"The Dark Queen may not be allowed in Genesi, but her spies are. Between the loud-mouthed siren passing through and the Dark Queen's rage about it, your little secret should be spreading halfway across the kingdoms by now."

Zafar and I traded a wary glance. What did this mean for me? For my safety? The only thing protecting me now was that no one knew what I looked like, but if anyone found out that Zafar had been entrusted with getting me through the desert...

"You never answered my question," Zafar said. "What do you stand to gain by allowing Briar to live?"

"The Dark Queen is dark, but she's not dark enough to go after someone just for the fuck of it. Maybe before, but not now. The fact that Briar's existence here is bothering her so much means something. Something is about to go down, and things are about to get interesting. I'd like her to stick around long enough to see what is so bothersome about this girl that the Dark Queen is losing beauty sleep over her."

"So you took the payment and failed to complete the job on purpose, because you want to see what kind of drama unfolds? If she finds out, she'll hunt you down. She'll detach your head from your neck and feed you to her hellhound."

"She'd have to catch me first. There's a reason she hired me." Her back straightened. "In case you've forgotten, I'm sort of the best."

"And yet you still live a life in the Pits. I haven't quite worked that one out either. With your skill, you could leave all of Kalopsia behind and live as rich as a lesser queen."

She drank deeply in response.

Zafar turned to me. "We're done here. We got our answer."

But Nilsa raised the hidden object in her hand to inspect it once more. Light flickered off it, and a golden oval embroidered with vines snaked in between her fingers. My hand shot to my chest. My locket. "That's mine." I took several useless steps forward.

"So she does speak."

"Give that back."

"What?" she asked innocently. "This?" The rest of the chain slipped from her fingers, and she dangled the locket in the air, showcasing it proudly. I took another step forward without realizing what I was doing. "It's mine, and you took it."

"I did, didn't I? Want it back?"

"Quit playing around, Nilsa. Give it back." Zafar stepped in front of me.

"I tried to sell it in the market. Couldn't get shit for it." She raised a brow in challenge.

"What do you want for it?" Zafar snapped. "I'm growing tired of these games, and you know if I wanted to, I could just take it from you."

"No, you couldn't, and we both know that." The truth of that seemed to appease her. "Anyway, I was speaking, and you interrupted. Rude. Besides, the stupid thing is broken. Did you know that, Briar? It won't open."

"It's never opened. Please, give it back."

"Oh sure, sure. I'll trade you for it."

"Nilsa." Zafar's tone was biting.

"For one of your horses."

Zafar's jaw gave out. "You want a whole ass horse?"

"Well, half of one wouldn't do me any good, would it?"

Zafar considered this, and I couldn't for the life of me understand why he was thinking about giving away a "whole ass horse" as he referred to it. Could he really not just manhandle the necklace from her? He had been so willing to threaten the bearded slaver in the market for me. He was a guard of the temple. The personal guard to the Sand Queen at that. Surely, he could handle this. But yesterday's events suggested maybe I was underestimating what she was capable of.

"The white one," he finally said. "You can have the white one."

"I'll take the black one. Matches my demeanor better." Before he could argue, she thrust the locket down. Zafar caught it easily. She was up in a flash, bottle still in hand, and leaped to the next ledge. And another and another and another, until she balanced on one directly above our horses. She jumped and landed smoothly in the black horse's saddle, whipped him around, and took off without a glance back. I watched, dumbfounded.

"You literally told her she could have it, and she still took off like she was stealing it."

"Like the loser she is." He handed over my necklace, taking a puzzled second look at his palm when it was empty, as if checking for a bite mark.

Instead of fastening it around my neck, I bent down and wrapped it around my ankle a few times. Zafar gave me a questioning look as I made sure the necklace was completely covered by my harems, but thankfully, he decided not to ask.

"We need to get out of here. I don't want to be caught in the Pits after nightfall, or else we might find our last horse gone, and we'll be walking back to the city."

The sky was turning dusky already, and I agreed. I didn't want to be caught here much longer either. I hooked my foot into the stirrup, and Zafar helped lift me onto the white horse. He followed suit, landing himself in the saddle behind me.

We rode most of the way back in silence, the sky fading to a soothing pink-orange, the Pits long faded away. The temple in the city ahead was coming into view, like a speck of land in the middle of an ocean. Zafar's body was rigid behind me.

"I can feel the stress radiating off you."

He didn't answer at first. "She's right," he said after a moment.

"Who's right?"

"Nilsa. If the Dark Queen wants you dead, there's a reason behind it."

I thought of what those reasons might be and could only come up with one theory. From what Darya had described, the Dark Queen only cared for two things—power and title. She wanted to make a statement. I was a visitor, an unwanted visitor at that. Elysian's whole creation had been set on the idea that my kind wasn't special enough to touch it. She was going to use me as an example, to show that no one came into *her* land uninvited. I explained my theory to Zafar.

"It's possible." He didn't sound convinced in the least. "I had something else in mind. You're right about the creation of Elysian. But somehow, you defied that." He pinched my waist, and chills blossomed under the fabric there. "She craves power more than anything, but the land won't give in to her. I think she wants to know how you did it. How you gained access, so that she can get in and out of Elysian too. She knows she's running out of time, and if Elysian won't give her power over this land, maybe another world would better suit her."

"But she hired the Assassin to kill me. I can't give her answers if I'm dead."

"Nilsa didn't say what the price was listed for you dead and what the price would have been if she turned you in alive. I'm willing to bet the price was higher to bring you back breathing. Lucky for us, Nilsa had no intention of delivering at all. All she had to do to get paid was fail and say she tried."

"Should I have thanked her for that?"

He laughed softly. "You're too kind. No, you should not have thanked her for that. Nilsa has her own agenda. But she's right, if someone like the Dark Queen wants you, there's got to be something special about you."

"I'm not special," I whispered, remembering his earlier statement.

Zafar snatched the reins, halting our horse so quickly I tightened my grip on the saddle. His hand came to my chin, turning my gaze to his.

"Don't ever say that again." I would have shrunk back had he not held me so firmly. "I'm not to hear anything like that come out of your mouth again."

I froze, too stunned to so much as blink at him. Too baffled to do anything but nod after holding his stare for too many uncomfortable seconds. Only then did he release my chin and allow me to face forward in the saddle. He gave the horse a light kick to continue.

I couldn't move, couldn't work out which emotion was flowing in my chest. No fire flicked awake, but there was something there. Something heavy and tight. I swallowed the hurt, refusing to let it rise.

It was the desert in him, I told myself. Years of working for the Sand Queen hardening him into what he paraded around as today.

Zafar leaned in and shifted in the saddle suddenly, closing the gap between my back and his chest. His hands closed over the reins, but he let them drop and rest on my thighs for the first time. I felt the weight of that touch coursing through every fiber of my body. Sensed the silent apology, as if he realized a moment too late that he'd been harsh.

I cleared my throat. "So you think she wants power over my world as well. World domination, not just of her own."

"Possible power over the universe. Right now, we don't know much about what lies beyond Elysian. I'll bet she is willing to play the role of God once she finds out."

I shuddered at the thought. This wouldn't end well.

"We need to get you to those scholars. Fast. Before the Dark Queen finds out Nilsa isn't coming back with you. We need to get you back where you came from."

*But I don't want to*, I wanted to say. Either way, I was damned. If I stayed, I'd be trapped in a world destined to fail. And if I returned, I'd be going back to the same empty, unfilled life. I'd have to start over. Again.

A dangerous idea crept through my thoughts. If the scholars were successful in getting me out of here, who was to stop Zafar from coming with me? He hadn't mentioned any family so far. Didn't seem to have friends. The desert couldn't possibly hold much for him. If I had nothing, and Zafar had nothing, maybe I could convince him to start over too...together.

It was a recipe for disaster—two species from two different worlds, and deep down, I knew I couldn't have him. I almost didn't care.

Zafar's thumb broke into my thoughts as it brushed my cheek, moving a strand of hair from my face and behind my shoulder. The contact sent warning bells down my back. I turned my head, and Zafar was close enough that his breath blew into my face. The hand at my thigh drew up, flattening on my waist, while his other hand came up to the side of my face. His eyes were dancing, daring, and when I didn't blink, his fingers clasped around my neck. He let a rough thumb drag from the cupid's bow of my lip to its full bottom.

"What are you doing?" I whispered.

He pressed forward, his lips hovering over mine. I didn't dare move a muscle.

"Do you want me to stop?" he breathed. I thought back to the moment we shared in the hallway, what could have been. What might have happened had we entered that room alone. Did I want him to stop?

The city rested sleepily ahead. We had a couple of minutes left until we'd be in eyeshot of anyone.

"No," I finally said. If I couldn't have all of him before I was to leave, I wanted just a small portion of a moment with him.

Before I was fully ready, Zafar's lips fell onto mine. If it weren't for his strong hand holding my neck in place, I would have jolted back. It was shocking at first, the way his skin felt on mine, the way he kissed just the way he looked at me—wild and pleading for more. The speed and desire behind the kiss were more than I bargained for, and before I could process that it was too much, too soon, our lips broke apart, and his mouth was at my neck. My breath hitched, caught between desire and confusion.

"Slow down," I whispered, almost too small to be heard.

"I have envisioned what it would feel like to ravish you since I first laid eyes on you. Can you blame me for making up for such stupidly wasted time?" His voice was thick and dangerous. But he obeyed, slowing down a fraction enough for me to enjoy it.

He found my neck again, and the contact of teeth and skin sent heat along my neck, my arms...other parts he was soon to discover.

I closed my eyes and fell back into him, letting him make my body react with each motion, each flick of his tongue on my neck. His tongue was like fire on my skin, lips like sandpaper. His hand fumbled with the layers of my cover-up. He'd only have to unsnap one button before slipping a hand inside to caress my warm, bare skin. My chest filled with heat, a different one than I'd grown accustomed to fighting off. This kind was one I couldn't send away. One I didn't want to.

I couldn't decipher which direction his hand would go, and then realized there was so much fabric to work through he probably couldn't go anywhere. I found the button to unsnap and then dropped my fingers to the next one, but Zafar's mouth abruptly left my neck, his body falling back in the saddle to generate space between us. My head was spinning. I was dazed and confused all over again by his suddenness. But then I heard it, the commotion and bustling from the direction we were headed in. The city.

My breathing was heavy as I turned forward again and snapped closed the undone button before we were close enough for the first creature to notice us.

I moved to lift my hood over my head, but Zafar's hand closed over my wrist, stopping me.

"Don't. If word has reached Kalopsia yet, it'll be more suspicious that you're hiding your face. Remember, you want to blend in here."

We moved through the crowd, the only silent ones in the streets. My breathing had slowed by the time the sandpit apartments came into view, but my mind was still racing at the speed of a warhorse. The kiss was one thing, but what I had been willing to do, how far I was willing to let him take things... I was speechless at what I had allowed. And how much I liked it.

I knew I had to go back. There was no choice in the matter. But that didn't mean I couldn't enjoy this, enjoy him, while I was here.

## CHAPTER ELEVEN

Zafar lingered at my door when dropping me off. I assumed he'd come in to finish what we'd started, but he left, a bit hesitantly, and then sent Keyon to guard my door for the night. He blamed it on an unimportant errand he had to tend to. When he returned from said errand, Zafar was going to ask permission from the Sand Queen to leave his duties at the temple for an unknown amount of time. Now that the Dark Queen was set out for me, Zafar didn't trust Kenna, or anyone who wasn't him, with my safety.

There was a possibility that would be a problem, since Zafar escorting me all the way to the scholars wasn't a part of the original deal. I was only promised safety during my stay in Kalopsia. To have Zafar accompany me through the forest meant one less guard in the temple and nothing in it for Cozbi. An unlikely scenario.

But Zafar didn't return for seven days.

I read the book a third time, my brain growing bored and guessing the next sentence before I got to it. I stared at the ceiling. By the third day, I needed fresh air and sun on my skin. I could only get a few minutes a day out of my room with Keyon close at my side before a set of hungry eyes had me retreating back underground.

I stared at the ceiling some more, thinking of Zafar's hand trailing along my stomach, his tongue teasing my ear. My breaths heavier than the sun's heat.

After the fourth day, Keyon walked in to find me in the same position he'd found me in last and offered to play a game of cards with me.

Their cards were different, though the games he went through with me were fairly the same. In place of hearts, spades, diamonds, and clubs, the cards were in suits of each realm.

It helped the time pass, but having Keyon with me didn't mean I'd escaped the quiet. He didn't have much to say at all, though I was starting to understand why. There wasn't much he could say in a language I would understand him in. But I didn't need conversation to stay sane, I just needed someone to be with. I came to look forward to Keyon rapping on the door and waiting for my response before walking in with his cards in hand. He wasn't like the others who lived here. His eyes never wandered, and even though he never smiled, I never felt uncomfortable when he was around.

I was just getting to a point where I thought I might actually beat him in a game, when he suddenly asked about my life before Elysian.

I remembered Darya's warning before we parted at the sandy border, but I couldn't find any harm in talking about people and things a world away. I kept my answers short anyway.

"There's not much to tell," I began. "I lived a quiet life. Worked a boring job."

"You left friend? Family?"

"I...didn't have much time for friends." A lie. "I wasn't close with my dad, and I haven't seen my brother in years."

"And what of mother?" he asked.

"She—I haven't seen her in years either."

"I am sorry."

I fanned out my cards, pretending to focus on them. "What about you? Have you always been a temple guard?"

It was hard not to study Keyon, the way he concentrated on each word before speaking them. Even the way he moved was carefully thought out and executed precisely.

"It is great honor to be guard for queen. Mother offered me at fourteen to temple."

"Fourteen?" He was just a child at the time, barely a teenager.

"Fourteen is manhood. Fourteen you learn to fight."

"Where I come from, fourteen-year-olds are only worried about the next video game release." A quizzical look was his only response. "Kind of like cards," I explained. "Just in a different form."

"Where you come from, fourteen-year-olds are lazy."

I laughed at that, which startled him, but then he let himself smile too. It was the first time I'd seen his facial muscles really move. It made him look even younger.

"Haven't seen mother in fifty-three years."

I blinked a few times. If he hadn't seen his mother in fifty-three years, and he left home when he was fourteen, that would make him sixty-seven, though he looked to be about my age, younger even.

"Do you miss her?" I missed mine.

He nodded, but his face returned to stone. "It is great honor to guard temple and queen," he repeated, as if he didn't want to be overheard through the walls that a part of him might miss his old life. I nodded in understanding and went back to my cards, shuffling the good ones to one side of my hand. If Keyon wouldn't press me, I would return the favor.

He laid a card down. "No boyfriends?"

I fought a smile, not wanting to offend him. "No boyfriends," I confirmed.

"Why? Briar is pretty and kind."

"Thank you." I let the smile surface this time, laying down Genesi's card. "I've had boyfriends in the past, but they never seem to work out."

He considered this. "Zafar is handsome."

My eyebrows went up in immediate agreement. "Yes, Zafar is very handsome." I should have regretted saying it, but something told me I didn't need to hide anything with Keyon. Keyon wasn't a liar, and he wasn't a thief or a drunk. He was just a lost soul who'd taken the job that would bring his family the most honor and probably the most coin.

"Briar." Seriousness coated his tone and captured my attention. We locked eyes. The cards in our hands stilled. A warning cloaked his dark eyes, and his face went more serious than usual. "Maybe, don't take first male to show little kindness."

I stared at him, working through what he'd said and not knowing at all how to reply. Was he trying to tell me there was better out there? Or was he trying to warn me?

Just then, the door swung open, and Zafar strutted in with a small duffel bag in hand.

Keyon laid all his cards down. "Winner." I double-checked the cards as he rose from his spot on the ground.

"Hey!" I shouted. I barely caught his sly smile before he gave Zafar a half nod and then disappeared without another word. I almost asked him to stay, to wait until Zafar left the room so we could finish our conversation, but the next thing out of Zafar's mouth made the disappointment of losing *again* and my curiosity vanish.

"We're leaving."

"Now?" I rose from the ground, collecting the cards.

"Cozbi authorized my request to leave the desert. For as long as needed."

I arched a brow. "How did you get her to agree?"

"Not important."

I crossed my arms. "How."

He rubbed the back of his neck, careful to look anywhere but my face. "I'll have to surrender my pay until I return. It'll be like taking an unpaid vacation."

"Zafar!"

"I like it when you yell my name."

I threw my cards at him. "You can't do that."

"I can do whatever I want." He bent down to pick up the cards that had bounced off his chest and fallen to his feet. "I told you before. I'm not hurting for funds."

I only scowled in response, feeling just as uncomfortable with this as I had when he bought me all those clothes, which apparently, I had needed in the end, seeing as I had spent much longer here than intended.

He shuffled through the hangers on the clothing rack and threw certain pieces over his shoulder into a pile. I bent down to examine the chosen. A few lightweight tunics, a clean pair of harems, and the hooded cloak. None of the plain brown dresses. He threw the bag on top of the heap and sloppily packed them in.

"It's a two-to-three-day ride across the desert, but we can make it in one and a half if we don't stop. That means one of us will have to sleep on the horses while the other leads. We'll take shifts." He was moving and talking too quickly, like we had to hurry before someone changed their mind. He zipped the duffel and grabbed my elbow, rushing me through the door and into the dimly lit hall.

"Wait." I jerked out of his grasp and made my voice big. "Where were you?"

He gave me an exaggerated puzzled look that had to be forced. "I told you. I had an errand to run. And then I had to get permission from Cozbi to leave. That took a lot of ass-kissing."

"You were gone for *seven* days. You said you'd be right back."

His face and his voice didn't match. His voice was strong and confident, but his eyes... Something there was uncertain, nervous even. Maybe he really was worried about the money, or maybe he just wanted to get going before the Dark Queen came to Kalopsia herself.

"I'm sorry," he said. "I didn't think it would take that long. I should have sent word that I'd be longer than expected."

He held my gaze. Were either one of us going to say it? Were we going to acknowledge what happened on our last ride together?

He broke eye contact first, taking off briskly before I could say anything else about it. I followed him into the night where there were already two horses waiting. Zafar quickly helped me into the saddle and attached the light duffel bag to a hook on the side.

I hadn't seen Kalopsia in the dark before now. The streets were less busy, but some still passed by at the same rapid pace, surely up to no good. Voices carried in the distance, drunk conversations in the night. Two bodies passed by, laughing loudly, with dark bottles in their hands. Their gazes found me, and an overly excited gleam cast over their eyes. Zafar cleared his throat, and the promise of a slow death sent the two hiding behind their hoods and carrying on without any more laughter. I didn't look back as we strode away from the Desert of Sin.

Sleeping on a horse was impossible. Even if it weren't uncomfortable with the saddle horn jabbing me in the ribs, the rhythm wasn't as soothing as one would think. I managed maybe an hour of sleep that night, and that was only because my body wouldn't allow me to stay awake any longer.

By morning, neither of us had spoken since leaving the sandpit apartments. I opened my mouth several different times, but an overwhelming awkwardness had me closing it every time. Did he regret what we did? Surely, he couldn't be upset with me for it. He was the one who'd initiated it, and from the way he held me, I had thought he enjoyed it just as much as I had. And truthfully, was it even a big deal? We hadn't gone all the way, or even half of the way.

Excuses and possibilities danced through my mind throughout the silent trek. Maybe he was playing it safe. He knew where he was taking me. Zafar knew this was going to end soon, the same way I did. Maybe he was just taking precautions and ending this flirtation before it went too far.

But did he have to be so cold in the meantime? The only time he acknowledged me was to draw his horse closer to mine so that he could pass me an apple or a slice of bread. Even then, he was careful to look anywhere but directly at me.

I gave up by the next nightfall, deciding I could be just as stubborn as him. But ignoring him out here was difficult. Horseshoe imprints going back and forth in the tan sand dunes and a blanket of dusty blue sky on the horizon was all to be seen for miles. There was only so much I could pretend to look at.

When he finally spoke, it was only to point me in the direction I was to stay in so that he could sleep. He fell back in the saddle, angling his legs around the horn and crossing his arms over his chest. I was annoyed by his insane ability to balance, and that it was not even close to the way I had tried to sleep.

A curtain of jet-black hair veiled his face from the sun and from me. I scanned his body and the way his chest slowly rose and fell. I had no way of knowing if he really slept or if he was faking, but I smiled to myself at the thought of him falling so deeply asleep that he slid to the side of the saddle and hit the sand.

He woke a few hours later. The silence continued.

By the second half of the next day, my back was stiff, and my shoulders ached. Tension was embedded in the air, and there was an unsettling feeling resting heavy in my chest. Intense anger grew as the hours flicked by.

There was no need for this, to be so childish about it. If he didn't want to continue anything with me, he could at least manage to be civil about it. I was reminded of Keyon's warning to steer clear of a romantic relationship with Zafar. This must have been what he meant, but was Zafar truly this immature?

I began practicing in my head things to say to him. *Hey, what the fuck?* was the first thing that came to mind. I readied myself and gathered the courage to confront him, but suddenly, *finally*, there was a change in the scenery.

# CHAPTER TWELVE

Green.

Clusters of birch trees littered ahead. My grip on the reins tightened as the border of trees drew nearer.

Neither of us spoke as the horses gingerly crossed into the trees. Birds chirped happily above us, and hoofs padded on the soft grass below. It was a nice change from the silence of the desert.

"It won't be long now." I jumped at the sound of his voice after hours of going without it. I wasn't sure if I was allowed to respond or not. This whole trip had not gone down the way I'd imagined it would.

"I thought you said it was called the Everwood for a reason?" I asked. His eyes hardened while his jaw clenched. His shoulders went rigid. "You did say it would take a long time to get through these woods, right?"

Zafar faced the trees again, his face relaxing. "It's just a name. If you know your way around, it's not difficult to navigate."

I nodded in understanding, though he never would have seen since he was avoiding looking in my direction so fiercely. As if I were a plague.

After a few hours, the silence between us no longer irritated me. It allowed me to notice how peaceful the Everwood was. Despite what Darya had said about the spreading curse, the branches swayed with life. Delicate purple flowers brushed across my horse's legs. Apart from birds and the occasional deer, we were alone here in an expanse of flourishing wildlife.

The chirping of birds faded to a cricket's choir as the brilliant sky darkened. As the horses traveled slower with fatigue, so did my thoughts. I'd worried the whole trip what Zafar would do once we reached the scholars. Would he stay with me to ensure I got answers, or would he say goodbye at the doors of Clive Steeple?

But as he unloaded bedrolls from his saddle and laid them out on the lush ground of the forest floor, I cared of nothing but sleep.

The stars were barely visible under the canopy of the trees. I wished for that night on the balcony. I wished for the constellations. As if on command, one by one, the stars floated down and flicked on and off inside the Everwood. Dozens upon dozens of them flickered like twinkling lights until they drew so near that I reached out and touched one. I smiled as a firefly landed briefly on my fingertip.

I turned my head to Zafar, hoping he was seeing this too, only to find his back turned to me. My smile melted. This silence had to stop. If he wasn't going to break, someone had to.

"Zafar," I whispered. His shoulders rose and fell with sleep, even though we'd just lied down. Surely, he couldn't be asleep already. I tried a little louder. "Zafar."

He rolled to his other side, his face suddenly in front of mine, and slammed a finger to my lips. The touch immediately sent betraying goosebumps up my arms, but I pushed his hand away, seething. "What is wrong with you? Why are you being so weird?"

He cupped his entire hand over my mouth. "There are things in these woods you don't want to wake."

Hand still blocking words from leaving my mouth, I let my eyes travel the forest again. I hadn't been afraid before. This forest had an aura to it, something woven in the air that made me feel safe. Now, with his warning, I fought off a shudder.

"The time for conversation is in the sunlight," he whispered.

I nodded, and only then did his hand come away from my mouth. I examined the woods with new eyes, looking for any sign of danger.

The fireflies floated lazily. The horses grazed. I laid my head back down and closed my eyes, not believing Zafar at all.

Zafar woke first. He sat with one leg stretched out, the other bent, and an arm draped over his knee. He stared out into the never-ending green. I wished I could get a glimpse inside his mind for just a moment.

"Good morning," I said, stifling a yawn and propping myself up.

"Morning," he replied, turning to me and gifting me a small smile. His face was softer than yesterday, his shoulders finally relaxed. Maybe he'd just needed sleep the same way I had. Maybe I had just witnessed Zafar in a bad mood. Even the soreness in my neck and shoulders had worked itself out once we had a night off the horses. Today, everything would be better.

"Is it safe to talk now?" I asked, testing his warning from last night.

He inclined his chin toward the soft, golden light filtering through the treetops.

"Let's wash first."

He reached over me for my bag, dug through it, and handed me a fresh set of clothes. "There should be a creek not far off from here." He stood and looked around before finally deciding on a way. "Come on."

We left the horses where they enjoyed a breakfast of apples and purple flowers.

In reality, we didn't walk very far, but it was long enough for my breath to start quickening. Zafar strode with ease, as comfortable as ever. Another reminder that he was immortal, and I wasn't. Another reminder that even if we could somehow work, we wouldn't.

When we came into the clearing, sunlight poured over the stream of water that trickled over mossy stones. Deer scattered from their morning baths as we approached to get our own. Zafar kneeled at the bank, cupping water in his hands and then splashing it on his face. He stood, water dripping from his chin, and removed his shirt. His eyes remained on mine the whole time.

It wasn't the multiple scars on his body that frightened me. It was how beautiful he still looked with them marking his collarbones, his chest, his stomach, his lower abdomen. My eyes roamed freely, and when they traveled back to his fiery gaze, my breath caught in my lungs. I froze, taken over by the glint in his eyes that was so familiar and yet so altered. I couldn't work out what was different between us, but it didn't matter. Nothing mattered other than getting him to talk to me.

He took one step and then another, until he was close enough that his hand came to my chin. I remained perfectly still, allowing him to come to me when he was ready. But his fingertips only lingered on my skin for what seemed like forever. I reached out to rest my hand on his bare stomach. His skin was warm, and the slashes of white were scattered along endless indentations of muscle. I flattened my palm, letting each fingertip connect with one of them.

His brows furrowed, and something clicked in his expression. Not in anger or offense, but something like confusion. Our eyes locked, each scanning the other for our thoughts and turning up empty. He took a step back, and my skin felt cold where his touch suddenly left mine.

"Change." His voice was hard while he turned his back to me for privacy.

I couldn't move. At first, because I was still frozen from the intensity in his gaze, but then...a ball of heat flared in my chest. This was unfair. Childish too, but just unfair at this point. I had emotional whiplash from going back and forth thinking there was actually something behind his games and teasing, only to be taught each and every time he was exactly as he appeared to be. My fingers balled tightly over the fistful of clothes.

I grabbed the hem of my shirt, yanked it over my head, and tossed it to the ground. I replaced it with the fresh one. Clive Steeple couldn't come fast enough, and when we got there, it would be me who turned their back first. I changed into the pants.

"There," I said. Zafar turned around, tugging a new shirt over his head and hiding those beautiful imperfections. "Now, what did you mean last night?" I asked. "What things are in this forest?"

"Haven't you ever heard that monsters live in the dark?"

"Technically, you're all monsters where I come from."

He half laughed, and the fact that my statement hadn't hurt him the way I'd intended it to pissed me off all the more.

It dawned on me then that I didn't know what Zafar was in this land of otherworldly creatures. What kind of monster was he?

"Will you ever give me a straight answer?" I asked.

A twig snapped, and we both turned in its direction. But no deer emerged from the trees. And then the birds stopped singing.

"What was that?" I whispered.

"Quiet." Zafar stepped in front of me, his hand finding his sword.

My eyes darted from tree to tree. I reached for him, my fingers touching the back of his shoulder when something snapped again. Then several more snaps.

A branch was shoved to the side, and an armored soldier stepped into the clearing with us. His eyes landed on Zafar and narrowed through a black helmet. Zafar lowered his sword a fraction.

When the soldier's forest-green eyes found mine next, there was a pause in his gaze. A calculation that lasted only half a moment, and then he tossed a shout over his shoulder, "Over here! I found them."

My gut told me Zafar had been right. The Dark Queen had come for us, or at least her army had. On their way to Kalopsia to finish what the Assassin hadn't.

"We have to run," I said, pulling on Zafar's shirt.

Zafar lowered his sword all the way, and I couldn't work out why. This was just one assailant. He could take him out before the others caught up. But then it was four others. I counted as they each stepped into the clearing. We were outnumbered and Zafar knew it. But we weren't surrounded. We could still lose them if we were fast enough.

"*Now*," I whispered to my personal guard. And then I turned and sprinted into the depths of the Everwood.

I wound through the trees, a small voice in my soul pleading with me to move faster. Faster, as I didn't think about where my feet landed. Faster, as the trees zipped by, each one a blur after the next. Faster, faster, *faster*.

I pumped my legs, willing them to move as quickly as a human's legs could.

An arm shot out from somewhere off to the side, wrapping around my waist and pulling me behind a larger tree. A rough hand pressed over my mouth, silencing my surprised yelp. A hard stomach pressed my body against the thick tree trunk, and fierce green eyes bore into mine.

I released my breath, letting my body relax into Zafar's.

"Shh," he whispered in my ear. His hair brushed against my neck, and his body crushed mine as his eyes darted from tree to tree. He slid his hands to my shoulders, steadying me with a promise to keep me safe. But the forest, even though it was deathly quiet, its air buzzed with something wrong.

He pressed a finger to his lips and then intertwined his fingers with mine. The touch was secure but unnatural, like our fingers didn't tangle correctly.

Zafar guided me with careful, light steps, his attention fixed in between the trees and listening for things my human ears couldn't pick up.

He was trained for this. This was the Sand Queen's personal guard in his element. But still, from the moment we left Kalopsia, everything about him had *felt* off. Something was different. Something was wrong.

And it wasn't just the tension between us. The woods. They were quiet too. There had been shouts before when I took off running. But there hadn't been heavy footsteps chasing after us. There hadn't been the clash of steel against steel, or the grunts of a struggle.

My hand came to Zafar's shoulder, hoping I could tell him my fears with just a look, but as we stepped around a cluster of trees, the breath left my lungs, and my legs stopped working.

*"Zafar."*

His grip tightened around mine.

Massive wolves standing on their hind legs blocked our path. Their shirtless, muscled bodies and giant heads were exactly like a wolf, even though they walked like men, laughed like men. Darya had mentioned a creature that matched their description, something I might see the farther I went into Elysian. A wulver. But as vile and upsetting as they were to look at, they were nothing in this moment. Nothing in comparison to who stood in the middle of them.

Somehow, I knew who she was without ever having seen her before. The way the pack of wulvers faded to nothing at her side. The way the trio of half-grown *dragons* looked unintimidating at her back. The way she held herself, the greed and hunger taking over her features like sunbeams, though, despite her fair skin there was nothing bright about her. A gothic crown rested on her head, and her hair fell in loose black waves, rolling down her curves and stopping at her waist. The faintest of red tinted the bottom ends.

A white-hot hatred burned like coals from inside her, spearing into me the moment our eyes met. It was a jealous, unkind, unforgiving hate that ran *deep*, and it was here.

The Dark Queen's black eyes were depthless. "Bring her." At her voice even the rustling wind dared not make its presence known in its own home.

Zafar remained rooted to the spot, still clutching my hand. There was nothing to do as the soldiers from the clearing caught up and cornered us from behind. We were surrounded, out of options.

"Zafar," I pleaded with a shaking voice, trusting him to come up with *something*, but he didn't budge. His fingers tightened around mine so tightly my knuckles squeezed together. When he dropped his head to finally meet my stare, they were still. The fire unlit. Those eyes of dancing green flame were deathly and apologetically still.

"No," I breathed.

There was no emotion in his voice. No pride, no teasing, but no regret either. "Turns out my vacation was paid after all."

My fingers loosened from his, but he held firm. "Zafar, let me go."

The Dark Queen's soldiers closed in. I tried to rip my hand from his, hurt and betrayal stinging my throat. "Let me go!" But he didn't let go until two sets of hands closed in on each of my arms and tore me from him. I turned to plead, to beg, to bargain. Anything to make him reconsider. But as I waited for his eyes to meet mine one last time, the only thing I got in return was the view of a brown sack so thick with coins the tie around the top was beginning to loosen. It landed in his waiting palm with a *clink*. And then another sack and another were offered.

He took it. He actually took it. And without an explanation, without another word or another glance, he turned his back.

Cold, long fingers wrapped around my chin and tore my gaze from him. Her black-painted nails were unnaturally long and sharp as they dug into my skin. I swallowed. Bottomless eyes that led to nothing peered into my soul, as if she could see straight into it. She said nothing, did nothing but stare. She was searching for something, like if she just waited long enough it would reveal itself to her. Moments ticked by, my heart pounding in my chest as I tried and failed to still my trembling muscles.

She gritted her teeth in something like frustration, and I knew then that she hated me. She pushed my face away from her touch and turned her back on me. Before the confusion could settle in, one of the wulvers stepped forward. As if the queen's dismissal was instruction enough, the back of a paw sailed through the air with enough force that I almost didn't feel it.

Everything went numb and dark before I hit the dirt. As unconsciousness greeted me, I wondered if she found what she was looking for or not.

# CHAPTER FOURTEEN

My eyes fluttered open. My head, too heavy and too painful to lift, rested on a jagged, rough surface. Hair lashed at my face as the wind tore through it, glimpses of the Everwood sailing by below. I dug my fingernails into the scaly back of a dragon.

"I would enjoy the scenery while it lasts if I were you," a voice behind me advised over the flap of black wings. Carefully, I lifted my head half an inch, the rest of my body still paralyzed. My arms shook with the movement, and I fell back to a flat position on my stomach.

I shut my eyes and breathed away the nausea. When I opened them again, the lush, green treetops had vanished. In their place hung a few drooping crispy brown leaves, hanging on for life, or what was left of it. But mostly, the trees were barren. We soared by dead trees, and the burnt landscape grew grittier with each wing flap. And then the tree line broke, and a wasteland stretched on. The destruction was enough to lift the top half of my body.

What Darya had described as endless hills of crops were now withered beyond repair. What looked like a once great lake now sat motionless and murky water slumbered in its own filth. Beyond acre upon acre of rot and decay, the lifeless Garden lay.

The Dark Queen rode her own dragon in front of us, her posture poised and confident. The false queen leading all of Elysian to its death.

A mist of gray populated the skies so thickly that the palace only came into view once we were upon it. The dragons swooped downward, and my stomach lurched as they crossed the distance of a long bridge and the water under it in a matter of seconds.

We landed with surprising softness in front of stony walls and endless turrets, most of which were empty. All but the one in the center. A lookout turret heavily guarded with soldiers and arrows at the ready.

I turned and locked eyes with the soldier sitting behind me. The forest-green eyes was the only identifiable feature of him I could make out to know it was the same soldier who initially found me. The same one who ripped me from Zafar. He took my arm again, gentler this time, and helped angle my body so that I could slide to the ground and land with a hop. The moment my feet hit the ground, a wulver was there to meet me, taking hold of my arm much more forcefully than the last soldier had.

We crossed the lattice of metal, my fate sealing with a solidifying *clunk* as the gate locked into place. My feet shuffled through old gravel while I was pushed along through a courtyard, and to a stony archway leading inside.

Any light that had been able to peek through the gray sky was swallowed up as I found myself inside the once great palace of the High Queen.

A cobblestone walkway, what was left of one, paved a path through a dirt-covered room. There was hardly any light inside to see much more. I tried to envision what the room might once have looked like, but it was impossible. Impossible to imagine the space as anything but what it currently was—an aftermath. The beginning of an ultimate end.

Our footsteps echoed off the walls, and that's when the moaning began.

Those were people—creatures, both male and female—chained to the walls. Most of them cowered in submissive fear, but a few brave souls dared to pull against the chains and beg for a trial. For mercy.

One reached as far as his chains would allow, coming within arm's reach of the Dark Queen's skirt. He screamed at her. Screamed that he was innocent, that he wasn't a part of any rebel group. He begged her to let him explain how he'd only been in the wrong place at the wrong time. I recoiled into myself at the wild desperation in his voice, in his eyes.

The queen glanced over her shoulder and flashed me a wicked smile, excitement brightening those obsidian eyes. A collection of smoke formed at her wrist, snaking down and around her fingers until it met at a point and became a small dagger. The blade formed into a twisted spiral of solid metal, smoke weaving in and out of it.

A bucket was placed underneath him, and without taking her eyes off mine, she lifted her arm and slashed it through the air, swiping the knife clean across the prisoner's throat.

I couldn't hear the noise that escaped my own mouth over the sloshing of blood pouring into the metal bucket. Time slowed while the body drained out. I squeezed my eyes shut, my stomach lurching violently at the sound of him choking on his own blood.

When his body stopped straining against itself, the Dark Queen simply flicked her wrist. The limp body crumpled to particles of ash, leaving only the bucket where a body had kneeled. A coppery tang filled the air while she bent over the bucket, letting her raven hair fall into it. Leftover droplets fell when the tips of her hair emerged, dyed in fresh blood.

I didn't want to know how much bloodshed stained those raven locks or how many innocents she'd drained before her tresses became permanently tainted in burgundy. For not even washing it to undo the things she'd done.

My stomach won and emptied on the cobblestones. I was pushed along, not given the time to recover. The moans and scent of blood disappeared as a set of doors slammed closed behind us with a soul-shuddering heaviness.

Tall windows lining the outer wall brightened the room only a shade, coating everything in gray. A lonely throne sat at the back, decorated in thorns and otherwise bare branches. A throne that so perfectly matched her reign. Ungodly beasts lingered in the shadows of the room, creeping out only far enough for me to catch the glint of teeth thin and sharp enough to cut through metal, razor blades for claws, and eyes in narrowed slits. Creatures I didn't know the names of, but all of them had come out of their shadowy homes to witness a trial that already had a verdict.

I tore my eyes from the nightmares and found the lacy train of the Dark Queen's black skin-tight gown snaking up the steps of the dais. She turned to sit, not breaking her stare from mine as she lowered herself.

She slouched in her seat, propping an elbow up on the armrest and letting the other dangle off the side in boredom. She took her time as she scanned my body from top to bottom, emotion unwritten on her features. Finally, the painted red on her lips parted. "Your name?" Her voice was smooth and cold.

She knew my name. There was no way she'd gone to all this trouble of capturing me without even learning my name.

When I didn't answer right away, the wulver released my arm for only the moment it took to knock his elbow into the side of my head, the same side that was still sore from the last time I was hit.

"Briar Clarke," I spoke, giving her what she wanted, my full name, so that this would all go by faster.

"Clarke," she mused, as if that was what she really wanted to know. She turned the information over in her head, but she never asked what I expected her to ask next. She didn't ask how I'd gotten here or what I planned to do. Instead, she flicked her eyes toward a door off to the side. "Take her away."

The word *away* echoed inside my head. I panicked. "Wait."

They didn't wait. They didn't falter for even a second. They hauled me out of the throne room. I lost it, begged just as those chained had begged. "Wait!" I screamed. "What do you want with me? What did I do?"

She said nothing, but she watched me go, revulsion coating every inch of her honed face.

On the outside, I mentally checked out. I didn't notice how many halls we crossed or anything about my surroundings. I was on the edge of losing every fiber of control in my body, too busy searching for a thought to hold on to. Searching for something deep within me that would hold me together. I found nothing. I forgot time, forgot everything. I didn't mentally check back in until I was peering down a gaping staircase that led to darkness.

Reminded of the Nothing, I stumbled and my knee crashed into the step below me. I was jerked upright so violently that I almost fell a second time. My mind reeled with each step. How had this happened?

With so few lanterns, my eyes barely adjusted once we reached the bottom step of the dungeon. Rows of steel-barred doors lined each side of the hall, markings of another language etched on the bars themselves. As if upstairs was just some kind of sport, a sick entertainment for the queen in her downtime. As if the things kept imprisoned down here were here for a reason, needing old magic strong enough to prevent the real threats from escaping into the world.

Most of the cells were bare, but some held creatures I could only guess at. We passed what appeared to be a used-up hag. Something that looked like a goblin hunched over, and broken looking. A gnarly monster with one eye in the center of his forehead. A few others so twisted and abused I couldn't look at them. The last few cells at the end of the hall held nothing inside them, but the markings drawn on and around them were more than the others. I was thrown into the last one, at the deepest end of the dungeon, and with the most markings on it. As if *I* were the most dangerous thing down here.

I landed on my shoulder, and the side of my head hit the stone floor, disorienting me.

My head pounded, but I managed to hold on to a bar and pull myself upright as the door locked into place. I peered down the hall with blurring vision. Arms stretched out of the cells, begging for water or a single moment of sunlight.

A deafening roar shook my heart and sent me spiraling backward.

Golden eyes glowered down at me. The creature foamed at the mouth, and the ravenous snarls escaping it had me suddenly thankful for the steel bars that separated us. Every last cry and plea ceased, and the begging arms retreated back into the safety of their cells.

A dog towered in front of my cell. No, not a dog. A wolf, an actual wolf this time, though it was the size of a car or perhaps a horse. I'd never felt a more pure terror in my bones.

The wulver laughed, his lips peeling back to expose thick teeth that matched his cousin's, and then nonchalantly made his way back toward the stairs. Footsteps trailed off and the heavy door above clicked shut, and the dog—the wolf *thing*—paced back and forth, up and down the dungeon hall. The only guard needed down here.

I scooted backward until my back pressed against the cold, windowless wall. I tucked my knees into my chest and lost all sense of self-control. My breathing was fast, too fast to keep up with my lungs. The edges of my vision blurred so that I could only focus on a tunnel of what was directly in front of me.

One...two...three... I tried to breathe in the seconds, but my breath hitched, and I had to start over again. One...two...one—

My head lightened, but just before I let darkness engulf me once again, a shadow shuffled into my tunnel. Not in my cell, but behind the set of bars directly across from mine. I didn't get the chance to see what was trapped there before blackness covered everything like a blanket, and my body collapsed to the ground, my limbs growing heavy and relaxed.

My joints were stiff, and even my bones ached from lying on the stone floor. The shoulder I'd fallen on was tender, and my head pounded with a raging pain I was all too familiar with.

A tray of food had been slid underneath a gap in the doorway while I was out. As if reminded of how hungry I was, my stomach growled. I hadn't had anything other than bread, apples, and cheese since leaving Kalopsia.

The food was cold, whether it arrived that way or had been sitting there so long that it had lost its heat, I wouldn't know. It wasn't much of a meal at all, just a stale piece of bread, cold soup of broth and carrots, and a cup of water only halfway filled. When I finished, my stomach didn't feel any less empty.

It was no use trying to escape, but I tried anyway. I searched and felt my way around the cell for anything I could use. I pushed on the walls, clawed at the corners, and patted the ground, looking for any flaw in the design. But there was nothing besides a section of my cell that ventured into a cave, the only thing there being a bucket to relieve oneself in. I almost scoffed at the ironic decency its designer had attempted for privacy. Standing now, I took a shuddering breath and risked a look outside my cell.

The wolf lay on his belly at the foot of the stairs, his head resting on giant paws the size of a bear's. His teeth poked out of his mouth, sharp enough to shred enemies to paper. His eyes were practically closed, the bright-orange glow of them seconds from disappearing as he slipped into a nap.

Escape didn't live here.

The door above suddenly opened, and the wolf lifted his horse-sized head to peer up at the newcomer. His pointed ears twitched, but then he rested his head on his paws again. Whoever was coming down was welcome.

# CHAPTER FIFTEEN

I had blacked out within minutes. When my eyes fluttered open, my arms were stretched above me, my head hung low. A blurry image of two bare feet inches off the ground, fizzled into view.

When I lifted my head, I wished I hadn't. My heartbeat pounded like drums inside my temple. A bitter, metallic taste coated my mouth.

Memories from the night before came rushing back. The memories were not pleasant ones.

I closed my eyes and waited for the next blow. As expected, the back of a hand connected with my cheek, and my face sailed to the side.

These beatings were different from what I had been trained to endure. What I'd gone through with my dad were quick fits of rage, moments he only might have remembered the next day. They were swift, single punches to the arm, smacks on the back of the head, just enough to get it out of his system before he just as quickly forgot what he was doing or passed out. But these moments with the Dark Queen lasted. They had passion and purpose behind them, as if I were the sole cause of all her problems.

"Look at me." Her cruel voice was monstrous in the dark.

I couldn't. I couldn't muster the strength anymore. Taloned nails sank into my chin as she turned my gaze toward her bared teeth. I couldn't tell if she was smiling or if she was exhausted from delivering one hit after the next. It didn't matter. Nothing mattered anymore.

I barely noticed the shadow that shifted behind her. It was the same movement I'd seen in the cell across from mine before. The shadow was too dense to make out a true form inside it, only a faint glowing of some sort sitting in the middle of it. The shadows glided from the back of its cell to the bars at the front. And then the glowing blinked.

"Look at me," the Dark Queen hissed acid.

But nothing could have torn my gaze from the intense, mystifying mix of colors coming from the eyes in that shadow cloud. I squinted, taking in a kaleidoscope. The center of its pupils were painted a midnight blue, and from there, they exploded into a burst of cobalt blue and amethyst. Flecks of white and gold scattered throughout the rest, like a universe of stars.

"Impossible," I breathed.

A sharp slap struck my cheek, and my tongue brushed fresh metallic.

*Look at me.*

The voice hadn't come from the Dark Queen this time. It hadn't been spoken out loud by anyone else either. The voice of velvet echoed from the corners of my mind, and I lifted my head toward it —toward the shadow. An overwhelming sense of calm rushed through me, like a bottle of sleep medicine. I didn't feel the hits that came after, and when I lifted my head again and again, it wasn't the queen's eyes I met.

The clasps around my bruised wrists were undone, and I fell to the ground with a heavy thud. I lay there and just stared at the wall. Waiting. For the next visit, the next cold meal, for death. I wondered how it would come, wondered if I would starve before she slit my throat the way she had that chained prisoner.

The dried blood caked on my face was itching. Dirt and blood coated my nails and my hair—it was matted. Ruined.

Nights passed, only counted by the one meal a day brought to me while I slept. I had a feeling some days were forgotten, and whatever tally I tried to keep was off by several days.

The tally I did have was up to day six now. Some days she would come, and some days she wouldn't. She never bothered those in any of the other cells, never asked me anything other than who I was. She never left satisfied with my same, unchanging answer.

Only once did she stop at another cell after leaving me beaten on the ground. The one across from mine, extra markings inscribed into every inch of steel there. She almost walked by it on her way out, but then half turned and paused, as if she'd forgotten it was there. She finally faced the darkness within. And waited.

Loose pebbles vibrated at my fingertips and at her feet. A warning. And yet she stood. A low growl rumbled. I glanced to the end of the hall, but the guard hound was nowhere to be seen. The ground shook more viciously with each passing second the Dark Queen remained there. Until thunder clapped, and the shadows from inside unfurled, dispersing with a blast of wind to reveal a silhouette of a magnificent pair of wings that took up the entire space of the cell. The colors between those wings raged like a storm, trained in on the queen, sending an undeniable message. They promised death. They swore it.

Sitting there on the ground, I leaned away from the blast of the wind and the sheer volume of the storm. My body tried to be afraid. I should be afraid, like I was of everything else, but a part of me was also overcome with an unnerving fascination for whatever beast was trapped in that cell.

A fascination that didn't touch the Dark Queen. She lifted her chin at the threat, though it wobbled, and there was no denying the way her body leaned away just as mine did. She took a step back and then finally retreated, despite the bars between them.

She hadn't come back to see me in three meals time.

I hadn't been offered an opportunity to clean up. There was still blood on my face, and my clothes were so worn they might soon turn to rags. I didn't want to know what a mirror would show me at this point.

The sudden absence of my captor made room to think of other things. My mind betrayed me, instantly going to Zafar. Cozbi had kept her end of the deal. She had, as promised, gotten me through her land safely. What Zafar did with me outside of Kalopsia was none of her business.

The image of him accepting the reward money sailed through my mind like one of the Dark Queen's slaps across the face. How had I not seen it? The errand that took him so long to return from was him securing a deal. He'd already been through those woods without me. He'd already traveled to the Garden to meet with the Dark Queen. To tell her he knew exactly where I was. To tell her that the Assassin had failed, but that he would deliver. To finally show his true colors—sandy brown, like the sin of the desert.

I had been so stupid. Stupid to have trusted so effortlessly, despite all the alarms inside me going off in warning. Stupid to have fallen so recklessly for the first attractive face that showed me a little kindness and a whole lot of charm. I'd been blinded by that, made excuses, made myself look so childishly *stupid* even up to the last second with him.

Tears collected in my eyes, but only one escaped. I swiped it away angrily. But the feelings swelled in my chest like a hurricane in a blender. Betrayal, sadness, physical and emotional pain. Hopelessness. They mixed together to make something that didn't taste right at all. I put my head in my arms and swallowed the burning in my throat. I would not cry. I would not cry over him of all things.

Collecting myself, I vowed Zafar would be the last male to ever disappoint me.

When I came up for air, those kaleidoscopic eyes glowed in my direction. I tensed and sucked in a breath as if those eyes could hurt me from over there. But they only stared silently. It took me several blinks to fully adjust to the darkness surrounding whatever lay in that extra dark shadow.

It looked like a man, though so many in Elysian did. But I knew better at this point.

His posture matched mine as he sat with his back against the wall, head leaned against it too with his stare pointed downward at me, his arms draped over his knees. I wondered if we had possibly looked up at the same time.

*What are you thinking about?*

His lips didn't move, not that I could tell, but somehow, I knew the question had come from him. That low, velvety voice tasted smooth and inviting. A voice that brought an alarming sense of curiosity, despite the mysterious creature it belonged to.

I was underfed and sleep deprived. I'd been hit on the head so many times over. I was going to die down here, I knew it. And now I was going to go out insane. At this point, I welcomed it. At least accepting it numbed the pain when the strikes came. If I fought the insanity, maybe I'd start feeling the pain again.

*Nothing. I am thinking nothing,* I responded.

There was no response to that, but his eyes remained locked on mine, searching.

*What are you thinking about?* I asked back.

*I'm not thinking. I'm eavesdropping.*

I furrowed my brows at him, not understanding what he meant.

The corner of his mouth turned up a little. *Want to see?*

I shook my head at myself and pressed my palms to my temples. I'd become so delusional that my own delusional thoughts weren't even making sense.

Even with my eyes squeezed shut, the vision played out in my mind. It was too clear to be imaginary, and yet the new room I was looking at was far too bright to be anywhere near this palace.

There were three of them in the room leaning over a table, their features too detailed to be made of my own creation. Each of them was so different, though their scowls were the same as they looked down at... That was a replica of Darya's map. A small glass bottle with what appeared to be smoke or fog slowly shifting inside rested on the corner of the table.

Maybe it was exhaustion, or maybe my senses were too overwhelmed to be shocked by anything else, but when I found a fourth figure veiled in shadows in the opposite corner, I knew this was real. But I also knew I—*we* weren't really here either, not in the physical sense, at least. We were simply visiting the space undetected.

The teal-haired one drew my attention first. With matching feathered wings sprouting from her back, she was too beautiful and captivating to miss. Her face was soft and young, and she clutched something hidden in her palm.

"We've got the pieces in place. All our forces and allies will be gathered in two weeks time. We'll move in from all sides, a united front. It's a foolproof plan."

"Until she obliterates us all," a tawny-skinned male scoffed. A mop of ebony hair sat loosely on top of his head, curls spilling over and covering his forehead, the edges trimmed close to the sides. He had a fresh, angled face that made him look like a warrior and prince all at once. His eyes were the strangest gray-green combination with long lashes even I was envious of.

Her hazel eyes, though small like everything else about her, shot daggers at the one who'd just spoken to her. "She can't disintegrate thousands of us at once. That's why it's imperative we march in at the same moment. We'll come in from all different directions. *No one* can be a footstep behind if this is to work."

"And then we find Ty and find his wings," another added. This one had dark, monolid eyes. His hair was even darker and combed away from his face. His warm beige skin was bright and healthy, but his nose looked like it had been broken a few times, hinting at the role he played here. This one was the troublemaker.

The teal-haired speaker, the only winged one in the group, puzzled over the map. She held her chin as she examined the access points marked on the map of this very palace. "There's not many left in the Garden to defend it. The easiest, clearest way in is through the front. That just leaves us to figure out a distraction to breach the courtyard."

"It'll take one hell of a distraction to buy us that kind of time," the warrior prince countered. She ignored him, studying the map as if her life depended on it. "What happens when we don't find them, Ara?" he added. The desperation in his voice seemed to capture her—Ara's—attention. "What happens when everyone I care about is cornered in that palace together? What happens when we take the biggest risk yet with a Wingless Night?"

The silence that followed was deafening. The two others waited for her answer, for some kind of direction. But there was only sadness and understanding in her eyes. She lowered her shoulders.

"We have to try, Ambrose."

The one with dark eyes watched her intently, and she furrowed her brows at him, suddenly annoyed. "What is it, Enzo?"

"You should leave," he said.

She tensed at that and looked to Ambrose, whose thick, dark eyebrows made his scowl the deepest of them all. He only lifted his chin slightly. A firm agreement.

Enzo continued, bringing her attention back to him. "You still have your wings. You can escape all this."

"How dare you," she snapped, and suddenly she didn't appear so young or small. She was much shorter than them, but she stood in a way that told the world she didn't notice her size. "I will not leave any of you. If you go down, *I* go down."

She gazed solemnly at her closed fist, spreading her fingers to show a winged figurine. The King of Valhalla's piece. When she looked back up her eyes glistened in despair.

I looked at the shadow in the corner, his eyes glowing brilliantly through the fog. But the anguish there surprised me. It filled his eyes, his posture even, as clear as this vision.

And then his eyes closed so slowly, so sadly, washing away the scene in front of us, and when I opened my own eyes again, I was staring back across the hall, through the dark, and into his cell.

*Who was that?* I asked eagerly.

I waited. He only rested his head against the wall once again, the beautiful mixture of colors hidden behind closed eyelids. His posture, his face—the very little of it I could see—was etched in burden.

*Who was that?* I tried again.

Even if I had imagined the whole conversation in my head, it had been comforting to hear another voice. To hear that voice specifically. I needed more of it to keep me rooted.

*I'm Briar.* I tried once more, hopeful for an answer. I waited for one, but none came. Only a wave of exhausted calm washed over me without warning, and even though I didn't want to, I leaned my head back and allowed sleep to grace me.

# CHAPTER SIXTEEN

The queen visited with a vengeance.

I knew from my experience with my dad that it was best not to make much noise. That any audible signs of pain are fuel to their fire, but it was harder to take hit after passion-filled hit in silence. It wasn't until she left that I clutched at my face and melted into the stillness of my cell.

Without meaning to, I eventually lifted my gaze and met *his* eyes. They blinked out at me like an animal in the woods. I held my breath at the terrifying way his gaze clutched my whole body.

But then his voice was in my head, and the velvety smoothness washed me in calm. As if he wasn't an anonymous voice cloaked in thunder clouds. As if I hadn't just had half the life beaten out of me.

*Sorry I disappeared before.*

I could only stare, marveling at what was happening between us, before deciding to shift so that I was facing a wall and not him. I sniffed and coughed on the blood that got stuck in my throat.

I sensed he was still watching me, and before I knew what was happening, an image flashed in my mind. It was just like before, a vision of sorts. A memory that didn't belong to me replayed in my mind.

Mountainous treetops rolled on for acres, their colors rich in autumn, and for just a single moment, I could smell the crisp appley air, feel the cool drop in temperature along my arms.

*My home.* His voice sounded over the treetops. *Valhalla.*

I sat up quicker than I should have and faced him again. *How are you doing this?*

*One of my many talents. Especially fun at parties.*

I didn't laugh. *Who are you?*

He didn't reply at first, but then, thoughtfully, *A weapon.*

I believed him. I didn't know exactly what that meant, but I believed he was meant for destruction. And if a queen of ash and terrors had him locked away down here... *Who are you?* I asked again, each word more meaningful than the last.

His shadow moved abruptly. It shot from his corner in the back of the cell to the opposite side. I whipped my head in the new direction, startled by the speed. He moved like an actual shadow and I suddenly wondered if there was a man in there at all. *Who do you think I am?*

I knew exactly who he was. The mysterious winged figure I'd seen twice now on two separate maps.

*You're the King of Valhalla.*

He dodged again, to the front of his bars, in a blink. I leaned slightly away, despite all the distance between us, and held in a breath.

*And you're the one they've been whispering about above ground. The one the Dark Queen would burn the entire Everwood to the ground over. What could you have possibly done to capture her attention in these times?*

I said nothing, only held very still, remembering everything Zafar had told me about this king.

*Your heart is stirring faster than a storm cloud.* I could have sworn a smile curved in that shadow. Was even more sure the way that smile leaned that his head tilted to the side, as if this pleased him. *Are you afraid of me?*

I should lie. I should lie and say I wasn't. Between the stories I'd heard and what I'd already seen for myself, I had every reason to be. Even the Dark Queen was terrified to face him without warded bars between them. But even then, something in my gut told me my fear wasn't real. *Should I be?*

He blinked once. Twice. But he never answered the question.

*What are you doing here?* I tried instead.

*I have something Xosha wants.* I tilted my head at that. *Her true name,* he added. *She is no queen, dark or not.*

Xosha. A name as fierce as she was. So he wasn't down here for something he'd done, but rather as a hostage, for something he had. *What does she want from you?*

His answers were slow, as if he didn't know if he should be speaking to me at all. *I could be of use to her cause.*

*World domination?*

His low rumble of a laugh sent heat down my belly. *That's the one.*

He was evasive in his responses. That, and the fact that I couldn't see him no matter how hard I narrowed my gaze, was unsettling. I dared to try again. *And you won't give it to her? Whatever it is you have?*

*I've been used as a pawn before. I won't be one again.* He held my gaze long enough that I let it fall to the stone floor. His voice instantly wrapped around my mind, grasping my attention and my gaze again. *And what is it she wants from you?*

His voice was honey. It was smooth and rich, coursing through not only my mind, but my veins. Warming me. But it was also catlike. As if I were a mouse just out of reach. It solidified the cold reality that even with bars between us, I needed to keep a safe distance.

*I don't know why I'm here.*

*Okay then.* There was definitely a smooth smile in that shadow. I could see it in the way his already glowing eyes brightened. In the way his shadow lightened just a tone. *How did you wind up on her bad side?*

*Can you read all my thoughts? Is that what this is?*

His glowing gaze lowered. The answer came slower than all the rest, so slowly that I thought he might not answer me at all. *I can't read your mind exactly,* he responded almost hesitantly. *I call it mind tapping.*

*Which sounds a lot like reading minds.*

For the briefest second, the shadows lit up again with a quick flash of teeth in that curve of a smile. But in the next blink, the shadows darkened again. *It's like a door. I can tap on your mind, and if you choose to keep it closed, then you can. Or you can open it, and we're able to communicate through a line of conversation or mental images. The moment one side closes the door, the connection is dropped on both ends. I can't invade your thoughts without your knowledge or permission.* His tone deepened when he added, *Trust me, I've tried.*

*And that room you showed me yesterday. You were able to see that because you...mind tapped into someone's head?*

Another beat of hesitation. *No. That's something else.* He didn't explain any further.

I flicked my gaze to the markings keeping him in his cell. *How?*

*These bars are made of Elysian steel traced with Elysian magic. I am not of Elysian.*

My mind reeled. He was a king of an Elysian realm, which meant a drop of Divine energy ran through him. If he wasn't of this world, how did he get here and find himself with a crown? His voice broke into my distracted thoughts. *The physical benefits of my shadows may be restrained behind these bars, but she has no control over what my mind can do. Magic is a cocky thing.* There was a misbehaving smile in his voice.

*You have questions.* He sensed. *Ask them.*

I did have questions, though none of them mattered. Why was I talking to him in the first place?

Because this conversation, as bizarre as it was, was possibly the only thing keeping me from breaking down here. If it distracted me from thinking about the sharp pain in my ribs, I'd be smart to let it go on as long as he allowed.

*You say you are not tied to Elysian's magic. That it doesn't have full control over you. How? You're its royalty.*

His laugh came out audible, instead of trapped within our minds. It was low and lighthearted, yet it echoed off the stone walls, sending a guard's head turning in our direction, though he didn't come to the farthest end of the hall to investigate.

My cheeks warmed. I didn't like the feeling that came with being laughed at. Like I was such a silly little thing.

*Only in this world.* The king answered in an overexaggerated voice. *In others, I am the son of Alaric, the Once Most Powerful. A Dark Angel's mutant son. I am the Angel of the Night.* He paused, his voice returning to a normal, almost familiar tone. *You can just call me Tynan.*

Tynan. Angel royalty and yet...

*They call you a devil,* I added hesitantly.

*Do they?*

*A ruthless one.*

*And who is they exactly?*

I paused, realizing my mistake.

*Exactly,* he said, and just like that, I felt silly all over again. I'd drunk in Zafar's every word like it was scripture.

*So there you have it. My name, my title. The rumors that come with it.* His shadows shifted a fraction as if reaching for the bars, but they stopped short just of touching them. *Who are you?*

Who was I? I was no one, and yet I was clearly someone in this world for so many to care about me.

*I...*

His gaze focused at my silence. *I've been down here at the end of this hallway for a very long time. Longer than I even know. And now you show up, dangerous enough to be my only neighbor throughout time.* His gaze flicked upward to the heavy markings on my cell. The very same that marked his. *I'd like to know who my competition is.* The glowing narrowed. *Do not make me ask again.*

Even if I had the words to answer him, I was growing too exhausted to speak, even mentally. So I tried something. I went back to the moment this all started, to the very beginning, and when the thought was fully formed, I pushed it. I sent an image to the other end.

I showed him Leah and I smiling up at the sun. And then there was no sun, and the world was tipped upside down, over and over until I landed on my feet and was staring into a vast Nothing. Two bright lights unraveled in the void—two choices. And then I tumbled into a world that wasn't my own. I lead him through an accelerated version of my time with Darya, her pointing to Clive Steeple on the map, the wind as it tied an invisible knot around her and Cozbi's arms. I only gave him parts of Zafar, a burst of emotions—mostly embarrassment—flaring in my chest. I flinched at the part between Zafar and I while the Assassin lingered quietly in the background. I showed him what we learned when we visited the Pits and our uncomfortable ride through the Everwood, and then, finally, I let him have the front-row seat to Zafar's betrayal. At the victorious look on the Dark Queen's face, I let the image fade.

The glowing tilted to the side. *You're human.* It was a statement, not a revelation. And then his voice suddenly altered. *How in the hell did you wind up with someone like Zafar?*

*You know Zafar?*

*I do... And that all sounds exactly like something Zafar would take part in.*

*Son of a bitch,* I muttered mindlessly to myself.

*Also, conniving, manipulative, slutty rat. But yes, son of a bitch would be one of his best worn titles.*

The surprised smile that overtook my face was uncontrollable. *Slutty rat?*

A smile so wide I could practically feel it in my very soul flashed through the shadows. His white teeth were the brightest thing down here other than his eyes.

*A human,* he said again, more revelation in his tone this time. More manlike. More...real. *Impossible.*

*So I've been told.*

*And you were headed to Clive Steeple?*

*Apparently, the scholars there are the only ones who can get me out of here.*

The metal door above clicked open and our heads snapped in that direction. We both already knew what was coming before she made it to the end of the hall.

*Tell me about your world. Tell me about your life before Elysian.*

My knees were tucked into my stomach. Bruises were already forming on my face from where the Dark Queen had just left my cell. Blood stained both my mouth and my thighs.

I'd always been irregular. The doctors said I may have complications getting pregnant. I never knew when my period would hit, and I sometimes went months without one. It was inconvenient starting my cycle at the most unforeseen times, but this was the most inconvenient timing of all. I clenched my fists into my shirt, never having experienced cramping this intense.

*Look at me.*

*No.*

*I said look at me.*

I was too tired to disobey. I swallowed the nausea threatening to rocket up my throat and lifted my eyes to meet his glowing pair. The whites and golds shifted carefully. Suddenly, the cramping around my lower abdomen softened. Not entirely, but enough that I couldn't help but to let out a moan of relief.

*How are you doing that?*

He didn't answer. Instead, he repeated his earlier request. *Tell me.*

I shook my head. He didn't want to know about before. No one did. *You first,* I dared. To my surprise, he let an image slip through our line of communication.

The sky in the image was odd. It was painted gray, but the dark clouds looming over us had nothing to do with the faint lighting in the sky. The trees were thin, the matted grass underfoot scarce. I thought at first it might be a realm most affected by Elysian's curse, but there was a feeling to the air here that sent shivers so deep they shook my spine. An eerie feeling had me looking over my shoulder even on this end of the memory.

Everything that should have color was washed-out in black and white hues. Until a flash of teal ran out into the memory. A small child around the age of eight or nine ran into the open field, arms thrown wide at her sides. Matching teal hair and feathered wings swayed as she ran.

I recognized the matching hair and wings and even the sweet, childlike face. I'd seen her already in the king's first vision, but this version of her was several years younger. Who was she?

She stopped, turned to face me, and smiled so big and so proudly that I knew she wasn't looking at me. *"Watch, Ty! Watch!"* Her head fell back to the clouds and she turned her palms upward. She closed her eyes, her smile radiating joy and innocence. I watched, waiting for something to happen. And then the sky dimmed even more, like God had closed Heaven's shutters and colored the scene in near darkness. Light droplets of water sprinkled down until they poured. She laughed, a sound like bells, as it rained and rained and rained.

*My sister, Ara,* he said into the memory. *This was the day the gifts she was born with clicked into place. The first time she showed me what she could do with them.*

His sister. My mind reeled, wondering if they resembled each other. If by looking at her, was I seeing anything of him? Without meaning to, I squinted into his shadows, trying so hard to see through the thickness of them. And then, as if in answer to my prayers, his smile peeked through the dark. A smile so bright I could feel it. It was warm and soft. A smile that couldn't possibly belong to a weapon.

*That place... Is that Valhalla too?*

*No,* he said. The drop in his tone matched the same eeriness I'd felt looking into the memory. *That place is not Valhalla.*

A thud sounded from the opposite end of the dungeon. I felt like a teenager all over again, flinching at what I knew was coming. But my cellmate did the opposite. His shadows were everything I wasn't. Curious and daring and brave. He was at the front of his cell in the time it took my heart to beat.

*It's not her.*

I shifted on my knees and slid over to the front of my cell in one movement, craning my neck to look down the hall. A metal door to one of the cages was hauled open by the guard on duty tonight. It filled the soundless dungeon with an awful screeching noise. He stepped inside the cell and out of view. I watched—we watched—in anticipation for him to reappear. When he did, he did so dragging out the old hag I'd passed on my way in. Dead. She had died down here, from starvation by the looks of it.

My gaze returned to Tynan.

*Your sister,* I said slowly, remembering the room we'd looked in on. They were planning his escape, along with an overthrow. *She's coming for you.*

He read the real question in my tone. Could she come for me too? Would he even care to waste the extra seconds getting me out with him?

The gold and white swirling flecks slowed even more. His shadows dimmed. And though he answered me in my mind, I could read the answer in those eyes before it sounded.

*It will be too late.*

# CHAPTER SEVENTEEN

"Put this on."

I lifted my head off my arms—the only pillow to use down here. A heap of fabric was tossed into my stomach. I touched the thick, heavy material, then looked to the guard in question.

He stood impatiently by the doorway. I hadn't seen this guard down here before. He peered anxiously over his shoulder, into my neighbor's seemingly empty cell.

"Are you deaf?" he barked when I didn't move.

I shook my head, immediately feeling stupid that I'd responded to a question not meant to be answered. I pushed myself off the ground, going to the deepest part of the dungeon where I wouldn't be seen.

It was so dark I couldn't tell what I was grabbing at. Taking my old clothes off was easy, but it took a few tries before I could work out what had been thrown at me. I shook it out, figuring out after a handful of shakes that it was all one piece of material—a dress.

"Hurry *up!*"

I stepped into it, pulled it up my torso, and eventually slid my arms through the correct holes. There were buttons at the back. My fingers worked at them until I couldn't reach them anymore, leaving the top two undone. I still couldn't make out anything of what I wore when I stepped into the front of the cell again. The dim lighting only gave me a few shades more to work with.

The waiting guard examined me, his eyes roaming my body with amusement. But the guard was so easy to ignore with a gaze like *his* planted on me.

The shadows around Tynan were still, but the gold and white flecks swirled with interest, the amethyst shining extra bright in his cave. I desperately wished I could see more of what lay in those shadows.

*You look ridiculous.*

For whatever reason, I grabbed at my hair. It was a mess. A tangled, crunchy, dirty mess slung over one shoulder. My bare feet padded against the cold stone as I made my way to the open doorway.

*Thanks.*

An open door. That meant freedom. It meant forgiveness from a sin I hadn't learned I'd committed yet. And still I found myself holding back a shudder as I walked into the hallway. A feeling crept over me. One that shouted this wasn't freedom. It was a trap. Any moment this guard would knock me unconscious or shove me backward. Another cruel game sent by a fill-in player. But the guard never laid a hand on me. Instead, he made toward the exit, nodding for me to follow.

*Think before you say anything to her.*

I glanced back. He was closer to the bars than he'd been just a moment ago. *Whatever this is, it's a game. And you've already lost.*

I squinted at him in confusion and a need to understand him. What was *his* game? Why did he care to warn me if he'd been goading me this entire time? But when his pointed, warning glare was out of view, it was all I could do to keep my heart from thundering out of my chest. The exit was near. For the first time in weeks, maybe months, the end was in sight.

I barely noticed the curious prisoners peering at me as I walked down the hall. Instead, I noted the loose pebbles that stuck to my blackened feet as I climbed each stair. The raised skin on my bare arms. The ruffling of the fabric I wore, shifting and swaying with every slight movement.

My eyes burned a little when the heavy wooden door opened. I blinked a few times, adjusting to the light I'd been denied. But even then, the light above was sparse. There was barely any of it left to push through the clouds and into the uncleaned palace windows.

I followed the guard, taking in everything I'd missed the first time I was here. The place was in ruins. No matter what it may have been—the great and majestic palace of a precious Garden—all that was left were dingy, empty hallways. The black and white checkered flooring hadn't been polished in years. There was the shattered glass of a broken vase at the base of a wall, and velvet curtains half falling off the wall as though one side had been ripped from the rod and flung down in the fit of a tantrum.

My eyes darted along each hall we passed, heart accelerating each time I saw a set of doors. I wasn't stupid enough to run for it, but I was hopeful enough to think freedom was still on the table. That by some miracle, I'd be led to the foyer and told to leave before the Dark Queen changed her mind.

But it wasn't the foyer I was taken to. Instead, we stopped in front of a dust-covered door that may have once been painted gold but looked a dull brass now.

"Are you going to stand there waiting for an official instruction on how to open a damned door?" the guard grumbled.

A game, the shadow creature had warned. One I'd already lost. I ignored the guard and braced myself for what I knew waited on the other side of this door. I could feel it, her presence humming from inside. A darkness tainted by blood and ash and suffering.

My arms felt small as I braced them against the heavy set of doors. I struggled against the fatigue and famine to push them open.

My hope changed direction, from a desire for freedom to a desire to eat when I realized where I'd been brought. A dining hall. A long table stretched throughout the middle of the room, with tall-backed wooden chairs around it. The chairs were all empty except for the seat at the head of the table. She sat with her back facing me, a black crown spiked above the chair.

My eyes scanned the rest of the room, taking note of every detail. There were no guards. She didn't need them. No blinking creatures lurked behind tattered curtains or dark corners. Tall arched windows lined one wall of the room, giving a view of the barren land outside. It was raining. In the middle of a drought, it was raining. Droplets of hope tapped the glass and sprinkled against the lake, sending its water dancing for the first time in decades.

She didn't speak. She didn't turn at the sound of my arrival. She only moved a wineglass gracefully to her lips.

Dread slammed into my chest and settled there. This wasn't freedom, it was a meeting. Or an interrogation, I wasn't sure yet. But the sooner it was over, the better.

Only one other place setting was laid out, at the opposite end. I guided myself there and lowered myself into the chair, the thick ruffles of the dress making the movement noisy and distracting.

The Dark Queen's gaze cut into me with feline interest. She sat so much like she did on her throne. Half slouched in a sideways position. Her elbow was propped on the arm of the chair, and her red-painted talons wrapped around a glass of dark liquid. Her blood-red lips slanted in amused rebellion. Her lips weren't the only thing stained. My eyes were drawn to the tips of her hair— burgundy the last time she visited me, but now a renewed brilliant ruby.

"You might look like a little dove in that dress if only you'd had the time to clean up."

I looked down at myself in response, seeing for the first time the pure white coloring of the dress and the silver tracings that lined down each petal-shaped ruffle.

When I met her stare again, her eyes were lifeless. My fingers tightened on the arms of my chair. Waiting. When she finally blinked, she leaned forward and set her glass on the table.

"That was my mother's dress, you know." Her eyes flicked to the ballgown I wore.

"This?" The shock of that statement was enough to get a single word out of me.

The corners of her mouth lifted in an attempt at a smile, though the gesture came out all wrong on her face.

"In fact, that's the one she wore to her coronation if I'm not mistaken." She lifted her dark eyes to the ceiling in thought. "No, wait. It must have been her wedding. With all the rules they used to impose on the High Queen, they wouldn't have allowed white at a coronation."

She lifted the lid of a silver platter before her and then reached for her fork. She motioned for me to do the same. "Do you know how long I had to dig through this palace to find something white? It was packed away in a forgotten room with her things. You certainly wouldn't find anything like that in my own wardrobe."

I lifted the silver lid, half expecting something to jump out at me. But there was only a thin slice of overcooked cow's meat. No vegetables or other garnishes on the side. How could there be? With no life in the Garden.

The Dark Queen was already tearing into hers. She ate like an animal, shoving forkfuls of meat into her mouth. I tried not to stare at her sloppy bites, but it was hard not to. It was the first time I'd seen her movements so...unthought out. Famine would do that though, even to royalty.

"Why?" It was the only word, the only thought that mattered since having the dress tossed at me. Why was I here? Why had she given me her dead mother's dress?

She chewed, creating enough time between my question for a heavy, uncomfortable silence. "I think we got off on the wrong foot, Briar. I'd like to get to know each other." She gestured her empty fork to my plate and then back to me. "Now eat."

Carefully, I lifted the fork to my left, the knife to my right. I cut a polite piece off the end, but I paused before bringing it fully to my lips. I stared at the meat with hesitation.

"If I wanted you dead, don't you think I'd have more creative ways to do it than poison?"

She was right. She could ash me to the nonexistent wind right here and now if she wanted to. I brought the fork to my lips and took a careful bite. I forced myself to swallow a dry, dusty bite, unable to hide a small cough at the end.

"You'll have to excuse the quality of the meat. It's been frozen for some years, and there is no fresh livestock in the pastures anymore. You'll get used to it in time."

Get used to it in time. I tried to keep my composure.

I reached for the wine in front of me, uncaring of my usual caution when it came to alcohol. I took the smallest of sips to wash the taste away, but even the wine was bitter.

"So tell me." Silence followed as she cut into her meal. Her teeth tore into it, but she did not speak again.

"Tell you what?"

"About yourself." Each word was sharp, like she was trying to be cordial, but she wasn't built for that. Her facade of pleasantries was a ticking time bomb.

"There's nothing interesting to tell."

She paused mid chew, her dark eyes deepening in annoyance.

My brain raced to come up with something. Anything to appease her. But there was nothing to share. I hadn't lived a life that presented much room for opportunity or experience. I'd been so focused on graduating high school and scrounging up enough part-time job money to buy my own hygiene products to learn anything about myself. Hobbies I might be obsessed with, hidden talents gifted to me.

"Dove." Xosha's voice was grating. "I'm trying my best to be nice here. Work with me. Things don't end well when my patience is tested."

Unplanned words fell from my lips. "I've lived a simple life. I serve food to make ends meet, and I live—used to live with my best friend."

"So you are a maid?" She questioned with a lifted brow.

"I worked in a restaurant."

"Ah. A kitchen attendant."

"Sort of."

"Well, we have very few of those left around here. Perhaps you'd like to fill a position."

I forced my lips to lift, though I knew it was too weak to be seen as genuine. The last hope of freedom evaporated in my chest.

"And your parents?"

The question was so unexpected that I didn't know how to respond at first. "Not in my life."

"That's vague."

I put another bite of food into my mouth, if only so I didn't have to respond right away. The food really was terrible, but the extra time was needed. I had no choice but to wash it down with another small sip. "My father isn't..."

"He's dead?" Her pitch heightened, out of excitement or alarm, I couldn't tell.

"He's living. We're just not close."

She dropped her fork onto her plate, finished. "A shame," she said dismissively. "And your mother?"

My skin crawled. Every fiber of my body screamed at me to

keep my answers as simple as possible. "Also out of touch. She left when we were small."

"We?" Her interest spiked, and I scolded myself.

"My brother."

"A brother." Her eyes sparkled with interest. I nodded. She folded her fingers underneath her chin. "Tell me more."

I bit down on my tongue, angry with myself for the slipup. I'd have to tell her everything. Despite all the things the Dark Queen was, she was also smart. She knew when I was keeping things from her and she knew how to get them out of me too, pleasantly or not.

"Our mother left my brother and I when we were small. It was just us two with our father for a long time. My father wasn't interested in being a parent, so we fended for ourselves until we too went our separate ways."

"And where did your mother run off to?"

"I don't know."

The Dark Queen gave me a chilling look. A final warning.

"Truly," I added quickly. "I never asked and never went looking for her."

Her eyes stayed on me for some time, long enough to decide my answer was acceptable. When she finally responded, her voice was deadpan, void of any emotion. "Tragic."

For a moment, she looked disappointed. She flopped into her normal reclined position, fixing her gaze out the window, though I'm not sure she was actually seeing anything of what rested beyond it. Whatever thoughts swirled around in her mind, they were so loud I could probably hear them if I listened closely enough. They screamed and clawed at her. Tormented her. Whatever her thoughts were, they ate her alive.

"I understand all about complicated family relationships," she finally said, only giving up a fraction of what she'd been thinking. Her lips turned, and for the quickest flash of a moment, I thought I saw sadness in her eyes. But it was only that. A flash. Gone just as quickly as it had arrived.

But it was then, in that unsuspecting flash, that I saw it. How very soft her face actually was. How...childlike it was. And then I realized something unimaginable. There *was* still a child in there. A scorned child holding on to deep wounds and hurt feelings. A child who, so much like me, had never been taught to sort through emotions too big for her little body. Until one day, she grew up, and it was much too late to fix anything of what her parents hadn't taught her was broken.

But it was there. Buried deep underneath all that hurt, and anger, and malice...there was a childlike softness.

Until her face moved. Until her brow ticked or her lip bared back in a grimace. Until her features curled in disgust and her eyes narrowed in on someone weaker than her. Then she was a hurricane of emotions. She was the Dark Queen. She was malice and pain, and she was a missile of all those things ready to strike the nearest target.

And I related.

"Tell me about them." I said, my heart rate speeding at my bravery. The Dark Queen also raised a brow in surprise. She responded quicker than I expected her to.

She smiled unconvincingly, and my hope flared to life yet again. Yes. This is what she was after. For someone to understand her. Companionship even.

"I'd like to think my parents meant well, but how could they have? They couldn't have been bothered to at least *try* to hide their favoritism." Her eyes slid to her glass and hovered there, her memory taking her to another time. Her eyes narrowed as she spoke through that memory. "I was simply an afterthought. The 'Oh yes, where has that other child of ours gone off to?' It was my sister they adored. Their heir. Their prized child of golden light. She couldn't have been more perfect unless she talked to animals."

"I'm sure they loved you," I tried, testing my bravery.

She scoffed. "They tolerated me."

Her teeth bared through her painted lips. She stared at the wine inside her glass and I could feel the white-hot rage boiling over inside her.

"I'm sorry," I blurted out and earned the Dark Queen's attention. "They had no business having children if they couldn't show you both the same love in different ways."

Her tight expression loosened, though I could tell it was a struggle for her to relax. She examined me curiously, as if searching for some trap. I kept my gaze on hers, willing encouragement in my features. My hope flared, surged almost. I'd gotten my foot in the door. I just had to keep steady.

"My gift was a disappointment," she continued. "When they learned I wouldn't be the heir, they at least hoped my gifts would be impressive. At the very least useful. Imagine their disgust when I withered life instead of created it."

Her chest rose and fell heavily with the barely contained rage swirling inside her. I wondered if she could burn things to ash if she pointed her gaze sharply enough.

But in that moment, I saw something more alarming.

I saw myself. The anger that filled me. It consumed us, living rent-free in our hearts. There was only one difference between us, and it was that I never let my rage surface.

"That all could have changed when my sister went missing. The worst was assumed of her. I expected the land's gifts would travel over to me fairly quickly, but they never did. And then I figured it out. The disappearance of my sister only meant the heir was missing, not the High Queen herself. It wasn't my sister that stood in my way then. It was our mother." She tapped her glass with a nail, churning over her words before they spilled out. Her dark eyes landed on mine, and her straight teeth flashed in a taunting smile. "And I was a very impatient child. Who knows how long it would have taken for her to pass and fully transfer her gifts to the next."

I could only stare. The nonchalant way she spoke made her confession hard to make out. I processed it over and over again in my mind, trying to convince myself I was misunderstanding. But the Dark Queen only stared at me with the slightest curve to her lips, waiting.

"Did you—"

"What else was I to do but kill them?"

I became very still. I didn't blink, didn't breathe. She took in my reaction, clearly reveling in it, and I wondered why she hadn't already announced her confession across the realms if this reaction satisfied her so much.

"I realized before my gifts could come to me as High Queen, there couldn't *be* a High Queen. No one suspected poor, orphaned Princess Xosha had been the one to sneak into their room and end their lives. All thanks to a special dagger of mine, poisoned with my very own ash that worked from the inside out once plunged into one's skin. Even if they did suspect me, no one ever challenged me. They learned not to soon enough."

She seemed unfazed by her words. Even as she admitted to killing her parents, she saw little wrongdoing in her actions, and that was the scariest thing of all. I thought her jealousy was the scariest thing about her, but it wasn't. It was that she didn't even see it. She was truly deranged.

My voice shook, but I found myself unable to stop. What happened to the Pale Queen was Elysian's biggest mystery. If I only dared to venture there, I could uncover the truth.

"Did you kill your sister too?" I tread carefully, knowing that associating her sister with her given nickname would only enrage the Dark Queen more.

She leveled her gaze on me. "If my sister is dead, it did not come by my hand."

So there was hope then. If not for me, then for the survival of this land. But surely not me, I knew that with a heavy certainty.

"Which only means one thing. My sister is still out there." Her jaw clenched. "She and the land are punishing me. This is all her doing. She's sending the plagues. The drought. The lifeless crops, all of it."

That was a theory no one had suggested yet. That the true queen was out there watching her sister. Tormenting her for a crime only the two of them knew about. I debated trying to talk her down from that ledge. I ran through the possibility of how well she might receive it—that the Pale Queen couldn't be behind this. She wouldn't punish an entire world, all because of a fight with her sister.

The Dark Queen looked out the window, staring blankly. "An ash kingdom," she whispered, and I wondered if she knew she was speaking out loud. "That's what she's given me. An ash kingdom for an ash queen."

Small droplets softly plastered against the window pane, rolling down in the slowest paced race. She stood then, downed the last of her wine in one gulp, and set the glass down much too carefully. The soft clink of glass against the table was somehow threatening. She sauntered over to the rain-splattered windows and gazed out in a dreamlike state.

"The fields are stubborn." The words were barely above a whisper. "But they will come back."

I swallowed before speaking, my throat dry. My fingers trembled, but if I wanted to make it out of here alive, I had to keep trying. "The rain is a good sign."

She huffed. "That isn't natural rain. *That* is the sign of a rebellion on the rise. A warning from the mountains."

The mountains. My cellmate. He could communicate with the teal-haired angel. With others outside of here. They were planning something. Something big. Something that might even the tables at the very least. If I could get this information to someone else before my fate here was sealed...

It's a game, and you've already lost. I reminded myself of that as I debated how far I wanted to push my luck.

She turned suddenly, expanding her arm out to me in welcome. "Come here. I want to show you something."

It's a game, and you've already lost.

My arms trembled as I put my weight on them to push myself up. I was so weak, but that's not why they shook. I left the barely touched meal and the undrinkable wine, and then took what may be my last steps. I stopped at her side.

She placed her hands atop each of my shoulders, much softer than I expected, and faced me toward the barren landscape. "What do you see?" she asked.

Immediately, I knew she wasn't talking about the view. My eyes were drawn to her reflection in the fogged glass. Every muscle in my body tightened. My skin prickled at her nearness.

"I asked you a question," she reminded me. "What. Do you see?"

Though every fiber in my body told me not to look away from her, I had no choice. I closed my eyes, feeling them prick with wetness. I was going to die. No matter what I did or said, that was my only way out of here. I opened my eyes to meet my reflection.

I'd been right about the hair. It was disheveled and knotted at the ends. But my face— There was more dirt than anything, but the old blood from her last visit was unmistakable. My eyes stung. My throat tightened. What I saw was nothing more than a punching bag. A thing to be beaten on for the remainder of my life. A discarded, unwanted item to be thrown about and tossed around. My gaze fell to the floor.

"I see nothing." My voice was barely above a whisper.

"Oh, don't be so modest." Her voice was cheery, as if we were merely gossiping over childlike crushes and wishful dreams. "You wish to be more. Don't you?" The last bit was a challenge. Yet another dare.

This is a game. I've already lost.

"I don't."

"Come now," she tsked. "No one wishes to be only a kitchen attendant."

I met her waiting stare in our reflection, and the color that her black eyes had deepened to—it was unlike anything. Unlike any creature that roamed the lands. Hungry and soulless and desperate for the truth. Her voice was bubbling acid. "Tell me."

I opened my mouth to repeat the same answer, to lie. To myself and to her. But when the words came out, it was a truth I'd never considered before now. It was a confession that was relief and a death sentence all at once. "I don't know what I want. But I do want more than what I have."

"Oh, Dove." She sighed heavily, as if the confession relieved her as well. She reached out, and I told myself not to flinch.

This is a game. I've already lost. *This is a game. I've already lost.*

My heart thundered as she took a section of my hair and tucked it behind my ear, showcasing more of my beaten face. Dirtied. Bloodied. Scraped and bruised. The contrast of my face against the white dress only highlighted those facts more. And that was the whole point, wasn't it? The revelation stung more than my throat. That was the reason I was here. It wasn't a chance at freedom or a plea to connect. It was to make a mockery of me.

This is a game. I've already lost.

"Such a pretty little dove."

She did something I didn't expect then. She reached both hands above her head and grasped the sides of her black pointed crown. I barely let myself breathe as I watched her reflection bring that crown to me. A tear slid down my cheek when she set it atop my head.

Her voice dropped to a whisper. "Does this little dove want to rule? Does she think she can bring the fields back to life?"

I shook my head, willing the tears that flowed to stop. "I don't want that."

Her eyes narrowed and the facade slipped completely. "Is that why you've come?"

This was all a game. And I just lost.

I turned from the window to face her with a pleading desperation. I shook my head rapidly. "I swear, I'm not after what you have. That isn't what I meant."

"*Stop* lying to me!"

"*Please.*"

This was all a game. And I—

My head jolted back, her claws suddenly in a knot at the base of my neck. The crown clattered to the floor. Her face pressed against mine, her teeth bared at my ear. "You can't have it. Not after all I've done to get here. *You cannot have it!*"

I was thrown to the ground, like the discarded item I was.

I blinked, and she was on top of me, clutching my chin with one taloned finger resting against my cheek. She pressed into my skin, and it burned. My skin *burned*.

A grunt of pain left my throat, and by the time I realized what she was doing—that her rage was spilling over and burning me with a simple touch—she stopped. Every muscle in her body stilled.

She blinked hard, as if coming back into the present moment.

"Oh, Dove." She snapped off the ground and smoothed wrinkles in her dress that weren't present. She laughed suddenly in a bewildered manner. "I lost my temper for a moment. I did warn you that may happen." She gritted her teeth, as though she couldn't hold back her anger no matter what she did. As though it truly were out of her control. "Here, let me help you."

I was hauled off the ground by the loose fabric around my

shoulders. Something ripped, but I was moving before I could place what it was. She hurried me across the room and through the double doors I'd first come from. She let go of me harshly, sending me crashing into the front of the guard who'd brought me here.

"We've had our fun, but it seems Briar here has gotten a bit carried away. Take her back." The bite behind her words was clear. I was being punished. For not giving her what she wanted. Or for giving her exactly what she wanted.

The guard's blocky hands came around my wrists, and I looked to the Dark Queen one last time. Despite the flashy attempts at smiles and the coolness to her tone she'd struggled to keep moments ago, an annoyed sort of defeat took over her expression. The door slammed shut and she was gone.

By the time I made it back to my cell, the top of the borrowed dress was torn. The sleeves dipped delicately off my shoulders, ripped from when she'd clutched onto the fabric to haul me off the ground. The bottom was torn from where I'd tripped after being rushed down the dungeon stairs. I could only assume the rest of it was no longer that perfectly pure white it had been when I first dressed in it. Not after I'd been tossed back into my cell. Not after I'd hit my head again and felt the blood trickle down onto the neckline. More dirt. More blood.

I was still dazed when I looked into my cellmate's prison just seconds after mine was slammed shut. Dazed from the fall and by the fact that I'd been brought back here at all. That I was still breathing instead of left as a pile of ash to be swept from an empty dining hall. But more important than my confusion over why the Dark Queen let me live was the information I'd learned. And that I had to share it with someone.

And there that someone was. Waiting. Curious.

The shadow creature crept close to his bars, peering questioningly at my strange return to the dungeon that neither of us expected.

My vision blurred, but I hung on to consciousness. Elysian was currently holding on to two of history's greatest unsolved mysteries, and I'd just learned the truth of one of them. He and I may never get out of here, but he had the ability to get that truth beyond these walls. To spread it to his sister through whatever mind communication he was capable of.

But my vision slipped just as my arms did. The hunger and exhaustion and pain forcing me back down. It was too much to explain.

*Did you hear that?* I asked, praying his abilities went beyond what I knew.

The shadow creature didn't move. Not a wisp of darkness shifted. Not a gold fleck stirred, but a velvety voice echoed in my mind.

*I heard every word.*

# CHAPTER EIGHTEEN

I didn't have a way of knowing how many days my meal had been skipped. It felt like weeks, though if that were true, my body would've been dragged out of here by now, just as the hag's had been, and now a five-tailed creature I couldn't name.

The hallway remained as it always did—dark and silent, even though my stomach's gurgling might as well have echoed all the way to the Dark Queen's chambers. The sharp pain each time I inhaled was all I could focus on. I was on my back, my arms holding each other over my belly, and my eyes closed, trying and failing to think of anything but food.

*Your stomach is very loud. It's quite distracting.*

My eyes snapped open and then narrowed. My head snapped in his direction. *Oh, I'm sorry. Is my near-death experience bothering you?*

That small, inaudible sentence was enough to drain the last of my energy. I couldn't even focus on his eyes this time, as all-consuming as they were. I felt faint even lying down. My arms were too weak to lift myself into a sitting position. I inhaled, slow and steady and deep, trying to regain the energy I'd just lost.

I almost used up that energy to snap at him again when a vision began unfurling in my mind. But this one was too captivating to send away.

A teenager, or someone not much older than one, with the deepest onyx hair, messy and grown out just enough for the ends to start curling around the ears. He had a beautifully defined face, one that had surely taken extra time to handcraft. I gasped, taken aback by the sight of him. His smooth, tanned skin. The faint dimple in his left cheek. Eyes of an endless starry night. A small teal-haired baby slept snuggly in his arms. He wore the most amazing smile in the world, one aimed contently at the small baby as if she were his own.

There was someone sleeping in a chair across from him, though I couldn't see her face. All I could see from this view was long jet-black hair braided down her back and a fist propped to her temple while she slept. And the not quite grown child, not yet...Tynan—he bounced his arms, keeping the months old baby and his exhausted mother both sleeping soundly while a fire crackled inside the hearth.

When the image faded, I stared into the void. Stared even though I could see nothing, but I suddenly felt I knew everything. Even if he still didn't drop his shadows, he'd shown me what he looked like, and he was devastatingly breathtaking. Not a terrifying thunder-shadow creature at all.

My gaze involuntarily flicked to what I guessed to be his back. I didn't see any wings in the memory. Didn't see where his shadows should drape around them now.

*Yes,* he commented, seeing clearly where my gaze lingered. *I had my wings then. They were just stored away. Another fun party trick of my kind. They sort of...morph into us when we need them to.*

*What do you mean...you had your wings?*

A beat of hesitation, but then, *I fell long ago. After that memory, but...before Elysian. What you saw me do in front of Xosha was just a shadow of what had once been. A reminder to her in case she has forgotten who she has caged down here.*

*What does that mean?*

*A long, uninteresting story.*

I doubted that. *Tell me anyway.*

*No.*

*Please?*

*After all the things the wannabe queen has done to you.* This *is when you finally beg?*

I was too exhausted to respond. I just closed my eyes and breathed.

*Briar.*

My eyes opened slowly, and I found his gaze again.

*You weren't... You didn't say anything for a while.*

*How long?*

*A few minutes.* I only breathed in response. In and out. Deep and smooth, despite the stinging sensation that came with it. *Ask me something else. Anything but that.*

Of all the questions I'd collected by now about this stranger, I couldn't come up with a single one now. Could hardly think at all. The only thought I could grasp on to was that his voice was different again. He'd gone back and forth, between man and beast. Between time and remembering he had secrets to keep cloaked in those shadows.

*What does the Dark Queen want with you?*

I thought of the beast he'd been just before I lost consciousness. Of every title he'd been given so far. A weapon, a mutant, the Wingless Night. *What is the Night? And I want a real answer this time. No more responses that make me think.*

*The Night is who I used to be. Who Xosha wants me to be again.*

I shook my head. It was another answer cloaked in shadowy half-truth, but I was too tired to question it.

*She'll come for you again if you get out of here,* I told him. *You know that, right? If she's so desperate for the two of us and whatever it is we have, she'll be relentless. She won't stop until she has what she wants.*

*Xosha will not come to Valhalla.* The playful beast again, though the two tones were beginning to blur together. *I can promise you that.*

*No? She seems more determined than that.*

His lip twitched upward, as if the thought pleased him. *Behind the veil of the Dark Queen is only a scared shitless princess who won't dare come near me or Valhalla.*

*If you're so big and bad, how did you wind up here then?* I managed to tease. *Captured by the very one too terrified to touch you?*

I could practically feel his playful smirk and felt every honey-dipped syllable in his tone. *Don't be so sure, Briar. I only found myself in this cage because I moved too quickly the last time. Rash decisions will not be a mistake I make again. I'm here today only because she used something against me that she knew I'd be desperate for. Something she knew would have me rushing out of my territory and straight into a trap. Straight into warded shackles etched in the very magic of these bars.* Tynan delicately tapped a finger against a metal bar. It sizzled hotly against his skin, sending his hand recoiling back, his shadows along with it.

It was working. With all this talk, all these images being traded back and forth, I'd forgotten what terrible shape I was in. I'd stopped wondering which time I'd go to sleep and not wake up.

*Can you keep a secret?*

I almost smiled. Almost. *I will tell everyone I know the first chance I get. Starting with the cyclops.*

His rumble of a laugh echoed through my mind. Only when the last one rolled over my shoulders and vanished along my spine did he continue. *I wish my sister would not come.*

My brows bunched. *Why is that?*

*Because right now, I know Ara to be safe. I can handle Xosha, but*

*Ara... Once she leaves Valhalla, I can't control what happens to her. I can't ensure she'll make it to me in one piece.*

*Can't you tell her that? You can mind tap—*

*I've tried.* There was silence for a beat, as if Tynan were bothered by something he wouldn't say. *It must be these bars,* he finally settled on. Which didn't make sense, because he was having a full-blown mental conversation with me now. But if he couldn't mind tap with Ara, then that meant he hadn't gotten the message through about what happened to the Dark Queen's parents. Though it really didn't matter. She was dead and there was no undoing it. The truth solved nothing.

*But if she doesn't come, what will you do? What's your plan then?*

*I stay here. Until Xosha gets what she wants.*

*Welcome to the club,* I said, already knowing that would not happen. *Now we're both dead.*

*We're all technically dead without the right ass on the throne. It's just a game of who falls first.*

I laughed aloud, delirious at this point.

*You need food.* He said it like there was something that could be done about it. *And I'm sure you have a concussion.*

*You're right about Ara coming here,* I said, ignoring him. *The Dark Queen will kill her if she gets the chance. She'll take whatever she can from you just to prove a point.*

A distant rumble of thunder rolled from somewhere far beyond the palace walls, and Tynan's voice darkened to that of something that wasn't man nor beast. It was otherworldly. His voice came from wherever gray place he'd shown me. *If my sister is touched, all of Elysian will have me to answer to.* Death took over that voice, an anger without rein lingering as the beat of thunder waves rolled to a stop.

*And what will that look like?* I dared to whisper. I didn't really need an answer to that. I had shivered against his eyes shining out in the darkness like a cave monster. Reared back against the thunder he produced from inside. Felt the rocks tremble at his wrath.

He shook his head. It's *your turn.*

The memories he'd shared with me up to this point had been pleasant ones. I could feel the warmth of them even in the coldness of this dungeon, feel whatever Tynan was feeling in those memories. I didn't have many memories that gave me that same warmth.

I closed my eyes, shuffling for memories, for a good place to start. I scanned for the happiest ones, the times with Leah, and almost sent through the one of the night on the balcony when the stars were alive. That moment of peace and belonging. But those brief moments with Leah weren't an accurate representation of the life I had lived. They were a facade, side roles I was barely in attendance to be playing.

And I was so, so tired of hiding. Of running. Of keeping it all in as if the sins of others were my best kept secret.

So I sent him the truth.

Like a film in fast-forward, I showed him the morning my dad realized my mom had left, the tears he sobbed as he threw her things into a fire. I showed him the fabric of my shirt clenched in my dad's fist as he pulled me close enough to smell tequila on his breath. He laughed loudly in my face. Laughed and laughed until I cried. I was seven. I showed him when I was eleven, when dad had wanted to get to Liam, but I was the closest thing to him, so instead, he took me by the shirt and threw me into my brother, knocking us both to the floor like bowling pins. I showed him when he grabbed me by the throat at fourteen and flipped me over the couch for not breaking eye contact first. I showed him when he called me a bitch the next day instead of apologizing. I was still naive enough at the time to believe that was something he might do. A rare fist to the nose at fifteen. The first time I had to hide alone at sixteen.

And in between them all, I showed him glimpses of Liam and I escaping through his iPod late at night or while walking home from school, sharing a set of earpieces and soaking in every normal minute we were allowed before we stepped into that house again. Until Liam left too and took the music with him.

Tynan didn't blink. Not a shadow stirred out of place while I sent image after image.

*That is what you are fighting to return to?* He asked after the last visual faded away. *Why?*

The question froze me. The truth was, I didn't have an answer. For as long as I could remember, I'd never really had a home, not really. I'd barely had a family. Everyone always left. It didn't matter who they were. I'd gotten my hopes up with Leah and her friends. I'd begun to believe that could be it. My home, my family. And I'd been wrong again.

*Because if not there, then where?* Realization settled in. The answer to the question I'd asked myself since arriving in Elysian.

When he spoke next, his voice had changed. It was the same, yet altered somehow. As if a mask had slipped. I may still be a mouse, but he no longer seemed interested in playing cat. His next question was coated in not honey, but disappointment. *Why didn't you go to anyone for help?*

*Our dad's family wasn't around, and our mom grew up in an orphanage. There wasn't anyone to go to. And when she left, our dad drilled into us that if we told anyone, we'd likely be spilt up. Taken into different foster homes, and we'd never see each other again. I don't know if that was true, but as a child, that possibility was much worse than enduring anything he could put us through together. At least Liam and I had each other.*

*And no one noticed something was off? No one helped?*

This. This was the part that pissed me off the most. *No. If anyone did notice, they never cared enough to ask or do anything about it.*

Tynan was quiet for some time, and I could feel when his curiosity turned to annoyance. *Your brother looked older,* he accused.

*By two years.*

*He never stood up to your father. He never tried to stop it.*

*My brother protected me the only way he knew how. He taught me how to keep my head down and my arms up. He taught me how to take the blows in a way that would hurt the least.*

*He should have taught you how to fight.*

I shook my head adamantly. *I was trained to stay down, and because of that, it might have kept me alive.*

The truth of what I'd just said settled into Tynan, and all the bright flecks in his eyes deepened to a deathly black.

Liam almost called the police once. I'd been hurt. It was the first time Dad truly lost all sense of self-awareness. He'd never come home that drunk before, and I was in the way. He turned around, and I was right behind him, a plate of homemade nachos in my hand. The messy chips spilled to the floor, red salsa staining the carpet. He only slapped me, but the force behind it... I woke up with my head in Liam's lap, a phone resting loosely in his hand with 911 already typed out. But he only stared blankly at the wall, wide-eyed. I think he was in shock. I don't know how long he'd been sitting like that, caught between calling the police and having them take us away—away from each other—and potentially losing me to the point of no return.

I didn't send that memory down whatever line connected us. But I sat with it. For the first time, I really sat with it and the feelings that it came with. My chest heated, and my breathing picked up. I hated my dad. I'd never let myself really think about that, because sometimes, something that was hidden in the deepest, darkest part of me, a part of me that would never be voiced aloud, wanted to kill him.

*And your mother?*

His voice was like a bucket of water, cooling my chest and bringing my attention back to the moment. *She left when I was really young.* I was going to leave it at that, but the honesty shared between us so far made it hard to keep the rest of it from surfacing.

*It never made any sense. I know I was young, but the little of her I do remember... It just never felt like something she would do. She loved us. I do know that. I remember how warm her smile was when she tucked me into bed. I remember the love in her touch when she hugged me. I'll never understand what made her leave without us.*

Tynan went silent, and the gap between our voices was deafening. *I'm sorry,* he finally said.

I shrugged.

As if sensing the shift in my emotions, the heat of my anger melting into a sorrow I didn't quite understand, Tynan sent another memory.

A child stood in a small kitchen. Little dark-feathered wings were tucked in close to his sides, too tightly to really see much of them. Those spectacular eyes glowing in the dimly lit room told me exactly who he was. Those eyes were even more striking on the face of a child.

Gray light from the only window painted the wooden floor, perhaps darkening the room instead of brightening it. There was an adult there too, the same one from his last memory. I only knew so because of the black braid running down her back. Tynan looked up at her, even with her back turned to him. There was a question in his eyes that would never reach his mouth. As if sensing it, she patted Tynan on the head, never turning to look at him and said, "Not now, son. I'm tired today." And with that, she left him standing in the room alone.

My heart ached as I watched this helpless child who was too nervous to ask his mother for even her gaze. It suddenly became impossible to imagine he'd been a spine-chilling shadow beast just days ago.

The memory faded, washing away Tynan's stare at the empty doorway and replacing it with the same child in a different room. A candle burned at his bedside, lighting a small space in the room. He leaned over a cradle pushed up next to his bed. Only the top of a baby's head peeked out, a tuft of blue-green hair. A door from another room opened and then shut. Tynan jolted at the noise. He blew out the candle in a panic, then sailed under the covers pretending to sleep.

The memory flashed again, and this time, Tynan was older. Much older. He was almost of grown age, but not quite. His wings were still tucked in tight. I wished I could see them, wished he'd spread them out wide for me to admire like the rest of him. He wore brown leather with black coverings over most of his body. He held his hands behind his back, chin lifted, gaze trained on the gray forest. Someone I couldn't see spoke into the memory, but his voice —I didn't need to see him to know what he looked like. His voice was as deep as the planet's core and as violent as stone.

"It's time you become useful, boy."

Tynan's face remained as stone as the cryptic voice.

"You've been gifted a great power. An ancestor has blessed you with a redeeming quality. Do not embarrass me today." At that, he handed Tynan something. Tynan's eyes flicked down to it without his head leaving position. A jagged spearhead tied to a pole. "Find me recruits. Strong and young. Bring back a promising army, whether they agree or not." Tynan's fingers wrapped around the pole, ready to take a step at the command, but was stopped short by a large hand to his chest. Tynan's gaze finally leveled on whoever spoke to him.

"Your failure is a direct reflection on me. If you bring me disappointments, you'll find yourself praying for mercy to the very ancestor who was foolish enough to waste their gifts on you." Tynan held his gaze and held in anything that would give away what he was thinking. I searched for it, but Tynan was good at it— keeping true emotion off his face. I wondered how long he'd been doing it.

He was the first to look away, returning his gaze to the forest. To his mission. He only took another step once the hand left his chest.

Tynan sent one more image after that. I recognized Ambrose just as he fell roughly to his knees. Thin cuts decorated his cheek, and a welt was forming over an eye. He shot his gaze up at Tynan. His scowl was so deep it looked permanently etched there. There were others lined in a unified row, but Ambrose was the only one I watched.

The face of the rough-voiced leader remained hidden, his back still turned from my viewpoint as he assessed Ambrose. "Stand up." But Ambrose did not. He glared with no fear in his eyes. With no loyalty or an ounce of obedience the way Tynan had shown. The leader turned his head ever so slightly in Tynan's direction, and with that one look, Tynan drew a knee up and kicked Ambrose so hard in the head consciousnesses was lost before he met the ground.

I blinked back at Tynan's glowing eyes, back in the dungeon hall with him again.

*You're not the only one who did what they had to do to survive.*

And that's when it hit me. That whatever creature Tynan may really be, we were doing something neither of us had meant to do. Somewhere along the way something had changed and over the course of a few days, we'd grown to know each other. Our faults, our weaknesses, the things that made us happy, and the things that didn't. He'd eased my pain time and time again when he didn't have to. And to some degree, maybe I'd eased his. Or helped to pass the time at the very least. But to what end? Why bother at all with each other when our endings would remain the same?

*Why are you telling me all this? Or...showing me, I guess.*

*Because...* Tynan blinked. The golds and the whites in his eyes slowed, and then his voice went flat. *You're never getting out of here. My secrets die with you.*

# CHAPTER NINETEEN

The next time I was visited by the Dark Queen, Tynan finally spoke out loud. His shadows appeared at the front of his cell, and his hands... Two tanned hands left those shadows and gripped the bars, ignoring the burns it gave him until he was forced to let go. He spoke to the Dark Queen, not me. He made demands, ordered her to stop, with so much authority in his voice. He swore of repercussions I couldn't imagine. The cruelness in her smile only widened at such caged outrage.

I turned to search for Tynan's gaze, but the view of my cellmate was blocked by a burly guard stationed outside. Without Tynan's eyes, I felt everything this round.

Cold fingers and pointed nails that had become all too familiar gripped my cheeks, tearing my gaze from the bars and forcing me to look into the depthless pits of her eyes.

She concentrated on my features like she was mulling over something. Like she still hadn't put together all the pieces of a puzzle. Her gaze dropped to my lips, and she ran a thumb softly over their outline. I didn't flinch from her touch. I just wanted it to be over.

"How did you get here?" she whispered full of uncertainty. "Just tell me."

I was half lying on the ground, partially sitting up from the last punch that had thrown me down. At least there were no chains today.

I'd given her this answer already. And still, I said, "I told you. I don't know."

Her grip dropped to my shoulders, her eyes pleading. "Liar!" Panic coated her features, and then it was gone in the next blink, as if she realized she was coming undone, thread by thread. We could all see it. With each visit, she grew more impatient. As if this was no longer a mere game to her. As if she was running out of time, and I was keeping secrets from her on purpose.

She straightened her shoulders, coming back to the cool, calculated queen she posed as. "What was happening when you came here? You had to be doing something specific. Tell me everything." She crouched in the perfect position to throttle me if I didn't respond the way she wanted me to.

I took a shaky breath in and spoke to the ground. "I was in a car accident. I don't know what happened exactly, but when I woke up, I was *somewhere,* and I don't know where that somewhere was. It was a dark place, that's the only way I know to explain it. I couldn't see anything except for two images."

Though I couldn't see the other inmates, I could feel the stillness underground, and I knew every ear within listening distance was straining to hear my story. "One showed my old life, and the other image... I didn't know what it was or where it led, but I stepped through it. It took me to Genesi." I stopped there, breathless, waiting for her to say she didn't believe me or to slap me again.

"It's impossible," she spat. "You don't belong here. Nothing that isn't specifically designed for Elysian can find its way here."

"I'm telling you the truth."

She shrieked. "You're a filthy human liar!" She wrapped her fist around what was left of the dress's neckline and pulled me in. One after another, she hit, clawed, and pulled at me. There were scratches on my cheeks, blood on my mouth, bruises on my arms.

I should fight back. Something in me roared to fight back, but I couldn't. I didn't know how to. That's not how I'd been trained. Instead, I turned my face and gave her access to my back and shoulders to beat on like drums.

*Briar.* His voice was pleading and hopeless all at once. He couldn't help me this time. No one could.

"You're a liar. You're a liar. You're a liar!" Her breathing was ragged as she punched me. She was blind with rage, some of her punches landing on the ground. Her knuckles cracked and caked with my blood. A fist collided with my temple. Blood trickled down my eyebrow.

The next punch had my arm buckling from under me, and I collapsed fully to the ground. The flare of emotion that cracked inside my heart was... I gritted my teeth, trying to hold back the angry tears. But with each pound, I saw my dad instead of her. And this time he wasn't stopping. He usually stopped. I could always endure it because it stopped.

With each drumbeat, the crack in my heart spread a little farther. A little farther. A little...

A cry escaped my lips, a broken sound of heartbreak and humiliation and fury. And with it, a familiar warmth seeped out of the crack. A beast kept caged for twenty-two years. Another pound, another, and the crack opened enough for the wild flame to burst through. And the hand that usually kept it reined in...slackened its hold.

It shot up my throat, and I cried as it neared the surface, not having any control over what would happen when it reached the top. I turned on the queen and screamed, giving the flame room to do what it must.

But nothing other than an unsettling roar came out. And where the flame stopped just beneath the surface, my skin glowed. My eyes burned. They thrashed with the fury I held for my dad, for the queen, for the world.

The Dark Queen jolted back, fear flashing along her face. I screamed louder than I knew possible, the fiery red glow of my skin brightening with it.

A screech of metal sounded, heavy footsteps raced inside, and my screaming was silenced with a boot to the head.

I wasn't unconscious for long. When I opened my eyes again, the queen still kneeled before me, her eyes wide and her mouth ajar.

I moved to sit up, and my leg brushed against her. She hissed violently, snatching her forearm to clutch it against her chest.

It was as if she knew before she even looked, her eyes going from mine to my ankle. She took a fistful of the tattered fabric and threw it to the side, exposing the golden locket wrapped there. Utter astonishment invaded every inch of her face.

"Where did you get this?" she hissed. I shook my head, confused. She dropped her voice to a panicked whisper. *"Where did you get this?"*

"It—I—it's mine," I choked out. She couldn't have it. She could keep me here until I died, she could beat me senseless, she could starve me, but she could not have my mother's locket. It was all I had left of her. All I had left of anyone.

"Who did you take it from?"

"No one. I swear it. It was my mother's, and now it's mine."

Her body froze to stone, but her features flashed between emotions—distress, pure revelation, and then...tears spilled down her face. She opened her mouth, but then closed it again.

And then she whispered, "Kill her." Her arms trembled, wet cheeks turning to the guard nearby. "KILL HER!"

While a pair of aggressive hands came under my arms and hauled me to my feet, the Dark Queen reached for the locket, snapping the chain and tearing it from my ankle.

"No!" I screamed. "Please, no!" I kicked and thrashed, not for my life, but for the keepsake. I was dragged out of my cell and into the hall. My heartbeat was in my throat. I was going to be sick. My skin itched until it *burned*.

The arms that held me fell away, and the dungeon was filled with screaming that wasn't my own.

I tumbled to the ground, grabbing my cellmate's bars for support. My breathing came out too quickly. I was dying.

"Briar," the honey-dipped voice spoke. "Don't stop."

*Don't stop dying?* But when I looked up, I saw my hands were blazing. Orange and yellow flames engulfed my skin, and the bars I clutched were *melting*. My hands fell to the ground as the bars disappeared from my grasp.

"*Stop!*" Furious, the Dark Queen rushed into the hall. Guards and soldiers barreled down the stairs at all the commotion but skidded to a halt at the fire that enveloped every inch of my skin. One whistled over his shoulder, and a rumbling growl of thunder charged down the staircase.

I didn't have time to think about it. On instinct, my hand shot up, a poor attempt to protect myself from the baring teeth and curved claws of the wolf. A stream of fire that crackled and roared shot from my fingertips, engulfing the wolf and two guards standing too close. A bay from the wolf, screams from males that shouldn't be pitched that high. They went up in flames.

Back to calculated moves, the Dark Queen took careful steps around me, emotion erased from her face now as if she were half in a shock. A few guards remained, but no one came toward me. I took the opportunity to lunge for the queen. She stumbled back, but not quick enough that I couldn't snatch the necklace from her fingers, the flames instantly leaving me. The warmth sank back into my skin, which was a little pink but otherwise unharmed.

There was silence and gaping. And then—

slow, echoing footsteps filled the hall. I didn't have to turn to know who was approaching from behind me. Didn't need confirmation as to why the Dark Queen's head was lifting slowly, rising terror quickening her breath. With my cellmate's warded bars left in a hardening puddle at our feet, I sensed who stepped from the shadows at last.

But as he stepped so close his arm brushed mine, I turned and lifted my chin anyway. And it was vengeance and murder that he gazed upon the queen with.

His fingers flexed, stretching out and curling back in. The few lanterns mounted to the walls flickered with the movement. My lips turned upward at the guards who took visible steps toward the exit.

"If you wanted a war, Xosha," his voice was laced in venom. "all you had to do was ask."

The last thing I saw was the Dark Queen twitch, and then the lights blew out at the same moment Tynan pulled me into his chest, shadows and fog curling in around our bodies. The floor disappeared, and I was grounded and unsteady all at once as those shadows pulled us away, away, far away from the dungeon.

It was over. How, I didn't know, but it was over. I closed my eyes and leaned my head against his hard chest, feeling safe maybe for the first time in my life. I didn't know what would come tomorrow, but for this moment at least, I could breathe.

Something shifted in the air as we moved into an unknown setting. Pine needles replaced soot. The stale air turned fresh and cool as it brushed my skin. Tynan held me to him firmly, keeping the strange wind from ripping me away. I gripped his arms for balance, and somehow, at that touch, it confirmed what I suspected. That for the first time in a long time, he could breathe too.

Tynan's arms loosened around me the moment our feet found solid ground. It had been like we were in a giant storm cloud, the fog lifting now and creeping off to evaporate into the corners of a brightly lit room.

My palms instantly went to my eyes, shutting out the sudden light after spending weeks underground. When the burning stopped, I lifted my gaze to finally get a true look at my cellmate. I only caught a glimpse of him, too much dirt and grown out facial hair to really see much of anything else, before he was already walking away.

I hesitated, standing alone in a woodsy, rustic hallway and watched as Tynan lingered in front of a room—a dining area with three familiar downcast expressions sulking around the table. They sat with untouched meals spread out in front of them. Ara had her hand propped on her chin and looked miserably at nothing, ignoring the lavish food right in front of her. My stomach rumbled at the smell of it.

"Oh please," Tynan said, teeth bared in an eager grin I caught from the side. "Don't wait on my account."

Three heads whipped toward the door, Ara's ponytail almost slapping her in the face.

"*Oh my God,*" she shrieked. Silverware clattered to the floor as she scrambled out of her chair. Her arms and legs moved too fast for the rest of her, as the others shot up from their seats as well. Ara sprinted the short distance and collided into his waiting arms. A heartbreaking mixture of joy and relief filled her voice as she cried. When Tynan finally let her feet touch the ground again, the tawny-skinned male I remembered as Ambrose stormed up to him and wrapped his arms around his friend in a violent hug.

"Took you long enough," Ambrose said.

A softness behind the warrior prince revealed itself as all the stress etched there from before melted away. It was a warm, genuine face, and I got the feeling I would like him if ever given the chance.

The second male approached Tynan after Ambrose was finished, and I could see Tynan's grin widen. "Enzo."

"Mother fucker." Enzo pulled him into one of those ridiculous bro hugs, slamming each other on the back more times than was necessary.

A sense of unbelonging overcame me. I turned, not taking the time to consider where I was going or what happened next, and raced through a larger room and out a door I only guessed to be the exit.

I stepped into a world of night lit up by stars and little lanterns that were attached to the railings of a porch. The porch branched out in different directions, wrapping around each side of the building and extending in the front. A brick hearth stood tall in the middle. I ventured out into the center, standing underneath bulb lights that hung over a set of outdoor furniture. In the distance, one of the side porches led to a set of declining steps that went on and on, with lanterns illuminating each step of the way to a gazebo sitting on a sleeping lake. And surrounding it all, there were only the trees.

The door behind me clicked open, and I turned. A wall of square paneled glass windows covered the entire front of the building and came together at a high point held by wood trim. It was an oversized, spectacular mountain-styled chalet. One so grand I'd only seen something similar on the front of magazine covers.

Ara walked out a door at the side.

Her wings, small and dainty, gave a rough snap inward and

disappeared. They were nowhere to be seen. I must have looked like a scared woodland creature, because she put her hands out in front of her, as if to show me she was just like me—no threat at all.

"Briar?"

I nodded, unsure.

"I'm Ara. You saved my brother." She closed the distance between us, and before I could stop her, she took one of my hands in both of hers. Silver lined her eyes. "I can't tell you how thankful I am for you. Please come back inside."

"I—" I didn't know what to say. After everything, I suddenly had no plan. I wasn't even sure there was a way back to one.

"I know," she said. When I didn't respond, she seemed to remember herself. "I know all about you. The entire world is talking about you right now. I know what you are, where you were headed."

I could barely think over the throbbing in my temple. "She knows?" was all I could get out.

"The world doesn't know about that last part, don't worry," Ara answered quickly, her hazel eyes pleading. "Tynan is the one who told me about Clive Steeple. We can help." She offered a small smile. "I know I'm a stranger to you, but you don't know how long I've been looking for a way to free my brother from that place. Let me feed you at the very least and give you a safe place to sleep."

Safe was such an unfamiliar concept. But unsafe was not. Living in distrust and on a constant edge was all I knew. The security that wrapped around me in her brother's hold and the way Ara's hand warmed over mine now did not feel familiar.

"Okay," I agreed, as if I had much of a choice. Her face lit up, her small eyes sparkling. With my hand still in hers, she led me back into the warmth of the chalet. I braced myself for questioning, but the room was empty, the other three having disappeared.

I hadn't noticed anything on my way out, but the space was a true mountain cabin after all. Mahogany flooring and wood-paneled walls lined the living room. A couch and two oversized chairs sat in front of a lit stone fireplace. A plaid blanket rested over each sitting option with a coffee table too small for all the papers that were spread out and spilling over it. Exquisite front windows towered from the floor to vaulted pine-beamed ceilings. The view would overlook the lounge area outside and lake beyond it, though the shades were rolled down for the night.

Whether it was all I'd been through lately or the soft crackle of the fireplace and the warm, low lights, my eyes grew nearly too heavy to keep open. Instead of stopping at the couch, Ara walked by it and back down the hallway. We passed rooms I only caught sight of briefly. A cozy kitchen area, and the dining room from before, but we stopped at a door at the very end of the hall, already open. Another guest room. Another temporary place to sleep.

"Ty barely had a chance to tell me who you are and what you did for him, before I forced him to find the shower. He has almost a year's worth of dirt and the Creator knows what else on him. I'm not sure how long you were there, but let's not take any chances."

Remembering what I must look like, my gaze snapped to the rags I wore. No longer were the layers piled precisely. No longer was its color pure. It lay flattened against me, the top so ripped and ruined that it exposed more skin than I was comfortable with. My fingertips went to my face, and I caught the black soot that stained them. I rubbed self-consciously at my cheek.

"Towels are in the washroom. I'll find you some of my clothes and have a plate waiting on the bed before you finish washing." She gave me a parting look, the strangest mixture of sadness and joy, before shutting the door with a gentle click.

I took in the room before me. It was small, but the perfect size for a visitor passing through. There was a bed dressed in a cream comforter and white sheets against the middle of one wall. A lone bedside table rested next to it with a reading lantern mounted over it. The light flickering inside it looked odd. I walked to the lantern, peered inside the glass, and squinted as I tried to work it out. There didn't appear to be a flame inside, but rather an orb of some sort, its orange flare glowing to give the appearance of a light.

A small closet door was tucked away in the corner, just big enough for a few things to hang. There was another door on the far side of the room, the shades up to show the trees outside. An exit leading to one of the wraparound porches. I crossed the room, drew down the shade, and made sure the back door was locked before stepping into the washroom.

The towels were, in fact, neatly folded on a stained wooden shelf. I grabbed one and set it by the shower, and then set the necklace that was still clutched in my palm on the shelf. Turning on the water, I slid out of my rags and left them on the floor in a dusty heap.

While the water warmed, I stepped in front of the mirror, and for the first time in weeks, maybe even months, saw what I looked like. I'd expected the dirt and dried blood etched onto my skin. I'd anticipated the dirty soot covering most of my skin, and the deep bruises underneath all that. I couldn't tell the difference between the ones that were healing and the ones just beginning to surface.

What I didn't expect was the alarming gloss to my eyes. I tried to label it with some kind of emotion—anger, defeat, sorrow, hopelessness. But no emotion seemed to fit. Oddly enough, they were brighter. Despite the gruesome mess I was, the green and blue in my eyes stood out more so than usual, and the yellow that surrounded the pupil like a ring of sun was glaringly prominent. The result of such a deep contrast to the deeper colors staining my body, no doubt.

My hair was atrocious. I couldn't even tell what color it was anymore. Beneath the layers of tangled, matted mess, the deep brown now appeared to be as black as the queen's eyes. I turned from the mirror, no longer interested in seeing the evidence of what my life had become.

Once the water was steaming I stepped in. Layers of grime flowed down my body and swirled around until it danced into the drain. I raked my fingers through knotted hair, using the lavender shampoo on the shower shelf. I scrubbed my scalp until it was sore, and when the shampoo had all been washed away, I reached for more. I used far too much conditioner, dousing it on my head and letting it sit before combing it through until my hair was once again smooth and sleek. The process probably took an hour alone. I reached for the soap next and abused it too. I washed every inch of my body, and then I washed it again. Unknown things slid off my feet and from in between my toes until I could finally see ivory once again. I was paler than I remembered.

I slid down the wall and sat. Leaning my head back, I let the water hit my face and thought of absolutely nothing.

"She burned up a hellhound." A familiar voice distantly sounded in my eardrums. I snapped my head up and peeked through the shower curtain, but only steam filled the washroom.

"How is that possible?" Ambrose asked.

The voices trickled in clearer. How I could possibly hear anyone over the stream of the water and from across the house, I had no idea. They must have been right outside my door or maybe they were yelling. But the voices didn't sound argumentative. If anything, they sounded secretive.

Tynan responded, "I don't know. She's just a normal girl."

"If she burned a freakin' hellhound to ashes, then she's far from normal." Enzo's voice this time.

"No, she's not. She's a badass," Ara joined in. A repetitive snipping cut between her words. "Stop moving, Ty. Kingdoms, you're going to make me cut you."

I had already forgotten the wolf—*hellhound*. That made sense. A beast like that could only have come straight from the very bottom of hell itself.

Ambrose picked up the topic again. "Normal fire doesn't just burn up a hellhound. They are made of hellfire itself. And the bars of your cell... Something ridiculous has to live inside her blood to be able to do that."

"There's a rumor that she was injured," Enzo said. "That's why she was going to Clive Steeple. To fix something. Something Xosha cares about?"

"Just a rumor," Tynan said. "She is who she says she is." His voice still had the honey-dipped hum to it, but it was obvious now. This was the relaxed voice I would sometimes hear from him when I caught him off guard. This was the voice he used amongst friends. His real voice.

"And how do you know that?" Ambrose's voice cut in.

"You think Darya would open her borders for a giftless dryad? You think a simple forest fairy has anything Xosha cares about?" Theory wasn't the reason Tynan knew I was human. He'd seen my past for himself, witnessed my life in another world. So why didn't he just tell them that?

Enzo blew out a breath. "She's beautiful enough to be dryad."

Ambrose questioned, "Why would Xosha give a damn about a giftless human either?"

"Enzo, you're in my light," Ara said.

"I don't know," Tynan mused. "But she was *beaten* down there." The snipping stopped. "From the day Briar showed up, it was like Xosha completely forgot I existed. She'd come down and beat the girl senseless until one day she just snapped."

"The girl?" Ara asked.

"Xosha," he corrected. "She found something on Briar, a piece of jewelry, and she flipped. And then Briar flipped. After all those weeks of staying silent and just taking it, Briar exploded. Literally. I was able to step right out after she melted the bars. Just like that, I was free."

"So you scooped her up and brought her here with you?" Ambrose's tone was accusing.

"What was he supposed to do?" Enzo shot back. "He couldn't leave her there. She's the reason he's here now."

"I don't like this," Ambrose said. "The whole thing. You declared war on Xosha."

"As if he wasn't supposed to?" Ara countered. "As if we haven't been planning that for a year already? She didn't just kidnap a King of Elysian, she kidnapped *Tynan*. Xosha decided the moment she sent that message to him that we were going to end this in a fight to the death."

"But she didn't know when to expect it," Ambrose corrected himself. "We had the element of surprise. And this girl complicates everything. We don't even know her. This could all be another trap."

I tuned everything out then, thinking about my very own skin on fire, the armed guards backing away from me, the terror displayed on the Dark Queen's face. What had I done?

I put my arms out in front of me and flipped them over, still looking for burns that had never shown up there. My skin was only bright pink from the heat of the water.

I brought a hand up to my cheek, feeling only a few light scratches and a cut on my lip, but no swelling around my eye the way there should have been. The way there just had been mere hours ago. When I wondered how I could have begun healing so fast, my head instantly hurt, and I gave up thinking about anything.

Starting out as silent tears mixing in with the shower water, it wasn't until I was shaking that I noticed I was crying at all. I listened, hoping I was far enough away that no one could hear me, but I couldn't hear their voices anymore. So I allowed myself to sob until my chest ached and my throat burned.

I stopped only when my stomach hurt from shaking and my eyes threatened to close where I sat. I finally stood and turned off the water, only halfway collecting myself. I needed to rest. I needed food in my stomach.

The ruined dress was gone, a fresh collection of garments folded on the countertop. I tried not to think about at what point Ara had walked in to replace those clothes. Before the crying, I hoped.

I held them up, a gray button-up sleep set made of cotton. My underthings had been replaced with a pair of lacy black ones, and a small folded-up cloth for my ending cycle. I had bigger problems to worry about than to think of blushing at what Tynan must have told her about that. Everything fit a little small, but I was thankful to just have a clean set on. I was thankful there was another female here at all. My necklace still rested on the shelf, waiting, but I left it there, too tired to make any more movements than I had to.

An inviting tray of food waited on the bed, as promised. I sat, with every intention of devouring it, but once the flavor hit my tongue, my chewing slowed. Like in Genesi, the food was better here, fresher and purer than the processed things I was used to throwing into my body. But this food was even more unique than the plates in Genesi. Every smokey bite of the wild salmon, every speck of the spices used in the bed of brown rice, and every last drop of lemon squeezed over it for garnish. Each and every flavorful nutrient on my tongue was a gift. I washed it down with a glass of ice-cold water, swearing I could make out the molecules in it. I refilled the glass from the pitcher provided on the nightstand and drank two more full glasses, reminding myself I was dehydrated.

When every last crumb disappeared, I set the tray on the table and lay down with still wet hair. My body—my *soul*—sank into the mattress. I closed my eyes, not allowing another tear to escape before falling into the deepest sleep of my life.

# CHAPTER TWENTY

Sunrays filtered through the shades, warming the room with their touch. I peeked over the covers, almost thinking I might find myself in my old room with Leah across the hall. But it hadn't been a dream.

I couldn't remember pulling the covers over me before free-falling into a dreamless sleep, but along with the empty nightstand, a new pair of Ara's clothes were folded on the washroom counter. The black camisole stopped a little too short at my hipbones, and the pants just above my ankles. I rolled the pant legs up so that it wouldn't be so noticeable.

My gaze settled on the shelf where I'd left my locket last night. The chain was damaged, broken from where it had been snapped from my skin. I fumbled with the chain for a few minutes, replacing it around my neck and securing it in a double knot. Once I was in my own world, I'd see about restoring the links as best I could, but for now, a quick fix would have to do.

I combed through my now smooth locks with my fingers, the mocha coloring visible again. Thankfully, my hair took minimal effort to maintain, but the ends were irreparable after being neglected for so long. I'd need a trim once I got back as well.

I washed my face in the sink and took one last look at myself in the mirror. The bruises were embarrassingly loud along my arms. I looked in the closet for a cover-up, but it was bare.

I cracked the bedroom door open, the rustling of kitchen cabinets opening and closing and faint voices drifting in. I closed it again without a sound, and instead of joining the strangers, exited through the other door in my room.

Time. I just needed a little time and the morning sun on my skin before facing what life would bring me next.

The chalet sat in the middle of the woods. Skinny trees littered the whole estate, their vibrant green leaves hanging over every pathway along the porch. A few of the leaves had already begun to fall onto the walkway, inviting autumn into the new season. In the corner, just out of eyeshot should anyone walk out onto the front patio, sat a round table small enough for two chairs.

A cool breeze leveled out the warmth, and I breathed in the scent of the very end of summer. Birds sang overhead, a deer and her fawn fed in the grass at the edge of the lake. Sunlight danced on the water while ducks waded in the morning glow. The scent of apples and oak filled my nose. Genesi had been soothing with its ocean's song, but this... My heart settled as I rested in the comfort of the chair. I could gladly get lost in a place like this.

A tall body suddenly stepped into my line of vision, blocking my view of the lake, and I nearly jumped out of my skin.

"Shit, sorry." Tynan lifted his arms in surrender, holding up two mugs.

I scolded myself for flinching. For going right back to the jumpy, paranoid version of myself I was before I came to Elysian. I guess that's what being beaten half to death will do to a person.

He waited for me to settle before coming closer, but his nearness only alarmed me more. I'd only seen him clearly a handful of times in moments from the past. I hardly recognized him, if only for his bursting eyes that were slightly less overwhelming in the daylight.

"Can I sit?" he asked.

I could only nod. He looked so much like the beautiful teen from the memories. Only older, obviously matured, and yet he couldn't be that many years older than me. He had a clean-shaven face now, but it was the same defined, slender cheekbones that drew down into a sharp jawline and the same strong chin. His nose was long and straight, his lips too inviting. Skin smoother than stone and golden glowed—a natural blessed tan that had nothing to do with the sun. I had to remind myself how to breathe.

He'd cut his hair already, the onyx locks now stopping just under his ears. The same length it had been back in the memories, only messier now, with more strands that curled out at the ends. I wanted to reach out and run my fingers through it. He pulled out the opposite chair to sit, and I took the opportunity to scan the rest of him. I could make out his shape underneath the fitted shirt he wore and noticed where it clung to him in all the right places. I made myself look in his eyes. He was breathtaking in a way no one else ever would be.

He offered me one of the mugs, and I had to demand my brain to transfer signals down my body and through my arms to take it. "Thank you," I said without a smile. He watched me as I sipped. Warm apple cider slid down my throat. It was somehow exactly what I needed.

His gaze dropped to my spotted arms, and his brow furrowed. I crossed an arm over the other, strategically placing a palm over the biggest bruise on my forearm.

Each movement of his was slower than it should be. Much slower than I knew he was capable of moving, like he wanted me to know what he was doing before he did it. Like I was a damaged creature.

"How are you feeling?" His voice was thick and sweet, the way it would sound if someone had just woken up.

"I don't think I have an answer for that," I answered truthfully.

"That's understandable." His eyes stayed on mine for so long I shifted in my seat, making some kind of movement to hide my nerves. "What..." I asked, suddenly aware of everything I hated about myself.

"I guess I should be thanking you. For whatever it was you did back there."

I shook my head and closed my eyes, not believing how anyone could have survived as long as he had with the Dark Queen. My chest was hollow after my short stay in comparison to his much longer one.

"How did you manage a year in that pit of darkness?"

He stretched an arm over his head, running fingers through the perfect mess of onyx. I willed my eyes to stay on his as his shirt lifted ever so slightly at the waist. "I'm well-suited for the dark, remember?"

It all came rushing back then. The dark and everything shared there. But the scales were uneven. I could tell there were parts of his memories he kept hidden. By the angles he let me see them from or the moments he cut a memory off. For whatever reason there were things he didn't want me to see, even if I'd soon be dead. But while there were things Tynan kept in the dark, I had let everything touch the light. I'd shared things with him I'd never shared with a soul. And that had been okay when I didn't think we'd survive to deal with the aftermath of opening up to one another. But now, with no bars between us, the shame of what he knew flooded me.

I sipped from the mug again, trying to keep my arm in a position that wouldn't show off the worst. Tynan cleared his throat, as if he too were remembering some of those memories.

"I um," I started, chewing on the inside of my cheek. "I need to get to Clive Steeple. Fast." The statement didn't feel quite right. I was enemy number one to a psychopathic, bloodthirsty queen, and still, I felt no rush to return to where I knew I belonged.

"Those shadows that took us away yesterday," I began. "Could they get me there?"

Tynan nodded slowly, his features stone. "They could get you anywhere you want." As if to demonstrate, a fog began to rise out of nowhere. It wrapped itself around his legs and up his torso until it began to consume him. But just as it wrapped around his shoulders like a friendly snake, he let it drop away. "As long as my eyes have seen it, I can get there."

"What is that?" I asked, eyeing the fog as it crept off.

"It's called shadow stepping."

"Can the Dark Queen do that?"

There was a hint of humor in his tone. "No, she can't shadow step." That didn't mean she wasn't quickly on her way, despite what Tynan thought. She had a dragon, a herd of dragons.

"Would you mind?" I asked, unsure. "Just dropping me off, I mean." It was uncomfortable asking him for help. I'd spent so long not even being able to see Tynan's face. And he'd made it clear then, even without saying it, he didn't owe me anything. He didn't even expect me to make it this far—alive, sitting on his front porch with a warm drink.

Tynan shifted, suddenly looking uncomfortable, and I instantly regretted asking.

"There is an immaculate breakfast waiting for you inside. You should go eat." He looked me over without hiding it, looking passed the faint bruises as if he knew my body didn't used to be as thin as it was now.

"Thank you," I said.

"Don't thank me yet." I eyed Tynan, at the dread that touched his tone. "My friend—*Ambrose*..." Tynan looked off to the side for a single second as if directing the comment straight to Ambrose's ears. "is a suspicious bastard. But he's a good friend, and I trust his council."

I wasn't following him. I didn't understand what his friend had to do with anything.

"Stakes are high for us. For all of Elysian," he said. "It was bad enough before, but now that we know about the High Queen..." he trailed off, looking discouraged for a moment before he shook his head to refocus. "Knowing that Xosha isn't responsible for the Pale Queen's disappearance means we're back to knowing absolutely nothing about the mess we're in." He lifted his chin so slightly I couldn't be sure he actually moved at all if it weren't for how regal he suddenly looked. "Ambrose has brought an important detail to my attention. A detail that involves a strange girl who the Dark Queen has taken such interest in and has now suddenly found her way into my home."

He watched me closely, and I sensed he didn't think I was going to like where the conversation was headed.

"Whatever it is, just say it."

He obeyed. "Ambrose thinks you're a spy."

"Is your friend stupid?"

Tynan's lip tugged upward ever so slightly, a single star in his eye lighting. "Because the costs are so high, you'll be staying under our supervision until we can confirm your intentions."

I smiled a smile I didn't know I was capable of. Spoke in a tone I'd never used before. "You're joking."

"If you are in fact who you say you are, then there should be no problem with that. You'll get to Clive Steeple, and we'll ensure your safety—and ours—in the meantime."

"You know I am who I say I am." A wick sparked from inside my chest, immediately extinguished from exhaustion. "How exactly would I even report back to the Dark Queen?"

"We don't know your gifts. Those memories could have been placed there or fabricated."

"I don't *have* any gifts." I wanted to shake him for being so stupid.

But Tynan's eyes flashed with a shadow of darkness, and a true king sat before me at last. His voice changed. It wasn't the shadow creature or a friend speaking to me now. It was a monarch. "Xosha had me down there for a year and was no closer to getting what she wanted from me. She's running out of time, fast. Maybe she thought it was time to try a different approach."

"You think she used me, to what? Learn about your mommy issues for fun?" It was a low blow. God, it was such a low blow coming from someone like me. If the comment touched Tynan anywhere he didn't show it, not one bit.

"This is what I think." He leaned forward in his seat, a random gust of wind stirring with the movement that sent me backward, pinning me into the chair. The shock of what he'd done had me stilling in a fear I was all too familiar with. "Those things I showed you were shared in confidence. Those memories were never supposed to leave that dungeon. And you mean to tell me that *you* had the ability to get us out of there the entire time? But you didn't. Not until you got information out of me first. About my home, my family, my sister's plans of an overthrow. You can't be so naive to think our caution is that outlandish. Simple-minded human or not."

I hated myself, *hated* myself for the burning in my throat that had nothing to do with any flames. I turned my head to face the lake, my body still pinned by an invisible force, and ignored the blurred vision while I pretended to focus on the grazing deer. I swallowed hard, and it hurt.

Whatever held me to the chair loosened, but I didn't budge out of sheer stubbornness.

"That's what you think? Or your friend, Ambrose?" I mumbled.

Tynan didn't speak for several moments, and I wasn't sure whether it was because he didn't want to satisfy me with the answer

I already knew or because he was nice enough to wait for the pink that had rushed to my cheeks to fade.

"If what you are and what you say is true, there's no issue here."

"And what if I'm lying," I muttered harshly.

Tynan went deathly still, and I remembered the threats he made to the Dark Queen, the violence laced in every word, the venom soaked in them.

"Right," I said to his silent response. "So I'm to be a prisoner all over again."

His starry gaze fell to his mug, his thumb rubbing the brim. I wished I could get inside his head without permission and see for myself what he was thinking.

"You can remain here. In the guest room," he finally said.

I looked at him with confusion spilling out of my pores.

"You're safe here," he went on. "No one can find this place, even if they were to come looking for it."

I rubbed my forehead, too exhausted for the games these villains adored to play. "So you'll let me stay here, make sure I'm comfy while I'm at it, all while you're worried I'm a spy who will somehow miraculously share your every move with your worst enemy. You have to know how naive *that* sounds."

Tynan shifted in his seat, annoyance seeping through his straight posture. "If you'd like to visit my own dungeons, just say so. Here or there, I don't give a damn where you choose to stay. But you will stay."

We stared each other down. I wished I could hate him. I wished I could take out all my anger on him. But logically, I couldn't.

Each and every memory he'd chosen to share with me involved younger versions of his sister and their two friends. Even if he didn't think I'd live long enough to do anything with that information, I'd learned that they weren't just friends, would never be just friends to him. They were his family. And if I knew that feeling, if I had a family to protect, I'd do everything in my power to keep them safe from a threat.

I had nothing to hide, and Tynan was offering to help me, even if it wasn't on my terms.

"Whatever." It's not like I had a choice in the matter anyway. It's not like I ever had a choice. I looked back at the lake, no longer caring for the apple cider.

"Look," Tynan said, his tone lighter. "If you have nothing to hide, there's no reason we have to make this difficult. When we decide it's safe for *all* of us, we'll get you to Clive Steeple."

"Fine," I said mindlessly, not caring anymore about any of it. "And when will you decide that?"

He set his elbows on the arms of the chair, holding his mug at his middle. He shook his hair out of his eyes and became that other version of himself with the movement. The other half of what I met in the dungeon. Something real. Something tangible. "If Zafar and Xosha were working together, I'm willing to bet he told her where you were headed. Xosha is not patient. If she thinks she can recapture you at Clive Steeple, she'll be headed there now. The way I figure it, if she shows up for you, that means the interest she seems to have in you is real."

His night eyes were deathly still.

I changed the subject, intent on proving my innocence. "And you're sure she won't find us here?"

"She will not step foot on Valhallan soil, especially not now that she's pissed me off."

"And she can't send someone else the way she sent Zafar?"

"If one were to stumble across us in the woods, all they'd see is a waterfall or a briar patch too dense to cut through."

"Let me guess, another party trick of yours."

Tynan fought a smile, pressing his tongue against the corner of his mouth. I tightened my fingers around my arm, a sense of betrayal flooding over me at the unraveling that his tongue was doing to me.

"My finest if you ask me."

Magic. It consumed this world, had built it, and a childlike piece of me ached to be a part of something so remarkable.

"So I guess I was brought here because you don't trust me."

"I brought you here because it was the first place my mind went to after being in captivity for an entire year. You've seen my home, whether I meant for you to or not. I can't just let you leave."

Surprise deepened my features. "This is your home? You're a king with no palace?"

"I have a palace. That doesn't make it my home."

I lifted my gaze to the wooded wonderland that surrounded us. The estate and its grounds were perfect, a place I'd be happy to spend every second of the rest of my life in. But surely a king wouldn't be content in a servantless, secluded mountain home. "This place is wonderful, but it doesn't seem fit for a king."

"You ask a lot of questions for someone who isn't a spy."

I rolled my eyes, unable to help it, and Tynan laughed. He actually laughed. Two deep dimples surfaced with that laugh and it threw me off all over again.

"I was many other things before I was a king. It's fit for me. There is a palace, but Ambrose wouldn't let me live in it even if I wanted to."

"Ambrose sure does seem to have a lot of influence over you." Distaste coated my tongue, one I didn't plan on, and I hoped Ambrose was listening to every word. Hoped he heard the suspicion in my own tone.

"He's a good friend. You may not have any, but that's what they do. They keep you safe even from yourself." I heard the message in his tone. It didn't matter how close we'd become in the dark. Things were different outside those bars, and he had information against me too. Information he'd use to put me right back in my place every time I attempted to cross the line.

Instead of speaking, I just gave him a look. One that questioned the entire existence of his friendship with Ambrose at all.

"He's more than a friend," he answered, reading the challenging look on my face. "He's my most trusted advisor. I trust his council above all others."

"And he doesn't want you to live in your own palace?"

"He doesn't *advise* it. That I live on display. I hold my business there. Otherwise, my whereabouts aren't publicly known, especially where I sleep."

It made sense, though the thought had never occurred to me, nor any of the other ruler's advisors apparently. "Most palaces trust guards for that."

"The High Queen herself was murdered by an assassin who made it undetected through the most heavily guarded palace in Elysian." *That* was because the murderer hadn't been an assassin from the outside. But...he was right, nonetheless. "Ambrose doesn't trust anyone. To answer all your burning questions at once, there is someone out there that makes Xosha look like a doe in comparison. Someone who, if they ever decided to come looking for me, could easily put down even the best of Elysian's guards with the swipe of a hand."

"Your father," I guessed. Tynan's face hardened, obviously annoyed that he'd shown me those visions. He'd shared so much with me. But not everything.

"Someone even Xosha should piss herself over if she crosses them," was all Tynan said.

I moved on, not wanting him to think I cared to remember any details worth repeating. "So Clive Steeple..."

Tynan assessed me and then said, "I've already sent sentinels to watch the area. If you prove yourself to be true, we'll go. Straight there. Straight back. And when we learn what it is you hope to learn there, how to return to your world, I'll even help you do that."

"Why?" I asked. "If your friend is so suspicious of me and you trust him so much, why help me at all when you have much bigger problems to deal with. You don't even know me."

"Don't mistake who runs things around here," Tynan's voice displayed a hint of that kingly authority, a warning. "I take Ambrose's council into consideration. That is all." At that last part, I wondered if the annoyance was directed toward me or Ambrose. "Precautions must be taken, but I do believe you. Who you say you are. If that proves true then it appears we suddenly have a common enemy. And if it involves wrecking Xosha's plans along the way, I'm in."

He watched me closely before speaking again, taking in my every movement, noting every inhale and exhale I breathed. "I do know one thing for sure."

"What is that?" I challenged.

"I know that human or not, you did something in that dungeon." I tensed at the memory, at the truth that I didn't want to believe. Or didn't know how to believe, maybe. "Everything Xosha did to you down there was because she was afraid of something. For whatever reason, you are a wreck in her plans."

"She has *nothing* to fear from me," I promised. "I don't know what that was down there, but it didn't come from me."

He assessed me with a look so similar to the one the Dark Queen had given me in the Everwood and then again in the dungeon. Like he was trying to work out some vital piece of information that was just out of reach. "I don't know you, not yet." His eyes didn't leave mine, and something warm as the sun shifted inside me as he said, "But I intend to."

## CHAPTER TWENTY-ONE

Tynan left me with advice and a warning.

He advised that I enjoy the quiet of the cabin before Enzo filled it with noise and mischief. And then he warned me that he had to leave—to announce his return to an anxious council—and that should I decide to venture too far into the woods, I'd only be lost and quite quickly found. If not by him, then by worse.

I only sipped smoothly from my cider, not giving him the satisfaction of a reaction as his shadows swallowed him and left an empty patio chair across from me.

I sat there until my cider grew cold. Eventually, I got up to follow the long path down to the gazebo. But even there, with a view so perfect for watching the wildlife lazily enjoying their morning, my mind could only focus so long before it wandered on to less enjoyable things.

I made my way back up the path, remembering the breakfast Tynan had mentioned. I came in through the front this time. With the shades all the way up, morning light spilled into the chalet, casting golden silhouettes along the furniture.

To the right, the kitchen peninsula was visible. I rounded it and stepped into the warm kitchen, some type of fresh bread just baked blessing the air. Cinnamon, I recognized as I breathed in the scent, apple soon following it. Only a gorgeous double doored stove, and a pantry filled the room, the rest of the space lined with granite countertops and wood cabinets. I set my mug in the empty sink and turned to place my hands on the countertop.

I stared at the hallway, stalling. I couldn't wander the way I had in Genesi. I was trapped again, in a much more comfortable way than I'd been in Kalopsia, but still confined. Not a prisoner, but not a guest either. I peered back into the living room area, looking for something I could clean. *Anything* to do. But the place was spotless, not a thing out of place. Even the papers that had been spilled out on the coffee table the night before had been cleared. I dropped my gaze to the countertops and ran a finger along it. Not a speck of dust.

I turned again to wash out my cup, but froze in place when it wasn't sitting in the sink anymore. Instead, it rested on the drying rack, fresh droplets of water running down the handle.

I whirled around, but the kitchen was empty except for me. I peered down the hallway, looking for what, I wasn't sure, but spotted another room that caught my attention instead.

There was a door cracked open that came right before my own. Tucked away with a hidden sliding door, the room could easily be overlooked had it been closed all the way. I slid the door the rest of the way to the side to find a miniature sitting room of some sort, smaller than my own room. A cream-colored chair and matching chaise sat with a wall of books behind them. A rolling ladder was propped on the wall to reach the high up books and a rolling cart sat in a corner with a decanter of some dark liquid and three whiskey glasses. A reading room. A place to get away in a getaway home.

I considered resting on the chaise with one of the books until I fell asleep. But first, I wanted to see what else there was in the house. Tynan's home was truly the most beautiful place I'd ever seen. Grander than any palace. I was enchanted by it. But when I found myself back in the main room, I realized there was only one other door left undiscovered. On the other end of the hallway, opposite of my guest room door. Excitement stirred over what else I might find on the other end of the house.

I glanced behind me, a sudden sense of wariness creeping along my neck. But there was no one else here. The mysterious door wasn't entirely open, but it wasn't clicked shut either. I could smell something slightly familiar from inside. Balsam and...something else. Something that could only be found deep in the hours of the night. Whatever it was filled my nose and drizzled into my chest. I lifted a finger to touch the door, unable to help leaning forward to smell more, to find what made that smell. My finger grazed the door as someone cleared their throat. I flung my body around to face Ambrose.

He stood there with his arms crossed and a deep scowl staining his face. Any warmth that might have been there before was hard to imagine now.

"Find anything interesting?"

"I—I just—" I didn't know why words failed me. Surely, I wasn't expected to sit in the same spot in the same room for who knew how long. If that was expected of me, Tynan would have locked me in the guest room before leaving the estate. But Ambrose's face and stance instantly had me feeling as if I were guilty of something. Ambrose, who already thought I was a spy. This wasn't a great look for someone trying to prove they weren't a double agent of some sort.

"I got lost," I lied.

"Right." His gray-green eyes inspected me in a way that practically screamed, *I don't know what or who you are, but I intend to expose every secret you have in you.* It was a look full of mistrust.

He shifted a single step to the side, and the door on the opposite end of the house suddenly became all too visible, as if to silently remind me where the guest room was. I said nothing, only made my feet move, Ambrose side-eyeing me as I walked by him. He didn't move a single muscle until I was behind my door again.

I leaned against the closed door, heart racing like I was hiding from my dad in a closet again. Every scenario of what Tynan had promised to do to the Dark Queen played out in my head of him doing to me instead. Which would be fit for a spy proven guilty? Which tactic would hurt the most?

I sat on the bed and waited for Ambrose to run to Tynan, shouting my verdict across the realms. I waited and waited, staring at the door until my eyes went dry.

And then it happened. A knock sounded, much softer than I'd expected. I didn't expect knocking at all. I took a deep breath in, ready to face Tynan's round of questioning. But when I opened the door, it wasn't Tynan's hard gaze I looked up at, but Ara's much softer one I peered down on. She held a plate in her hands.

"I noticed breakfast was still out earlier." It was then that I noticed the light was different. The hallway was lit with those odd lanterns. I glanced behind me to the only window in the room, a warmer, fading sunlight pooling in.

"It didn't look like you got around to it. I wanted to make sure you got something to eat." I blinked at her. It was a kind gesture. Much too kind for someone who was posted here to make sure I didn't leave. I took the plate when she stretched her arms a fraction.

"It's a roast," she offered. "I didn't know what you like, but... Well, who doesn't like roast?" She added a lopsided smile at the end, and I instantly felt lighter.

"Thank you," I finally said.

"Would you like to join me in the dining room? You don't have to eat alone. Someone will be here with you at all times."

This was the oddest hostage situation imaginable. Captors who were friendly, at least some of them anyway. Captors who wanted to make sure I knew I didn't have to dine alone. Who cared about my dining at all. I'd take it over my last captive situation. "Sure."

I followed Ara the very short distance, just around the corner through the open archway, and came into the dining area, where a large mahogany table with room for six took up most of the space. The kitchen could be seen through another archway.

Windows lined the front wall, overlooking the lamp-lit gazebo. The string lights from the patio were just barely visible from this side of the cabin. It was really quite cozy. The cabin was spacious and yet conservative all at once. I sat down at the chair closest to me, and Ara grabbed a plate that was already at the end of the table and moved it to the seat across from mine.

My plate was topped with a mixture of roast, carrots, and pota-toes, all speckled with a blend of onion and garlic flavors and drowned in red wine and broth. I poked my fork into a savory carrot and stacked it on top of a small piece of roast. I took a careful bite, holding back the urge to tear into my food the way the Dark Queen had. But when the flavors hit my tongue, I breathed a contented sigh. This was the third time since I'd been here that I was convinced food could be art. I caught Ara's smile as she hid it behind her own forkful.

No one spoke for a long time. The minutes were filled only with metal clinking against glass plates. I knew what she was doing and silently thanked her for allowing me the quiet to just eat in the afternoon glow of the room.

I scanned the room in between bites, my gaze catching on the stove. It had a classic appearance to it, with two deep-blue doors at the front and accented gold knobs resting above those. But it was also a bit modern, with a sleek design and grills resting on the top.

"I'm confused about something. I don't see any outlets around here." I looked to the lantern on the wall behind Ara and nodded toward it. "Or light switches. How is all this stuff powered? The lights I see are lit by some kind of flame, but the stove... I don't understand."

Ara's eyes lit with excitement, ready for conversation. "I don't know how things are charged in your world, but in ours, Elysian's power runs underground."

"Really? But then how does it come through the walls?"

Ara took her last bite of potatoes, set down her fork, and clasped her hands as if giving a lecture.

"In Elysian's earlier years, many millennia before I came to be here, a geologist discovered an odd substance in the world's core. It was some type of dormant energy source that he extracted out of the ground and experimented on. What he found was that if it was left alone and whole, it seemed to have no use. But if one were to break the substance in half, something odd happened. The insides seemed to be made of two parts, one with an orange glow, and one with a blue one. And when broken apart, their energies were strengthened, like they were reaching for each other. He named the orange energy Celestium, and the blue one Divinium. Don't ask me how he figured this out, science was never my strong suit, but somehow, this geologist learned that if he were to plant the Divinium back into the ground, as long as it were planted close enough to Elysian's mantle, the two halves would still search for its other part. The Divinium's energy travels along the crust looking for its counterpart."

Ara placed her palms flat on the tabletop to push herself up, and went to the closest lantern. She stretched on her tiptoes, opening the little glass door and reaching inside.

Gently, Ara cupped the orange globe and carefully brought it out of its home. "This isn't a flame. This is a celestial light. Right now, a Divinium is traveling along the ground and up through my toes to power this Celestium orb. Ara shuffled her toes and peered at them. "But..." She smiled, and her wings suddenly appeared, softly snapping out at her sides where they hadn't been before. She gently lifted herself two inches off the ground, and the orb went out, the room darkening a tone. "Now there is no connecting point between the two." She let herself back down, and the orb lit once again.

"Fascinating, right?" She replaced the orb back in its glass box, where it gently flickered as somewhere a Divinium's energy invisibly traveled along the wall for it.

"It really is," I admitted. "And resourceful."

Ara took her seat again. "It's harder to extract out of grounds like Kashmir, so sometimes they will buy it from other places. But the orbs are expensive. If you ever find yourself in Kashmir, you'll find that a lot of their citizens are pretty set in their ways and content to live as they did before the orbs were discovered. And they thrive well enough. You'll find a lot more wood stoves and light by candle, but here in Valhalla, our ground is so rich that we're able to generate so much of it. It's our most profitable export. Ty could make Valhalla a lot more coin for it than he's charging."

"And where is Tynan now?" I asked, remembering what he'd said about not sleeping in his own palace.

"I'm not sure, honestly. He's going to be pretty busy after his time away."

"I'm shocked he isn't taking a day off after...everything."

We looked at each other then, as if silently agreeing neither of us wanted or needed to acknowledge what "everything" was.

"I know it's hard to see it now, but my brother isn't all that bad. And he's a good king. He cares about this place."

I dropped my gaze to my plate. She was right. It was hard to see Tynan in any admirable light. I'd seen through Tynan's own eyes what Ara and he meant to each other, but that was their relationship. It didn't extend to anyone else. Ara had to know the Tynan she knew and loved wasn't the Tynan I was getting to know.

"I would imagine at this hour he's somewhere in the mountains attempting to balance out what's been undone. He probably won't make it back here for some time. He'll be out there all night. Either that or he's regrouping the troops to—"

"*Ara.*"

I nearly jumped out of my chair, both of us snapping our heads toward the voice. Ambrose stood in the archway, his arms over his chest, and a special scowl aimed just for her.

Ara's eyes flicked to mine, an apology there before she scooted out of her chair. "I'll just…"

"Good idea," Ambrose finished for her. She made to slide past him, but he stopped her with a harsh tone. "I'll be taking over things around here from now on."

She paused at his side and lowered her voice, though it came out just as harsh. "Leave her alone. You can watch things around here without harassing the girl." Ara matched his stare without wavering, and suddenly, she was that commanding officer positioned over a map again. A rebel. A fighter who wouldn't back down. "At least let her enjoy her meal without your prying."

I was shocked when Ambrose was the first to blink. He moved away from the archway, following Ara, but he made sure to give me a particularly nasty side-eye on his way out. Their hushed bickering faded down the hallway and into the next room over.

I didn't waste any time. I scooped up the last few bites of food and then took mine and Ara's plates to the kitchen sink. I didn't need to make eye contact through the partial open floor plan to feel Ambrose's suspicious glare on me while Ara whisper screamed at him. I only washed the plates and silverware, gently setting everything on the drying rack, intent on regaining some of my innocence by minding my business. My feet became the most interesting thing in the whole chalet as I moved to return to my room.

I stayed there, with no plans on leaving it again. I almost didn't know who to dread more—Ambrose or Tynan. But for whatever reason, the thought that Tynan may not return to the chalet tonight, and I'd be sharing a roof with Ambrose instead, made the answer extremely clear. Tynan may be teetering on the edge of doubt with me, but it was Ambrose who was going to make my stay miserable.

# CHAPTER TWENTY-TWO

I stayed true to my self-pact. I didn't leave my room again. Not through the side door to get some fresh air the next morning. Not even to slip out just long enough to grab a book from the next room over, though it was hard to talk myself out of that one. For the first time, I found myself missing things like television and my cell phone.

I considered stepping out only once. After all, it wouldn't be hard to cure my boredom with just the view, but it simply wasn't worth Ambrose's menacing glare. I'd almost rather die of the boredom.

I sighed heavily, resting my head against the headboard. I raised my hands to my face and inspected them. Flames had come from these fingers. I flipped my hands back and forth, flexing my fingers in and out. Testing how such a thing could be possible.

It wasn't possible.

And yet...I could feel the ever-present warmth beneath my skin. That heat was almost like a comfort at this point. It had been there all my life to keep me in check when I would almost lose control. I squinted at my fingers, willing something to happen. Nothing did. I flopped my hands onto my lap, giving up. This fire in my veins, it was no power, it was just anger. Anger that was never allowed to see the light of day.

A small series of tapping came from the other end of my door.

"It's Ara! Can I come in?"

I swung my legs off the bed and leapt for the door. I didn't realize I was smiling until Ara's face lit up as I opened the door wide.

"Hi!" It was the first time she'd spoken to me with true enthusiasm. The first time it didn't seem like she was walking on eggshells around me.

"Hi."

She wore a loose fitting pair of pants rolled up at the ankles and a casual shirt a few shades darker than her hair. So unofficial compared to the previous times I'd seen her. She smiled for a moment longer, then seemed to remember herself. She cleared her throat. "Um... I'm supposed to say this with a bunch of authority or whatever, so...you're coming with me." Her voice dropped and her eyebrows bunched at that last part, but her contagious smile quickly resurfaced, unable to help herself.

"Where are we going?"

"Into town. For...very important things."

"Kingdoms, Ara. You really are bad at this, aren't you?" Enzo appeared, propping an arm in the doorframe, looking far too handsome for his own good in a loose linen shirt. It was cut low enough for his pectoral muscles to peek out.

Ara shrugged. "I told them to let you do it. It's not my fault no one around here listens to me."

Enzo stepped the rest of the way into the room and put a hand on her shoulder. "You'll have to excuse her. Little Ara has also been held prisoner in a way, and now that she's free, she's a little wound up."

"Yeah, prisoner to a royal council who has been hassling me

nonstop for a year." She glared at him. "'Princess Ara, we need your signature'. 'Princess Ara, how will your brother be retrieved?' 'Princess Ara, there are bats in the library again.' Now that Ty is finally back, it feels good to *breathe* again. I do not envy this role of his."

"What's in town?" I asked.

"Shopping," Ara answered matter-of-factly. "Shopping is in town."

"I'm allowed to go shopping now?" I asked, surprised with myself for the pushback.

"We're on supervision duty today, Briar." Enzo rubbed his hands together. "And no offense, but I'm not sitting around doing nothing. No need to waste such a day."

"I've been in way over my head," Ara added. "I'm taking a well-deserved day off and intend to devour every high-end store on the east side of Valhalla with it."

"But Ambrose—"

"Ambrose apparently needs beauty sleep and shouldn't have left me in charge if he didn't want me to invite you along."

"But Tynan said—"

Ara grabbed me by the hand, and led me out of my room. "No more questions. Come on."

"You'll adore the shops in Valhalla." Enzo followed us. "The fashion is ahead of its times."

"It's true," Ara added as we walked down the hall. "You couldn't pay me to live in a different realm if my brother didn't already rule over Valhalla."

Enzo snorted. "Please. If the males in Empyrean wore cardigans, you'd be all over that." She smacked him but didn't dispute the accusation. I noticed the disappointment quietly fade from Enzo's face. I noticed that Ara hadn't noticed.

Ambrose was stretched out on the couch when we came out into the living area and crossed the room, like he was guarding the chalet from its center. He opened only one eye when he heard footsteps. I slowed my pace as he opened the other to properly stare me down and the sudden weight of his feelings toward me landed with full force. Ambrose didn't like me, not at all.

"We're going shopping, Ambrose," Ara announced.

"I don't care where you go," he said. "Just don't let her out of your sight for a single moment."

Ara glanced to me with a silent smile of apology. "You sure you don't want to join?" she asked him.

Ambrose closed his eyes again as he spoke, arms folded under his head. "I've been given one day off after a year of plotting, stressing, and avoiding every meltdown that could possibly be had. And you think I'm going to waste it shopping with *Enzo*?" His lips pulled upward. "That sounds like a whole different kind of hell I've never been to."

Enzo punched his shoulder and then swerved out of the way before Ambrose could return the favor.

Ara shrugged. "We'll get you something pretty while we're out then."

I didn't dare look back to see if Ambrose's stare was on me as we walked out of the chalet and onto the porch.

"How far is town?" I asked after breathing in a lung full of fresh morning air.

"Not far. But we won't be walking," Ara responded.

"Security reasons," Enzo added.

I looked to Ara's wings, suddenly visible again, though last night the teal feathers had been morphed, somehow disappearing when she needed them out of her way. But hers were so small, even now with them out in the open, they didn't take up much space.

"Oh, don't worry," she said when my gaze landed on them. "Something tells me you'd rather not travel the way I prefer to."

"No, I don't think I would like that at all," I agreed.

Enzo put a hand in his trouser pocket, pulling out a small glass vial with a dark, murky substance floating inside it.

"Some of Ty's shadow," he answered my unspoken question. He threw the vial at our feet, and the glass shattered on the porch. The hazy mist lifted from the ground, snaking around our feet and looking for the one that had called it. "Let's go, ladies."

Ara rolled her eyes. "You do know you can just open the bottle and let it trickle out, right?"

"This is way more dramatic." Enzo put an arm around each of us, tucking us into his sides. He smelled warm and grassy, like someone who spent all their time outside.

The mist wrapped around our shoulders, engulfing us completely until it washed away the trees and we were hidden inside the dark cloud. The wind started out faint, Ara's teal hair tickling Enzo's shoulder, but then it swept us away—the weirdest sensation that we were moving, but somehow also not. Like maybe only the things around us were. And then the ground was under my feet again.

It had been easier than the first time, but still unsettling. I stumbled a little to the side, and Enzo steadied me with a strong arm. As the haze crept off, the woods we'd been standing in were gone, replaced by mountains piled on top of each other that overlooked the charming town we now stood in the middle of.

For a moment, I was thrown back in time. An expanse of stone brick made up the walkways where horses clip-clopped by. Children chased each other freely, and creatures strolled with shopping bags or coffees in their hands. Cream, yellow, rust, and purple shops lined each side, creating somewhat of a direction to walk in. Pointed roofs and little handmade shop signs hung over each door, and Victorian-like lampposts were stationed at every corner. Patio tables littered every other corner, some even in the middle of the street, where creatures sat to enjoy tea and cakes from the local shops.

A clock tower chimed in the distance. It was so oddly human, and yet so vastly not.

Enzo grinned proudly. "Welcome to the town of Bramberg."

I didn't have time to wonder over the goat-legged male carrying boxes of delicious-smelling pastries before Ara pointed excitedly at a shop across the street with after-season dresses modeled on sale in the window. The circular sign hanging above the door said "Victoria's".

Once inside, Ara took a deep inhale of the store, theatrically breathing out its scent. "Oh, it's been too long."

A saleswoman looked up at Ara's voice, surprise flashing across her face, and then rushed over. "Princess," she chimed. "I haven't seen you in ages!"

"Yes, Victoria, and it's high time I made up for the absence. I need to spend lots and lots of coins today, do you hear me?"

Victoria, a silver-haired, wide-eyed female, appeared torn between the professionalism required when dealing with someone with Ara's title and being familiar with what was obviously her regular customer. She settled with a closed-mouth smile and enthusiastic nod.

"I'll hold your usual dressing room for you." Victoria gave Enzo a too obvious look over and ignored my presence altogether before scurrying to the back of the boutique. She moved like a dancer, her long legs making her movements swift and poised.

"A fox shifter," Ara whispered at my curious stare.

Enzo left us for the back of the store, immediately taking his post at the dressing rooms while Ara and I ventured toward the dresses. The handful of customers in the shop suddenly found themselves ready to check out after doing a double take at the king's sister. When the last customer walked out the door, I noticed the owner flip a door sign from open to close.

Ara shopped in silence, a crease of concentration forming between her brows. I shuffled through some racks, gliding my fingers along the smoothness of the materials, just to keep busy while Ara draped dresses over her arms.

I scanned the shop, my eyes indulging each section. There was a little of everything, though it was all of tasteful quality. From casual everyday dresses, to the more formal wear we were standing in now, to exquisite jewelry stands and display counters with glittering insides. My eyes landed on a section in the back of the store where intricate pieces of lingerie decorated a wall. Bold reds and tempting blacks popped and demanded attention. My gaze traveled along the lace hems. I tried to picture something like that on myself and once again came up short. For a moment though, I let myself linger in that thought. How I might look. It was everything I wasn't. Daring and alluring and fearless.

"Hmm."

I turned back to the formal wear section. Ara rummaged through dress after dress, thinking out loud. I swiped through the rack mindlessly.

After a while, I noticed Ara's eyes strategically darting to different sections of my body every few minutes, the last look aimed at the pants I wore with their ends rolled up too high. I hoped I wouldn't be here long enough to need to borrow anything more, but wouldn't dare ask.

When she was ready for her dressing room, Enzo was already sitting on a bench, waiting semi-patiently.

Each dressing room was as big as my guest room alone. I took a seat next to Enzo, and after only a few minutes, he sighed heavily. Leaning back on his hands, his head lolled lazily toward the ceiling, he said, "Are you ever going to come out or what?"

"I'll come out when I think something is worth showing off," she yelled back at him.

Enzo rolled his head dramatically to the side in my direction. "If you take as long as she does, I might scream."

"You're in luck," I said. "I'm not trying anything on."

A teal head popped out of the curtain. "What fun is that?"

A memory of Zafar's hand nudged my back, and his breath caressed my ear, urging me to pick something out in the market for him to buy. My heart panged at the shadow of his touch.

"Even if I had Elysian coin, I'm leaving soon."

Ara frowned at that and retreated behind the privacy of the pink and white striped curtain, but her voice came through clearly from the other side. "Must you though? I could really use a new companion around here. Ambrose forever has a stick lodged up his ass, and Enzo annoys me most days."

Enzo scowled at the curtain. Ara giggled as if she already knew the reaction he wore.

"What's the hurry?" he asked me. "Have someone special to return to?" He started to run a hand through his combed-back hair and then seemed to remember how much styling gel was in it.

"Not even close." I grinned at him, matching his laid-back posture. Here in this shop, it was almost like we were all friends. Or like we could one day be friends. It was hard to imagine them as those serious-faced warriors stressed out over a map. This is what they looked like outside of leading wars and being heroes. "And there won't be in the future either. Not after the whole thing with Zafar—"

Ara's head poked out of the curtain before I could finish my sentence. I waited for her to come the rest of the way out, to show us what she had on, but she just stared at me. "Continue," she instructed.

I blinked. "Zafar?" Ara only nodded and I gave a nonchalant shrug. "I thought we were more than we were, that's all. It's no big deal."

"You've been here for what, a few months? And you've already gotten yourself tied up with *that*?" Enzo asked, a bit dumbfounded. "How?"

"Tynan said the same thing," I speculated.

"Ty knows about this?" Ara balked, even more taken aback than Enzo.

"I mean...I mentioned it to him, yes. That we... I don't even know what we were. Obviously, nothing. I thought he liked me, but then he turned me in to the Dark Queen."

Ara and Enzo's voices merged. "He what?!"

I glanced between the two of them, not sure who to direct my answer to. "He was supposed to be taking me to Clive Steeple, but he arranged a detour on the way."

Ara gritted her teeth in frustration. "That snake! God, he's just —Oh! I can't even believe this!" She disappeared behind the curtain again, ranting loud enough for the whole store to hear her had it been full. "Actually, you know what? I can totally believe it. That lying, full of shit, snake! That big-headed, two-faced *slut*."

Enzo raised his eyebrows, and his lips curved enthusiastically, like he loved it when she did this.

"So I'm guessing she knows him?"

"Oh, yeah."

She came fully out this time, drawing the curtain wide and revealing a glittering deep-blue dress with flecks of sparkling white etched into the fabric like stars at midnight. The neckline was modest, and the sheer sleeves dipped off her shoulders and ended at her wrists. The bottom flared out behind her in a court train. Enzo's smile slowly faded, and he just looked at her, raw emotion slipping through the cracks for a moment too long. Still not long enough for Ara to notice.

"I think I'm going to wear this to dinner tonight."

I got up from the bench, walked to her, and took the fabric of the skirt in my hands, admiring it. "It's stunning," I said. She smiled up at me.

"I'm starving," Enzo said, the brief awe erased and replaced with cool nonchalance. "Can we wrap this up now and go to lunch?"

"Kingdoms, yes," Ara said. "But Briar gets to pick where we eat."

We went to a few more stores after lunch and then back to the chalet afterward. Between the two of them, they'd accumulated so many bags that even with me helping, Ara had to have some of them set up for delivery to her suite at her brother's palace. Most of the bags on my arms were Enzo's purchases. How he'd run up such a large bill while spending such a short amount of time trying anything on was beyond me.

Tynan and Ambrose sat at one of the patio tables outside, talking in depth, both their brows furrowed when they looked up at the cloud that appeared before them. My face froze, and a hammer of dread slammed into my gut.

"Whoa," Enzo said. "Did we walk in on something?"

Tynan and Ambrose exchanged a tense glance before at least Tynan attempted to loosen his shoulders.

"Nothing at all," Tynan replied. "Seems like you're putting your vacation to good use." He stood and kissed Ara on her cheek, and my mind flashed to my own brother. Of what our relationship could have been had things turned out differently. A future stolen from us.

Enzo took all the bags from us, pushing them up his arms to make them all fit. "I'll drop these off for you, Ara. Briar, will you be joining us tonight?"

"For?" I looked to Tynan for confirmation, not sure if I was invited to their dinner table after Ambrose's interruption last night or if I was expected to eat in my guest room from now on.

"A celebratory dinner at the palace in honor of my return." He glared at Enzo, who had an innocent expression plastered on his face.

Ambrose cleared his throat, gaining everyone's attention. "Maybe we should save the rest of this conversation for later." He eyed me.

Ambrose wasn't wrong. I was a stranger, an outsider, being invited to a fancy dinner at a palace full of important titles I didn't belong to. Even if Tynan had admitted that, for the most part, he believed me. Even if his sister kissed the ground I walked on because I was responsible for her brother's freedom. Even then, Ambrose's caution wasn't misplaced. I knew that. But the hostility in his eyes when he looked at me was a bit much.

Enzo tried again. "So Briar won't be joining us then?"

Tynan gave him a warning look.

"But I bought her a dress," Ara pouted. I snapped my head in her direction. "I bought you a couple of things actually. I ordered them and they'll be delivered in what I hope to be your size," she added with a guilty smile. "I feel terrible that I've dressed you in high-water pants."

"Ara," Tynan said, the warning in his voice growing.

"That's my cue." She turned to leave, tugging on Enzo's sleeve. On her way passed me, she whispered, "Don't worry, there will be other occasions you can wear the dress to." She winked.

With a soft snap, she let her wings unfurl, and the blue-green feathers rustled as she gracefully pushed off the ground and took for the sky. Enzo struggled with his pocket, pulling out and fumbling with another vial before tossing it on the ground. It was only seconds later when he faded away after her, a playful smile the last thing to be gobbled up by the cloud of gray.

I watched Ara soar until she was only a speck far above the tree-tops. When I looked to Tynan and Ambrose again, a hint of sadness, or maybe longing, touched both their eyes.

"Don't worry," I said. "I know I'm staying here."

"Obviously," Ambrose huffed under his breath. I blinked at him, feeling an urge I'd had so many times before. The urge to snap back, to stand up for myself. An urge I'd never acted on until recently. But I bit my tongue and swallowed the retort.

He turned to leave but stopped short, directing his next sentence to Tynan. "Xosha was seen leaving Clive Steeple late this morning."

I looked to the horizon, where the treetops kissed the skyline, and noted the hues of the sky. Still bright, but just beginning to darken, ready to transition to an early evening. Tynan voiced my exact thoughts.

"And you thought to tell me this just now?" An edge coated his tone. They'd definitely been arguing.

"I had more pressing matters to discuss with you first." Ambrose's eyes cut to me and I shrank.

Tynan made his irritation and his dismissal clear by letting a beat of silence go by before saying, "Thank you."

At that, Ambrose strode off aimlessly into the woods.

"We'll talk more later, Ambrose," Tynan called after him, but Ambrose showed no signs of having heard him. When Tynan met my gaze, the stress lodged between his brows was back.

"I get the feeling he doesn't like me very much."

"It's nothing personal."

"Isn't it though?"

Tynan shrugged. "Don't let it bother you. I told you Ambrose has trust issues."

I changed the subject, almost not caring what Ambrose's problem with me was. "So. I've proven myself. Xosha cares about me, so I can't be a spy. Can we go now?"

"Tomorrow," he said.

I frowned. "No." I startled myself at the taste of the word on my tongue. It felt unfamiliar and slightly satisfying. "Ambrose wants me gone so badly. Why wait?"

Tynan blinked in faint surprise, but brushed it off just as

quickly. "Fine. Let me take care of a few things around here, and we can go in an hour or so."

"No," I said again, more forceful this time. "I'm done waiting around. I've been given every single excuse since coming to this world about why I have to wait one more day, one more week. I'm done waiting for everyone else to tell me when they want me gone."

The stress mark deepened, and his shoulders tensed again. Guilt flooded me instantly. It was his first day back as king after having no idea what was going on for the past year, and I'd clearly walked in on what was a fight with Ambrose. And now he was getting attitude from a strange girl demanding even more from him. A girl who truly wasn't his problem.

But I had been held back, shut up, and forced into doing things I didn't want to do for far too long. There had been one obstacle after another stopping me from finding my way to Clive Steeple. I couldn't allow myself to continue to be walked on, all for the sake of not wanting to be an inconvenience.

"Damn, I can't even eat something first?"

I crossed my arms, ready to stand my ground for once in my life. "You can do whatever you want, but I'm leaving."

"Clive Steeple isn't going anywhere."

"I want to go home," I said, my insides recoiling at the meaningless word.

Tynan's annoyance spilled over, a long and stressful first day back on what sounded to be an empty stomach getting the better of him. "Is this place not a palace in comparison to where you come from?" His words were true, but they bit. Hard. "Do you not have everything you could ask for here? A secluded place no one but my most trusted know about? Food constantly supplied when you need it. Your every move cleaned up after?"

I remembered the mug I'd placed in the sink, how it had magically cleaned itself, and I was momentarily sidetracked by curiosity.

"Yeah, what's up with that, by the way?"

Tynan paused, confused by my change of subject. Irritation still lingered in his voice, in his shoulders, but he answered anyway. "Dryads. The very thing you came here pretending to be."

"Dryads," I repeated, thinking of the tree nymph I'd seen in Darya's palace with flowers for hair and ivy for skin.

He nodded. "They rarely leave their true form. I'm surprised you even noticed her."

"And you have one as a maid," I finished. "To clean your dishes for you."

The slow shift of his features as he recognized the insult to his character was satisfying to watch unfold.

"Yeah," he finally said. "I'll tell her you said thank you. Wouldn't want her to think you're ungrateful or anything."

"Excuse me?"

He shrugged, hands finding his pockets. The fact that he still looked utterly breathtaking while we were going at it was infuriating. "I'm just saying."

"Remember just last morning when you were thanking me for saving your life?"

His eyes went skyward, his voice unbelieving. "That was one time."

I clenched my fists. We could do this all day, hurl insults at each other until one of us ran into a wall. But I didn't want to play these games anymore. I had played them with Zafar, and that had ended horribly. I was exhausted of games in disguise.

"I'm going. With or without you."

He halfway smiled and motioned toward the forest. A challenge. My heart raced as I realized I'd been the one to hit the wall first, but pride overwhelmed me. I turned away from him, staring at the trees and biting my lip as I pondered what my next move would be. I could feel the smirk at my back and refused to meet his eyes.

"Oh, did you need directions?"

Smug, arrogant, *Angel of the Night.*

"No," I snapped. The word gained more strength each time I said it. "I didn't."

On Darya's map, Clive Steeple had been in the Everwood, just on the border of Valhalla. Southeast. I needed to head southeast.

Which way was Southeast...

I'd rather get lost in these woods than make him feel like I relied on him. Like I needed any of these charming, unreliable males. I stared at the forest, the harsh reality sinking in deeper that he was winning, and he knew it.

Tynan's low laugh was infuriating. His arm barely brushed mine as he walked ahead of me. "Maybe when you're able to show me how grateful you are, we can talk about Clive Steeple."

My heart sank, realizing what I'd just done. I'd pissed off someone willing to help me.

"So what? I'm to be your prisoner until I kiss your ass enough?"

Tynan turned, continuing to walk backward. He spread his arms, showcasing his shadows as they lifted from nowhere and gathered around his body. "Gratefulness, Briar. It's a nice ass. You could kiss worse."

# CHAPTER TWENTY-THREE

I glared at Tynan until the last shadow engulfed him at the tree line and spit him out hopefully far, far away from here. It was only then that I let out the biggest, most immature groan I could muster to the sky. I spun around, my flame igniting with the movement, and marched for the opposite end of the tree line.

No way. No way was I staying here a moment longer. I didn't care that I was basically his captive. If he wanted me a prisoner, he should have put me behind bars again. I didn't know where I was going, but I would figure it the hell out. I walked with no real destination but away, pushing passed overgrown branches and stepping over uneven ground. Branches from two different trees reached out to graze each other and I tore through them too, flinging their greenery apart to reveal—

The back of the cabin.

I stared at it. My brows creased. I must have made a circle, though what a perfect circle it must have been to have wound up right back where I started. I turned and stalked off, not knowing whether I was headed for Empyrean or Kashmir or right back to the center of the Garden itself. The woods were unchanging as I continued on a straight path, no obvious landmarks to let me know where I was headed. My flame quivered at the realization that I was going to lose myself in these woods, but it was much too late in my temper tantrum to turn back now. I ducked under a branch and stepped into a clearing.

A sleepy lake rested before me with a lantern-lit gazebo in the middle of it, and just beyond that was…Tynan's cabin.

"What?" I breathed.

I shook my head and turned from it, making *sure* to walk straight, never straying an inch from my path. When a tree or a boulder blocked my way, I stepped out of line only long enough to move around it and then get right back on track. I stepped over a moss-covered log, and when my boot hit the ground again, it wasn't the summer leaves they hit, but a wooded deck. I looked up at the front door.

I cursed at the sky. I kept cursing as I flung myself around and ran, calling Tynan every name I'd ever heard in my life. Some names I made up. I was out of breath and *seething* inside, my fire never so ignited. I already knew what I'd see as I got ready to rip open a new canopy of lively branches. I opened my mouth, ready to yell so loud Tynan could hear me from whichever corner of whichever realm he'd shadowed off to. I nearly choked on the breath that caught in my lungs as my mind reeled at the beast I looked at instead.

My attention caught first on the shiny obsidian scales. It was coated in them, from the tip of a nine-foot tail, along a feline body, and up the neck that flared out into hoods. At the sound of my breath, it turned a reptilian-shaped head toward me. The eyes were darker than the Dark Queen's. Darker than Tynan's hair. Darker than the Nothing itself. My gaze nervously flicked to its massive feet as it took a pivoting step.

Claws shaper than knives tipped each of its toes. Its neck vibrated in low rumbles and clicks as it took me in.

The four-legged snake moved like a panther, with slow stalking steps and an unblinking stare. The fight or flight instincts left my body, freezing me instead. My legs went numb. I was going to faint. That or my heartbeat was going to thump straight through my chest, and I'd die right here on the forest floor.

I was frozen solid when its snout stopped in front of my nose, and it *sniffed* at me. The line of its mouth curved into a smile and something like satisfaction filled its colorless eyes, recognizing prey over predator. But it wasn't until it hissed, its head shaking with the movement, and a black tongue flicked out to graze my nose, that a noise somewhere between a scream and a whimper left my throat.

*Briar, run!*

I bolted.

Whatever the thing was, it was after me so fast it was a wonder it didn't swipe my head off before I took my first step. I took off faster than I knew I was capable of, pumping my legs until I cried out. A set of razor-sharp claws swiped my ankle, and a searing flash of pain tore through my skin. I tripped, unable to bear any weight on the foot, and fell. The ground dipped at the perfect moment, a hill rolling downward. My body tumbled with it.

I hit every root and rock on the way down, the scorching pain in my ankle forgotten as a rock sliced through my brow. I clawed for something to grab, something to stop myself from rolling, and grasped a particularly thick root. My palm burned as it caught my weight. I groaned against the pain and gritted my teeth, begging that inner flame in me the will to hold on, but when I looked up at the top of the hill, the cat-like reptile was strategically making its way down.

The thing thrashed like a deranged animal, barely allowing its claws to sink into the soil long enough to steady its footing before taking the next leap. The next bloodlusted pounce sent it only a few feet above me, and its scaled tail curved around and swiped at my cheek. I opened my palm at the strike. I fell and fell, sliding through the dirt until something heavy and solid threw itself into me, knocking us both off course.

Tynan's fingers gripped me so hard it hurt, his thumbs digging into the soft muscle of my shoulder blade. He'd arrived so suddenly and so harshly that it stopped us in our tracks. My knees hit the dirt, my palms smacking into the loose, wet ground to steady me once he released his deathly grip to crouch his body in front of mine.

With his back to me and his arms shielded out in a protective stance, Tynan was every bit of a creature as this snake thing was. Or maybe he was just steadying himself after moving at the speed of a lightning bolt.

The creature came to a stop at Tynan's arrival. It paced on the hill, assessing the situation. Its tongue flicked out every few seconds, as if it could taste me on the nonexistent wind. But its eyes kept returning to Tynan. Me, it had attacked on sight, but Tynan... It was as if it knew him. Knew what Tynan was and debated who might win. Tynan tilted his head, as if to dare it.

And then the creature decided, lifting a taloned foot in our direction. Tynan struck before it planted that foot on the ground again.

Droplets of darkness left the sky. They came in from all sides, pulled from any corner of the forest that even a hint of darkness touched. It flooded in until it became a monsoon, meeting together and pooling at Tynan's fingertips like they were called there.

They were.

And then, without Tynan moving his arms, the darkness shot toward the creature, engulfing it. The rumbles and clicks and roars turned into an ear-splitting squawking. The shadows tightened and twisted around the beast, sending its body thrashing and wailing. It tried to find relief in any loose space it could use to slither its way out. But the shadows prevailed. The creature choked.

Its tail was the last to drop against the ground. Tynan relaxed his arms and his shadows took their time wandering back to their places in the woods. I couldn't stop staring at the creature's eyes, so black I couldn't tell if they were lifeless or not. But its tongue hung out of its mouth and its body was limp. Its stomach still as death.

Tynan lifted himself out of his crouch, and I shuddered as he turned to face me. All the stars in his eyes were fatally still.

"What is wrong with you?" Each word was spoken so slowly and so sharply I prayed for the bars that used to sit between us.

I was barely able to lift myself off the ground, my legs still numb, my heart beating so rapidly I couldn't feel it. I opened my mouth to speak, though I had no words. It wouldn't have mattered if I came up with a response anyway, because more of Tynan's shadows sucked away my next breath. His arm came around my wrist. I closed my eyes, unsure what fate I was about to meet. Whatever it was, I deserved it. But the wind only thrashed in a violent gust, and then the shadows lifted. Lifted at the back of the cabin.

Tynan glowered at me, and that look...I hated him for it. I hated him, and yet I hated that he was capable of looking at me that way. I braced myself for the yelling, for the name calling, for the torture promised in his eyes. But he only turned his back on me, heading for a set of steps leading to the back door.

"Wait." I followed after him, my ankle searing in pain at the step. I stumbled and hissed. Tynan looked over his shoulder. I tried to stand, but it *burned*. His eyes glimmered in interest. "Were you bitten or cut?" I couldn't tell if it was alarm or scolding in his voice.

"Cut."

"Fangs or claws?"

"Claws."

"You're lucky," he spat. "One bite from that thing, and you'd have been dead before anyone could have gotten to you." He turned his back again and muttered loudly enough for me to hear, "You're going to be the death of us all."

"Hey." Tynan kept walking, and I pushed past the pain to follow him up the steps. "Hey! This wouldn't have happened at all if you hadn't been such a jerk!"

Tynan whirled on me so fast I stumbled to a stop. I hated that my body still shook from the attack while he towered over me from two steps above.

My voice shook, but I spoke anyway. "I thought you said nothing could find its way here."

"It *didn't* find its way here. *You* found *it*." But even as Tynan said it, his eyes flicked up toward the forest, and watched it with suspicion.

"What was that thing?" I asked, bringing Tynan's eyes back to mine.

"That was a najaonca, and you should be thanking the Creator it wasn't also your ending. If your heartbeat wasn't so damn loud, I wouldn't have heard you at all."

My shaking was visible, and the pain in my ankle was excruciating, but still, I struggled to take the extra steps so that I was the one looking down on him. "I didn't ask for you to come running, Tynan. I was trying to get the hell away from you."

"And look where it got you." Tynan took a single step up to level his ground, and took his turn to glare down at me. But then he seemed to change his mind and took another step and then another, not stopping again. He walked all the way up, making his way inside without me. I chased after him into the living room, so riddled with adrenaline that I wasn't thinking about what I was doing. "Why bother with me at all then? If I'm such trouble, you could have just let that nah-yuh whatever kill me for you and be done with it."

"Maybe I should have. Now I know for the next time," Tynan said, turning to me as he said it. But he quickly looked down, as if his gaze betrayed him, and he eyed the foot I couldn't bear all my weight on. Blood poured from the slash marks, soaking my pant leg. "You need salve."

I paused, every muscle in my body tensing at the confusing confession. I assessed Tynan so intently that when he lifted his eyes to mine again, he blinked in surprise. "Oh my God," I said, baffled at the revelation.

"What?"

I cracked a smile, an unkind one. I was finding that the longer I remained in Elysian, the better I was at those, and I didn't know if I liked that or not.

"You care."

Tynan sneered.

"No," I said, a cross between astonishment and humor coating my tone. "You actually care, don't you?"

Tynan's sneer faded just a second or two after the mocking gleam in his eyes did. I had trouble focusing on his gaze, that amazing, impossible gaze, but I pressed on. I took a step forward, and Tynan instantly stepped back with it.

"You didn't have to send me any memories in that dungeon. You didn't have to lift my pain when I was dying. You didn't have to take me with you." With each step I took toward him, Tynan took a matching step back. And with each word out of my mouth, Tynan's eyes widened a fraction more. "You could have left me there to deal with the Dark Queen on my own. You could have thrown me in a cell all over again when Ambrose pressured you to. You don't have to care about my bruises or my ankle or anything. But you do."

Tynan's back hit the wall. His mouth fell open, taken completely off guard, and it pleased me. For whatever reason, the fact that his stone features cracked under my gaze, it pleased me.

He started to speak, but I cut him off before his words could escape. "For whatever reason, Tynan. You care about me." I teased with a smile I knew had to be infuriating.

But at that, whether it was the smile or the words behind the smile, Tynan's eyes darkened. Before I knew it, there was pressure on my shoulders, and my smile was wiped clean off my face while I was whipped around, my back hitting the very wall Tynan had just been pinned to. Maybe I could have kept up the arrogance if the breath hadn't been audible as it left me

"I'm sorry if there was some confusion somewhere. Allow me to clear things up. I care about one thing, and one thing only. And that's those inside these walls. That is all. Do not be mistaken. You might have proven yourself innocent, but you've also proven yourself a pain in everyone's ass and a threat to the very few I do happen to care about. And I think you'll have no trouble at all guessing what I do to those I deem a threat."

I watched him carefully, a little less cocky than I'd been seconds before and much more afraid.

"You said it before," he added, as if the message weren't clear enough. "I'm a ruthless devil."

I was pinned to the wall, palms pressed against it. Tynan's chest brushed mine each time he took a breath. He was taller than me, and yet his face was far too close to mine. I was in absolutely no position to provoke him. Still, my eyes stubbornly remained on his as I dared to whisper, "Ruthless devils don't apologize."

A mix of emotions crossed his face, and I waited for what would come next, but suddenly, Tynan pushed off the wall. Instead of letting his shadows envelope him, he walked away on foot. Wordlessly, he crossed the living room and threw open the front door, leaving me there breathless.

Only then did I sink down the wall and collect myself on the floor. I grabbed my ankle and gritted my teeth, groaning against the pain soaring through it. It wasn't until I looked down at it that my head throbbed. I put a hand to my head, remembering the rock that had sliced through it. My hand came off bright red from the gash.

Tynan was right about everything. I would never give him the satisfaction of knowing that, but he was right. I would be the death of anyone who tried to help me. If I didn't get myself killed first.

"*You* have been bad." Ara kneeled in front of where I sat on the couch, my foot propped up on the table. She'd shown up shortly after Tynan left with a tin of salve that smelled of tea tree and honey. The pain soothed instantly. She wrapped my ankle now in a beige covering, gently tucking the end piece into the folds as if she'd done this a million times.

I stared at the ceiling, half embarrassed, half pissed off. "This isn't necessary. I don't need to be babysat."

"Apparently, you do." Enzo said from his seat in the neighboring chair.

I turned my gaze to him. "You really think I'm a flight risk? With things like *that* out there? I've learned my lesson, trust me."

"I would hope so," Enzo said. "You look like you've just returned from battle."

I sort of felt like it too. "How did you guys know to come back here?" I asked. I'd seen them shadow and fly away from the chalet, but they both reappeared just minutes after Tynan had stormed out of here. Enzo had come first, finding me bracing my ankle on the floor. He lifted me off the ground, supporting my weight at his side while helping me carefully over to the couch. Ara had come in soon after that.

"Ty and I were talking in the palace, and he froze midsentence," Enzo explained. "He whipped around like there was something dangerous at the door, but it was just us in the room. And then he shadowed off without a word. I could tell something was wrong by the look on his face, so when he didn't come back, I figured I'd come here to make sure everything was good. I was about to leave the palace when he barged in. He snapped at me to find a healing salve for you and to cancel dinner tonight. I tracked down Ara for help with the salve."

Ara's hands dropped into her lap with a soft thump of disappointment. "He canceled dinner?"

"He briefly muttered something about there being too much to do to stop for celebrating."

Ara huffed in annoyance. "Cullen was going to be there."

Enzo's jaw tensed.

"I looked magnificent in that dress," she added in a mutter.

Ara left my ankle to come up to my face. She reached out, gently applying the cool ointment on my brow. "It's not deep enough to scar, thankfully. Just deep enough to hurt for a few days," she assured. It throbbed at the touch, but a few seconds later, the burning eased. I breathed out the relief I felt and then looked at her, thanks in my eyes. She smiled kindly in return.

"He warned me not to go out there," I admitted. "I thought he was only trying to scare me."

"He *was* only trying to scare you," Enzo confirmed.

"Well, then how did that just happen?" I asked. "Tynan promised me nothing could find its way here."

Ara and Enzo exchanged a long glance, and it was Ara's shoulders who slackened first. "What did he tell you of the magic surrounding this place?" she asked.

I recited the words carefully. "That if anyone were to happen upon us, all they'd see would be a waterfall or a briar patch."

"Yes." she said. "But the curse..." She paused as if debating saying more. She shook her head at herself and continued anyway. "The curse has spread farther into Valhalla. It's killed our side of the Everwood and has recently hit some of our towns. The facade that Tynan placed around us stood strong, but now looks completely out of place surrounded by all the death. That creature normally wouldn't be found anywhere near here, but lots of things are wandering farther off their path looking for food. It must have gotten curious when it found a random patch of life."

"It took a chance and went exploring," Enzo said. "And it found you."

Dread hit my gut. I was the last thing on Tynan's priority list. Why push my survival to the top when he had an entire kingdom's survival to figure out? I was never going to get out of here before the whole place went down.

"And no one is any closer to finding the Pale Queen?" I asked.

Enzo responded, "She's not here."

Ara shot him a look.

"What? Everyone else is too afraid to say it, so I will. Things are only getting worse. She's dead. Like really dead."

"Enzo," Ara hissed.

"And this drought," he ranted on. "Kingdoms, the drought is going to be what takes me out. The air is as dry as Ambrose's humor."

A thought occurred to me. "But your rain," I directed to Ara, thinking back to the rainstorm she produced to threaten the Dark Queen. "Can't you do something about it with your gift?"

Ara spun the lid back on the can of salve and set it on the table. "I'm afraid not even my rain can help. I can shower this estate and maybe the forest surrounding it, but an entire realm is beyond my reach."

She lifted herself off the ground to sit beside me, resting her head against the cushions, and for a while it was silent. We sat there for some time, each in our own thoughts, until Ara broke it.

"It's things like this, just sitting here with my friends. Doing nothing at all. I think this is what I'll miss the most. This and the feel of rain on my skin."

I tried to imagine it. The feeling of rain on skin being enjoyable. I'd always run through it as quickly as possible, trying to get out of the cold, sticky wet before it soaked my hair and clothes. "What?" Ara asked, and it was then that I realized I'd been making a face at the thought.

"Oh, I just was thinking about it. How that feeling could be something worth missing."

Ara lifted her head after a beat. "What do you mean?"

"I mean, rain on skin? That can't be comfortable."

Ara just blinked at me. "You've never...had rain fall on your skin?"

"No, I have," I said. Ara stared at me until time dragged, and I suddenly worried I'd offended her. The rain was her gift after all. "I mean, you said that's what you're going to miss the most. I'm just trying to imagine what rain must feel like to you for you to enjoy it so much. It's just rain."

"Just ra—," Ara scoffed, leaning up urgently. "Nothing is just anything. Not when you've really experienced it."

"I haven't experienced much of anything to be honest."

"Nothing at all? Haven't you ever felt something so...so...magical that it filled your very soul? Gave you purpose and a will to keep going?"

I pursed my lips, thinking, and came up with absolutely nothing. I finally shook my head at Enzo and Ara's anticipated waiting.

Ara's brows bunched. "Oh..." I could see her thoughts play out on her face, the disappointment and then the astonishment.

"Briar," Ara scolded. "You mean to tell me you've never danced in the summer rain?"

I reluctantly shook my head, as if I'd done something wrong. Ara gave me a sympathetic look. She stood and then reached out her hand for me. "Come here." I put my hand in hers and she pulled me up before I could process what was happening. Ara escorted me out onto the patio, Enzo following.

Ara looked up to the sky, her arms spread out wide, just like in the memory Tynan had shared with me. Her smile was just as excited and bright as it was then. Even though I knew what must be coming, I still asked after a few seconds of her standing like that, "What are you doing?"

"Just wait," Enzo leaned in and whispered to me, a mischievous grin tugging at his lips.

And then the rain shower came. Without easing us into anything, she let it pour and pour on our heads. I screamed, scrunching up my shoulders at the sudden chill. My entire body tried to collapse into itself, as if I could become so small the rain couldn't touch me. Ara laughed, and before I knew it, so did I. She took my hand and spun me, lifting her arm as high as she could reach, allowing me to spin under our bridge of arms like a ballerina. I had to bend a little to make it happen considering how much shorter she was than me. She took my other hand then and moved us in exaggerated ballroom-style circles.

We didn't need music for our dancing. The rain was our music. It pittered and pattered against the wood deck, our laughter filling between it to create the most natural duet there could have been. We twirled and twirled, the burning in my ankle long forgotten. It was somewhere in those silly, overdone movements that I noticed I was grinning widely.

Ara was right. Just because I'd felt the rain before, didn't mean I'd experienced the rain. The sudden coldness of it was short-lived. When I stayed there in it, I found my skin wasn't prickling uncomfortably at the droplets, it was simply reacting to them. Adjusting to the touch, recognizing the sensation, and breathing it in. And my hair wasn't sticking to me, but rather allowing my whole body to be drenched as one in the euphoria.

The rain soaked me, cleansing what I didn't know needed to be cleaned. Freeing me of a weight I didn't realize I was bearing as it all invisibly slid off my body and sank into the wood grain beneath our dancing feet.

Enzo's laughter was a harmonic note that sounded like him—loud and carefree and witty. I glanced at him for what was meant to only be a second, but I stopped dead in my tracks. Ara pranced along the patio, skipping through the rain in a solo ballet, but I stood motionless, staring beyond Enzo's shoulder.

I blinked through the rain at Tynan.

He stood way in the shelter of the trees, watching us with his hands shoved in the pockets of dirt-stained pants. His stare captivated me even from a distance as his eyes glowed, the clouds draped over the sky giving his stars their moment. And then I saw it. He wasn't watching us. He was watching me. There was no clear expression on his face, but his unblinking eyes were trained on me, drinking me in in a way I wasn't sure I liked.

I turned at a sudden shift in the music. Ara doubled over in laughter, the sound like chimes as Enzo walked onto the dance floor and gave a dramatic bow. She curtsied back before taking his offered hand, and they danced and danced in my absence. I grinned uncontrollably, and when I looked back to the trees, Tynan was gone.

# CHAPTER TWENTY-FOUR

Everything was gray. My skin prickled. I couldn't tell if it was because of the temperature or the strangeness of this place. I looked down. I couldn't see myself.

Voices echoed into the corners of the gray expanse—an open, lifeless field lined with skinny trees. The voices spoke, but I saw no one.

"Dispose of him."

There were panicked breaths between the repetitive words "no" and "please".

"Father..." That was Tynan's voice.

The response came slowly. It came audacious and challenging. "Boy?"

"He didn't know what he was doing. Perhaps we give him the chance to make it up to us."

"You do not make suggestions." Steel and stone raked through each word. "Do what I say."

"No." The response came after a few beats of silence. Somehow, the motionless field went still. "This isn't right."

No response came after that, but I could feel it. The look that the stone face must have worn... I felt it as it crawled up my spine and grasped my shoulders. It was agony waiting in that deathly silent response.

Finally, I blinked, and I was somewhere else. Somewhere inside. Dull light, if you could even call it light, barely squeezed through what was meant to be a window. It was only that one window, a small rectangle cut through a stone wall. There was nothing else inside those walls but a beat-up prisoner, his back tied to a wooden stake and his hands bound behind him.

"You look at me when I speak, boy." The voice had been stony before by nature, but it hadn't been truly mad the other times I'd heard it. This time the voice behind the faceless speaker was out for blood. He'd been bruised, or perhaps only his ego had. And he was getting even now, that much was clear.

The bound prisoner looked up, and I gasped.

Tynan's eyes... His bright, beautiful, alive eyes were different. They were simply...sad. Defeated.

The bottom half of his face was covered in blood that poured out of his nose. It was beginning to run down his neck and toward his collarbones. His shirt had been removed, and his stomach shook on the next breath. And that simple breath was what gave it away. This was what fear looked like on the Angel of the Night. Fear and sadness. I looked upon Tynan and saw true sadness in his stars, and it broke me.

Tynan's father walked forward. Apart from seeing that he was tall and dark-haired, I couldn't see anything else of what he looked like. He rolled up the sleeves of a black linen shirt as if he were only walking into his home after a long day of work. His knuckles were painted in fresh blood. Tynan's blood.

He sauntered up to his son, as if just to talk. He stood there, assessing the damage from their last talk. I wished I could see the expression he wore. Wished I knew what he was thinking. Tynan's father abruptly punched his son in the stomach.

I reached out for him, but when my own body didn't move, I understood this was a dream. I wasn't really present and there was nothing I could do for him. No way I could help or change the outcome. Tynan's breath shot out in a pained huff, one leg slipping out from underneath him. He doubled over as far as the ropes would allow.

His father grabbed him before he had any time to recover and forced his weight back up. He grabbed Tynan's face in one hand, so similar to how the Dark Queen had grabbed mine.

"The next time I give you an order, you don't even blink before you submit."

I'd never tried to control a dream before, but I tried now. I willed one of Tynan's hands free from the ropes. Tynan would only need one free hand to get a hold of him, to get himself the rest of the way out of this. I focused my mind, but Tynan's wrists remained bound.

His father planted his fingers over the spot on Tynan's abdomen that just took a hit. All he did was push, and his fingers lit, illuminating Tynan's skin to show a blackness that seeped into him with that touch. Whatever it was, that electrifying smoke seemed to push into Tynan. His stomach lit in the murky smoke, and Tynan bellowed out, the sound soon swallowed with the pain it took to make any noise at all. "If you ever disrespect me again, I'll kill you. I'll kill you in front of your mother. I'll kill you in front of the entire kingdom."

He pushed his fingers inward some more, and whatever dark abilities his father had been gifted burned Tynan from the inside out. Tynan's bright teeth were coated in red as he grunted against the pain.

"Stop!" I cried out, desperate. Tynan's father released his hold, and Tynan's strained frame slumped over, gasping.

I blinked, and I was outside again. My skin was sticky despite the constant chill that coated this place. My cheeks were wet.

I blinked through tears I hadn't noticed were there until the new scene in front of me was clear. Tynan was unbound and clothed again, back in those brown leathers and padded armor everyone in this place wore.

Enzo was there, and Ambrose too, along with a line of other soldiers similarly dressed. They stood in the background, slightly out of focus in my dream. It was Tynan standing before them all, and a kneeling figure at Tynan's feet that took up the focus of the dream. The hunched over soldier—his breaths were raspy, his body shaking, and the top half of his clothes were soaked in dark liquid that pooled slowly from one side of his mouth. Whatever had happened before I joined, he could hardly hold himself up because of it.

"That's enough," the stony voice said from somewhere out of view. Then his voice grew louder for the others watching. "This is the result of insubordinate behavior. Should there be others considering to follow his example, remember what you've seen here today."

In a command directed to Tynan, the voice said, "Now finish him off." Tynan didn't hesitate.

I was going to look away. I expected torture, drawn out and relished the way I'd just seen Tynan go through, but I didn't have time to look away before it was done. It was quick, possibly painless. Tynan crouched to grasp the poor male's head between his hands. He moved in a blur, and I only knew what happened by the harsh click of bones. And that was it.

No one reacted. No one shifted in the background. And somehow, when the stony voice spoke again, I detected a hint of disappointment in his tone. "Your friend."

Tynan twisted his body from where he crouched to look at his father. His tired gaze looked straight through me, and I knew he didn't see me. "What?" he breathed.

"The cocky one," Tynan's father replied from somewhere.

"Remind him who you are. Remind him you have no friends here. Only sergeants."

Tynan turned to the lineup behind him. Enzo stood tall, taller than I knew him to normally stand. His hands were clasped behind him in order, his chin lifted.

The voice of stone dropped. "Do we need another lesson, boy?"

Enzo's eyes flicked to Tynan, only briefly. But in that brief half-second, it was enough. Enough for even me to read the message there. That it was okay. That Enzo understood.

Tynan rose to his knees tiredly and moved toward Enzo before anyone else could read the message shared between them. I never saw what Tynan did, only heard Enzo's breath rush out in an attempt to keep from bellowing. And that noise, it was so vivid. As tangible and real as the ache in my gut when I heard the impact. It was the sound that left Enzo that told me it hadn't been a dream as I jolted upright.

I woke gasping for breath, my chest slick with sweat. A thump sounded from outside my room, a door banging off a wall. Without thinking about the black silk nightgown I wore that Ara had bought for me, I swung my legs off the bed and made for my own door. I jerked it open, my other arm clutching to the doorframe for support. Tynan stood on the opposite end of the hallway, his stance surprisingly matching my own.

His eyes met mine, and in that instant, we both knew.

"What did you see?" He shot out, his breathing panicked and his eyes wide.

My gaze dropped to his stomach, his bare skin on display from a shirtless sleep. Dark smudges stained his stomach and his chest. Scars from another world's magic.

"What was that?" I gasped, even though I knew. Knew by the marks on his skin I'd just seen in the dream. *His* dream. It wasn't a dream at all. It was a memory playing out in a nightmare.

"Briar—" Tynan reached out for me, taking only a single

lopsided step before tripping into the doorframe. I shot backward and slammed my door shut before he could regain himself.

I locked it, uselessly. As if he couldn't bang it down. I stood at the far end of the room, my hand on the doorknob of the exiting door, ready to bolt. Bolt to where? Into the midnight-cloaked woods? Into the teeth of another wandering beast? I stood there, my hand trembling on the doorknob. My breathing was the only noise, loud enough to fill the whole cabin. But Tynan never came. He never kicked the door in or blasted it away into splinters. I waited and waited, but Tynan's wrath never came.

I never found sleep again that night. I eventually heard Tynan's door click shut. The sound of it was chilling. How soft it was. How calm it was. He'd taken a step toward me, had reached out for me. I had hours to replay that in my mind. Hours to come to the conclusion that Tynan hadn't been ready to punish me for what I'd seen. His step had been unstable. He'd stumbled on that single step. And his eyes, his stars had been out of control. Tynan had been a different kind of scared in that moment. The Wingless Night had been afraid of what I'd seen. But why?

It was only because of that realization that I was brave enough to venture into the hall when I heard a quiet clinking of glassware. After dressing in a cream knit sweater and pants that finally fit, I rounded the corner of the kitchen, my footsteps light and unsure. Tynan's back was to me, but I could have sworn he tensed as I entered the room.

When he turned, I took in a deep breath.

I didn't know what to expect the next time I encountered Tynan, but I didn't expect the mug outstretched in his hand. An offering.

"Do you like coffee?" he asked.

"Not the poisoned kind."

Tynan rolled his eyes. I'd expected that even less. "Good thing it's the hazelnut kind."

I took the cup, wondering if I'd be able to decipher the difference in taste if it were tampered with. If I'd have time to see it coming before choking on this so-called coffee.

Tynan leaned back against his side of the counter. I leaned against mine, cup in hand. He watched me. But I didn't taste the coffee, not even to be polite. Tynan smirked and pushed off the counter. He took painfully slow steps toward me, his eyes buried into mine. I hated that I was intimidated, but I'd choke on this coffee before I let him know that. I only allowed my head to move as it lifted to keep eye contact when he got close. Much too close. So close that his chest brushed my fingertips as he inhaled. Close enough for that faintly familiar scent to rush my lungs—balsam at midnight. He reached for the mug clasped in my hands, his fingers coming over mine. It was near electrifying, that touch.

He was doing this on purpose, moving so slowly and blinking so little. That was another thing I hated about Tynan. I hated that when his eyes landed on mine, he had full control. He brought the cup to his lips, and I noted every movement and sound that came with it. I watched his throat move and heard the liquid as it made its way down. He placed the mug back within my fingertips, the faintest tug at his lips.

I hadn't realized I was gripping the countertop with my other hand and holding in a breath that hurt until he turned to walk back to his side. I used that opportunity to collect myself, to hold the mug with two hands if only to preoccupy them.

I cleared my throat. "Busy day?"

"How did you sleep?" He ignored my question, somehow managing to cut right to the chase while also beating around the bush.

I stared into my cup, debating my next words. "That wasn't a dream, was it?"

When I finally dared to look up again, Tynan was watching me intently, and I knew he was wondering the same thing I was. What was the best way to handle this? Did we continue to dance around the topic or be honest with each other here? I took advantage of his hesitation.

"You know for a fact I'm not a spy now. I have nothing to report to anyone."

Tynan nodded so slowly I wasn't sure he was aware of it. "It was not a dream."

"So what was that then?" I dared. "What you... What you did to Enzo."

Tynan's gaze dropped to the floor, and I caught the shift play out on his face, even if he didn't mean for me to. When he looked up again, it was a king's face. And a king's authoritative voice when he spoke. "I've made a new life for myself here. I'd like to keep it that way."

I watched him, unable to tell if that was a threat or a request. And while Tynan waited for my response, I remembered the way he looked at me last night. The way he reached out.

I noted the way he took me in now. He was assessing me in the same way, trying to figure out if I was being defiant or considering his last statement. I was just about to reassure him when Tynan gave in. His shoulders slumped a fraction, and he said with honest eyes, "My sister. Just don't tell my sister what you saw."

And there it was. That's what Tynan was so afraid of. I tilted my head. "Ara doesn't know?" The honesty in his eyes turned to pleading. "How could she not know?"

"Ara is too bright for that place. And for the things that happened in it. She never belonged there. I dedicated a massive amount of time to giving her a normal childhood in a place where those didn't exist. She knows our family was feared, but I sheltered her from the worst of it. I don't want that to change now."

And of all the things I'd seen of his memories, that was the one thing that added up. Of the things Tynan was, he was an older brother first. It might be the only title he actually did care about. "I won't tell Ara," I said, meaning it. "I won't tell anyone."

Tynan leaned against the counter slowly. "How can I be sure of that?" When I didn't answer, he crossed his arms, and his features turned defiant. "If you think I'm going to kiss your ass now just to ensure—"

Just then, the front door of the chalet opened. Tynan's attention fixed over my shoulder, and I turned to see Ambrose entering the living room. He caught sight of us and halted, his entire demeanor changing when he noted it was only the two of us in the kitchen.

"Well?" he said from a distance. He fumbled with his sleeves while he spoke and nodded his chin toward us. "What are you two talking about?"

I looked to Tynan. He had nothing to hide from Ambrose, who had been a part of that dream. They'd worked alongside each other, in the same army. But Tynan only looked to me. I turned back to Ambrose and answered sweetly, "We were just discussing when Ty here would take me to Clive Steeple. This afternoon seems to work well for both of us."

Ambrose squinted at me. He actually squinted his eyes in suspicion, like he smelled the lie but couldn't work out the truth. He finally directed to Tynan, "So, I guess I should cancel the council meeting planned for this afternoon, huh?"

I watched Tynan closely. I almost thought I could make out the faintest hint of a smirk, one he might not have wanted to give. "Yes. Do that for me."

I never turned to look at Ambrose again, but heard the expression he wore clear on his face. "Uh-huh. I'll get right on that." He scented the bullshit, and the anger in his voice was unhidden. He knew we were keeping secrets, and he didn't like it.

Tynan reached for a cabinet and pulled out a second mug. He took the kettle from the stove and poured himself a cup. I only knew Ambrose had gone by the sound of the front door clicking shut again, a bit too loudly. Tynan leaned back against the counter, his gaze returning to mine over the brim of his mug as he sipped.

"Is Ambrose into you or something?"

Tynan nearly choked as he laughed into the mug. "Say that again?"

"It's just... He seems very protective over you. In a way I can't explain."

Tynan wiped his mouth on his wrist. It was so...out of character. So unlike anything I could have imagined him doing when he was all glowing eyes and mysterious shadows. That simple movement was so natural, and yet nothing about Tynan was natural. Nothing about the way he moved or spoke or the way he looked at me was how anyone else could move or speak or look at me. Or maybe it was just me paying too much attention. Because I did. I wasn't oblivious to the effect he had on me. I took in Tynan's every movement as if it were my own. I didn't just see Tynan when I looked at him. I assessed him. I admired. I feared him. I practically breathed him in, and despite all the mistakes I'd made since coming here, I couldn't help but make this one too.

"What?" he said in a light tone. "Two males can't have a close bond without being into each other?" He smiled wider, *both* dimples popping out. "There's such a long history between the two of us."

"Clearly," I replied, and Tynan frowned at that. I'd seen too much. I knew the very things he wanted to keep hidden.

"There is a lot to be protective over, is all I mean."

"I never thought you to be the sentimental type."

"And what do you think of me now?" His expression was serious, his dimples hidden. The question was genuine.

I tapped my mug as I considered how stupid I must be for the response that waited on the tip of my tongue. I let it slide off anyway. "I don't know, Ty. I guess I think you must be grateful." Tynan's features deepened in curiosity as I set my mug on the counter and pushed myself away from it. I aimed for my room, twisting my head so that he could see the mischief on my face as I said, "Grateful that you could have worse asses to kiss around here."

And despite everything, when I turned my head away from him, I was smiling.

# CHAPTER TWENTY-FIVE

I made it down the hall and a few steps away from my bedroom door before a cloud formed in front of it, stopping me from reaching for the doorknob. Tynan appeared in that cloud with a devilish grin before closing the gap between us in one stride.

The ground pulled out from underneath me like a rug. My hands shot out, palms landing on his chest. His arm came around my middle too confidently. Balsam and midnight filled my nose as I begrudgingly leaned into him for support. The tug of his smile was so loud I didn't have to see it to know it still rested on his face.

Charming. Why did they all have to be so damn charming?

Our feet settled on the ground just moments after taking off. I pushed away from him before the clouds departed and stepped into a clearing in another part of the forest. I glared at him. He smirked cunningly.

"What the hell?"

Tynan put his hands on my shoulders and turned me.

A church-like building rested at the far end of the clearing, a steeple basking in the trickling sunlight. "It seems my afternoon was cleared," he said at my ear.

It appeared as any normal church would, but Darya said these scholars were older than she was. "This is Clive Steeple?" It was impossible the building could still be standing in such pristine condition. And yet I knew by the goosebumps along my arms that the magic holding its stones together was old and strong. It stood with pride, importance radiating from across the field.

"The very one."

I left Tynan, my feet bringing me closer and closer to the thing I'd been chasing all these long months, one silent step at a time.

I swiftly made it up the handful of steps and reached for the handle, but I stopped short, my fingers retreating in on themselves. Behind this door was the answer—hopefully—to how I could return to everything that was normal to me. *So go in*, I shouted at myself. But still...I didn't reach for the handle.

Tynan stretched his arm ahead of mine and pulled open the door. I blinked up at him, his eyes sparkling down at me with a tense expression I couldn't read. I ignored the slowly swirling stars there, the easy distraction, and took the first step inside.

I was expecting to be blown away, by what, I wasn't sure. Darya had made Clive Steeple sound like a grand historical library of some sort. But...it wasn't.

Warm, dull light from the late-afternoon sun spilled through tall stained-glass windows. Rows of empty seats led up to a bare, unimpressive altar at the very back. A few cloaked figures sat in front of lit candles, their heads bowed and hands clasped in prayer. But nothing stood before them. Whatever they prayed to—whoever they prayed to—didn't need an overexaggerated statue or shrine.

But as far as history books full of long-kept secrets, there were none in sight. It was simply a quiet church on a lazy afternoon.

A gray-haired scholar with faint wrinkles around his eyes rushed from behind the desk to greet Tynan. With his head bowed deeply, he took one of Tynan's hands in both of his. He wore a set of brown robes held together by a cord, the sleeves hanging delicately off his wrists. I struggled not to stare. He was the oldest looking thing I'd seen in Elysian so far. And yet between the tiredness in his face and the gray in his hair, his movements and posture were still youthful.

"Your Majesty." The scholar raised his head, tired eyes filling with awe. "You're back."

The words echoed in the cathedral-like room.

"Scholar." Tynan didn't comment on being away. "I was hoping you could help me with an urgent matter."

The scholar eyed me at his side, taking a small sniff of the air, and then nodded. "The girl. Yes, we've long been expecting you. Darya's letter came months ago."

Darya. She must have lost her mind when she learned what happened.

"Do you think you might have what we need?" Tynan asked.

The scholar's attention fixed on me and he nodded slowly. "I think I know where to start." He turned his body to face a bare wall, and waved his hand. In response, the wall shifted to the side with a stony, ancient grind. A spiral staircase curved downward like a snake and lamps lit the way into the depths.

"For the answers you're seeking, we must start at the very beginning. In the creation times." The scholar took a step down, his shoes clicking on the stone staircase. But I didn't move, my mind flashing back to the last time I took a step down a darkened staircase. Tynan's elbow brushed past mine and brought me back to attention as he stepped ahead of me. When I didn't follow, he paused at the doorway.

I knew I wasn't in the Garden's palace, knew I was somewhere deep in the Everwood, but I still struggled to bring myself back to the present, to reality. Suddenly, I could *feel* the Dark Queen's presence here. It still coated the air from her visit just hours ago, staining everything that was good about this place. I couldn't move my feet, couldn't hide the slight shake that found its way to my arms.

*Say the word, and we'll leave. We can try again another day.*

I snapped my eyes to his, and that was it. My fear and my anger lost their strength at those words. A sense of calm trickled through my chest, strengthening with each inhale.

This was the Tynan I'd gotten to know in the dungeon. That voice of comfort in my head when I needed it the most. I closed my eyes and took a steadying breath in. I was okay. This darkness was different. It wasn't going to hurt me. When I opened my eyes again, it was to take the first step toward answers. Toward a fresh start.

The staircase twisted into a never-ending descent, diving deeper into what was undoubtedly underground. The lamps were few and far apart, and with my weak human eyesight, I had to take slower, more careful steps. I placed a hand on the clay wall to help guide each footstep. The old scholar was gaining distance between us, and I knew I was holding Tynan up behind me. But the deeper we went, the fewer the lights appeared, and the slower I stepped.

Tynan came to my side, and his fingers caught in mine.

I snapped my head up. The amethyst in his eyes glowed in the dark, like that cave monster I knew he wasn't. "What are you doing?" I whispered sharply at him.

"Relax. If you keep falling around here, the whole kingdom is going to run out of salve." His white teeth flashed in the damp, dim basement. Charming. So damn charming.

I glared accusingly at him, and in doing so, missed my step. My toe touched the edge, and I stumbled, like an idiot, into his waiting arm. When I righted myself, he was grinning. Like he'd expected the fall. A flicker lit inside me, but I glared in front of me, shrugging the flame and his arrogance away.

Finally, we hit the last step. A room expanded at the bottom, and I understood why we'd been led so far underground. Textbooks slept inside shelves of earth. Up, up, up they went until the rows were so high we couldn't see them anymore.

There were no ladders, no possible way to reach some of the books, but the scholar lifted a robed arm over his head like he'd grow and reach what was at the unseen top. Nothing happened.

For a few uncomfortable moments, we just watched that waiting hand. Nothing happened for a long time, but then...a book appeared. From the top, wherever it lay, a book gracefully floated down like a dust speck into his waiting fingertips.

A way to protect their secrets, I realized. Only the oldest, most trusted beings in Elysian had access to these words, just as Darya had said.

More floated down, all leather-bound replicas of the first. One by one, the scholar tucked the desired books under his arms. As I watched the growing stack, it registered that my hand was still in Tynan's. I jerked my fingers loose. I tried not to look directly at him, at the amused grin that radiated off his stupid, perfectly shaped face.

The scholar led us to a circular, gray study table and let the books spill out onto the surface. Every inch of table was covered in books, each one thicker than the last. The scholar readjusted an unlit lamp to shine over the table and then waved a hand gently over it. A spark lit inside it, brightening the area.

"Elysian owns only one entrance point. One that is inaccessible to humankind. That is supposed to be through the sky, where the Creator's angels used to visit. But—you did not come through the sky. If there is another way into Elysian we have not known about all this time, there may just be a way out we haven't discovered either. Your answer may be difficult to find, but you will find it in the beginning."

The beginning, as it turned out, consisted of six books—all three to five hundred pages.

"Whoa," Tynan said.

"This is all on the creation?" I asked, dumbfounded.

"Most of it, yes," the scholar responded. "I retrieved some additional text I thought might be useful. Darya said in her letter that you arrived from the ocean. First, we must discover how you came to arrive there in the first place. I think the answer on how you might leave would soon follow."

"Alright." Tynan slammed a hand on one of the books and pulled it toward him as he took a seat. "I guess read until something jumps out at you."

And that we did. With no windows to see through, we turned pages until I could only assume the light outside had begun to fade. We read until both our mortal and immortal necks ached.

No one spoke for hours, the sound of pages flipping and the occasional deep sigh the only noise. My eyes were dry from staring at text after text, and my neck burned. Eventually, one scholar was switched out for another, even though Tynan insisted they didn't need to stay and help. When one showed up anyway, he didn't send them away.

The reading was anything but dull. To me, this place was fiction. The workings of the beginning were fascinating, like a math equation I would never solve, no matter how long I studied it. One book in my stack included a passage I recognized immediately, and my heart pounded. It was the most popular line in the most famous book from my own world. *In the beginning God created the heavens and the earth. And the earth was without form, and void; and darkness was upon the face of the deep.*

Why would there be a passage from the Bible of my world in the library of another? I scanned the following lines, hoping to find some tie between the two worlds. Anything that would explain how I could have wound up in a world meant to be unfound, but I only came to a dead end. The next pages oddly switched directions and went into an in-depth history of the first Divine—the fire-gifted one—taking its first breath.

At one point, I read so much that I couldn't remember what I had just read. I wasn't retaining the information anymore. The last thing I remembered reading was information on the closed east end of the Garden of Eden back in my world. The entrance was guarded by the Archangel Uriel, with a flaming sword to ward off explorers. The text flip-flopped between both worlds, but there was no mention of the two pieces of land being linked, or where Elysian was located in relation to mine.

One minute I was reading, and the next I was opening my eyes again. My head rested on a closed book, the one I was supposed to be reading stretched out in front of me. I popped my head up.

Tynan and the newest scholar watched me with half-bored faces. They glanced at each other. "Humans," Tynan commented, and they both lowered their heads back to their reading. I ignored them both and opened the book I had been using as a pillow.

It was Tynan who later broke the silence. "Got it." The old scholar nearly jumped in his seat.

"Here." He pointed as he read. "*And so, it has been spoken that Elysian is a special land. That of what not a human may touch. As Eden was destroyed by man, man can never touch this new soil. This soil was meant for God's other creations and beasts. May they come only by design and go as they choose, but never to return to paradise again. And no human being to have the ability to set foot upon it. So it will be this way until the Creator calls Uriel from his post, and all worlds collapse as we know it.*"

He pushed the book to me so I could read it for myself. While I did so he pulled another open book to him and began reading.

"*Once a creature is banished or has left Elysian, reentrance would be lost forever, with the exception of the ruler of all rulers and those who travel the skies.*"

"Banished?" I asked, reaching for that book too.

The scholar hastily reached for a book to his left, hovered a hand over it until the book flipped to the desired page by itself, and then pushed it to me as well. "There is a stone archway in Empyrean," he explained while I examined a picture of that exact archway. "Bristol Gate. There have been...things...that have been sent away through the Bristol Gate. Things that have grown much too evil to remain in Elysian. Or sometimes things grow bored of this place and seek a new land. But this gate is a one-way exit. Those banished things never come back."

I blinked at Tynan. "You knew the whole time about a way out?"

He shook his head, frustrated. "Bristol Gate isn't *your* way out. We don't know where those banished things go. We just know that they go."

"Ruler of all rulers," I repeated while scanning the text for myself. "And those who travel the skies."

"The text is vague," the scholar supplied. "But we assume the book is referring to the Creator. Those who travel the skies would be his favorite." The scholar looked to Tynan and gave a playful wink. "His angels."

"The only angels who are here now didn't come by choice," Tynan said, implying only the fallen wandered here. "The others haven't bothered with Elysian since the Creator originally left this world. Neither have been seen in millenniums."

"So what does this mean?" I asked.

"It means," Tynan stated. "It truly is impossible for you to be here."

I rolled my eyes and fell back into my seat. "And yet here I am."

Tynan dragged a hand through his shaggy hair in either frustration or exhaustion. A pang of guilt hit me.

"I wonder—" the scholar started and then stopped, staring at the table in deep thought.

"What?" I pushed.

"The creation of witches is somewhat new," he pondered.

"What do you mean...the creation of witches?" I asked.

"Witches weren't born into creation, not in this land anyway, until some hundreds of years ago. With so much crossbreeding, a new species was born, and with that, a different source of power. Their power comes from a mixture of Elysian's natural elements and the fires of Hell. It was around the same time things like hellhounds suddenly found their way here. A coincidence, maybe, but one can't be sure."

"I'm not following," I said.

"It could be possible that with this new magic, witches found a way to summon things from other worlds. Things that don't belong. Perhaps someone has discovered new magic in Elysian and has kept these advancements to themselves."

"Who would do that? Why would someone bother summoning me here?"

Tynan's eyes dropped to my locket. "Where did you get that?"

"You know where I got it," I snapped, suddenly on edge.

"And have you or your mother ever...practiced?"

The scholar cleared his throat and shifted uncomfortably.

"Are you calling me a witch?"

"You did emit an impressive fire for a normal human girl."

The scholar raised his eyebrows with this new knowledge, full attention on me.

"I'm not a witch," I shot back. "That's insane."

"So were those flames."

"My mother is very human, and my father isn't anything more than a piece of shit. I'm not a fucking witch." It came out the same way the fire had—unpremeditated and *hot*. A heat rushed to my cheeks, but there was nothing supernatural about it. Tynan's lips peeled back for half a second, almost as if he were pleased by my outburst, but he wisely let it fade.

"Maybe she is indeed human," the scholar offered, attempting to gain control over the direction of this conversation. "Maybe not. There has to be some explanation for this fire you speak of."

"Let's forget about how I got here for a second and the one time any fire might have been involved. So what if it's said to be impossible? I'm here, and all I care about is how to get back." I stared at the drawing of the stony archway and at the odd symbols etched into each stone. "What are those symbols?"

It was the scholar who answered. "An ancient language no longer used. Their meaning is lost to even us today."

It didn't matter what the symbols meant. "I have a theory," I said. They both waited. "Where I'm from, we have fairy tales. Myths and legends we imagine up and create movies and books about. Like mermaids and ogres and other creatures that don't exist. Except here, they do. All of them and more. Every single one of my world's make-believe stories is living and breathing in Elysian. What if when things go through the gate in Elysian, they wind up on the other side where I live? What if the glimpses of mythical creatures humans have claimed to see...are actually what you've sent to us?"

Tynan looked to the scholar, who rubbed his chin at the thought, nodding to himself. "It's a solid theory," the scholar said.

"Can we get those symbols translated?" Tynan asked him.

"It would take time. Months to even track someone old enough to have had the training. Those symbols are older than all the living scholars today."

"We don't have time." I stood from my seat, cutting the conversation short. "The gate is the answer, I know it."

Tynan shook his head. "It's a theory, not a proven fact. If we send you through, you could wind up anywhere."

"The scholar said it himself. It's a solid theory and the only one we've got."

"For all we know, the gate could be sending those banished creatures straight to Hell."

My eyes grew wide. "You'd really send someone through if you thought there was a chance it could be to Hell?"

Tynan didn't bat an eye and his calm demeanor to my urgency made me itch.

"The things we send away don't get sent away for no reason, Briar."

I shoved the thought away, along with the sound of my name on his tongue and how it sounded like it belonged there.

"I have a target on my back, and this world is a dying one. My fate here is sealed either way. I'm willing to risk it."

"You'll have to excuse her, scholar." Tynan stood, tapping his temple. "All those knocks to her head have gotten to her." I squinted my eyes at the same time he did.

"What do you even care where it sends me? What say do you have over anything I do?"

The scholar stood too, already inching away as he spoke. "Let me know if you'll be needing anything else, my king."

"Wait," Tynan said. The scholar reluctantly turned back to us, one hundred more years aging him on the spot. "Actually, I do need just one more thing."

"Anything." The scholar sent me a cautious look, practically begging me not to start yelling at him too.

"Has anyone else been here asking the same things we have?"

A wary look crossed the scholar's face. "I cannot say, my king."

"Xosha won't be a queen for much longer. It's of the greatest importance that I know what she came here to learn."

"My sincerest apologies. You know I truly cannot say even if I wanted to."

Tynan nodded, swallowing his irritation. "Thank you for your time. We'll show ourselves out." The scholar bowed and huddled over the books, gathering them in his arms to send them away and mark them accounted for.

To me, Tynan explained, "The scholars are bound to secrecy on the comings and goings of others. The books, and who visit them, are Elysian's greatest kept secrets." His features were hard, his eyes narrowing on me, as if I were a problem. I wanted to shrink back and stand tall all at once.

"Let's go." Tynan turned for the stairs, not bothering to wait for me this time.

Clive Steeple was built with invisible wards etched into its construction to prevent anyone from entering without going through the front doors first, including the King of Valhalla himself. So we had to make the long, silent trek back up the spiral stairs on foot.

Despite his mood, Tynan stayed close enough to steady me each time my foot caught on a step, but he didn't take my hand again. And when we stepped into the fresh air of the night, he pulled me into him without warning, and we shadow stepped back to the front porch of his cabin. The sky was dark, well past dinner time. I retreated from his touch and stormed off without a glance in his direction.

He'd accused me of being a witch. I knew exactly where I came from, and it wasn't from any source of magic. I came from broken homes with broken dishes and plenty of other broken things. My father abused me, my mother walked out on me, and even my own brother—my best friend for most of my life—abandoned me without so much as a goodbye. If I had any magic in me, I would have figured it out by now.

But there was the fire I'd used to burn a hellhound to ashes. I still had no answer for that. I had never done anything like that before, and it wasn't something I could summon again, even if I tried. And I had tried. Not just in my free moments in my guest room, but again when I was out shopping with Ara and Enzo. They'd been bickering over which store they'd stop at next, and my eyes had caught on a streetlamp, the interiors unlit with the sky full of daylight. I'd focused on it, trying to light the flame with a stare, with an inconspicuous flick of a finger. But once again, nothing happened. So the fire couldn't have come from me. It had to have been something else using me as a pawn.

I was so mad that if I could produce any flames, I would now. I was so sick of following the lead of someone else, exhausted of the trickery and the lies disguised as charm. I had been physically abused, verbally lashed out at, lied to, and tricked. I was done with it. I was done with all of this.

I whipped around to tell Tynan just that, swinging my body around to meet his glare from where I'd left him on the porch. But he wasn't where I left him. Instead, he came to an abrupt stop, narrowly avoiding colliding into me.

"I'm sorry." His words flew out and stopped me cold. I held his stare, searching for the sarcasm. There wasn't any to find. "I didn't mean for it to sound as though you need my permission or approval. The decision is yours, not mine."

I frowned up at him. "You're right, it is mine."

"I know that." He seemed to be struggling with himself, his next words forced. "I'll take you to Bristol Gate, as promised."

I blinked. "You will?"

He nodded slowly, like he was still thinking things through.

"Okay." I didn't know what else to say. I had been so prepared to tell him off, and he'd just taken every reason I had to do so away.

"I can't be away from Valhalla right now. Xosha isn't stupid. She knew we'd head to Clive Steeple, and she very well may have come to the same conclusion you have about Empyrean. There isn't room to fall into another trap or get involved in another scheme. I can send Ara with you if you can't wait, but..." He scratched behind his head, as if he knew it sounded like he was making excuses. "Zafar isn't the only treacherous scumbag out there looking to get paid. If you can wait for me until this war is over, I can guarantee you'll get there safely."

"In order to make a promise like that, you'd have to be pretty confident about the outcome." I said in a softer tone.

His voice lifted to a strong, sure volume I wasn't capable of reaching. A voice that didn't quite meet his eyes. "I am."

Despite everything, I couldn't help but have a fondness for Tynan. He raised such rare emotions in me, even though I *knew* better. He was so damn good at putting on such a convincing front, but he kept forgetting that I knew things about him that possibly only three others in existence knew. Or maybe he hadn't forgotten and just hoped I had. But I hadn't. I couldn't. He may not want to acknowledge it, but it was because of that front-row seat into his mind that I knew his deepest secrets. Yes, he was capable of terrible power beyond my comprehension. Yes, he was a monster. He was dangerous, arrogant, and unpredictable.

But he loved. He quite possibly loved his sister more than anyone could imagine. He loved his friends, and his friends were incredibly loyal to him in return. And he loved his kingdom. Though I hadn't seen him in action, I'd witnessed him behind the scenes. He was a diligent king who cared more about his subjects' well-being than he did his own mental health—putting aside even a single day of rest to learn what the kingdom's immediate needs were. He barely returned to the chalet after a full day of work so that he could stay up throughout the night to push the winds in hope of balance. To try. For Valhalla. For all of Elysian. And to me... He was no one to me, but for weeks we had been all the other had. And instead of abandoning me at the first breath of freedom, he was now pushing aside some of that responsibility to help me too.

Escape had been in question for so long. I don't think he was prepared for the pressure that came with it when it was finally a reality. It was too much for one to bear, even a king. Tensions were piling higher and higher. Could I really blame him for all that stress affecting his mood?

And everyone else I'd met along the way... What would happen to them? To Ara, Enzo, and Ambrose. To Darya, Remi, Mavi, and Bly. To all of these living, breathing, *good* creatures.

"Do you think the Pale Queen will return after it's all over?"

His expression turned sullen. The crease between his brows returned as he looked away. "She has to," he said.

My heart panged for him. For everyone here. If she didn't, it didn't matter if they were successful in the coming war.

"How do you plan to stop the Dark Queen?" I asked, not much caring for the secrets Ambrose had worked so hard to keep from me. I would be gone soon enough. Tynan knew it too.

"We'll surround her. We'll come at her with more numbers than she has. She can only turn so many to ash at once."

Chills spread across my skin. In other words, many would have to die first.

We were quiet for several moments as our minds worked separately.

The Dark Queen was a monster. There were stories in my world of what we thought monsters looked like. We were wrong. A true monster was willing to kill off an entire population if it meant even a chance of bending the laws of the land. She would fight, even if it was only her left standing in a land of death and ruins. A queen of nothing and no one.

"We have to stop her," I said. He tilted his head. "I mean, not we. But someone has to stop her."

His jaw clenched. "We will," he said. "And then we're going to get you home."

# CHAPTER TWENTY-SIX

A few days passed, each growing slower than the last. The supervision and company that had been promised dwindled. Someone made an appearance each day, though only for a few minutes at a time before they had to be back in a sparring ring or busy on top-secret business of some sort.

Ambrose's distaste for me grew more apparent as the days went by. Not that he ever spoke all that much, mostly only when Enzo began to say too much. And then I realized that's exactly why he showed up at all, to gatekeep conversations.

It wasn't just me who Ambrose was short-tempered with. Tensions in the cabin rose beyond the vaulted ceilings. Ambrose was snapping on all of us, instead of solely focusing his hate on me. Enzo and Ara bickered more than what seemed normal, less teasing and more bite in their tones. And Tynan's presence grew rarer altogether as he spent his days at the palace and his nights in the woods, sending the winds as far as they would go. Though from a conversation I overheard between Ara and Enzo, it was too late for that. Tynan never stopped trying anyway.

Sometimes I'd hear him shuffle into the cabin in the early

morning hours, and sometimes I wouldn't hear him come in at all. The one time I did catch him in the kitchen just a few minutes after I was waking for the day, he passed me a cup of coffee, and then rushed out before I could ask any questions, but not before I could spot the darkening circles under his eyes and noticed the clothes he wore.

The last time I'd seen him, he'd worn a cotton shirt as black as his hair that hugged him in a way that displayed every dangerous and perfect line on his body. The sleeves were pushed up to his elbows, the top two buttons left undone to show off a smooth, tanned chest and neatly tucked into black dress pants, a belt bringing too much attention to his hip area. The amethyst in his eyes was striking in those clothes. But now he wore black leathers and fingerless gloves and tall boots. Leftover smudges on his knuckles he didn't have the time to clean off. Though no one confirmed it, Tynan was no longer getting a kingdom back in order. He was preparing soldiers.

Ara did find the time to trim off the damaged ends of my hair, but as war quickly approached, so did my seclusion, and worrying thoughts had room to flood in.

Whenever they did move in, how long would I be left alone? Would the battle take hours? Days? A week? What if no one returned at all, and I was trapped inside the chalet, the dying land finding me in even a place the Dark Queen couldn't? Would I be able to find my way to Bristol Gate on my own?

So far, food had arrived magically on the dining table at around the same time every day. But tonight, I had to find something other than reading to keep my thoughts at bay.

I wandered into the walk-in pantry for the first time. I wasn't a cook, never had been. Any cooking had been done by Liam when I was too young to do it for myself, and afterward, I was too tired after working double shifts to cook anything without instructions on a box. Usually, I wound up eating discounted food from the restaurant. I had no clue what I was doing in the kitchen, but I suddenly found myself with time to fill. I didn't expect to get it right on the first try, but if there was ever a time to teach myself something new, it was now.

The shelves were stocked with everything I needed to make anything I wanted, and the back of the pantry held a type of covered cooler that held perishable items. I filtered through the contents of the cooler and decided I had what I needed to make a pizza. I found the ingredients for the toppings and even a container of premade dough.

I spread out some flour on the bare countertop, flipped on the oven dial, and plopped the dough on the counter, shaping it with my knuckles into a perfect circle and folding the sides up to make the crust.

A breeze rustled behind my ear, so gently I almost didn't pay it any mind. But I turned, finding several fern-colored leaves swirling in the air, almost too quickly for the human eye to catch.

"There you are." The leaves slowed when I noticed them. They moved in collectively and took the shape of a small, leafy female standing not even a foot high. Her bare legs and slender torso were brown as an oak tree, with fern-colored leaves merging into her body that covered any revealing areas. Green, veiny vines wrapped around her arms. Her hair was dingy, somewhere between brown and green. She bristled at my wrists, shooing me away.

"You can have the night off. I've got this." But the small woodland fairy ignored me, and instead broke apart to swirl around my hands and tickle my wrists. I gave a gentle brush at the air, insisting.

When I was done with the dough, I placed it on a pan and slid it on the top rack of the oven. The leaves danced around my waist, and I remembered I'd forgotten the sauce. Sauce and toppings should have gone on it *before* it went in the oven. I think.

I rummaged around the pantry again until I found a stack of tomatoes, some basil, and other spices I thought might work well together, and a bowl to mix it all in. When I returned to the counter, the leaves had formed into the figure again, and she'd moved on to my toppings. The mushrooms had been cut and the cheese shredded that fast.

"Stop!" The dryad startled for half a second, splitting apart into individual leaves, but then shifted back into formation, continuing with her work. I set my supplies on the counter and swatted at the air. "I *want* to do it myself."

"What are you doing?" I whirled to find a disheveled Tynan in the doorway. "Why are you yelling at my dryad?" The skin under his eyes were even darker than when I'd last seen him, the dirt on his knuckles now matching the smudges along his face.

"I wasn't yelling at her. I'm trying to make a pizza, and she won't stop helping."

He raised his chin slightly in the air, eyebrows raising. "A what?"

"Pizza. I'm trying to make homemade pizza."

"Who?"

"Excuse me?"

"Never mind," he decided. "You're mad because someone is trying to help you?"

I bent to pick up a fallen tomato and set it back on the counter. Tynan answered before I could, a crossness dripping from every word. "Never mind again. That sounds like you."

An irritation of my own washed over me. "What the actual fuck is your problem?" I shot just as he turned to leave.

The stars in his eyes swirled, his honey voice dipping to a dangerous level. "Careful, Briar, or you might show off a little personality there."

I laughed, fuming. "Fine. She can make the damn pizza if it makes everyone so happy." The timer on the oven went off. I closed my eyes in frustration. I'd put the dough in before it was even done preheating. I turned to take the pan out of the oven, but stopped short to see that the dryad was now working on mashing the tomatoes for me. I clenched my teeth.

"When all the work is done of course."

My body froze, teeth bared, as I fought the instinct I'd fought my whole life. But Elysian was changing me. I thought it had been Zafar who challenged me and brought out something I'd never known. But it wasn't him or anyone else here. It was this place.

"Don't act like you know my work ethic. You're the one trying to convince me to let someone else do the work for me."

He gestured to the dryad, hard at work on my sauce. "You're insulting her by not letting her help. She *likes* it. By telling her to stop, you're taking away her purpose."

"Says the one sitting on his ass getting waited on hand and foot." The timer was still going off, and I became more flustered with each beep.

"Speaking of ass, you have some flour on yours."

Heat rushed to my face. I growled out my frustration, not able to compose myself with everything going on at once, and I reached into the oven for the pan without a mitt. The heat scorched my skin and I yelled out in pain, dropping the pan and sending it clattering to the floor.

I never actually saw Tynan move, only caught a blur that was gone in the next blink. He was in the doorframe, and then he was in front of me, taking my hand in his. He assessed the damage and pulled my body with his over to the sink, flipping the faucet on and holding my pink fingers under the water. They burned with relief, the water cooling my insides too, and I suddenly felt so stupid. Like the simple-minded human I was.

"Why would you do that?" He kept his eyes on my palm, flexing the fingers back so that the water ran over each of them.

I bit my lip and turned my head away. "I wasn't thinking," I muttered.

He turned the sink off and examined my bright pink hand, blisters already forming on the palms of each finger. He reached for a dish towel and gently patted the area dry. Every brush of his skin on mine was intensified, my senses on high alert, and not just because of the burning pulse in my fingertips. I accidentally made eye contact, and his gaze held mine.

*Does it hurt?*

I wanted to answer him, but pride, and stubbornness, and so much frustration got in the way. I was so angry. Angry that I wasn't able to control such big emotions that I allowed others to pull out of me so often. Angry for letting Zafar get close enough to me that he was able to turn his back on me. Angry for choosing the wrong portal to walk through in the first place.

"I can't do this." I pulled my hand back.

A single muscle shifted and changed his expression from concern to confusion. "Do what?"

"I'm leaving. I've been patient long enough, and I can't do it anymore."

I left Tynan, and the kitchen, and the mess behind.

"Wait, *now*?" Tynan followed me down the hall, a surprising alarm filling his voice. He was in front of me too quickly, blocking the path to my door.

"Tynan." The start of a headache crept on, and I was suddenly very tired and not hungry at all. "Move out of my way."

"You can't be serious."

"I'm dead serious. Move."

His eyes scanned my face and the seriousness he found there. "Look, we're all tired. Let's just calm down for a second."

"Tynan," I said sharply. "*Move.*"

His body moved to the side as if commanded, though his face filled with near grief in doing so. I didn't hesitate to walk right by him and into my room, my fingers grabbing hold of the door, ready to close it behind me.

"Wait, wait." Tynan took a single step forward, his voice leveling out. "Okay, I'll go with you."

I whirled on him. "No." This time, the word didn't feel satisfying. "I don't need you. I don't want you." The words froze him. "Send Ara with me tomorrow, or don't. I don't care. I'm leaving tomorrow for that gate. I'm getting the hell out of here."

I didn't give Tynan the chance to unfreeze himself before letting the door end the conversation between us.

# CHAPTER TWENTY-SEVEN

It was the ass comment that had done it. Anger wasn't an emotion I was unfamiliar feeling, but one I was very much unfamiliar with expressing. I was so used to keeping it contained that I didn't know what to do with it once it reached the surface, but I knew this wasn't it. I knew it as soon as the lock to the door sounded.

I squeezed my eyes shut in frustration. As much as I had been through, Elysian had been through worse. Tynan had been through worse. And I had been so unfair to think of only my needs and expect him to put his aside, all for the return to a home that had never been kind to me.

Minutes passed while I built the courage. I ventured into the hall and found it and the kitchen to be empty. He didn't come when I knocked on his bedroom door either. I tried outside, hoping he hadn't shadowed himself away by now. The stars were plentiful, a countless array of them dusting the night-veiled sky. Had it not been for the attention they demanded, I never would have noticed him on the rooftop.

"What are you doing?" I called up.

His chin was lifted to the sky, and he didn't look at me as he said, "Thinking."

"Not eavesdropping this time?"

He lowered his gaze then and despite knowing exactly what was coming, I sucked in a breath at the intensity of the amethyst that glowed back at me.

"Not this time."

"How did you even get up there?"

One moment I was standing alone on the ground, the next his arms were around me, and in a gust of wind and fog, I was on the roof with him. I gasped several seconds too late and gripped his biceps tightly. His nose was a mere inch from mine, those eyes holding me in place. His arms slid away, quicker than I would have liked, and he returned to his spot on the roof, a wine bottle sitting there with several gulps missing from the top. I took careful steps and sat next to him, making sure there was a little distance between us.

"So what are you thinking about?" I asked, praying he couldn't hear the speed of my heart with those inhuman ears of his.

His voice was hollow. "Everything."

I readied the words on my tongue, guilt cloaking me like one of his shadows. But I faced him, made sure the words came out steady and accountable and said, "I'm sorry. I've never...used my voice before. I'm learning how to now. I might not always get it right, but I'm trying. And I'll do better."

A beat of no response and then, "There are many apologies I'm waiting on." Only a hint of softness reached his face. "Yours isn't one of them."

I breathed in the cold night, feeling better already now that I'd said the words, no matter how little they were. Even the smallest of tension between us weighed heavy.

Following Tynan's gaze, I'd never seen more stars in my life. They stretched over our heads like an ocean of constellations. And

Tynan, oddly, looked even more striking in the darkness that wrapped us. I couldn't help but watch him, to take in the sort of dark beauty he held. He was art painted to perfection, the night sky reaching for him like a long-lost friend.

Tynan must have felt my gaze, because when he finally looked at me again, the movement was hesitant. His eyes shocked me. The cobalt coloring that was more prominent in the daytime was gone, swallowed whole by the purple hues. They were pained, so heavy, as if he held the weight of the entire universe in those eyes. The white and gold flecks shifted around their center, like the stars above.

And then it clicked. An Angel of the Night, whose eyes held the reflection of the very universe itself. I tilted my head, wonder filling me. "What does son of Alaric, the Once Most Powerful, mean? Who are you really?"

Tynan tensed at the title, but then reached for the bottle and took a long swig, like he knew this question was coming. "My father was one of the most powerful Dark Angels in existence. I was his mutant son and greatest disappointment. Now, I'm just a fallen, and he's only a myth."

I shook my head, not buying it, and pursed my lips. "No lying on the roof. Those are the rules."

The words took him by surprise, and just a hint of a curious smile lifted, a swirl of a star brightened, and then dulled.

He didn't answer me right away, and for a moment, I thought he wouldn't. But then he filled his lungs with a breath of night air and spoke with a heavy, tired voice.

"The Dark Angels are a particularly nastier strain of our breed. They were made and used solely for the purpose of the Archangels' dark-ops team—a team of celestials tasked with overseeing the supernatural crimes of other planet's inhabitants. They mostly hunt demons running loose in realms they shouldn't. Alaric was made with a cruelness imbedded so deep within him that I don't think it can be unwound. He was stronger, more brutal than most, and because of that, he was placed at the head of his legion. Alaric played his role well for a time, but then he started taking things into his own hands. Started making friends with the things he was meant to hunt.

"The Archangels took notice, and they warned him. But he'd driven himself mad with a hunger for power. Instead of falling back in line, he organized a small overthrow. There weren't many stupid enough to try it. Needless to say, it didn't go according to plan for him. He was stripped of his title, his wings, his grace massively weakened. And then he was banished to another land altogether. Now he's weak and exiled to remain where the homeless supernatural go, and he's pissed about it, to say the least."

"Where was he sent?"

"Purgatory. An in-between place one can only leave once their soul cleanses. But a Dark Angel's soul isn't one meant to be purified. They are ruthless creatures meant for destruction and war. The Archangels knew that when they sent him there. And to add insult to injury, they gave him a new title. They crowned him Prince of Purgatory. Never king." He flashed a brief smile at that, like he applauded the Archangels for it. "He found my mother there. They saw something in each other no one else could."

"What was that?" I asked.

"He saw someone pretty enough to sit next to on a made-up throne, but not quite pretty enough that he could develop true feelings for. She saw someone who could hand her power and a title without having to work for any of it. For those two, it was the perfect arrangement."

"That's heartbreaking," I said, meaning it.

"To know you're in a loveless marriage?"

"To accept it."

"Alaric doesn't believe in love. Or maybe it's that he's afraid of it.

If something can be taken away or used against him, it's viewed as a weakness."

And suddenly I realized that's exactly what I was doing. In an attempt to keep myself safe, I was keeping everyone from getting too close. I was doing exactly what Leah had told me not to do. And the only thing it had gotten me was the very heartbreak I was trying to avoid.

Tynan's voice interrupted a revelation that stung. "I'm the son of the Prince of Purgatory. My birth was supposed to promise his power restored, but he was wrong. I didn't turn out to be the Dark Angel prodigy that was expected. Alaric blamed my mother for some ancient bloodline on her side interfering with his. So I was deemed useless. I was to stay home with my mother, help keep up the house, and when Ara came along, I helped with her."

I smiled at the memory of him rocking Ara to sleep.

"From what I can tell," I said, pulling from the information I'd seen from all his memories, "you didn't just help with Ara. You practically raised her."

He gave a soft smile. "I even named her."

"You named her?"

He nodded. "I couldn't believe how easy it was to convince our mother to let me pick her name." Tynan frowned. "It took me a very long time, but I finally figured it out then. Neither my father nor my mother wanted to be parents."

An eyebrow rose. "And you? Who named you?"

"I was boy or lieutenant for a long time. But he liked boy. It was demeaning and reminded me that I was lower than my species to him. Not worthy of my class. Eventually, when my gifts clicked into place about a hundred years later, I picked my own name."

My mind spun, my thoughts and his words working to catch up in the middle, and when they did... I only gaped at him. Tynan gave me a lopsided grin.

"You went *one hundred years* without being named?"

"My mother was tired...always so tired. And my father had no interest in me until I showed some talent. When I did, he was determined to make me what he wanted. And he did, for a time." An eclipse came and went over his eyes.

I hadn't known until now that Tynan and I had more in common than I could have ever guessed. Both our parents had let us down. I wanted to know more. I wanted to know everything about him.

"What is the difference? Between a Dark Angel and an Angel of the Night?"

"I am—" he paused. "I was *the* Night itself. Made of cosmic dust, dark matter, and the light of the moon. I could take a night form, become one with the constellations and travel through galaxies. All through the night and anything the darkness touched with its shadows."

"I've never heard anything like that."

"It's like..." Tynan tried to put it in words, like it was only a distant memory to him now. "The daytime is just the daytime. The stars are always there, but they're faint. But when darkness comes, their best attributes are on display. I become a different being altogether in the night. My senses are heightened. I'm swifter, stronger, more comfortable there. On the loneliest of nights, I've become the stars themselves."

I glanced up at the bright moon on full display, picturing Tynan in the stars. "So you left then. You came through the stars of Elysian to start over." It was a guess, but what else could the explanation be? I was glad for him that he'd found a way to get far away from Alaric.

"I...didn't come by choice." Embarrassment flooded his tone, and I was finding that I was thrown off each time Tynan showed me another layer of emotion. I never would have dreamed he was capable of having any upon our first meeting.

"I'd been hidden away for so long, but when my gifts fully

developed, Alaric suddenly had something to prove to his subjects. The nameless son that had only been rumored up until that point was truly a weapon in training, finally ready to be wielded. I was basically his experiment. A Night Angel with Dark Angel blood? The two are rare breeds to begin with. Mixing those bloodlines was unheard of. Alaric had to see what he could get me to do and how far I could take those gifts. Or how far they could take him really."

Nothing on his face showed that he was proud of that. "I was so excited by the sudden attention and too childish to see that I was his pawn. I carried out every order without question, no matter the cost." Disgust crinkled his nose as memories I couldn't see, but could now guess at, played out behind his eyes. "In the rare moments I wasn't terrorizing Purgatory, he'd send me away on these missions that lasted months at a time. No one knows where exactly Purgatory lies in existence. But when I took to the skies, I was always somehow...out. Far away from there and suddenly somewhere new. A different galaxy possibly. It was like its sky was a portal. My eyes would shift to adjust to the new sky, and I was able to navigate my way without any effort." Tynan's gaze flicked shyly to mine long enough for me to understand. All the stars in his eyes were real. His eyes were a map of the universe he stood in. "I was to find his old base. Alaric was disappointed I wasn't like him, but I think after seeing what I was capable of with both bloodlines, he saw the potential there. He became obsessed with revenge. Direction was lost to him, but I could find anything. It may have taken some time, but I would find it. And together, we would take back everything he lost and then some."

"Why did you leave all this out when you showed me those memories of your past?"

"I heard your heartbeat when you first saw what was in my cell. If you weren't terrified of me already, you would have hated me at the very least." He attempted an unconvincing smile and then added, "More than you already do."

"I don't hate you, Tynan." I said reassuringly, ignoring that he'd accidentally admitted that he did in fact care. "You're not so bad, even if you try to be."

"I'm not good though." Now that he'd started, it was like a river of confessions. I couldn't tell if he wanted to get these things off his chest, or if the alcohol wouldn't let him stop.

"When things in Purgatory were meant to be punished, it was my face they trembled at the sight of. I did terrible, dark things by my father's command. And the few times I did hesitate or question an order, it was me who received that punishment five times over. So I stopped asking questions. I stopped thinking altogether. I was a mindless, trained animal. You can't come back from the types of things I did. I was so desperate for something I couldn't give a shit about now and my soul is forever tainted for it."

"You're being hard on yourself," I said, even though I knew there was more to it than what I'd seen. After all, he'd cut the memories short on purpose. "You obviously left Purgatory. A place you said you can't leave until your soul is cleansed."

Tynan shook his head adamantly. "It's different for me. I was born into Purgatory, not banished there. My soul wasn't tied to it." He took another drag from the bottle. "May the Creator help us all if Alaric finds a way to untie his soul."

"Is that possible?"

Tynan immediately took another drag, longer than the last. "I fucked up." He tilted his head to the sky as if silently asking for forgiveness. "When wings and grace are detached from each other, it's only flight that is lost. But if it's grace that's removed, an angel's very essence is wiped. There would be nothing left to make them an angel. Which led me to an idea one day. If I could take the essence of an angel who was born into Purgatory, and switch it with my fathers, not only might he be able to leave his throne, but maybe I'd gain his respect too. In the end, I stole from another for nothing."

"So it didn't work?"

"Even with a grace returned to him, it wasn't *his* grace. I was successful in disconnecting his soul from Purgatory, but any traces of his old power were switched out for something much weaker. After being punished for that little detail, he had me take him with me from then on when searching worlds—another perk of my Night that works the same way I can pull from shadows and take you with me in them. We'd been gone for what seemed like forever. He knew what to look for, so it caused for less stops. But then we passed over this planet, and it felt...interesting. There was a pull to it, unlike any I'd brushed before. And I stopped. For whatever reason, I stopped. Before my father could order me to move on, he felt it too. The creatures there, the *life* there. It was different, and I never got a chance to figure out why. Alaric took one look at the world below, and I could see it playing out before his eyes. The thirst in them. The desire to conquer. And despite everything I'd seen him do, I was most afraid of him at that moment." Tynan drank deeply. "They were so far below us that we couldn't see them, but we could feel their energy. I don't know if he thought it would be a bonding moment or what, but as celebration, I was to smite them. Something he couldn't do in his weaker power."

"Smite them?" I hadn't taken my eyes off him the entire time. The expressions he wore, the thoughts that raced through his mind. It was the most transparent thing I'd ever witnessed.

"Obliterate them."

I was almost too afraid to ask. "And did you?"

"Almost." He raised the bottle to his lips again, avoiding my gaze, but the shame written there was clear. "I wanted to. I was so desperate for just his tolerance of me. I think I would have done anything."

"So then what stopped you?"

He shook onyx hair from his eyes and glanced at the stars, as if he were speaking directly to them. "They say every being in existence has a soulmate of some kind. Sometimes those souls never cross paths, and they go on to live good lives, but a part of them will always feel off. Unfilled in a way they can't place. Something I would have laughed at before it happened to me."

A strange wave of disappointment crashed into my gut. "You've met your soulmate?"

"Kind of." Tynan winced. "That night."

"Oh."

"She was somewhere in that world and close enough that I would have killed her had I followed orders. I've never felt anything like it. Like my soul was a loose string, and it had just been tied into an invincible knot. I fell to my knees and clutched at my heart. I thought I was dying. Alaric knew somehow what was happening, and that bonding moment was gone. He was enraged and went in for the kill himself, but I grabbed him and traveled out of those skies so fast. I've never moved that fast in my life. My mother and sister screamed when we appeared suddenly, landing on the floor in a cloud of struggling darkness, his hands around my neck. We struggled for a bit against each other before he did something worse than killing me." The longing that flashed across his face as he watched Ara fly off before matched the sorrow there now. "To an angel, losing your wings is a disgrace. He ripped mine from my back, and I fell. I landed in Elysian."

"How did you not die?" I asked, unbelieving.

"I'm still an angel with his grace. I still have the power of those two strong bloodlines, it's just my ability to fully connect with the night sky that is gone." He gestured to his back, where his wings would have rested. "The pain from the loss of my wings was unbearable. I lay in the woods of Valhalla for days. I didn't find out until later, but the King of Valhalla before me died a few days before my arrival. He never married or had offspring of his own. There was no legitimate heir to fill his place, and with a missing

High Queen to fill that void, Valhalla was momentarily in an uproar.

"When these things happen to lesser rulers, the magic woven throughout Elysian's soil will scour the lands, looking for a worthy soul. And the land chose me. For whatever ridiculous reason, it thought I was worthy of the title. I remember the trees bowed to me, and the wind whispered my name. It asked if I wanted to be something great. If I would swear to do right by the once-perfect creatures of this land. I thought I was just delirious from the blood loss, but I accepted. And the next time I breathed in, it was a gust of new power that coursed through my veins. It was also then that I realized my Night was gone. I could gain control over the shadows on the land, but the darkness in the sky wouldn't connect to me."

"And then what happened?" I felt like a child being told a fantasy, but I needed to know more. Or maybe I just wanted it.

"I picked myself off the ground for the first time in days, and somehow, my body knew where to go. It was like the wind changed course just to guide me to where I belonged, to the palace in the hilltops. When I arrived at the gates, they knew. The guards, the council, they all bowed."

"They just took a wild guess that you were their new king?"

"The storm of wind I brought with me didn't hurt." He managed a quick smile.

I suddenly remembered the others. If Tynan was thrown from Purgatory... "Did the others fall too?"

"Not Ara," he explained. "We're of the same blood. We'll always be able to find each other because of that. She doesn't have any Night in her, not any that's awake at least, but we do share some connection through the sky and its weather. Me, only to an extent, but with a combination of my new wind abilities, her rain, and my connection to the skies, we can sense each other. An unnatural rain here. A sudden, single rumble of thunder there. It's almost like a silent form of communication in a way."

"Like mind tapping," I said, slightly confused.

Tynan paused, the same way he had when I first asked him about that particular ability. "Differently than that, but...sort of, I guess. She begged and pleaded and cried to my father to bring me back, and when he refused, she left. Once she portaled into this sky, it was easy for her to sense me. Ambrose and Enzo though, not so much."

"So they weren't bound there either then."

He shook his head. "Also born into Purgatory, cursed from a fate before their lifetime. Honestly, I think they were only friends with me because they were terrified of me. I recruited them. Basically, forced them to be my henchmen. And for that, my soul is also tainted, but...somewhere along those years, we actually became friends. And then one day, family. It's a blessing I don't deserve, but—" He shrugged before continuing. "Alaric displayed my wings behind his throne. A bragging trophy showing what the Prince of Purgatory would do to even his own son should he be defied. When Enzo saw, he lost it. If you haven't noticed, Ambrose has always been the more level-headed one, and he tried to intervene but got caught in the crossfire. My father did the same to them that he did to me, only worse."

Regret tightened his throat, even though he swallowed to hide it.

"He didn't just rip Enzo's wings from his back. He shredded them and then burned what remained while Enzo watched, bleeding out. He was handed off to the border patrol and discarded of. I don't think he meant to send him to Elysian, but that's where he landed, staining the snow in Kashmir with his blood. He was found by an arctic fairy there and eventually healed. She took care of him, taught him about his new home. And then she mentioned King Tynan of Valhalla, the fallen angel turned king of the mountains. When he traveled to Valhalla to see if it was true... I don't have words for what that reunion looked like." The smile that spread at that told me enough.

"Ambrose's arrival happened a bit differently." I don't think he meant to display such confusion on his features, but the transparency he allowed tonight was riveting. I wondered if he'd ever allow me to see it again. "His wings were also burned, only he was sent someplace far darker. Somewhere it should have been impossible to escape from. But he did."

"Where did he go?"

"Hell." Goosebumps coated my arms and crawled up my neck. "He won't talk about what happened there, but months later, he clawed his way out of the ground in Empyrean. Scared the hell out of some kids playing in a meadow. To this day, I don't know what he had to give up to get here. But he's different now."

"How?"

"His grace... I can't feel it anymore. There's something else there now."

I didn't want to know what it was that tainted Ambrose's soul. And if even Tynan didn't know... I shuddered. "So," I started, melancholy filling my voice. "they'll never get their wings back."

"Never," Tynan replied with equal sadness.

I let my eyes rest on his back, envisioning what he might look like sitting here now with wings. Ara's wings matched her personality and even her hair. If hers were dainty and teal, I imagined Tynan's being strong, intimidating, and as dark as midnight. Like the Night Angel he was.

"Does it hurt?" I whispered.

"Not anymore. I don't feel like myself, but...I'm starting to get used to it."

"Does your Night have anything to do with the Dark Queen needing you?"

"I don't know how she did it," Tynan said it like he still couldn't believe it. "but she has my wings. Maybe Alaric discarded them and has no idea that everything he's getting rid of is going straight to Elysian? I don't know. But she has them. She sent a dove to Valhalla with a single feather from them. I knew it was mine. I could feel the power radiating off it and reaching for my grace. I was rash. I didn't stop to think. Ambrose was with me when it happened, and he tried to stop me, but I shoved him off and shadow stepped to the Garden. Obviously, it was a trap. The only thing that waited for me were ancient markings in the soil and cursed shackles around my wrists that burned. Any power I still possessed was sucked away the moment I landed. Once she had me on her turf, I wasn't leaving until I agreed to a deal. I could have my wings back, in exchange for obedience to her for just one year."

"Tynan," I gaped unbelieving. "Why didn't you take that?"

"The Night will bow to me if ever returned. Think about that. Xosha would have used my Night to cover this place in a blanket of darkness, slaughtering anyone who stood in her way, and then she would have used me to do the same in other worlds too. She would have used me down to the last second, and then ordered me through my vowed obedience to run a dagger through my own heart. You have to be very careful with your words when making a deal." He tipped the bottle up, looking to me just before his lips met with it. "And then the human girl finally showed up and revealed herself to be my knight in shining armor." His sudden teasing smile was a weight momentarily lifted.

"Yeah right. If anyone did any saving, it was you," I admitted. "You talked to me down there. You kept me going when I was slipping away." He didn't respond, and the soundless night lingered between us. "You did something else too, didn't you?" His head turned to mine, and he waited as if he knew what I'd say next. "You took the pain away." He looked away in response, affirming everything I'd put together since then. "I felt every one of the Dark Queen's punches until I made eye contact with you. Then it was like my body went numb. I could feel something make the contact, but the pain was somewhere far away."

"I didn't think you'd notice that was me," he said to the moon.

"Where did you take it?"

"I...absorbed it."

I blinked at him.

"It had to go somewhere. So I took it." He shrugged. "I can usually transfer emotions without any problems, but physical pain takes more concentration. I need to make eye contact to focus hard enough on it. But it has to go somewhere."

Everything I should have felt when meeting his eyes instead of the Dark Queen's...he had felt in my place. He took those punches. He stepped in, the way no one else had before.

Someone who hadn't even known me. "Why would you do that?"

"After losing a soulmate, physical pain is nothing in comparison. Maybe it's what I deserve for the things I did in Purgatory."

I reached out and placed my hand on his shoulder. The contact caught us both off guard. "You were surviving."

"I was weak."

"No." I suddenly felt the same aggressiveness to protect him that I felt for Liam. "We all make decisions that we have to deal with. But our past mistakes don't define us. They do not control the outcome of the rest of our lives. We have the opportunity every day to make better choices, to *be* better. And you've done that. Even before you came to Elysian. I saw for myself in your dream. You could have made that soldier in Purgatory suffer before you ended his life. But you didn't. You ended his misery quickly and without pain. Because you aren't bad, Tynan. You aren't your father. If anyone's soul is tainted, it's not yours. I refuse to believe that."

He stared at me, transfixed, as if the words had hit some deep nerve ending and settled there. But then he cleared his throat. "Enough heavy talk. Tell me something ridiculous."

"Like?"

"Like the amount of men waiting in line for you once you return." Tynan stretched his arm to the side, bottle still in hand, as if to demonstrate the long waiting line.

I laughed so loud it startled even the stars above. "God, no. None. No men."

"No?"

"Not interested."

"Why not?" He was smiling wide now, dimples driving inward.

"That is not a story you want to get into."

"Oh, I very much am interested in this story."

I tried to match his smile, to hide behind it, but I could feel it slipping. Feel that the wall I had spent years building was failing this time. Tynan's own expression shifted too. He was almost examining me, trying to crack a code of some sort.

His tone softened, truly curious. "Who has disappointed you so much?"

"Everyone." The weight of the word hung heavily in the air between us.

I side-eyed the bottle of wine. Tynan stretched out his arm and tilted the bottle in my direction. My eyes went from the bottle to his starry gaze. For him to even offer knowing about my dad...

*Whatever it is, you're safe here.*

I believed him. I knew enough about what unsafe felt like to know that this rooftop was safe. He was safe. Ara and Enzo and maybe...*maybe* even Ambrose. They were safe, even if they didn't all want me to know it. There'd been so many opportunities for Tynan to not only hurt me, but to let someone else do it for him, and he'd gone out of his way every time to keep me from harm. My arm reached out, and my fingers curled around the bottle. Maybe I was being stupid, but careful and guarded had never gotten me anywhere. The bottle came to my lips, and I turned it upright, just a little, and the red liquid brushed my tongue. It hit my veins fast, and my legs tingled with the smooth, sweet taste of berries.

"Were you in love with him?" Tynan asked, watching me drink.

"I don't know."

"That means no. You know when you're in love with someone. Without a shadow of a doubt." He knew that feeling. He may not know who it was exactly that he was in love with, but he knew what his love for her felt like.

"Well, I guess no then."

"Huh."

"What?"

"I just find it hard to believe someone hasn't swept you off your feet yet."

I took another swallow, refusing to feel embarrassed over the heat in my cheeks that the wine was already creating.

"Tell me about him," Tynan said. It sounded like an order.

"I'm about to make myself sound pathetically naive," I fore-warned, "But...he was insanely charismatic. The good times were really good. I think I could've been happy with him if those times outweighed the bad, but mostly there was just yelling. Usually over nothing, and an apology from me was never enough. He'd just go on and on until I'd *finally* snap back. Then all of a sudden it was me who was insecure and needed to get professional help." I stopped to laugh ironically. "All the while, he was doing the things he was accusing me of. I can't count the number of times I was cheated on in that relationship. I'm not sure why I put up with it for so long. Maybe I was so inexperienced I didn't know any better. Or maybe I thought the fighting was romantic in a way. But as embarrassing as it is to admit, that relationship was the closest thing to normal I'd ever had. I just wanted normal and thought a boyfriend that cared enough to fight with me was it."

I stopped, but Tynan didn't respond, as if he was waiting for me to finish, so I did. "There was one night, I couldn't sleep. I was just staring at the ceiling wondering how I'd gotten to the point where I slept next to someone who talked to me the way he did. I don't know what clicked, but I just got up and left in the middle of the night. I went to the only person I knew in town. Leah." I smiled at her name. "She'd quit the restaurant after a while, but not before we'd gotten to know each other during our shifts. I refused to do much talking outside of taking customer orders and she'd refused to let me be the outcast. She basically forced me to be friends with her." I smiled at the truth of it, remembering how warm and accepting and perfect of a friend she'd been. "At two in the morning, I knocked on her door and broke down. It just so happened her current roommate was moving out at the end of the week. She still needed someone to sublease the second room. Leah is the closest thing to a home I've ever had."

"The girl from your memory."

I nodded slowly. "Now there's nothing." I raised the bottle, taking a larger swig. "So that was my miserable first and last try at dating for an extremely prolonged amount of time."

"I can promise you we're not all scum."

"No? Have you been listening? My past experience with men proves otherwise. Fathers, brothers, boyfriends. Almost boyfriends."

Tynan grinned and leaned in, brushing my shoulder with his as he took the bottle back. My insides sloshed with wine.

"If you've only dated once, surely you've had other...experiences?"

I stared him deep in the eyes, and maybe it was the wine, maybe I just wasn't bothered by the fact anymore, but I said, "Nope."

Tynan's jaw slackened, and he covered his mouth with a hand in mock surprise.

"Shut up," I said.

"You're lying."

"I'm not." I sighed, returning my gaze to the stars.

"Why the hell not?"

I laughed, unable to help it. "Unlike you, I'm sure, sex means something to me. I don't really do the whole meaningless hookup thing, or because I'm bored, or whatever reason I can come up with." I shrugged to myself. "I don't know, that's just not me."

"I never said sex doesn't mean anything."

I rolled my eyes playfully, and Tynan gave a smirk that was just as playful but far more pleasant to look at. It felt a lot like flirting, but also a lot like two friends joking around.

"So your only time was disappointing. That's a shame."

"Disappointing." I grabbed the bottle before he'd taken a turn. "What a word for it."

"You have to tell me."

My face fell. Tynan's smile dropped, taken aback. "What?"

My insides felt weird, and I wondered if it was the wine. "There's not much to tell. It's not some grand, romantic story."

"Most of our first times are awkward."

I nodded, feigning agreement.

Somehow, Tynan saw right through it. "What else."

I suddenly felt gross. I'd always felt uncomfortable thinking back on it, but now that someone was asking me to speak the words out loud...something didn't sit right in my stomach, in my chest. I wasn't sure I could even transform the feeling into words. "Apart from it just totally not being worth it, I don't think—" Shame filled my entire chest, burned with it. "I didn't really want it to happen."

Tynan watched me, listening with his whole body, and something about that made it easier. "We'd been together for a few months, and he brought it up. Again. I was hesitant about it." I went deep into thought, my mind going back to that moment, searching for whatever it was that felt so off about that night. I had spoken unsurely, had avoided eye contact when he asked me. Had *said* I didn't think I was ready. And he... He'd rubbed my arms lovingly and was uncharacteristically sweet. I had stared at my feet as he said, "Let's get a little alcohol in you, loosen you up and see how you feel then." He was smiling a lot in a way he only did when he was getting what he wanted.

Out of everything, the only thing that stuck out was that I hadn't said no. I'd made it clear I was uncomfortable about the whole thing. But I hadn't said no. Why hadn't I just said the word?

I didn't realize that I'd opened my mind and accidentally let the memory slip free until I saw the look on Tynan's face. The way the lines were hard around his mouth, jaw set back, the movement of his stars nonexistent. The purple so deep it was almost black.

"So he had you get drunk in order for you to be willing to have sex with him." His voice was flat, words slower than honey.

I flinched. "Well, when you say it like that—"

"I'm not saying it like anything. I'm saying it how it is."

"I mean," I started, flustered. "I was sober when he offered that drink. I've seen what alcohol does to some people, the way it makes them different. And I willingly took it anyway, knowing what might happen. It's just like the cheating. Sure, he did it, but I knew deep down. And I just let it happen. Everything I allowed to happen was my own fault."

Tynan stole the bottle back. "You're wrong. You're not responsible for how someone else knowingly decides to treat you. He knew what he was doing." He lifted the bottle toward his lips but stopped short and set it on the roof instead with a *clink*, holding it there. His tone hardened. "Partial consent is not consent. Offering alcohol to someone with the intention of 'loosening her up' is not consent. That makes me sick to my stomach."

I grabbed the bottle from him in a hurry, and then immediately realized he didn't mean because of the wine. I shouldn't take another sip, but I did, like it would wash the confession away.

"You shouldn't have had to give away anything to bargain for his love. If he'd wanted you for the right reasons, he wouldn't have asked for anything in return," he added.

"I know that. Now at least."

His jaw clenched so hard that surely it would shatter, and his knuckles went white in the dark as they wrapped around his knee. He met my eyes with a startling sincerity and said, "I can't control what happened in your world, Briar, but I swear as long as I'm around, no one will ever take advantage of you or lift a hand to you again."

My skin tingled as the air warmed, as my breath quickened at the passion in those words. Despite my teasing before, Tynan did care. Maybe not for me specifically, but in general. Tynan cared deeply about right and wrong. And the fact that he was letting me know it now meant he trusted me. I looked away. "Okay, spill," I said, desperate to change the subject.

"About?"

"I just told you the most embarrassing thing I could about myself. That in twenty-two years, I've only slept with one person."

"That is not embarrassing. Stop stealing my bottle." He snatched it back.

"It's highly personal," I said. "So it's only fair."

He hummed in thought. "In Elysian?"

"Settle down there, player," I said, only to keep my disappointment from showing.

"What? You try being perfect in a span of almost two hundred years." He raised the bottle to his lips and then looked at it with a scowl when he realized it was empty. "It's probably less than what you're thinking," he added. "I can't be redeemed from what I used to be, but Elysian gave me at least the chance to be a better male. I'm trying to live up to that."

"How many in this world then?"

"Just one."

"One?" I challenged skeptically.

"I haven't been in Elysian very long. And don't forget, I was locked up for one of those years."

"What happened?"

Tynan tapped the empty bottle mindlessly against his shin while he mulled over his thoughts. "Whoever that soul was, she has mine, even if she'll never know it. After experiencing something like that, no matter how brief it was, it's been hard to settle for anything else. I was half-assing my feelings with anyone that came after. Eventually, I felt I had no other choice but to end things before they really even started. It wasn't fair to give someone only half of my attention."

I smiled.

"What?" he asked.

"See? Better decisions."

He laughed. It was a soft, unconvinced one, but a laugh in the midst of all the heaviness. And the sound of it melted me. I tried and failed miserably not to envy his soulmate. I was unsure why it bothered me, and I didn't want to explore it.

"So what...you're to be alone for the rest of your life because your soulmate is out of reach?"

"I hope not. I hope I come close to being in love one day. But it hasn't been with anyone here."

I thought for a moment and then asked, "Do you think that's why our fathers are the way they are? Because they never met their soulmates and are miserable because of it?"

"I don't think there is always some deep, psychological reason for everything. I think in our fathers' cases, they are shit just because they are. Not everyone cares enough to try to be anything different than that."

I hummed my agreement, turning my attention to the thousands and thousands of stars that sprinkled the sky. A canvas just as breathtaking as Tynan.

"I truly can't work out a reason for you to go back," he said after some time. "You've said it yourself, there's nothing there for you."

"I can't stay here. Elysian isn't for me."

"I think Elysian has changed her mind on that one."

"Doubtful."

"Says who?"

"Says everyone! Darya, the scholars, the Dark Queen." I rolled my eyes. "Who doesn't say so?"

"You're making a decision for yourself based off what others you barely know are telling you to do?"

Every single time I thought about going back, something in the pit of my stomach told me it was wrong. But Elysian wasn't a true option. Not without the return of the Pale Queen who kept it breathing.

"I think," Tynan added, leaning in to softly bump my shoulder with his, "it just may be time for you to speak for yourself."

"I do speak for myself." I scowled and ignored the lie on my tongue. "It doesn't matter," I said. "I've always been homeless in a way. Wherever I go, it won't really be mine."

Tynan tilted his head so slightly I hardly noticed, his eyes filling with sympathy. I shook it off, not wanting anymore pity from him over how unfulfilling my life was.

"Do you really think I have no personality?" I asked abruptly, and Tynan burst out in a laughter so rich and deep and true that my whole face shined. That sound... An entire world *needed* to exist to hold that sound.

"I just think there is more to you, that's all. I think there is so much that you're keeping inside. Like you're afraid to show too much of yourself."

"What do you mean?"

His gaze was so intense that it made me anxious. "You aren't so delicate the way you have everyone including yourself fooled into thinking you are. You aren't weak or small. There's a fiery warrior in you. I saw her in the dungeons. I see her on the verge of surfacing when you argue with me. Hell, I think I might be the only one to have ever seen her. And when you finally realize it too, and you pop off one day, I hope I'm there to see it again and again." Even with one corner of his mouth lifted, a part of him was searching again for some missing puzzle piece.

I pushed at him lightly, shoving his attention away. "You're drunk."

He laughed huskily and lay back on the roof. "I am."

My eyes grew heavy with the wine, but I didn't want to sleep. I had learned so much about him tonight, more than I ever thought I would. And I liked it. All the parts. Even the ones he wouldn't show me.

I lay down too and listened as Tynan pointed out different constellations, telling me their names and origins. My eyes drifted closed for a moment, just one moment, and I may have started to drift off to sleep before his smooth voice pulled me back in.

"The First Night," he spoke softly, pointing to each connecting dot of a large constellation directly over the chalet. It formed the shape of a horse reared back on his hind legs, mighty and fierce, with wings stretched out at his sides. "He was recorded so long ago that no one remembers his name today. But they say he loved his night form so much that he never left it. He galloped through the galaxy until he traveled so far that he found new galaxies altogether."

The next morning, I woke in my bed, the covers tucked just under my chin, my shoes removed and placed at the foot of the bed. I didn't remember getting off the roof last night or walking myself to my room. I didn't remember us saying goodnight or anything other than the stars in the sky, the stars in his eyes, and the stories told between us.

I wasn't sure what exactly had changed during our conversation on the roof, but when I woke, I knew we could never go back to before it.

# CHAPTER TWENTY-EIGHT

I expected Tynan to be long gone when I woke in the early morning. Instead, he found me outside where I lounged on one of the cushioned couches. Amongst everything else, the morning was too untroubled to miss by sleeping in. I'd wandered out here alone to soak in the crimson sunrise, until Tynan sauntered out and took the opposite couch. We smiled at each other in good morning, and then just lay there like that, neither of us feeling the need to speak. Out loud or silently.

I witnessed the morning sky brighten, only thinking of the newest constellations I'd learned of, when a blue speck appeared. My eyes trained on it, questioning, until it grew bigger and flew close enough in our direction for me to recognize it as Ara. I knew something was wrong before she landed gently on the porch.

Tynan shot to his feet. "What happened?"

Ara's face was pale, and for a moment, the words wouldn't come. Enzo and Ambrose rushed out, as if they too had seen the dread etched on her face from inside.

"Word was just sent from Kenna's court." Tears welled in her eyes. "The meadowlands are no more."

Ambrose sharpened his tone accusingly. "What do you mean the meadowlands are no more?"

"The fields." She blinked, and her breath rushed as if she'd flown here as fast as she could. "All of them. Every inch of Empyrean's meadows withered up and died in the middle of the night."

Enzo looked to Tynan, his face paling too.

"That's not all," Ara's voice wobbled, as if nervous to deliver more bad news. "The twin leaders have been captured. I don't have details. All I know is Xosha has them imprisoned in the Garden as we speak."

Tynan swore under his breath, turning from the conversation.

"But their troops—" Enzo protested.

"Most of their troops have pulled back and are relocating. Xosha's visit to Empyrean wasn't clean. Creatures are hurt. They're scared. Only half of what was expected are moving on as planned, but if they don't come in time—"

Tynan's arm moved in a blur, a glass lantern from a table soaring through the air and shattering against the hearth on impact. No one budged at the outburst. Ambrose didn't seem to care I was around anymore as he directed to Tynan, "No more waiting for the perfect moment. We have to move *now*."

"What good will that do?" Tynan whirled on him, sleep deprivation and layers of stress taking over his body. "Genesi and only a small portion of Valhalla are the last lands standing. Our markets are depleted from sharing with crumpled realms. What happens when the curse reaches all of Elysian? We last maybe a few years off what's been stored and what's in the water, but then what? We've run out of time. Even if we win, we've lost."

"We can't just quit because things look bad," Ara chimed in cautiously.

"Empyrean had our largest numbers. Every soldier counts, and we've just lost a hundred thousand of them."

"We'll make do," Ambrose cut in. "Valhallan and Kashmirian

armies are already in position. All we have to do is move them. Empyrean will catch up and join us after a few days and increase our numbers at the final moment."

Tynan shook his head. "I promised Briar I'd take her to Bristol Gate after this is all over. But things are different now. I have to take her before in case... In case we don't come back."

Ambrose pinched his nose as if he were in pain. "I swear to God, Tynan."

"It's not optional. If we don't come back, she's on her own here."

"And you just *have* to be the hero, don't you?"

"What is that supposed to mean?"

"Why do *you* have to take her?"

"You think I trust she'll make it there on her own?"

"She won't be on her own, moron," Ambrose hurled. "One of us will go with her."

The two had taken steps closer to the other, and Enzo placed himself in between them. At Ambrose's insult, Enzo put a hand to his chest, forcing him back a step. "Watch it, Ambrose. That's your king you're talking to."

Ambrose laughed humorlessly. "He's our *friend*. And I'm not going to let our friend do anything stupid. *Again*." He shot a pointed gaze as sharp as glass to Tynan.

Tynan seethed, but Ambrose simmered just as hotly. "I'm done with all of this. I've been through *hell* and back to keep my friends breathing and in return you both walk straight lines to your death year after year. And now, you bring some girl into the only safe place we have and—"

I didn't hear whatever came next. All I focused on were Ambrose's last words. Tynan had been distracted because of whatever debt he felt he owed me. He'd been away from his throne for me, away from the woods last night, because his priorities and focus were altered. I wasn't surprised Ambrose blamed me for it. I blamed me for it.

It wasn't until I couldn't breathe that I realized I wasn't sitting on the couch anymore. My knees were on the wood planks, and I was bent over, searching for air.

"Briar." Tynan's voice came from above me, his thumbs pressing into the soft part of my shoulders. Ara was there too, coming to her knees beside me and placing a steadying hand at my back. Enzo came to the other side, blocking the little air I had access to. I struggled to get the rhythm of my breaths back in order, overwhelmed. And then Tynan somehow pieced together what was happening.

"Back up, back up."

The two bodies on each side of me disappeared, and it was just Tynan's form in front of me. "Briar, look at me."

I shook my head, only able to focus on the planks under my shaking hands.

He pushed my shoulders back, forcing me to straighten and meet his eyes.

*Breathe with me.* He was so close, his touch firm, his gaze firmer. He didn't blink, as if he were afraid the connection would break if he did.

*In.*

*Out.*

*In.*

*Out.*

My chest moved with his, as if our lungs were in sync, like some machine. He instructed me like that, over and over, breathing so deeply and leaving some seconds in between each inhale and exhale. But it wasn't just the breathing exercise that leveled out my anxious heartbeat. He had added something. I was too flooded with a calm sensation to tell him to stop, but the wild panic he tried to hide behind a collected face—the way the frazzled, unstableness was taken away all at once and now glazed over the cobalt in his eyes. He had once again taken away my panic, and this time I knew where it had gone.

My breaths smoothed, coming back to their normal state, but I held his gaze and put my hands over his to keep him kneeling there with me, as if it were only the two of us here. His instructions went silent, his hold on my shoulders shaking underneath my hands, even though he fought to hide it.

I took over, not able to transfer any emotions, but at least able to guide him through the exercise the same way he had for me.

*In.*

*Out.*

*In.*

*Out.*

*In...*

I didn't stop until the nervousness in his eyes subsided, his breathing evened, and he shook no more. I sat back against the couch and let his hands fall loosely from my shoulders.

I ran a palm over my face. "Sorry."

"For what?" Enzo asked.

For causing a scene. For forcing an anxiety attack on Tynan. For being a colossal burden to everyone who came in contact with me.

"You don't have to apologize, Briar." Ara said, coming closer again and returning her hand to my back in comfort.

Ambrose hadn't moved an inch the entire time. His arms were crossed, his face set in disgust. He turned and stormed off, not back into the cabin, but into the woods. Either to cool off or to sulk for the rest of his life, I wasn't sure and didn't care. Neither did anyone else it seemed.

"So what's the plan?" Enzo asked, returning to business.

It was Ara who took over as Tynan and I stood. "I'll fly into the Everwood to inform both armies that we're moving in without Empyrean at first light. While Xosha is distracted with the ambush, I'll get Briar through the gate." Tynan opened his mouth to argue, but Ara forged on. "No, listen. This may be Elysian's fight, but everyone is looking to you to lead it, Ty. I'm the only one of us who can afford to be away from it. I'll get Briar through and race to the fight directly after."

No one spoke while we each thought through all the things that could possibly go wrong. But there was nothing to add. Valhalla and Kashmir would move in together, their less than expected numbers still more than Xosha's dwindling forces in the Garden. And my passage through Bristol Gate was ensured. Even if I was wrong about the gate, even if I wound up somewhere else, at least I wouldn't be anyone's problem anymore. Something I had been since I first touched Elysian. Since even before then.

My eyes flicked to Tynan, who was already watching me expectantly. "I'll be fine with Ara," I assured him.

He looked like he wanted to argue. Like he wanted to fight the same way we had about this at Clive Steeple. But whatever he was holding back behind his clenched jaw, he finally swallowed it. "Fine. Everyone leaves at first light." His tone couldn't have sounded more unconvinced.

My heart raced. For the impossibility that this was actually happening. For the uncertainty that suddenly clouded over my theory. And for the realization that once I left, I'd never know what happened to any of them.

I straightened my posture and steadied my voice, hoping I sounded confident. "First light."

# CHAPTER TWENTY-NINE

Ambrose was freaking out.

Upon delivering updates to both armies in the Everwood, Ara had a near run-in with a herd of dragons. Only it wasn't the false queen and her wulvers riding on the backs of those dragons. It was minotaur with battle axes, cyclopes barring massive clubs, and *Zafar* at the head. Some flew in the direction of the Garden, and others, without riders, flew away from it as if they were using the dragons for transport.

Suddenly, Ambrose was questioning just how much of a surprise this ambush was, and at what point Kalopsia had promised their loyalty to the Dark Queen. If the barren Garden had suddenly found itself an army, Elysian's most ruthless army at that, the odds had tipped yet again, even farther from our favor.

Ambrose wanted to call back the troops. To plead with Darya to break her pact and join them with her army at their side. But he had been right before. Elysian didn't have any more time to wait, as the last tree of Valhalla met its death just an hour after the dragons were spotted. Tynan's warding around the estate was now pointless, as all the trees outside it withered and died before our very eyes.

The curse was here.

Hours after the news spread and Valhalla was in an uproar of panic from border to border, we all pointlessly sat in various places in the chalet, the air thick. Ambrose stood by the windowed wall, gazing out at the darkened lakeside as if envisioning it decaying by morning. Not that Ambrose didn't always look as though he hated the world, but this was different. Whatever was rolling around in his mind about tomorrow's odds was troubling beyond words. His usual scowl was deeper than should be possible.

Ara sat close to me on the couch, staring at nothing. Tynan sat alone on the hearth of the unlit fireplace, elbows resting on his knees and fingers interlaced under his chin. Lost in thoughts so deep his mind was probably in another room altogether. But Enzo... He couldn't sit still. Enzo was probably the only one of us who wasn't nervous about tomorrow. Battles, as Ara whispered to me earlier, excited him, and he was talking. A lot.

"Xosha is going down." He smashed a fist into his palm. "Is it bad I hope she doesn't yield? I want to watch Ty choke the air from her lungs."

Ambrose glanced back from the window, allowing a small break from his thoughts and letting an amused smile slip.

"That is if I don't get to her first." Enzo bared his teeth, hopeful for the chance.

"Enzo," Tynan spoke with an edge. "We have a big day tomorrow. You should rest. We all should."

Enzo's excited features melted, hearing the dismissal—and the shift—in Tynan's voice. That was a king's voice Tynan had just used.

"Good idea, brother." Ara shifted off the couch and said to me, "I'll be back just before the sun is up, so be ready. We'll be flying." I swallowed a wince. She crossed the room to Tynan and the way they embraced sent a pang through my heart. Tynan put a hand to the back of her head and pulled her into him. His gaze flicked to mine, but I quickly looked anywhere else.

"Enzo," Ambrose said. "You should shadow step to Kashmir's location. Just to make sure everyone is still in good standing. You can come back here for me after, and we'll head to our own troops."

Enzo nodded and then crossed the room, surprising me with a genuine hug. "Well, Briar, if I don't get to see you again, it was an honor. Valhalla owes you a huge debt for what you've returned to us." The smile that surfaced on my face was just as genuine. The way they made me feel, all but Ambrose, was the way I felt with Leah and her circle. Except this time not an ounce of me wished to keep them outside my wall. Enzo turned back to me halfway across the room and added, "Oh, and for Kingdom's sake, when you do return to your world, please start with a better taste in males."

I had to laugh at that one. "It's a promise."

He flashed a charming smile before following Ara out the front door, Ambrose the last in line. I didn't expect a parting speech from him, but he paused in the doorway. With a hand holding the frame, he turned, looking past Tynan as if he weren't even there, and staring me straight in the eyes. I sucked in a breath.

"If you are to one day learn how it is you came to be here, Briar —" his gaze sharpened "—don't come back." And then he stepped through the door before I had time to process his words.

I huffed in near humor at this point. "Let me guess. Don't let it bother me?"

Tynan's features didn't shift. "You should get some sleep," was all he said.

I wouldn't. But he was right. I should at least try. I started down the hall.

"Briar," he said again before I'd made it to my door. "If Elysian's circumstances were different, I think you could have made a home here. Wherever you wind up tomorrow, I hope that's what you find."

A small shred of hope flared in my chest at his wish for me, but I couldn't find anything to say in return. Finding home would always be a dream just out of reach. I only nodded and quickly retreated to my room for the last time, crawling into the bed and pulling the sheets up to my shoulders.

It was hard to control the direction of my thoughts, so I didn't. I let them wander and explore the possibilities of what was to come. If I was right, would I wake up from my coma in a hospital bed? If I was wrong... My mind spiraled at the horrors I might face if I was wrong. I must have spent hours second-guessing myself. How was I even supposed to continue living a normal, mundane life after... this.

A clattering of metal sounded from outside my room, pulling my mind away from made-up scenarios.

I shuffled out of bed and cracked open the door. The kitchen was illuminated, and freshly baked scents of some sort filtered down the hall. I followed the path of light and rounded the corner into the kitchen, where Tynan was busy working over the stove.

I leaned against the doorframe with my arms crossed and watched as he grabbed ingredients off the counter to add to whatever he was working on.

"Couldn't sleep?" I asked.

He turned, shaking wisps of hair out of his eyes. "Did I wake you?"

"No." I suppressed a sigh. "My head won't shut off."

The circles under his eyes told me his own head hadn't shut off in days, weeks. A year. We stood there staring at each other for a moment, his colorful eyes searching for something to say. There was so much uncertainty for both of us. Was this to be our goodbye? Would I see him in the morning before I left with Ara? He hadn't said when he'd be leaving to join his troops.

"Ara decided to stay put," he said.

"Where is she?"

"She's around." He looked up. "She figured you wouldn't be able to sleep and wanted to be close if you needed her."

"That was considerate of her. She should be getting her rest."

"So should you."

I ignored the impossible request and nodded at the counter behind him instead. "What are you making?"

"Oh." He smiled, dimples appearing, and grabbed the hot pan with a mitt to proudly hold his work on display for me. The stars in his eyes danced wildly, waiting for my excitement to match his own. I came closer, examining the creation thoughtfully, wondering what kind of otherworldly cuisine it could be.

A toasted crater of dough sat on the pan, the edges raised and curved inward to form a bowl. A large, whole tomato sat in the middle of the dough bowl with sliced mushrooms and black olives sitting carefully between the tomato and the dough, a surplus of shredded cheese sprinkled all across it. When I couldn't come up with anything, I asked as politely as I could muster, "What is it?"

He frowned. "It's...pizza?"

I closed my eyes, holding back a smile and the dumbfounded "oh" that was on the tip of my tongue.

"This is pizza?"

"Well, yeah, I mean..." His features turned shy, a lovely expression I'd never imagined on his face. I adored it. "I felt bad for ruining yours the other night. I figured it would mean more if I made it myself rather than have someone else do it while I 'sit on my ass.'" He gave an unsure smile. I could only stare at Tynan's version of pizza. And then I lost it. I burst into laughter, ending up with my hands on my knees.

"Did I do it wrong?"

The sincerity and innocence reflecting off him... I laughed louder, tears blurring my vision. I laughed so hard my stomach hurt, beyond the point of fearing what I looked like. But when I reined it in enough to wipe my eyes, there was only amusement in Tynan's.

"You were so close," I said, walking up to a drawer that held silverware and grabbing two forks.

We ate the homemade not-really pizza outside. If I forced myself to ignore the suddenly dead trees around us, it almost felt like we were in our own little world out here. Here, in the middle of the woods beneath the string lights and starry sky. The end of summer warming the night chill. Like tomorrow and everything that would come with it didn't exist. We sat facing each other on opposite ends of a couch with the pizza bowl in between us. Tynan picked carefully around at the ingredients, avoiding the tomato entirely and scooping what he could of the rest into his mouth.

"You know," I said, "this really isn't bad."

"It's terrible," Tynan said, his mouth full.

"You're right." I laughed through a bite. "It is."

"It's the thought that counts." He lifted a shoulder. "Have a real pizza for me when you get back to your world."

I hummed my agreement. I'd give up all the pizza in the world for a place like Elysian.

"Are you nervous?" I dared to ask.

He shook his head. "I've seen enough of war and violence in general for the idea of it to not shake me anymore. Doesn't make it fun though. Unless you're Enzo. Sometimes I think he thrives off the drama." I laughed at that. "I'm mostly worried for Ara. She's never been a part of something like this. But you try telling her to sit out while everyone she loves is out there fighting for their lives."

I stared at the dough, pushing the contents around aimlessly with my fork.

"What's the first thing you'll do when you get back?" he asked.

"Order proper pizza."

His laugh was a rumble vibrating through the night, and I couldn't fathom never hearing that sound again.

"When are you leaving?" I asked, the question driving me wild. When would I have to officially say goodbye, and how was I supposed to thank him properly for his help?

"I should be there now, giving some inspirational speech to drive their passion."

"So why aren't you?"

Tynan set down his fork but kept his gaze fixed on it. "Something about this doesn't feel right."

"The war?"

"Not the war."

A part of me didn't want him to finish what he was going to say. A part of me knew our conversation on the roof had changed the relationship between us. Along with half of our lives being shared with each other through a chord of memories. We knew each other far too well to have only known each other for a few weeks. A part of me knew that he had a right to be brutally honest with me, like he would any of his friends.

"Something doesn't feel right about you going through that gate."

I fiddled with the fork still in my hand and looked anywhere but his eyes. I didn't trust myself, not after being so careless with Zafar.

"You said it yourself in the dungeon," he added. "You admitted that you had a choice to go back after the accident. It speaks volumes that you chose not to return when you had no idea where the other portal would take you."

"I know," I admitted. "But I've been thinking. Maybe there's a reason for all this. Maybe I was supposed to come here to truly realize all I've lost and still could lose. Maybe once I go back, I can start over in a way I haven't tried before." I paused, considering if it was something I actually wanted or if it was just something I felt I should want. "Maybe I'm supposed to look for my brother and patch up whatever went wrong there."

Tynan's breath of a laugh was humorless. "He never tried for you. Why bother?"

My brows furrowed on instinct. "He's my brother."

I flinched at the disapproval on his face and the glimmer of hostility that reflected there. He was too still, even the rise and fall of his chest barely noticeable. He was holding something back, something that took everything in him not to say.

"What?" I asked, a bitter whip sharpening my tone. He shook his head, keeping the words in. I squinted, daring him. "Say it."

And he did. "You're making the same mistakes again. You're giving parts of yourself up for someone undeserving of it."

My heart sank like stone so fast and so hard it physically hurt. My fork dropped. For a moment, I just stared at him, my mouth slightly open. I waited. Waited for him to either take it back or add something to somehow alter the entire course of the sentence he'd just spoken. But instead, he only added, "I just mean he's not worth it, is all."

Of all the things he'd say to someone he considered a friend, why would he use the biggest mistake of my life and throw it in my face after confiding in him?

"Ara would do the same for you. She *did* do the same for you." I threw back what I could of his own past, the sting not anywhere near equal enough to feel satisfying.

"When Ara came for me, it wasn't because we'd abandoned each other."

Abandoned.

I didn't know why a burning sensation lit my veins. I didn't know why Liam left in the middle of the night without a goodbye. I *didn't know*. But Tynan didn't know Liam the way I did. He wasn't there when Liam cared for me when I was sick, when he taught me how to ride the secondhand bike *he* bought for me. When he cooked meals for us when I was too young to do it on my own. When he filled every role a parent should have. When he protected me from our father the only way he knew how to at the time. Tynan didn't know enough of the good to speak on the bad.

I stood above the King of Valhalla and glared down at him. "I don't care how much of my life you *think* you know about from things you had the displeasure of seeing in my mind. You don't know me, Tynan. And you don't know my brother."

When he didn't say anything in return, I decided I wouldn't sit back down, my temper too out of hand to smooth over tonight. I'd promised him I'd do better with my words when I got upset, but I didn't feel that control in me right now. I took two steps toward the door before his hand came over my wrist, the touch as gentle as a spoken apology itself.

"I didn't mean to upset you."

"What the hell did you mean to do then?"

He rubbed his temple and closed his eyes, like he knew he was making this worse and didn't know how to backtrack. I flinched at a raindrop that hit my nose, and then another, and another, but a rain shower wasn't enough to dampen the fire coursing through me. He thought I was weak, that I wasn't capable of standing up for myself. That I let everyone walk over me. For the most part, he was right. That's really what set me on fire, that he was right.

"Why do you always think you can be so brazen with me? Who do you think you are?"

A muscle in his jaw twitched, and then he slowly stood, until he towered over me. I had to raise my head to match his stare, and for the briefest moment, I thought he was going to tell me exactly who he was. The King of Valhalla, a fallen angel, but an angel nonetheless. An Angel of the Night with Dark Angel blood in him too, someone who could show me exactly who I was in comparison to him if I wasn't careful.

But he didn't say any of that. He didn't say anything at all. His eyes locked on mine, and he only gave me the silence I needed to continue, to let it out, to fight back for once.

"My life and the decisions I make are none of your business. I'm so sick of everyone's *boldness*. What is it about me? What do you all look at and see that tells you I can be told how to think. I keep my mouth shut, I do what everyone wants me to do because it keeps them happy and avoids a bigger problem. I let others control when I speak and when I don't speak, and what words will come out when I do. And if I ever go off the script, then I'm either a nuisance or challenging. But when I do what I'm told, I'm a pushover, a doormat, a fucking simple-minded *flower*. Everyone else can do and say what they damn well please, but when I do it? Oh God forbid I even think of it. No fucking more. I have a voice of my own, I get to use it, and you will hear me."

The few raindrops splashing against our bodies turned into several, dampening our hair and clothes. Neither of us seemed to care.

Tynan put his hands in his pockets and sharpened his gaze on me. His continued silence was my only indication that he wasn't going to interrupt or argue. The rain fell, not a single drop dousing my flame.

"I'm going through that gate because I want to. Not because Darya told me to, not because of Liam or some obligation to him, not because Elysian isn't giving me much of a choice," I lied, I lied, I lied. "And when I cross over, no one will tell me how I'm supposed to live anymore. If I want to find my brother, I'll do it. If I never want to acknowledge his existence again and shut everyone out for the rest of my life, it'll be because *I want to*. And I don't give a damn anymore what kind of picture that paints of me."

Rain slammed against my eyelids to the point it was hard to see clearly. Tynan's hair stuck to his forehead, his hands still in his pockets, and he just...listened. There wasn't a hint of disapproval or whatever his personal opinion may be over my rant. He allowed no emotion to seep through, and it irritated me even more.

I moved around him, out of breath and out of words.

He wrapped an arm around my middle, spinning me back to him. I spun so fast I put a hand out to catch myself as I landed solidly against his chest, our faces meeting too close. Tynan went utterly still, any emotion on his face barely readable. His stars swirled, but there, just beyond them, I could see it. The hurt and understanding, and maybe a little confusion, though I didn't understand what for.

His grip loosened around my back, but he lingered there, giving me a chance to control how this played out. The skin exposed from his rolled-up shirt sleeve brushed my bare arm, and the trickle of heat it left in its wake... My breathing hitched when his gaze flicked to my lips. He pulled me in slightly. When I didn't pull away, Tynan closed the small gap between his mouth and mine.

It's not as if the list of lips I've kissed is very long. There was Zafar, whose sandpaper lips were too crazed to even feel. There was my ex-boyfriend before that, whose kisses were fine, but they were simple things. They were normal. Between two normal people settling for the lips in front of them. Before him there was my first kiss, an embarrassing first attempt in high school. The guy had made out with my teeth, and my mouth came out sopping wet. I thought it was me, thought I might never kiss again.

But no one and nothing had ever felt like this. Like Tynan. This wasn't normal or simple. It was like unraveling and coming together all at once. Like his kiss had sent shivers of his very essence down my body, traces of moonlight floating down farther and farther until they reached whatever made up my own core. They tangled together and *pulled*, and something deep and guttural and ancient flared to life inside of me.

I might die because of this.

His satin lips brushed mine softly, maybe even reluctantly at first. His lips were just as warm and smooth as his honey voice. The rain soaked our clothes and his shirt pressed to him so tightly it was practically skin touching skin. I moved my mouth with his, each movement a driving force of whatever power was surging through me. He must have felt it too, as he drew his free hand up to the side of my face, the one at my back curling into the dress that clung to me.

The want that washed over me was just as heavy as the rain that poured and poured and poured.

My fingers wrinkled in what they could of his wet shirt, pulling the neckline lower so that I could graze the chest underneath it. His body reacted, his lips parting. It ignited me, sent the hot flames of anger deepening to ones that raged with a desperate need for more. More of this. More of him. More, more, more.

His tongue slipped in and brushed mine, flooding my tastebuds with something I'd never tasted before and couldn't place now. My fingers moved to his hair, finally weaving them through its silky texture. It was softer than I'd guessed.

There was a sureness about this kiss, about his hold on me. Our bodies fit like a puzzle, our lips so impossibly right together, like his were meant for mine all along. Like we'd waited years for this. His teeth dragged over my bottom lip, and the hand at my back dropped to my hips and gripped them with promise. I broke the kiss to look at him, keeping one hand in his hair and one tangled up in his shirt.

I gasped, blinking through the rain. My entire body buzzed with the passion pouring through my veins, my lips heavy still. My hands dropped. Tynan seemed to read and process whatever I was feeling as it coursed through me. Of course, he had. He could feel the emotions around him. He opened his mouth to speak, but whatever he was going to say got stuck there. I stepped out of his hold.

He didn't reach for me a third time.

I turned for the door and moved my legs as quickly as they would go without breaking into a run. Tynan might have whispered my name, but I was too focused to know for sure. I only just barely caught the ruffle of teal shuffling out of view from the rooftop. I didn't have time to be embarrassed. Couldn't even be upset with her for the stunt with the rain. I just had to get out of here.

When I stepped through the door and into the incandescent lighting, I ran. I didn't stop until I was safely behind my bedroom door. I stood in front of it, just staring at it as if it had slapped me. I ran my palms down my face, my fingertips lingering at my bottom lip.

There was a knock. I took a step back.

"Briar." His voice was hesitant. His sigh floated in, and I pictured him on the other side of the door, head resting against it. That kiss... It scared me because it was different. It hadn't been forced, and it hadn't been a lie like all the ones before it. It scared me because it was real.

I could open that door right now. For once, I could do something that scared me. I could be bold and fearless, and I could *live*. I could cross the room and slam my mouth into his. I could pull him inside and let whatever happens unfold naturally. I could risk staying. I could start over. Again.

"I don't know why I did that."

My fingers fell from my lip.

"I don't know what that was, but it was a mistake."

Or I could ignore him. I could go to bed and leave with Ara in the morning and never have to face this again.

When I didn't answer, he didn't try again.

A mistake. My mind reeled, wondering how something that felt like *that* could be a mistake. And then I remembered, breathless and unbelieving, that I wasn't his. It didn't matter how that kiss felt, because it wasn't meant for me. That kiss had been reserved for a soulmate an entire world away.

I could feel the emptiness on the other side of the door.

I never slept. I sat on the bed, the covers wrapped around my legs, and watched the light from outside shift from the blueish-black of midnight to the cusp of a violet twilight.

# CHAPTER THIRTY

My stomach twisted while the first tinge of color brushed against the dark sky. I swung my legs over the side of the bed when Ara's winged silhouette came into view at my side door. By the time she'd lifted her hand to knock, I was already there.

Despite the steel armor that covered her body, she still looked far too delicate to be dressed that way. The deep-green fighting leathers underneath made her hair stand out less, though the teal strands were pulled back into one thick braid and held together with a tight black ribbon.

Her hand lingered in the air before she slowly dropped it, eyeing me warily.

"Are you ready then?"

I nodded, but Ara shuffled in the doorway tentatively, as if she were waiting for something. "I didn't know if you wanted to say goodbye to anyone before we left." She didn't say it, but I was thankful for the unspoken kindness. That if I wanted to make a quick, painless exit, this was it. I loved her a little more in that moment. Even if she had indirectly been a factor in the awkwardness I was now avoiding.

"No," I said before I could change my mind. It would be easier this way. He wouldn't have to explain anything, and I wouldn't have to pretend it meant nothing. "Let's go."

She only nodded as I stepped out and shut the door behind me for good.

"So," I began, immediately feeling insecure, "how does this work exactly?"

"Well...you might want to keep your eyes closed if you're scared of heights."

I shook my head. "I'm not scared of heights."

She took a step forward in response and offered her arms for me to step into. But Ara was shorter than I was. There was no way her tiny form would be able to lift me, let alone carry me from one border to another. Enzo was going to have to do this. Or worse, *Tynan.*

"Are you sure you can—"

Ara swiftly scooped my legs off the ground, firmly supporting my back without even a breath of struggle. "Never underestimate me." Her eyes sparkled and her wings splayed out, and then she pushed off the ground. I sucked in a sharp gasp and gripped her as tightly as I could.

I didn't *think* I was afraid of heights until the clouds touched me. My legs went numb like I'd taken a double dose of sleep medicine. I clung to her, and if I hadn't been fighting off a heart attack, I would have worried I was hurting her, but she breezed through the sky, unfazed.

My head stayed buried in her shoulder the entire time we flew, but I could *feel* the height. The wind was surprisingly calm up here, and it smelled...new and cold.

"You should look." Ara's voice was level, confident. "We're almost there."

I peered up gradually. Dawn was just an inch from breaking. The mountainous valleys that dipped and rose were nowhere in sight, the dead, level treetops of the Everwood standing in their place. And all around us, clouds drifted.

I dared to stretch out an arm, reaching for a wispy cloud, but I felt nothing as it passed through the spaces between my fingers. A thicker cloud lay ahead, and Ara flew straight through it. Airy cotton candy hit me in the cheeks and the broken-up bits peacefully scattered in different directions behind us.

"This is unreal," I whispered.

"It's real, Briar. Every bit of it." Ara's smile was radiant, and I suddenly understood why she was so comfortable up here. I wished I could fly. I wished I could stay here in Elysian for the rest of my life. I wished I had said goodbye to Tynan.

I glanced down at the wilted treetops. The once-full forest was drained, the death of it like a darkened bloodstain spilled out from the Dark Queen's chalice.

Ara raced above the browned landscape, the sun threatening to beat us to Empyrean. Not the first light of the day though. That had already come and gone, and at this very moment, Tynan's life and thousands of other lives were on the line.

The tree line broke, and a brown field spilled onward onto the rest of the expanse. The curse's graveyard. We sailed over it for some time, not one sign of life in sight, until finally, there was something to look at. Ara dipped at the collection of stacked stones that came into clear view. They were piled high and rounded at the top to create an arch. It was old. *Ancient.* My heart lurched at the symbols etched in each stone. The markings pointed in odd directions, in a language no one could read anymore. I stared down at the only ticket out of Elysian. Bristol Gate.

Ara landed soundlessly a few feet before it and set me down, my legs feeling wobbly at first. Neither of us spoke as we scanned the lethargic meadow. Once gold clusters of switchgrass that would have touched my kneecaps now drooped and hung sadly at my ankles. We stood in a completely dead place, no breaths other than ours filling the air. No buildings. No dragons. No birds. No enemies. Just a paradise in apocalypse.

The pre-morning light and emptiness sent eerie shivers down my spine. I scanned the tree line that was barely visible in the distance, remembering what Zafar had said when we spent the night in the western part of the woods. It was early enough still that those things he'd spoken of could still be lingering around, spying for the Dark Queen. How did we know those things hadn't caught sight of us and followed while it was still dark?

I tugged on Ara's sleeve, whispering, not taking my eyes off our surroundings. "Someone told me there are things I didn't want to wake in the woods."

"Who told you that?" she whispered back.

I hadn't wanted to say his name, not with the reaction I'd gotten from her the last time I'd done so. Not with whatever wound was there. "Zafar."

She puffed out an annoyed breath. "He's full of shit. The Everwood is harmless. Probably the most innocent and magical thing about Elysian."

Of course, Zafar had lied, telling me the Everwood was dangerous at night, so that he didn't have to speak to me when I wanted to talk.

Ara's chin lifted, her skin brightening against the warm light that suddenly trickled into the meadow. "Ty and the others should be infiltrating now." My heart sped at the mention of Tynan and didn't slow as I pictured him clothed in swords and armor, battling head-to-head with an enemy who could turn him to ash in the time it took him to blink.

Ara took my hand and then turned my attention to Bristol Gate. "Ready?"

I gave a weak smile, doing my best to look convincing. "Okay," I said, more to myself than to her. "I'm ready." But as we drew nearer and nearer with each footstep, I couldn't shake an uneasiness that buzzed at my skin. *Wrong, wrong, wrong.*

A patch of dead grass to our right rustled. We halted.

The antlered head of an oat-colored rabbit popped up, its small black eyes landing briefly on us, but then it leapt for the small steps of the gate's dais and dove headfirst into the archway. It was there, and then it wasn't, not even a ripple in between. Its lean hind legs were the last thing to disappear into thin air, leaving the motionless meadow on the other end unchanged.

"It's only a jackalope," Ara said. "Traffic around the gate has been more active lately. The farther the curse spreads, the more things are deciding whatever lies on the opposite end is better than committing suicide by staying here."

At that, Darya's words echoed in my head. *The land isn't suicidal. If she were dead, it would have no other choice but to turn to the Dark Queen.* I eyed the gate and then scanned the emptiness around it.

"There's not a soul here. Does no one guard this place?"

Ara's brows crinkled. "Why would they?"

Every cell in my body froze over, my eyes wide with disbelief as the powerful revelation rippled through me.

I gaped at her, dumbfounded. "You mean to tell me no one monitors who goes through Elysian's only exit?"

"No," she answered simply. "If a creature wants to leave, they're free to. It's only when we force things out as punishment that we accompany them."

"Ara." I splayed an arm out toward the gate. "I know where the Pale Queen is." She followed my gesture but didn't seem to follow where my mind had gone. "The land *isn't* suicidal. And it isn't moving on to the next in line, because it isn't the next queen's turn yet. Elysian is dying because the High Queen that fuels it is disconnected from her land. Her power isn't here, but it's *somewhere.* Just somewhere that isn't within reach."

I watched in agony as the information, the truth and sense

behind it, sank into Ara's mind, deepening her confusion but then lifting to something else. Astonishment. "She hasn't been hiding," Ara said, working and processing through the information I'd unveiled. "She hasn't been hiding and she isn't dead. The land is refusing Xosha, because it can feel the true High Queen's presence—"

"Just out of reach." I said at the same time Ara looked at the gate again.

"Holy Kingdoms," Ara breathed. "*Holy Kingdoms.*"

"She's not in this world, Ara." I said it with almost annoyance. How had no one come to this conclusion already?

"No, wait," Ara said. "Why would the Pale Queen banish herself? Everyone knows what this gate means. This entire area stays clear unless there's a sentencing."

Ara's body was suddenly a blur as something barreled into her head from behind us. Her body rocked to the side, unconscious before she hit the ground with a solid thud.

It happened so quickly and silently that my mind didn't catch up in time to even gape at the towering beast of green, bumpy skin and teeth too large for its jaw. Stringy wings hung from his back. An absolute monster stood over Ara, a thick club clasped in its blocky fist. I already knew before I fully turned to see where he'd come from while we'd been distracted by the gate. I knew who was there before my eyes landed on her freshly blood-stained tips. The Dark Queen's tunnel-black eyes bore into mine, an unkind victory spreading across her lips.

"You were so, so close, little human."

CHAPTER THIRTY-ONE

Three small strides, and she was there, claws reaching out and grasping my jaw, pulling it to hers the way she'd done so many times now. Like the rag doll I was to her. Like the punching bag I was to my dad.

"I've been looking for you."

My heart pounded in my chest while the world spun. She knew all along. She'd figured out the same things Tynan and I had at Clive Steeple about the gate. The same thing I'd discovered here about the Pale Queen just now. But *how*?

"You won't be surprised to hear of the uninvited guests I have waiting for me back home. How pleased I will be to make such a grand entrance once I'm done here with you."

I scrambled to catch up as she half dragged me up the steps of the dais and tossed me at the foot of the archway. She left me there to gaze longingly at the gate, to trail her fingertips along the stone, feeling the cracks and edges in the odd lines marking them. Its magic echoed off a warning: *stay away, stay away, away.*

Her eyes fluttered closed, a memory playing out there.

"If you want something from me, just take it," I spat. I was so, so sick of being thrown around like a useless, unwanted shirt. Of staying quiet in hopes it'd help me survive. I was so *sick* of it. If she would just tell me what she wanted she could have whatever measly, unimportant thing it was. "You can have it. I am nothing and no one."

At the sound of my voice, her eyes snapped open, that white-hot hatred blazing again. She hauled me to my feet, and even though I struggled against her grip, I could feel it inside me, that ember flicking awake and growing, so desperate to be allowed to surface.

"Did you think I wouldn't come back for what was mine? Did you think I wouldn't figure it out, who you are?"

*For what was mine.*

A dumbfounded confusion flooded over me, a look I couldn't help that basically asked if she was stupid. And instead of it enraging her more, her features slowly fell, almost as if she were disappointed. "You really don't know then?"

"*What* are you talking about?"

She released her hold on me, allowing me to take a single step back. "Tell me what you think happened to my sister."

"I don't know," I replied carefully, and then lifted my voice a little as I went on. "No one knows what happened to her."

The dark sister barely nodded. Her voice lowered and sharpened. "I know what happened."

I eyed her, daring to venture back to what we all feared. "You told me you didn't kill your sister."

She laughed, as if the accusation were preposterous. "No, I didn't kill Zara. Not that the thought didn't cross my mind."

"Why?" I truly wanted to know what had made her heart so dark. Had her parents really disappointed her this badly?

"Zara was born with the most power in her blood, and the most room in our parents' hearts. The land called to her in ways it had never called to me. I knew from her sixth birthday she would one day have the crown that should have been mine. When a lily simply turned its head in her direction."

"But that's not how it works," I tried to reason with her. Had anyone tried to reason with her? "The soil decides who takes the crown based on their heart, not birth order."

"Zara didn't deserve Elysian's gifts. Elysian was wrong," she barked. "She was an irresponsible, carefree child. She was a dreamer and would never have ruled with purpose."

"You're describing a *child*, Xosha." The Dark Queen's features cracked, as if I'd disrespected her by not using the nickname she most likely adored. "No child is meant to be responsible or anything but carefree."

"She was insufferable! You didn't know! You were not there, you disgusting half-breed. No one understands what it is like to be the eldest and to be the least favored. For your birth to be celebrated from the moment you were conceived. For an entire world to adore you. And then for someone else to come along and for her gifts to bud at the same time yours do. Only one was twelve, and her hands turned the gardens to ash when she felt passionate and the other was six and the sun worshiped her. To see your parents' faces melt at that revelation, their precious roses dead before my feet. Zara stole *everything* from me. *I* was the beautiful one. *I* was the treasure. I do not regret anything I did to get where I am today."

"You just looked me in the eyes and told me you didn't kill her."

"I didn't kill my sister, I sent her away." Her sunless eyes flicked to the gate, lips curling in a wicked grin.

Something about that grin, the victory in her eyes as they flicked back to mine... Something about where this conversation was headed made my veins catch fire and then freeze over...

"I watched her take what was mine for three years, until I couldn't watch it any longer. So I plotted. A few weeks before her ninth birthday, I visited Kalopsia. I told my parents I wished to get to know the realms firsthand so I could properly stand beside my sister, my *High Queen*, and advise her with the best knowledge and judgments. And they allowed it." She laughed humorlessly. "They never would have sent their precious Zara to the Desert of Sin alone. But I knew what I would find there. I purchased an ordinary locket from a merchant and then took it to the Black Market, where witches and heathens sell their illegal goods for a high price. I found a desperate witch who took payment in the form of deals instead of coins. She put a curse on the necklace, and in return, I swore she'd never have to worry over coins again for the rest of her days. Despite the cloak I wore, she recognized me for who I was. She knew I had the resources to fulfill that promise, magic bound or not."

Xosha walked along the dais, gazing at the archway, reliving yet another dark memory. "The spell she placed on the necklace was meant to dampen the powers of anyone who wore it. Their abilities would live trapped inside it, so long as it rested on their skin."

"What happened to the witch? Where is she now?" I interrupted, thinking of the scholar who thought there was a chance I could have been summoned here.

The Dark Queen's full lips curled until they ran out of room. "I fulfilled my end of the deal. She never had to worry over coins again. She never had to worry about anything ever again." Just as she would have done with Tynan. She held up her end of the bargain with the witch.

"I gave the necklace to Zara on her birthday, thinking if her powers were smothered, the land would pass its gifts to the next sibling in line. But even with Zara's abilities trapped inside the pendant, nothing changed. I still had nothing but this useless ash, and Zara remained the golden child in our parents' eyes and in the kingdom's as well."

*Useless ash.* The things she could have done with that ash. The protector she could have been to her family, to her kingdom. If only she'd seen her worth, what she could have been capable of doing with the gifts she was given.

"So I formed a new plan. One night, I woke Zara from her bed and told her we were going on a secret adventure. We left through an old passageway that led out the back of the palace. No one saw us together, no one knew we'd even left. We took a pegasus from the stables and flew over the Everwood in the dead of night. I told Zara about the magical arch in the meadows of Empyrean and spun a tale. I told her whoever looked into it would be shown their future.

"Oh, she was delighted when we stepped onto this very dais. She could barely contain herself. When she was close enough, I pushed her through. And that was it. She was just gone. I came back home, brushed the dirt off the pegasus and stabled him, snuck back to my room, and faked a sickness the next day. As far as our parents knew, Zara had just vanished from her bed."

I shook my head, not believing how nonchalant she was over this. "You're disgusting."

"Thank you," she replied sweetly.

"Can't you see?" I asked. "The land still hasn't chosen you. You put all this blame on everyone around you and try to justify your actions, when all this really is, is you being so jealous of someone else that you can't stand yourself." Her nose twitched at that. "You're so envious it makes you sick. And now look. All that you've done, and you still don't have what Zara has. You will *never* be High Queen."

"Oh, yes, I will be. I made several mistakes as a teenager, the biggest being not killing Zara when I had the chance. I thought if only she weren't in Elysian, she wouldn't be a choice. But her lifeline still exists. The land feels that existing power within her, still waits for her return. As you seem to have figured out by now."

"Wait." I was forgetting something. Some vital piece of information that was essential to the story. It was like being pulled under the ocean and coming up for air, only to be met by another wave and crashed back under. I was almost there. Almost...

"The locket." I touched it as I spoke of it.

"I should have known when I first laid eyes on you," the Dark Queen said. "Those lips. You have your mother's lips. And her earthly eyes, even though the locket dulls them."

I shook my head, visualizing a memory of my mother's face. "My mother's name is Sarah."

"Your mother's name is Zara," Xosha corrected, a challenge on her face that matched her tone.

"My mother's name—" Sarah. Her name is Sarah.

Xosha had pushed her sister through this arch and Zara... She landed *somewhere*. Scared and alone in a foreign place. And only a child. I was right. The place that banished things went to is...my world. All the legends and stories and monsters... They came from Elysian. My mother had come from Elysian.

The puzzle pieces suddenly fit. Whoever found her, on whatever lonely street she had turned up in—she must have tried to tell them her name was Zara. She must have tried to explain everything. And of course, she would have sounded like a child with a wild imagination who'd probably gone through something traumatic. My mother was found on the streets and turned in to authorities and they must have thought she meant her name was Sarah, not Zara. And Zara—my mother—must have eventually believed it was all her imagination. With her gifts suddenly not working and being told what she was saying was impossible, she must have learned to believe it.

"My mother is Princess Zara," I breathed. "The Pale Queen."

"That's right, my sweet niece." Xosha grabbed my hair. I barely felt any pain from it. "You stupid nothing girl. I built this empire, and you are not going to ruin everything I've worked for." A murderous gleam glossed over her eyes. "I guess I never questioned where my sister was going, only that she was going. I never imagined her having a child of her own. And I certainly never imagined that child coming back here. Did you bring her with you?"

I didn't answer. My head was still swimming in the revelation that this *monster* was related to me. The Dark Queen was my aunt, and she was screaming in my face now. Asking—demanding—where Zara was. I didn't know. I hadn't known where my mother was for over a decade.

Something snapped at my collarbone, and I barely came to as the locket was ripped from my neck once more. A surge of energy blasted through me. The fire that had rumbled beneath the surface for so, so long—the raging, screaming flame in my veins—it unleashed. And it was the biggest mistake the Dark Queen had ever made.

A burst of noise left my lungs—a roar I didn't know I was capable of emitting. A flash of disturbance invaded Xosha's face. Her eyes went wide, and she thrust me back. I threw my arms out to catch myself, grabbing the sides of the archway before it was too late. But the way the Dark Queen looked at me was almost equal to the way she'd looked at Tynan when he was set free from his cell. She kicked a leg out, her foot thudding against my chest and pushing *hard*. My fingers slipped, and I fell back, back, back into a pit of darkness.

The meadow disappeared, Xosha's unsettled face with it, and I fell so long that for a moment, I thought I might be back in the Nothing. And then I realized I *was* in the Nothing, right back where this had all started.

Little flickers of light came alive all around me, taking form much quicker than they had the first time I was here. I fell in an eternal depth, familiar scenes playing on both sides of me like a movie reel.

My mother, with her snow-white skin and sun-bright hair, tucking me into bed with sad, pale-blue eyes. My father, staggering and passing out cold after he'd slammed my face into a wall for looking at him too long. My brother, showing how much he loved me in the only way he knew how. His own fists meeting with my arm in an effort to teach me how to survive the life that was given to us. My ex-boyfriend's voice as he spat verbal abuse and manipulation. His mouth forming the word "crazy" when I thought I saw... I thought I had seen him leaving an empty room with a girl at that one party.

I would show them all crazy. I would not be silent anymore. I would not run, I would not stay down. More images flashed by.

Leah, Ian, Rhett, and Viv—the pictures they'd send me as they danced between light beams, teeth the brightest of all the colors. The nights when they didn't feel like doing, rather than just being, and being together was always preferred. The laughter and conversations that had lasted far longer than the moon could stay awake.

And then metal crunching in and darkness invading. Three hands grabbing at my body, pulling me out of one world and into another. Dangerous eyes in the desert that looked hungry for anything but food. A hopeless look in a pair of honey-brown eyes.

Zafar. His hand on my waist as we rode through the sand. His teeth at my ear and his hand dropping lower. The lack of fire in his eyes when he betrayed me. The last male that would ever use me or make me feel less than.

I closed my eyes, not able to take any more playbacks of my life, but the images didn't stop. An alternate reality flashed through my mind instead. The life I could have had. A normal one. The one stolen from my brother and I. And it was too much to bear.

My eyes opened, and I screamed. A dark, vengeful noise that echoed until I landed with an impactful thud.

I choked on dense, gritty dirt, its dampness pressing against my arms, my legs, in between my fingers. I inhaled and coughed immediately after, my brain processing that I was somehow underground. Panicked, I clawed my way for a surface, only for more dirt to cave in on me.

But I would not die today. Not after everything I had survived. I held my breath and shoveled my arms through the thick, wet soil, scraping past worms and roots. I fought with everything in me until fresh air hit the tips of my fingers. I climbed the last bit until my elbow was out, and then my head. I should have been coughing out dirt and gasping for air, but I came out a vengeful banshee. I was a psychopath, and God help anyone who found themselves in my path next.

I tumbled to my stomach and grappled the rest of the way out of a makeshift grave. It took only one blink to recognize exactly where I had turned up. I was in my fucking backyard.

The first thing in my line of vision was the kitchen window. Lying on my stomach, I watched through it, to where my father stood, tipping his head back to bring a beer to his lips. The wrong one. He was the wrong one to run into today.

The roar found its strength again and resurfaced, regenerated. A deep, earthy war cry left me as I pounced up from the ground and ran. Everything but my father standing in front of the window grew fuzzy.

The back door could have been unlocked, I didn't bother to find out. I threw it open with such an inhuman force that it splintered off the hinges. My father's head whipped toward it, toward me. Whatever wild thing he saw standing before him was enough to make the color drain from his face. He went as pale as I remembered my mother's skin being.

He stumbled back, the beer bottle slipping from his grasp. "Briar?"

My body moved of its own accord. My fists were balled in his shirt, dragging him from where he was rooted in the kitchen. I threw him backward, clear across the house and into the front door so hard the bare walls rattled. But they were used to that.

I closed the distance faster than should have been possible and hauled him off the floor with ease.

"Briar!" he shouted at the daughter he hadn't seen in six years. This hard, cruel man that had once found such things humorous was now frozen in a wide-eyed terror. Good.

There was so much I wanted to say, but something at my core raged against me, fighting for my attention, and for whatever reason, I listened.

"Where is she?" It came out a bitter snarl. I pushed my hatred and sorrow aside for just this one moment, to learn where another world's queen was. To get her back.

When he didn't answer, I lifted his body toward my face. "Where—" I slammed his back against the door, "—is my mother?" It wasn't until he gargled out some noises that I realized his feet had left the floor, and my dirt-coated nails pressed far too deeply into his neck. I loosened my grip and set his feet on the ground.

"I didn't—" He gasped for air, *tears* in his eyes. "I didn't mean to."

"What do you mean? What didn't you mean to do?"

His eyes widened, blinking about like he was waking from a dream. "H-how?" His confusion was so different from his usual cruel, lopsided grin and hostile laughter. He actually stumbled over his words. "You were dead. Liam heard it on the news. He confirmed the identity of your body and then he came here to tell me. You were... I—"

"Buried me in the backyard because you're too cheap for a headstone." It felt nice to *say* something back to him for once. To not feel powerless.

I pushed inward slightly, and maybe it was the sight of a ghost come back to haunt him, but my emotionless father crumpled in fear. "She was going to leave with you two," he cried. "I didn't mean for it to happen. I was just trying to stop her from leaving."

I paused. Every cell in my body tingled with nerves. But I said nothing and waited for the awful truth to come out.

"She had bags packed and was waiting for you kids to get home from school, but I left work early that day. I walked in on her packing. I thought if I could just hold her down long enough to get her to listen, but I—"

My heartbeat sped too fast. It pounded in my throat, my whole body sweating. "You what?"

All it took was a single display of fear on my face for his bravery to return. His own resentment washed over him. "That girl ruined my life. I got so close to living the dream. I could have made a good life for us, better than she'd ever had, but she was careless and got pregnant and it ruined everything. She thought I was going to let her ruin my life and then walk away like she'd never been here? I lost control, I admit that."

He lost control. That was all. Like he'd done no harm. Like there was any way to pin the blame on her.

I blinked, and tears spilled out one after the other. All these years, my mother's quick departure had never felt right. I hadn't thought about it too much until I left. But my mother took nothing with her. She left her clothes behind, along with the necklace that was so important to her. She left us behind. She left it all. And I had doubted her anyway. Her kind, warm heart that I knew deep down could never willingly leave her kids with an abusive alcoholic. All this time, all these years, I had wondered what life she'd found after us, and she had never left us at all.

"Did you know?" I whispered. My soul was drained, the fire nearly spent. He only stared at me, his usual coldness returned. "Did you know where she came from? Who she was?"

He wheezed out what had always been his cruelest laugh, the one he used when he was making fun of someone. The sound of it sent the dying embers flaring. "You mean her stories? She would dream. Call out names I'd never heard, talk of places that didn't exist. The one time I asked her about it, she said she'd had the same dream since she was a child. A place she'd invented." He laughed again, already forgetting that a wraith was before him.

I gritted my teeth. "You didn't answer my question. Where is she?"

His eyes flicked over my shoulder subconsciously. Another squeeze had him spitting out, "Buried. Deep in the woods."

Buried. Along with the fate of Elysian. The earth-shattering truth vibrated through me, and it was the only thing I could hear. It was over. It didn't matter who came out the victor in this war. Elysian's fate was sealed. My mother was never coming back.

My father fell to the ground, not catching himself, and the loud thud sent me blinking. I hovered over him. His body was limp, his eyes open, but unmoving. Their deep-brown center darker than usual.

"Get up." I sniffed. He would show me himself. He'd walk me to the grave, and I'd make him face what he'd done. He didn't move.

I closed my eyes, pointlessly trying to stop the tears from trickling out. "Get. Up."

But he didn't move, didn't blink, and the red semicircles imprinted on each side of his neck made me watch his chest. It never rose. Never fell. I kicked him. Still nothing.

I turned my palms upward, examining my dirt-covered hands. I hadn't felt the scratches he left at my wrists trying to fight for air. I hadn't felt anything at all, just that blinding sorrow and rage finally allowed to unleash. I waited for the guilt to take over. For the realization of what I'd done to overwhelm me, to send me to my knees in shock and grief. It never came.

I didn't remember sitting down. I just came to at some point, sitting on the couch and staring at the wall. It was the flat-screen television I noticed first. We didn't have one when Liam and I had used the living room as our bedroom too. I blinked, my eyes heavy and my throat dry. I found the remote stuffed in a couch cushion and pressed the power button, the news flicking on. The date sat in the lower right-hand corner of the screen. September thirteenth. It hadn't even been the beginning of summer when the accident happened. If time worked the same here, I had been gone for almost four months.

My gaze landed on my dad's cell phone and car keys on the coffee table. I reached for the phone, pulled up the search engine, and typed in my name and last known location. I don't know why it mattered. Of all the things I couldn't fix, this was yet another one of those things. But I scrolled through the results anyway until I found what I was looking for.

### 2 Dead, 1 Injured in Multi-Vehicle Collision

*Two people were killed, and one injured following a multiple vehicle collision Friday afternoon in Wake County. First responders arrived at the scene of the accident on Crossroads Blvd at 12:17 p.m. Troopers reported a pickup truck was traveling eastbound on Crossroads Blvd when it was hit by a semi-truck that ran through a red light. Driver, Briar Clarke, 22, died in the hospital after days in critical condition. Passenger, Leah Culver, 21, was killed instantly. The pickup truck rolled several times before coming to a stop on its hood. The driver of the semi-truck suffered minor injuries and faces charges from both the state and Culver's parents.*

I fell back onto the couch, the phone's screen dimming as I swallowed the burning in my throat.

Leah had died instantly. I would never know if she'd felt any pain, or if she'd had time to realize what was happening. I hadn't even been given an opportunity to say goodbye.

I didn't look back as I started my dad's truck and pulled out of the driveway. I didn't care that someone would eventually come to look for him. Didn't care about the door blown off its hinges as evidence that something wrong had happened here. Didn't care that they'd find his body slumped against the door with his dead daughter's fingerprints around his neck. It should have bothered me that none of that was bothering me. But I felt nothing as I drove.

# CHAPTER THIRTY-TWO

It only took a few minutes of searching the internet to find where Leah had been laid to rest.

I walked through the rows of headstones. It came quicker than I was ready for.

*Leah Culver. Cherished daughter, faithful friend.*

That she was. Faithful to the very end.

Flowers flooded her gravesite, the petals drooping. My heart cracked at the silver chain draped over the side of the headstone, the same one that used to hang around Ian's neck.

The unfairness of it all hurt too much. Ian and Leah hadn't even been given a chance. I was the one who left no one behind. I was the one who wouldn't be missed. I didn't have parents that mourned the loss of me or a boyfriend who was made whole by my existence. Why had I been the one spared?

I knelt, placing a hand on the ground and allowing the tears to fall freely. "Leah," I whispered. "I'm so, so sorry. This is all my fault. It should have been me."

The wind blew, rustling the grass, and a soft, quiet voice hummed words in my ear that weren't actual words.

*But you* are *needed, child. An entire population is dependent on your existence and is suffering by your absence.*

I ignored the impossible voice and its impossible words. A tear splashed on my hand, reminding me to wipe my eyes.

"I'm sure you know all about the mess I've gotten myself into," I said to Leah. "Everything is so screwed up, and I don't know what to do next. Where do I go from here?"

*Elysian,* the wind whispered.

"I can't go back to Elysian," I said to the wind, to Leah, to whoever was listening. "I don't belong there. And something that wasn't meant for Elysian cannot stay." I repeated what Darya, the scholars, and Xosha had drilled into me.

The wind lashed at that. *Wrong, wrong, wrong,* it seemed to say.

I wished I did belong there. With everything in me, I wanted to belong.

*Don't you see?* the wind said in return, as if it could read my mind. *You* are *designed for Elysian. Your family has reigned the soil longer than you know.*

My insides squeezed at the truth of it. My mother was the Pale Queen, and she had died, leaving only one daughter as a successor. But no one knew better than I how wrong that was.

"I am *not* a queen. Haven't you been paying attention? I'm not a leader or a fighter. I'm not built to be special."

The wind laughed, a soft, breathtaking sound. *You doubt the very soil itself?*

I wiped at my eyes again, unable to stop. "I *can't.*"

How did Elysian expect *me* to stop the Dark Queen? I couldn't even get back there. No one could after they left.

*Oh, but you can.*

"But *how?*" I pleaded, since the wind seemed to have all the answers.

But it was Tynan's words as he read from ancient text that breezed through my mind over and over and over. "*This soil was meant for God's other creations and beasts. May they come only by design and go as they choose, but never to return to paradise again."* And then a separate piece of text... *"With the exception of the ruler of all rulers."*

"Ruler of all rulers," I whispered.

*Yes...*

We had thought the text was referring to God, but... "Ruler of all rulers. The text was talking about the queen of all queens. The High Queen."

*And you are queen of all queens.*

I felt for a locket I no longer wore.

I had worn my mother's locket around my neck since the day she died. I hadn't known at the time that the day her gifts had transferred to me, they had also been dimmed and trapped inside that same cursed locket. The fire I created in the dungeon had only ignited once the locket was snatched off my skin. And even with my abilities trapped inside that locket, Elysian had recognized me, had still reached for me in the Nothing. Begged me to come home.

*All you need to do is ask, and you shall return home.*

Home. My body didn't recoil at the word like it usually did.

I could go back if I chose to. My presence alone without the cursed locket resting on my skin could save Elysian. I could bring life back to a dying land.

But I was scared. My stomach knotted, not only at the possibility of facing my aunt, at even attempting to somehow stop her, but about what came after. Was I really to believe I had impressed the Core of Elysian enough to rule an entire kingdom? To sit on a throne and expect masses to listen to me?

The memory of Mavi wrapping his arms around my neck in a hug before I left Genesi washed over me. Of Bly dancing in the water. Of Ara and Enzo playfully bickering. Of Tynan's lips on mine, fitting so, so perfectly.

No one had to know the Pale Queen was dead. No one had to

know the truth of who I was. I could simply return, come up with a plan to incapacitate Xosha, and when life returned, no one had to know it was because of me. I didn't care who sat on the throne, as long as it wasn't a murderous heart. And I was now a murderous heart.

But as far as going back, I couldn't lie to myself. It was what I had to do. What I wanted to do. I would restore peace and then I would live quietly.

*We shall see*, the wind spoke.

An odd determination I'd never experienced before filled me. I straightened. "I'll do what I have to. But first," I told it, "I have some goodbyes to say."

I flattened my hand on the ground, my palm and the grass fully connecting. There was no work to it, it just happened naturally. The soil responded to my touch, and far below, I could *feel* it, roots driving deeper into the earth as buds sprouted open. It was such a small act, and yet there was so much vibration underground as stems rose up, up, up, all while roots moved in the opposite direction. Green stems calmly poked through the soil and awakened, continuing to grow until their leaves unfolded, one after the other, and then, at the top of each stem, yellow rose petals unfurled, blossoming with life. My fingertips tingled as I drove the magic—*my* magic—deeper, adding Elysian's extra magic in the seeds to make the roses live longer than what this planet's soil could give them.

"I love you," I said, because goodbye was too hard. "Forever and ever and ever."

I drove back to my father's house.

Cutting through the backyard, I walked past my unmarked grave, with only a quick nasty glare at it, and into the woods. I kept walking until the sunlight had difficulty pushing through the thick brush, until I passed two sets of old boxing gloves resting together in the dirt. They'd been there for a long time now, unbothered by mine and Liam's problems.

I walked until I found what I was looking for. I'd realized at the cemetery that it had to be in these woods. I walked until a massive redwood tree blocked my path, stretching taller and grander than all the other trees around it. I dropped to my knees at the sight of my mother's grave. Her missing redwood tree from the Garden.

For a while, all I could do was stare, at a loss. I barely remembered my mother, and that made me sad. I knew she was warm. I knew she loved me. And that was all. "You didn't deserve any of this," I spoke to the tree, my throat tightening. "I'm sorry I doubted you." My body buzzed with an awareness it didn't have before. "Show me what to do, and I swear I'll fix this."

The wind thrummed with glee, and suddenly, the forest was alive. Treetops swayed, and my hair whipped at my face. The soil murmured louder and louder until I touched my hands to its slightly damp richness.

All you need to do is ask. That's what the wind had said.

I closed my eyes and tried to imagine what the Sand Queen felt like when she connected herself to the earth. I tried to imagine my feet rooted in the soil as if it were a part of my own body. I breathed in deeply and said the words, meaning them with every fiber in my being. "Take me home."

The ground shifted, and my knees sank. I kept my eyes closed the entire time as the earth turned inward like quicksand and swallowed me whole. When I was fully submerged, I couldn't tell what was happening, but somehow, the earth *moved* for me, creating a pocket of space to breathe. I sank and sank until the world tilted and upside down became right side up, and when I flipped on the other side of that mirror, I could feel it—a magic woven throughout the soil that matched my own. Elysian. As if it had so simply been there all along.

I let the earth read my mind, flipping through different places I'd seen, each image carrying me there with just a flip of a mirror. My sense of direction stilled once I landed in a place with tiny, grainy particles of sand and a saltiness coating the air above ground. Here, I let the earth carry me upward until I broke the soft, white surface and rose from it like Cozbi, sand pouring off of me and repelling from my body easily.

The air was feathery, and I filled my lungs with it. If I thought the scents and sights were intensified before, they were unbearably sweet now. The vanilla musk and beachy forest were so much more than that, but I didn't have time to properly take it all in. I had to move. I had to find someone to help me. And Darya was the only ally I had, regardless of the rules she'd put in place against crossing the border.

The cluster of trees that separated this part of the beach from the palace lay ahead. But they looked...different. They were stiff and gray, on the verge of death. That quickly, the curse had reached the farthest ends of Elysian.

I ran. Swiftly and painlessly, unlike my first trek up this hill. My legs pumped, and when I made it to the palace gates at the cliff's edge, my breathing remained steady. If I had time, I would have been taken aback by the ease and speed of it.

I sprinted for the two guards standing watch, both of them stiffening at my approach.

I set aside pleasantries. "I need to see Darya," I demanded before either could speak. One of them bunched his eyebrows in offensive, and I thought he was going to turn me away, but then the other stepped forward and looked me over.

"You're the human girl."

Half human, apparently. "Yes," I replied. "That would be me."

"I remember you." The girl Darya risked her kingdom's safety for, his eyes seemed to say. But he only turned to the other guard and nodded. "She's good. Darya called her a friend."

"Thank you." I moved to walk by them.

"You won't find her in there." His words stopped me. It was then that I noticed how empty the courtyard was, how the ocean carried no sound other than its own soft roaring. "You'll have to wait for Remi to return."

"Why?" I asked. "Where is Darya?"

"Briar!" a chirpy voice called from the courtyard. I knew that voice. Only one naiad in this entire kingdom had a voice like...

"Bly!" I called as she ran up to me and clasped my forearms.

"Ohmigod, Ohmigod, Briar, Briar, Briar! You've come back!" She bounced on her toes, all the nerves and excitement inside her too much to contain.

"Bly, I—"

"Where have you been? Did you make it to the scholars? I have so much to tell you! Have you heard?"

"Bly, listen. I—"

"They said Kalopsia turned you over to the Dark Queen. We were worried. Quick! You must tell me everything!"

"I will—"

"Oh, it's terrible news, Briar. You should have seen—"

Blythe!" I yelled.

She halted dead in her tracks, her features melting into a puddle of pure distress. I'd never seen anyone look so double-crossed. She pouted and threw her arms down at her sides, stomping one foot like a child. "How could you!"

I grabbed her wrists in an effort to keep her attention on one thing for more than a second. "I need you to listen to me. Okay?" She didn't speak. "Bly?"

Her bright, over-the-top, bubbly voice flattened into a monotone annoyance. "I'm listening." If I had known using her full name would get this kind of reaction, I would have used it a long time ago.

"Where is Darya?" I asked.

"The Garden."

I shook my head, confused. Darya had been dead set on not having anything to do with the rest of Elysian. "Why did she go there?"

"Well, she didn't have much of a choice after the Dark Queen came."

My head spun. I led Bly farther into the courtyard, away from the guards standing close by. "I need you to tell me everything in detail. It's really important, Bly."

"Everything?" she asked, reminding me that she didn't know where I had been all this time.

"Start at when Darya left Genesi."

Bly leaned forward, unable to keep still or upset with me for long. "It all happened so fast. The Dark Queen—"

"Xosha," I interrupted. Bly's eyes widened. "She is no queen," I repeated Tynan's words. "She's an imposter who killed her way to the throne."

Bly eyed me at the vagueness of what I'd just told her.

"Xosha..." She started again, seemingly uncomfortable using Xosha's real name. "She came through the barrier with a cart from Kalopsia. That deal Darya made to get you through the desert, it allowed Kalopsian carts access to the water's edges to deal their trades. It allowed Xosha to come through undetected." If there was any question over Kalopsia's allegiance it had just been answered. Kalopsia had been quietly loyal to Xosha this whole time. "She forced Darya to come back to the Garden where she is to stay until she bends the knee to the D—to Xosha. She took Kenna and Keagan too. She's coming for all of them."

"And she just expects everyone to pledge their loyalty?" Doubt crossed my tone.

"She...made a bargain with Darya."

"There's no bargain that could possibly make Darya pledge her loyalty to Xosha."

"It..." she said very slowly, like if she didn't say it out loud, it wouldn't be true. "involved Mavi."

My blood ran cold, a nervousness clutching at my heart. "Where is Mavi?"

"A siren approached him on the shore. It only took a moment to lure him to the water close enough to drag him in. They waited for Xosha to arrive with the carts and then handed him over to her. If Darya went quietly, and if she bends the knee when asked, Mavi will be returned safely. If not..."

We all knew what Xosha did to her prisoners.

I put a hand to my mouth.

"It was awful. Darya went with her and ordered that the towns be put on lockdown until her return. Only a few guards remained here to guard the palace, and I... I didn't follow orders. I couldn't leave. This palace is my home. Remi has been in and out all day, going back and forth between the towns and the palace, waiting for either Darya or word from Darya. He's worried sick, Briar."

So that was Xosha's newest plan. With the lesser rulers behind warded cells, the little of the true power Elysian still survived on would be trapped, and that would speed up the death of the land. Xosha thought she could back Elysian into a corner and make it more willing to give in and crown her so that it could live. A last-ditch effort. She was desperate now. But Xosha didn't know that her sister's lifeline had ended and had already been passed on to someone else. Someone whose gifts were no longer smothered. She'd have to kill me for her plan to even have a shred of hope at working. But first, she'd have to figure it out.

"How long has it been since she left?"

"Two days. No word from Darya yet."

"Two days and you haven't heard from her?"

"Something happened. There was an attack on the Garden. King Tynan and Queen Zima's armies invaded before she could get to them too."

"How long has it been since they invaded?"

"Word arrived just hours ago." She tilted her head at me. "You have odd timing."

"I'm going to stop Xosha." A look of hopelessness crossed Bly's face, and I took her hand in mine. "But I need your help."

And then I told her everything, leaving out the incriminating parts. With a guilty consciousness and a whole lot of hope, I told her the only plan I had.

# CHAPTER THIRTY-THREE

I couldn't risk leaving to search for Remi in case he came back to the palace while we headed for the towns. We sat in absolute agony for two hours. Two hours of me swimming in thought over how much longer Elysian had. Two hours of me dwelling on which hour Tynan would face Xosha and which minute he would fall.

Until Remi finally trudged through the double doors, combing a hand through his hair, face strained with so many emotions I couldn't pick which took the forefront.

Bly and I straightened from where we sat at the bottom of the staircase when he glanced up, his pace quickening when recognition hit.

"Briar? I don't believe it. Where have you been?"

"It's a long story," I replied, meeting him halfway.

"Darya reached out to Kalopsia for an update a week after you left. We were told you'd been delivered safely through the desert. But then news traveled that the Dark Queen had the human girl."

"I was delivered safely through the desert. Cozbi's personal guard escorted me through the Everwood himself, and then into the hands of Xosha."

A slow transition from understanding to anger hardened Remi's expression. "She kept her end of the deal."

I nodded. That she did. "I escaped."

"How?"

I shook my head, tucking away the small details that might hint toward what I wanted to keep hidden. "Another long story. I've been with Tynan in Valhalla, and we got separated. We have to get to the Garden. Quickly."

Remi shook his head. "We can't."

"We have to."

"Briar, we *can't*. The Dark Queen has Mavi. She wins. It's over."

"No, it's not," I said, taking a step closer. "I have a plan."

Remi gave me a cautious look.

"It's a good plan, Remi," Bly said softly from around my shoulder. He looked at her like it was the first time he'd noticed she was there, but the unusual calmness in her earned his attention.

"Okay," he said. "Let's hear it."

I spent the next several minutes rehashing the last conversations I had with Xosha. That she was responsible for the murder of the High Queen and the disappearance of the Pale Queen, how she'd quickly realized the mistake she made. How she needed a clean slate in the royal family in order to get what she wanted. And then I told him about the locket. What it had been created to do, and how we could use it against her. If only we could get to the Garden and into the palace without being detected. If we could find the locket and somehow get it to touch Xosha's skin long enough to render her ash useless, we could put her somewhere she couldn't hurt anyone else.

"You told me once that you have the ability to shift forms when under a great amount of distress," I finished.

"I did." Remi's tone matched the wariness in Bly's eyes.

"How much distress?"

He understood then what his part in this would be. While they didn't know I could get to the Garden on my own, I needed support in this plan, and towing that support with me underground would surely lead to questions and suspicion.

"A lot," was all he said in response.

"Then we'd better get outside before we poke the dragon."

We tried everything. From attempting to piss Remi off, to threatening him, to bringing up the saddest memories he owned. Nothing was enough to get him to change forms. At one point, he told us to hit him. Bly refused immediately. I, however, was willing to do anything to get to Tynan. If it wasn't already too late.

I marched up to Remi without warning and punched him in his strong jaw with everything I had. Everything I had turned out to be a shocking amount of force that rattled me to the core. I had to stifle my bafflement when his face shot to the side and he stumbled backward.

Bly screamed and covered her mouth. The guards stiffened behind me. They'd already been given instructions by Remi that they were not to intervene no matter what happened. When he faced forward again his expression was a mixture of stupor and a hint of irritation.

"How the hell did you—"

I let out a frustrated groan. "This isn't working, and we're running out of time."

"I haven't turned since the last war. It's been hundreds of years. This isn't going to be easy. Maybe if I'd practiced shifting often, but I haven't."

"Think of Mavi," I said, as if he weren't already. It was a low blow, but I was desperate. "What if Mavi doesn't make it out of this?"

"That's not going to happen. Darya is going to surrender."

"But what if not all the rulers surrender? I know Tynan won't. What if Xosha keeps her word but Mavi gets hurt in the crossfire?"

He considered it. "I'll kill her."

"I know you will," I said. There was no doubt in my mind. "What of Darya?" I pressed on.

Remi looked at me as though he didn't know me. He didn't, not this version of me, at least. "What of her?"

"What if she's hurt too? Xosha has kept every deal she's ever made, with an unexpected twist at the end. What if Xosha takes everything you've ever loved away from you, just for the fun of it?"

He gave me a stone-hard look, arms crossed. That look as though he had never met me before was just as set as his jaw was.

"You love her, don't you?" I challenged.

"Of course, I do. We share a child together."

"No, I mean you're *in* love with her."

Remi said nothing, but his jaw flexed just a tick.

"It's obvious. You love being around her, but you hate it too, don't you? You hate playing family without truly being one. Seeing her every day is torture, and there's nothing you can do about it, because she doesn't want you."

There was no sign that anything was changing, internal or external, but I knew I had to be close. I just had to chip away a little more, had to find that nerve he didn't know was there and hit it. I gave a mean laugh under my breath and felt Bly go rigid beside me.

"You're unbelievable," I said with disgust. "You might be old, Remi, but you're still just a kid."

"Briar." Bly inched closer to me. "Maybe—"

But I could see it then, the quiver of change behind those cool-blue eyes of his.

"Darya has known you her whole life. You've had *hundreds* of years to do something about it, and you haven't. Why would I expect you to do anything now? You're a coward."

"Briar," Bly whispered. She slipped her hand into mine, either to bring me back from the rampage I was on, or to keep herself from running from the flicker we both witnessed in Remi's eyes. An internal shift.

"No," Remi spoke, keeping his eyes on me. "Let her finish. Let's see how quiet little Briar really feels."

I smiled unkindly. "Oh, I haven't even started yet. You know what I really think of you?" I left Bly's side and stepped closer, not stopping until I couldn't walk any farther without bumping into his chest. "I think you're pretty." I flicked a tuft of white hair. "Perfectly sculpted." I pushed his chest, and he unfolded his arms to catch himself, taking a hard step back. A brief hint of bewilderment flashed across his face and then disappeared as the anger pushed back. "Perfect hair." Another shove. Another flash of fury. "Perfect charisma." Shove.

And then it was there. The near violent rage I needed from him. "And that's it. A pretty face to flirt with. That's all you're good for." I shoved harder, and he took two steps back, almost tripping on the last step, but he quickly rounded on me, his face hovering above mine.

"Enough!" he yelled. "You've made your point."

And that was when I knew I had him. He'd forgotten what we were doing here.

"Have I? Is it enough?" I didn't shrink back like I was so used to doing. "Because you've failed to protect your family, and it doesn't seem to bother you at all."

Smoke fumed from Remi's nostrils, his shaking so violent I thought he was going to be sick. For a split second, I was nervous he might lose all control in the middle of transition and shove me back. But he fought to hold on to any last bit of him that wasn't animal as he fell to the ground and convulsed, his skin ripping to reveal another layer underneath that was not dermis, or any layer of skin at all.

Somehow, someway, right before our eyes, Remi's body took shape into another creature altogether. A body that was not Remi towered over us so high that he blocked the sun from view.

Bly screamed again. The guards scrambled backward, never having seen Remi this way with their own eyes. They drew their weapons, but I lifted my hand to hold any further action, and for some reason, they listened to me.

Remi's white-scaled body towered above us, his wings outstretched so wide they blocked the sun. He was larger than Xosha's three dragons combined. He angrily flapped his wings.

"Remi!" I called up with a triumphant smile. "I was only kidding!"

For a moment, he looked like he was going to eat me, but then I saw the shimmer of recognition in those familiar blue eyes. His wings calmed, and he lowered his long neck to the ground, bumping me with a giant nose so that I fell into the sand.

I couldn't help but laugh. Bly found nothing funny about this, and her sudden lack of overbearing personality sent me into a greater fit of laughter.

He lowered his body to the ground in invitation.

I stood and grabbed Bly's hand. Her feet stuck in the sand, and for once she was speechless. If I'd been wearing the locket, she may have been able to resist me, but without it, I was stronger, braver. I was a new being entirely.

Bly only halfway protested, mentally stuck somewhere in her disbelief over what had happened. I was able to push her up onto Remi's back thanks to that disbelief and then climb up behind her. Remi pushed off the ground before anyone could change their mind, and in only a few blinks, we were leaving the gaping guards on the ground far below.

Bly dug her nails into Remi's scales, her body frozen in terror, but something came over me. If we weren't trying to stay under the radar, I would have screamed with joy, with victory. It felt like hope in these clouds. Like there might actually be a chance I could walk out of this alive. For the first time in my life, I wasn't afraid. And in that moment, I knew the old me had died along with the human part of my soul in that accident.

We flew over the Kalopsian desert, and soon after, the Everwood. Only it wasn't the same Everwood that had greeted me the first time I crossed its border from the west. There wasn't even a speck of green below us. The scene below was deafening—a bareness that matched the Garden. Where the thick trees had once canopied the forest floor, it was now see-through, the purple flowers brown and dried into the ground. It caught Bly's attention too.

"The main towns perished after Darya left," Bly spoke for the first time. "Elysian only has a few days maybe before the last of the life in Genesi dies. Before it all dies."

My newfound bravery wavered, familiar fear sinking into my stomach. What if this didn't work? Stupidly, I didn't have a backup plan. If we couldn't find the locket or couldn't get to Xosha within a safe range...

That wasn't an option. "No." I sat taller on Remi's back, willing the flicker of flame awakening inside me to reach my voice. "It won't."

# CHAPTER THIRTY-FOUR

We heard the battle before we saw it.

Thousands of raging bodies poured throughout the entrance point of the Garden. The fighting began on the front lawn and spilled out onto the bridge and in the courtyard. Some of the battle just began to spill out farther along the palace's walls, but had not yet surrounded the entirety of the massive estate grounds.

The land was speckled with the deep-green armor of Valhalla's warriors, the frosty white and gold of Kashmir, the blood-red of the Garden, and the dirt-brown armor of Kalopsia that practically blended in with the battlefield.

A mixture of sweat, dirt, and gore had me crinkling my nose as we flew over them all. We breezed down the side of the enormous palace, a symphony of colliding swords and clubs and spears zipping by until only their echoes reached us. Remi flew a slow circle around the back of the empty palace grounds, giving us a bird's-eye view.

The Garden was made up of acre upon acre of crops—or what should have been live crops—to supply food to lands like Kashmir, who couldn't grow certain things naturally. But with all the death in the land, there was nothing growing. Nothing that could provide any cover for a secret entrance into the palace. No ivy walls to tear through, no grown-over flower beds that may hide any doors. Apart from the lake and a lone weeping willow tree, the grounds were empty. Remi dipped low to the ground, close enough to allow Bly and I to run our hands along the lower stones. He flew slowly while we inspected the exterior walls for uneven surfaces or gaps that might be a secret door-way. I tugged on a broken trellis, but it only crumpled to the ground.

Xosha had admitted she snuck out undetected with her sister through an old passageway that led out the back of the palace. The most heavily guarded estate in the world at the time. I scanned the area over and over, Remi flapping in place patiently, waiting for direction. For a moment, I froze, unsure. What if she'd lied? What if she'd misspoken or I'd taken her words too literally? I scanned farther out to the endless hills of soil rolling on for miles, but there were only mountain cliffs in the farthest corners and rows of bare fruit trees scattered throughout.

Those tree branches had once flourished. These hills had once been full and ripe for harvest. Would they ever thrive again? I glanced around the space with new eyes, picturing what it would have looked like during the High Queen's reign. During the time of my grandparents.

My eyes darted back to the weeping willow, or what was left of it, the closest tree to the palace. Its darkened limbs drooped low to the ground. The lack of fronds left the inside of it transparent from here, showing a lonely bench inside its cover, where someone once could have enjoyed reading in complete privacy. I visualized it— two young children peeking out of the fronds, barely revealing themselves for the split second it would take to run into the start of whatever crop lay ahead. Far enough from the palace that a guard might miss a figure in the night retreating from under its once full branches.

I leaned toward the tree, and Remi was so focused on my body language that he instantly picked up on the movement and changed directions.

I pointed. "There. The willow tree." Remi soared for it, landing in front of it and lowering his belly to the dirt for Bly and I to slide off. Our feet hit the dirt with a soft thud.

We ducked under the naked branches. "Look for anything that seems off. A trap door, uneven dirt. Anything."

I went for the tree, while Bly ran to the bench, looking for an inconspicuous lever or anything deceptive about its design. I worked my hands around the wide trunk, my heart pounding with the passing seconds. I scraped my nails against the grain of the bark and all around the tree in different places until a piece shifted. Bly's head snapped up at my gasp. She raced over to my side and put her palms next to mine. We pressed into the bark and pushed our weight into it as a hidden door silently slid open.

I took Bly by the shoulders, the panic inside me too real to hide on my face. "If something goes wrong, you forget about the necklace. You run. We'll find another way."

Bly only blinked at first, as if she couldn't believe she were a part of something other than pretty dresses and flower crowns. I kept talking. We didn't have time to mentally prepare for any of this.

"She won't have it on her, but she wouldn't have gotten rid of it either. She'll want to keep it close by to use on the Pale Queen again. Find her chambers, tear it apart if you have to. There won't be many in the palace now, but if someone does see you, you are a new maid who got lost looking for somewhere to hide from the battle outside."

That was Bly's purpose here. I was the most wanted face in all of Elysian, but no one here knew of Bly's identity. And with her current experience as a handmaiden to a queen, no one would question her acting skills should she be caught roaming through forbidden rooms.

Her poor face had lost all its color, but she steadied her voice. "I'll find it."

I nodded more for her encouragement than my own. Doubt crippled me as I stood and watched her disappear into the dark tunnel. How could I have just sent the doe-eyed, free-spirited river nymph into an evil queen's lair?

I left the door open for her return and reemerged from the dead canopy. My stomach tangled as I climbed onto Remi's back. When Bly came out, we'd have to move quickly. Remi watched the skies, his restlessness apparent as he blew out impatient huffs every few minutes. The nervous energy in me didn't settle as I realized I needed to come up with a plan B. Fast. If I couldn't take Xosha down by using her own weapon against her, I'd have to somehow make it so she couldn't use her hands. All the images that trickled into my head on how that could be done... I didn't want to think about it.

Time ticked by. I glanced back at the tree for the hundredth time. "I should have gone with her."

Remi puffed out a breath and shifted on a foot. No. He was right. I was too known here, and if Xosha was inside and we crossed paths without the locket... It was too risky. I couldn't face her without it. Plan A was the only way.

A screeching sounded from the skies. I lifted my gaze and found a smaller dragon with no rider on his back speeding for us. Time. We'd run out of time.

Panic scorched my veins. I leaned into Remi and gripped on tightly with my thighs, desperate to keep our discovery of the hidden tunnel unknown. Remi seemed to have the same thoughts. Debris ricocheted off the ground at the beat of his wings, and he shot up, soaring into the battle ahead and away from Bly's mission.

Weaving in and out of abandoned turrets, we dodged streams of fire sent for us from behind. His scales pierced my skin as I clutched on with every sharp turn. Remi made a circle around the front of the battle, moving sharply in an attempt to gain enough distance between us and the other dragon so he could find a safe place to drop me off.

A whoosh originated below, much too quick to pinpoint from where, and a trail of green fire rushed through the packed battlefield, sending bodies tumbling down and screaming in its wake. The fire barreled on with no signs of fizzling out, until it met with a wall of ice that wasn't there a second ago. At the foot of the bridge, a fighter stood dressed in impressive white and gold armor and a ring of icicles crowned her head. She lifted a brown hand, and the green blaze struck against her ice barrier that was much too thick to shatter. Her long hair was as white as the ground of her land and the white bear that stood by her side. His mouth stretched open, emitting a hungry roar that shook the ground around him. Queen Zima of Kashmir flung out a stream of razor-sharp icicles spiraling for the next opponent stupid enough to charge in her direction.

Remi shot up and then down again, twisting out of the smaller dragon's range and changing our direction again. My eyes found Tynan like magic. It was concerning how they seemed to just know exactly where he was. A sword in his hand and Ambrose at his back. No helmets covered their dirt-coated faces, allowing all to see exactly what they were on this battlefield. They were different beings altogether here. Long gone was the angel I'd grown to know and his complicated best friend. It was the Wingless Night and the warrior prince and all their glory from a shared past life.

They moved like magnets, parrying and thrusting as they plunged swords in between red and brown suits. Any creature or beast that approached them fell soon after. It was easy for them. Every move they made was as if they'd been built for it. Tynan *had* been built for it. Sculpted into something deadly and without morals. Sculpted into something he'd worked hard to bury deep, only letting it loose on days like today.

Not far off, a pattern of dropping bodies caught my attention. A lone figure zigged and zagged between each of the fallen. The way he moved... It was as if this warrior were dancing rather than fighting. Three opponents approached him at once, and he stopped long enough to assess. Long enough for him to turn and reveal his face.

With dirt and blood smeared across his features, Enzo was actually smiling as he plunged his sword into the thick, wooly throat of a minotaur. He pulled back and whirled, sensing rather than seeing the next one to make a move. His sword met its target, slicing into a stomach at the same time a third attacker lunged. Enzo dropped to a knee just in time, arching his back toward the misty sky to miss the flash of silver meant for his neck. Twisting his wrist to angle the sword, he thrust backward and up, into the Kalopsian soldier's ribcage. As he fell, Enzo was up again. He dropped his sword, and I watched as he took on the next enemy, making a series of quick maneuvers that ended with him choking the assailant with his own shield. He fought with his bare hands then, simply to show off.

"Can you get me to the ground?" I called up to Remi's alert ears. In response, he dived, veering off in the direction my body leaned to.

To Tynan.

Tynan's gaze flicked to Remi's incoming wings. He glanced up for what was only meant to be half a second, but then his eyes caught mine, and he froze.

His body slowly relaxed, and there was only a flicker of a smile before it fell. Before he realized that not only was I back, but I was on top of an impossibly oversized dragon.

Bodies scattered as Remi's wings sent hard dirt bouncing off the ground. Everyone but Tynan and Ambrose. My feet had barely hit the dirt before Remi was off again. I spun around to face the two soldiers staring at me—one in awe and the other in outrage. But it was Tynan I looked to. And I smiled.

Tynan didn't smile back. He only stared, his gaze fixed just above my shoulder. I read the alarm in his eyes. I barely heard a slash of silver sing at my back as Tynan's arm came up, and a blast of wind flowed around my sides. I whipped my body around, throwing my own hand up at whatever was there.

A sphere of Tynan's wind rotated around me, stopping a sword from cutting into me. The sword connected with the invisible shield, the force of it ripping the weapon from the Garden soldier's hands and hurling it several safe feet away. But even if Tynan hadn't moved as quickly as he did, my fire would have scorched the assailant. Instead, my raging storm of orange and yellow flames rushed through his bubble of wind, trapped there. The fire danced wildly through my hair and weaved in and out of my legs.

*Hold on to it.*

Even in the midst of the battle surrounding us, his voice was clear and calming. It steadied my heart and sharpened my focus.

*Not yet.*

I held firm, even as the wisps of flames begged to be set free. I closed my eyes, barely feeling the tinge of warmth on my fingertips, but the warmth inside my chest raged on while the pleading inten-sified. I breathed deeply, steadying myself and my emotions. This was my fire, and I controlled it. Not the other way around.

*Now!*

The wind barrier broke off, and I flung my eyes open, allowing the trapped flames to run free. Tynan sent pathways of wind around my fire, making tunnels for it to follow that took our enemies down with it. Bodies tumbled, starting with the Garden soldier who hadn't been smart enough to run while he could.

A hand I knew all too well wrapped around my shoulder, turning me around forcefully. His eyes were wild, and somewhere behind the murder in a warrior's brutal face, there was terror buried there too. Murder and terror and yet relief in those eyes. I stumbled when he pulled me into him, my body not sure what to do with the contact. I only allowed one hand to slide along his covered arm, suddenly feeling way too calm despite what was going on around us.

"You're back," he breathed into my hair.

Ambrose's fury was in my direct line of vision, and I pulled free of Tynan's embrace simply to get away from it.

A rapid flapping sounded at my ear, a small shadow dropping next to me a second after. My chest flooded with relief.

"Holy Kingdoms, Briar!" Ara took me by the shoulders, scanning me from top to bottom as if to ensure I was in one piece. "When I came to, I looked for you, but you were gone. I didn't know if you made it to the gate or if Xosha took you. Eventually, I didn't know what else to do except to come fight."

"It's okay. It's not your fault. I'm fine," I assured her.

Ambrose remained a few paces back, eyeing me suspiciously. He was too quiet. He was always too quiet, examining the situation and surroundings intensely, as if to make up for the lack of speculation from everyone else. But this was different. He looked at me as though I was nothing that I'd presented myself to be. He was right.

"Where *were* you?" she asked. "I searched everywhere."

Ambrose finally stepped forward, and Enzo broke through the stream of warriors filtering back in from the wind blast that had cleared a path. He didn't stop fighting to marvel at my arrival. He might not have noticed at all. He was in another headspace completely, a ruthless machine slaughtering anyone, anything, that came across his path. He fought with his sword again, around our circle, as if protecting us while we paused to regroup.

"Xosha pushed me through the gate."

A stunned silence froze the air, and Ara was the first to break it. "But that means..."

"That means she came back," Tynan finished, dimples

betraying him. I never thought I'd see those dimples again. "That's twice now." It almost sounded like pride in his voice.

Ambrose gave me a look that was both curious and untrusting.

"The Pale Queen is dead," I said in the rush of things and immediately faltered at the mistake I'd made. Too late. It was too late to take the words back.

Those words even seemed to filter through the air and over to Enzo, who I could have sworn missed a step but then quickly recovered himself and was back at it. The other three around me stilled, not a muscle flexing, and a pang of guilt coursed through me. In their minds, that meant Elysian was choosing to ignore the next in line. It meant that no matter what happened today, they would eventually die of starvation anyway.

"I know that sounds vague. I—I can explain more later," I added, not sure how I was going to do that exactly. "Right now, I have to find Xosha. I think I know how to get her under control long enough to detain her."

All heads looked to Ara. "I still haven't spotted her. As much as I've been in the skies, it's like she's not even here."

"She must be hiding inside," Tynan replied and then shot out a hand and blasted away an approaching attacker who had slipped through Enzo's defenses. The body sailed through the air and into another. "The line holding the entrance point is strong. We haven't been able to force our way in past the wulvers."

"Can't you shadow your way in there?" I asked, confused.

"I can't get in there." Tynan brushed the back of his forearm across his cheek, dragging a mixture of blood splatters and dirt farther along his face. "It's protected by some warding. It's like running into a brick wall. She must have added it after we escaped."

Anxiety twisted around my stomach. If she was inside and had run into Bly... "Then we lure her out," I blurted.

"With?" Ambrose shot an eyebrow up. A challenge. A taunt.

"Me." I held his stare as I said it. Ambrose didn't bother hiding the slight curve to his lips.

Tynan looked to Ara, as if he hadn't heard me. Or as if he had and didn't dare give me the chance. "Ara, get Briar out of here. Take her to Valhalla and stay there with her."

"No, I have a plan." A half plan without that locket. "You need me."

Ambrose cackled, and I cut my eyes to him. I knew what they were all thinking. I'd been nothing more than a helpless damsel this whole time. I understood why the idea of me helping them was preposterous. Not to mention, how out of place I looked standing in my regular clothing—the bare skin on my arms covered in dirt from my own grave—in this sea of steel and blood-smeared armor. But Tynan watched me with purpose in a way no one else did. He'd already admitted to me that he thought I was holding back. That there was a fiery warrior in me.

*Your eyes are nearly glowing.*

Because I wore no locket to dull them. Because I'd been capable all along even if I hadn't known it. I glanced around, eyes darting from one end of the battlefield to the other. There was no sign of Bly. Remi still soared above, battling not one, but two other dragons now in the sky. I didn't have the locket as planned, but I had the Core of Elysian on my side. Even if no one else knew it.

I met Tynan's eyes once more. *Do you trust me?*

"This is crazy," Ambrose interrupted our silent conversation. "She has no role here."

As he spoke the words, a minotaur's gaze met the backs of Ambrose and Tynan. Enzo was too busy fighting off multiple soldiers at once to see the new one approaching. Before Ara could open her mouth in warning, I shot up my hand, aiming just an inch over Ambrose's shoulder.

The minotaur caught aflame, his battle-ax falling to the ground.

Ambrose flinched at my raised hand but then whipped around at the minotaur's deep bellowing.

Slowly, Ambrose turned his body back to me, the astonished look on his face leaving me the amused one.

Tynan smirked. "What were you saying, Ambrose?"

Ambrose's face hardened. "Fine." He stalked over to the fallen ax and handed it to me. I took it with two hands, the weight of it sending it falling heavily back into the dirt. Ambrose sneered. "We're all going to die."

"She doesn't need a sword or an ax," Ara smirked. "She's got hands."

*Yes,* Tynan finally answered. *I trust you.*

I left the ax and looked down at my hands, flexing them in and out, testing everything I felt under my skin. I could feel more than just the fire now. I distantly felt the other elements swirling around in there, somewhere, not quite sure of their origins. I had felt the ice before, freezing over my veins in a moment of revelation and stunned sureness. And the water must have been flowing freely all around me. But the wind... That was weightless. It was everywhere and nowhere all at once. It would be easy to summon. My fire raged on, having been there all along, cursed locket or not. It was what I felt the most comfortable with. It's what I would use to fight my aunt.

*I don't know what you have planned, but we're right here with you, whatever you need,* Tynan said. I nodded at him and just barely caught Ambrose doing a double take at our exchange, like he didn't think he'd seen correctly.

I eyed the turrets above us. Xosha had asked if my mother was in Elysian, if I'd brought her with me. If she really believed that, she would be waiting. Watching. "Just get me to the front of the palace and keep me there."

Tynan was unstoppable. The way he moved, the way he ordered and directed soldiers he passed with a simple command. The way they listened to him without question, without a flicker of doubt. And Enzo... He was as beastly as any wulver. All the teasing from last night and every other night had vanished. Now he was all steel and grit and otherworldly *might*. He was so locked into his role that it took Tynan three times to get his attention long enough to show him our next move. Even calling his name hadn't been enough, but a sharp *"Commander!"* had his head whipping in the direction of Tynan. In the direction of me. His steely face only flickered in surprise for a millisecond before the warrior in him returned.

Ara fell back to assist a fallen Kashmir soldier, who an arrow had gone through just as we breezed safely by in the protection of Tynan's wind shields. It was simple numbers alone that this war wasn't over and done with already, with the way Tynan blasted his way to the front line. When we made it there, my heart pounded, knowing that once I started this, there was no going back.

"Just keep this area clear for me. That's all I need from you," I directed to Tynan.

So vague. I was being so vague with them all, trusting them to just believe in me. Even Ambrose was allowing me the chance to hold their fate in my hands, and all I had for them were half answers and murky instructions. I saw the flash of unsureness in Tynan's eyes too, but it was gone a moment after, and he simply nodded.

Ty, Ambrose, and Enzo turned their backs to defend the area I'd chosen—the front lawn, just before the bridge. The would-be road that led from the Everwood to the palace gates. The front row seat for the lookout guards who watched for incoming visitors in the top turret.

I looked up at that turret, only an empty, dark void staring back. I watched it anyway. Watched and waited until I had to hold back a shiver as a haunting aura crept over me. Even then, I stared. At anyone lurking in its shadows. And then I turned my back and set to work.

With both hands in front of me, I planted my feet in the decayed soil and let my fire rain from my fingertips. There was nothing to burn but the ground itself, which of course, wouldn't keep a flame. I didn't need it to. Mini wildfires raged and roared for only seconds at a time before they went out, just long enough for the flames to stain the dirt with the letters I needed. A shadow of a message. Six little words. When I was done, I marveled at my work, the text smoking. At the words written there that could only be made out from above.

I turned my body to face the palace again, to that turret. I stared into a deceptive nothing and lifted my chin.

I threw myself around and ran into the battle, stomping over the words,

THE HIGH QUEEN IS NOT DEAD.

# CHAPTER THIRTY-FIVE

For the first time in all my life, I'd have to fight, but I would not fight with an audience. I would not face off with my aunt in a place where those I'd come to care about could get hurt in the process.

I took off for the Everwood, sprinting before the others had a chance to notice I wasn't there anymore. I ran as fast as my new inhuman legs would pump, covering so much distance already that when they did notice, they'd have to fight through an entire sea of soldiers before they got to me. I ducked underneath an incoming attacker, a swing that wasn't meant for me, and didn't allow myself to take the time to be shocked at how easily I dodged it. I kept running, making for a break in that sea of bodies where I caught a glimpse of the tree line ahead. My heart leapt for it.

I was so focused on the destination that I didn't see the dragon amongst the others, and its tail lashed out and slammed into my side. My body sailed, the breath leaving me. I landed on my stomach. Hard.

I groaned, pushing past the sharp stinging in my stomach, and forced myself to lift off the ground. In another life, I would have stayed down. I never would have stood back up, even if my body were able to. But this new body, this Divine body, was made with a whole new set of boundaries.

A challenging snort drew my attention to the dragon. He pawed at the ground, eyes so soulless they told me he was driven by pure hunger alone. I wouldn't make it to the Everwood after all, but I was far away enough from my friends that hopefully it wouldn't matter.

My hands tingled at my sides, and I eyed him, waiting. Each second that ticked by was another second that the fire inside manifested and grew into something bigger, hotter. I held it tightly as each second passed, just like Tynan had instructed. When the dragon's giant jaws snapped open, I was ready. Our fires collided.

I groaned against the force and gritted my teeth, my feet sliding in the dirt. My groan turned into a roar as I tried with everything in me to dive deeper into the source of my power and will every last drop of it out of me. It wasn't enough.

I started to angle one foot to the side and timed the perfect moment to let go and run for it. But when the opposing flame went out unexpectedly, I stumbled forward. A rush of relief and exhaustion left my lungs.

I wasn't ready for another go. I eyed the dragon, panting. I wouldn't blink first, wouldn't let him know that I would fall if he struck again. But he didn't strike again. His unblinking eyes stared into mine for seconds that felt like minutes. He seemed to sneer before shooting to the skies, flying to some other end of the battlefield that I didn't bother to track.

A chill swept over the sweat-coated air. For a moment, I just stood there, and the movement on the battlefield seemed to slow down only for me. Warriors stumbled and fell at an unnatural pace. Roars drowned out to a distant cry. It all slowed down as I watched, untouched by it all, waiting. And then she came.

She arrived as a shadow at first. A blurry image beyond the sea of clashing steel and leather suits. But the frame was unmistakably hers. The confidence of her shoulders, the bold determination in her steps. The spiked crown atop her head.

A body made its way toward her, and my gaze traveled to it. All I saw was Valhallan armor, some warrior bravely but stupidly taking advantage of what he thought was an open shot. His hands gripped his hilt, his arms lifted, preparing to sweep his blade for her head.

I breathed a word I couldn't remember as soon as it left my mouth. No, or stop, or please. It didn't matter, because it was over before it started.

Xosha flicked her wrist to the side. The end of the blade stopped short, falling to the barren ground mid swing. The soldier was there, and then he wasn't—crumbled to nothing more than ash in the wind.

Xosha stepped into full view, unfazed by any of it. She'd changed from her usual form-fitting black dress into unscathed, sleek fighting leathers the color of soot. Her raven hair was pulled back into an extravagant bun, the crown of spikes confidently sitting around it.

Time returned to normal speed, and Xosha lifted both her arms, clutching her fists in victory. When she drew them back down, a pounding of power hit the dirt in wave after wave after wave. The bodies before her disappeared into thin air. Ashes. Yards of soldiers dropped to nothing more than ashes. She hadn't even looked. She'd had no way of knowing which soldiers she took out —her own warriors, enemy warriors, or her allies from Kalopsia. The particles drifted like black snow.

Her eyes cut into mine with a fury so wicked and fierce. A ravaging smile quivered at her red lips. She'd paved a path for us, nothing but bulk pieces of leftover armor to easily step over.

"Your death won't be so kind." Her words were acid. "It won't be quick," she seethed, anger bubbling over to the point her body couldn't contain it. "You will die by my dagger in your heart. And you will feel everything as the life pulls from your core. Just the way your grandparents did." Her eyes lit with excitement and rage.

A ball of fire formulated in my palm at the same time a dagger slipped out of her sleeve. Spiral strands of metal wound from the hilt to meet at a pointed tip, smoke weaving in and out of the strands.

"If you stop this," I tried one last time, "you'll get off easier. Stripped of your powers but allowed to live. Stop the killing, end this fighting, and you can move on with your life."

Xosha's striking face twitched with rage. "I should have slaughtered you on sight. I won't continue to make the same mistakes."

For some reason, the corner of my lip went up, amused.

Xosha didn't move at first, as if thrown off by the oddly placed confidence. She finally took a step forward, her steps lacking the arrogance they usually held. But then she stopped short, her gaze landing on something just beyond my shoulder. She frowned.

I wouldn't take the bait. She'd promised to kill me without her magic, promised to end me with pain, but that didn't mean she wouldn't use tricks and cunning to get her there.

The shouting around me softened, and while silver still clashed, it too eased. And then, out of nowhere, it stopped. I locked my eyes on Xosha, refusing to give her the chance to come at me when I wasn't ready.

But her face crumpled in defeat, a small tear rolling down her cheek. Her voice was barely a whisper. "*No...*"

Her fingers tightened around the dagger's hilt, readjusting. "You want this kingdom?" she snarled. "Come and get it."

She ran, and despite the promise of suffering on her face, I met her halfway. She swung the ash dagger's point wildly. Each move was sloppy and poorly aimed, as if she'd never actually used it in this way before. I dodged it with a swift slump of my shoulder, and then another and another. Each time she attacked, I made just the slightest move out of the way. The movements came naturally and I wondered if this was how the Assassin felt when she moved. I liked it. I liked it a lot.

Xosha let out a frustrated cry, and I saw it in her eyes, what she was about to do before she was able to raise her free hand. I lifted mine faster, sending a whip of fire lashing out and wrapping around her wrist like a lasso. She screamed at the heat scorching her skin and dropped the ash dagger.

When her knees sank to the ground, I reined in the whip, leaving it tied around my own wrist, ready for if she tried it again. She clutched at her wrist, rocking and seething in pain. When her dark eyes lifted to meet mine again, I grinned. An overwhelming sense of pride in myself made it so that I couldn't contain the smile if I wanted to. The one thing she had that everyone feared, as long as I paid attention, she couldn't hurt me with it.

When she stood, still clutching her wrist, I noted the dirt staining her leather-clad knees. It was the first mark on her since this fighting had begun all those hours ago.

"You've never fought a day in your life, have you?" I called out. All this time, she'd been watching from above, letting others fight her battle for her. Her reign had been feared, not because she owned admirable skills or was a well-known warrior, but because she had a gift no one could defend themselves against. But when it came down to it... "Without your ash, how strong are you, Xosha?"

Murder filled her lungs as she charged for me. I was too busy focusing on what her hands were doing that I didn't stop her from pummeling into me. Our bodies crashed into the soft turf.

As if to prove herself to me, she shoved my face into the grass and punched me. Hard. The second blow had my vision blurring. The third had me realizing my mistake and regretting it. Despite my taunting, I was just as defenseless without my gifts. Just like her, I had never fought any battles, always taking whatever blows came my way.

The fire inside me died out with the next hit. I scrambled for it, for that power in me, but as Xosha's wild flailing and screams mixed together, I couldn't get a grasp on it at all. The next time her fist came down, I saw it coming down in the dungeon instead. Blood coated my tongue by the time those fists in the dark became my father's.

I looked for Tynan's amethyst eyes in that darkness. For that anchor. They never came.

Instead, teal flashed by, flapping over the darkness, and when it was gone, so were the fists. I waited for them to come again, but only the returned sounds of shouting and silver clashing remained. I blinked until the gray sky came back. I stayed in the grass, my breathing slow and even, as if I were so rattled that the only option was to remain calm.

Someone fell to their knees beside me, their own breathing labored. "Get up."

I couldn't get up. Not after the reminder that deep down, no matter what abilities I possessed or what confidence came with them, I'd always be the same. I'd never be a fighter.

"Get *up*," the voice snapped, desperate.

I blinked up at a warrior wearing the red armor of one of Xosha's Garden soldiers. He scanned the battlefield in a hurry. And when he looked back to me, it was forest-green eyes that met mine through a slit in a helmet. I'd met those eyes before. Briefly. In an enchanted-like forest as I ran through the trees. On a dragon's back as I was taken to this very palace to be beaten and starved for weeks.

"I can't," I faintly got the words out.

He stood, as if he were running out of time. "If you don't get up now and kill her, she'll obliterate me for this." He stretched a hand out to me, his fingertips begging for mine.

I stared at his hand, stunned. Never once had I fought back, but never once had I had someone encourage me to.

"*Please*, get up." He tried one last plea, not tearing his dark eyes from mine.

A million possibilities flashed in my head of what could happen if I took that hand reaching for mine. And out of all of them, the only one that stood out was the one possibility that would happen if I didn't. They would all go down with me.

All my life, I had been exactly the thing people saw when they looked at me. A flower. A little bird easily crushed. They had trained me to stay down. I wouldn't stay down any longer.

I clasped his hand, and the Garden soldier hauled me to my feet, relief flooding his eyes. He nudged me forward. And then he was gone.

I stood and waited, taking as many breaths as I could fit in, knowing Xosha would find her way to me again. Ara had bought me time. The soldier had bought me a second chance. The rest was up to me.

A line of bodies evaporated as Xosha ashed a clear path to me. She stopped, teeth bared, and thrust out her arms. A wave of dust coated the air and rippled for me, but I was ready. I threw mine up, and instead of summoning fire, something else surfaced. A wall of wind was thrown up like a shield. The ash slammed against it and fell to the ground. Xosha didn't seem surprised as she advanced, only stopping long enough to reach down for the fallen dagger.

Murder glinted in her eyes, but it wasn't the never-ending promise of death that sent my heart plummeting. It was Tynan, finally catching up and making his way toward us. His sword knocked down a body before his eyes snapped to mine, a determined willpower forcing his way through.

The fear of losing one more friend I cared about was the worst possible thing I could think of. Worse than anyone detecting who I was. Without thinking twice, I threw both my arms back, fire lancing around them. I drew them around in a circle, the fire following, and in under a single second, Xosha and I were completely cut off from the rest of the battle. It was her and I in a ring of fire, the walls so high and so hot that not even Tynan's wind could get through them.

Xosha glanced behind her, meeting Tynan's petrified gaze at what I'd just done.

She turned her body smoothly back to mine, satisfied. "Your emotions will be your weakness."

Before I could respond, she whipped out an arm, a wave of ash rocketing for me. It was met with a force of wind. Her ash came to a screeching halt, turning to nothing before it could meet the ground. Wave after wave she sent, and each was met with another block of my own. It was easy, so easy to summon it, but I was tired. Sweat coated the air and our bodies, and my legs shook from using so much power I wasn't trained to use. My arms trembled even as I pushed on.

Xosha screamed in frustration. For the first time in all her life, she couldn't use the only weapon she had that instilled so much intimidation and fear. She readjusted her grip on the ash dagger and started walking.

A shadow too big to be a cloud covered everything in darkness. We looked up at the giant white dragon that flew above our heads. And on his back... *Bly*. She'd made it out. Her eyes locked on mine, a nervous pleading in them. With a simple lift of her hand, she revealed the locket clutched safely in her fist. My eyes widened at the sight of it. There was no time to communicate anything more. Her fingers loosened, and the locket slipped from her grasp.

When I looked to Xosha, there was victory and malice in her eyes, and her teeth were bared victoriously. A mere handful of strides away from me, she drew her elbow back to deliver the final blow. I swallowed and looked back up. The locket was falling, falling, falling. Not fast enough.

I reached up anyway, whispering a hopeful prayer in the wind. But instead of waiting to catch it, I sucked in a deep breath, and with that breath, I took hold of the wind. My wind grasped the locket, and I thrust it as if I were throwing it with my own hand straight toward Xosha's chest, a mere foot before me.

Time itself paused. My fire wall fell.

Xosha staggered back at the force of the blast. She rasped in a pained breath as the gold of the locket glowed against her skin, tasting this new power for the first time and then dimming, as if thinking it bitter. My wind held, pushing it to her body without letting up. Her fingers loosened, and the ash dagger dropped at her feet.

Her eyes went wide, and though she struggled, she slowly dropped to her knees at the shock and force of her power being sucked from her very core.

It wasn't until I hovered over her that I truly realized the power I held in this moment. There was pure silence around us, only distant noise from a battle too far away to witness the Dark Queen's fall.

"I want to let you go," I said, despite everything. Too many had died because of all this. Some even at my hands. "I want to give you a second chance. Please let me give that to you."

My wind didn't falter for a moment, allowing the locket to taste her to its fill. She didn't scream, couldn't scream. Her fingers scrambled for the dirt, looking to retrieve the dagger. I was spent, but I was able to catch an ember swimming in the heart she had meant to stab. I let it rise through my other hand and sent a river of flames sweeping for her. I only let my wind drop once the flames were touching her skin.

She did scream then. I let the flames ignite the locket just enough so that the gold began to melt into her breastbone. Melt into her tanned skin. This was the only way to let her live while making sure she couldn't hurt anyone again. If she was smart, and I knew she was, she'd walk away from this fight with the locket permanently burned into her flesh. It would be ugly to look at, and she'd hate me even more for it. But it would heal, and no one else would have to suffer at her hands.

As the locket sank deep enough to become one with her forever, the last drop of her power drained from her core to sleep inside the locket. I dropped my flames then and Xosha sputtered at the relief and the pain that came with it. With the locket permanently embedded in her skin now, I could step close enough to reach for her crown. She swatted at my hand. Maybe my aunt wasn't so smart after all. I stared at her, letting her read the disappointment there. It was the last warning she would get before she took this too far.

When her own message remained one of clear death, I closed my eyes with sorrow and regret. My fire met with her chest again, melting the locket further into her. The scream that left her was one that would haunt my dreams. Perhaps even the Garden itself.

Xosha's mouth moved as she searched for the strength to speak. "I...will...*break* you." Somehow, she managed a sick smile.

I paused. For a second, I considered sending her through the gate. But I wouldn't do that to another world. Even that world, with all its faults and sins and all it had done to me, I wouldn't return the favor. But her words stuck with me. Her threat to break me. I almost smiled. Not a malicious one to taunt her, but a real one, because I'd realized a truth that was probably my greatest weapon of all.

I leaned in, whispering so only she could hear me. "You can't break me." A quiet laugh slipped through the statement. "I'm already broken."

She'd lowered herself while I leaned in to whisper those parting words, her fingers curling around her weapon. I only realized it once the ash dagger was shooting toward my ribcage. My fire seethed instinctively, slamming full force into her chest. Xosha shrieked an inhuman noise.

The tip of the dagger nicked my side, leaving a faint trail of smoke as it singed through my clothes. But the dagger fell again, the force of her attack sputtering out before it had reached far enough to do any true damage.

Gold and flesh fully bonded, the locket no longer visible. Xosha's screams of defeat struggled to make any noise at all while that liquefied gold betrayed its maker. The ash within it imploded, seeking a new cage cursed to keep it contained. Instead, it only found one it could destroy.

Xosha's screams faded, her face permanently stilling. And then it caved inward, cracks spearing out like broken ice and stretching until they ran out of room. The Dark Queen shattered. As if she'd only been a sculpture this whole time. Pieces of her fell away, tumbling to ash and rock at my feet.

For a moment, all I could do was breathe. Breathe and exist until I remembered to check my side and make sure it was only my clothes that had suffered. But I found the dagger amongst the rubble in doing so. My breath caught in my lungs as I examined it resting on the heap of ash and rock...in a bed of luscious, green grass.

I snapped my head up, finding an arena of soldiers who had stopped to watch Xosha's fall. No one moved. No one spoke. Weapons either rested motionless in hands or discarded at feet. And beyond the motionless soldiers...hill upon hill of green so vibrant it couldn't possibly be real rolled on as far as the eye could see.

The gray, polluted sky broke apart, and sunrays sprinkled onto the battlefield. They bounced off the lake, and the water glinted and moved again against the slight wind.

I turned in a circle, taking in the acres of *green*. I stopped short when I came back around and faced Tynan. There was a strange revelation in his eyes as he stood breathless—one of wonder and disbelief and somehow, total belief.

For whatever reason, I looked to my feet again, just in time to witness a collection of daffodils sprouting from the earth next to the fallen dagger.

# CHAPTER THIRTY-SIX

Tynan's knee was the first to hit the grass. Enzo dropped immediately after, and then, to my astonishment, *Ambrose*. It didn't matter what color painted their armor, every single soldier who had been close enough to see Xosha's fall followed without hesitation. The rest dipped shortly after simply because of what the return of life in the Garden meant. Wave after wave, weapons clattered in surrender while warriors and beasts alike kneeled.

I was too stunned to move. Maybe if I was still enough, I could disappear into thin air.

"Hail," a voice said, snapping my body awake again, and I met the mysterious glint in Tynan's eyes as he pressed a fist to his heart.

I shook my head in a panic. *No.* This wasn't what I wanted. I wasn't here to reclaim a throne.

Tynan stared at me with unwavering devotion.

*Don't you dare, Tynan.*

The corner of his mouth twitched up in a knowing smile, and his voice boomed into the battlefield. "All hail, High Queen Briar."

I stepped back, mouth agape as if he'd insulted me.

The voices rang like a choir. Or a taunting chant. "All hail, High Queen Briar."

*No, no, no.*

The choir of beaten-up soldiers only spread across the reborn land, strengthening with each round. "All hail, High Queen Briar. All hail, High Queen Briar."

Shit.

AFTER

Saint Briar. That's what they called me now.

Saint Briar, the High Queen of Fortitude and Restoration. A title worthy of the new throne room I sat in. Gone were the broken branches and thorns my aunt sat on for over twenty years during her reign. From the moment I sat on the throne, the branches regenerated to life with blood-red roses that would bloom for as long as I did. I still didn't know how to sit, even after a week. I shifted in the velvet-wrapped seat, trying to get comfortable. I slumped, resting my wrist lazily on the arm but then quickly caught myself. I sat up straight, back stiff, and uncomfortable. I sighed and glanced around the empty room, nervously tapping a thumb on the armrest.

That day on the battlefield had changed everything. I'd hardly been given the time to take a breath after those chants had finally stopped. I'd had no time to process what was happening before some of those warriors had inched in, some with praises and others with a sudden desperation for forgiveness.

Tynan had shoved his way through the starstruck crowd, pulled me into him, and shadowed us into the front courtyard to make a run for it into the palace... The palace that was now mine to hide in. Enzo caught up, helping Tynan bar the door, only allowing Ambrose and Ara through. It was a full day before the Garden was cleared, before any of us were able to establish some type of order. And then only half a day more before I was put to work.

Reestablishing order in a fallen kingdom was about as challenging as taking it from Xosha in the first place. But Ara and Enzo, it seemed, were up for the challenge. Both hadn't left my side, even spending nights in one of the dozens of bedchambers in this insanely magnificent palace. Tynan and Ambrose hadn't shown their faces since they left at the end of that first day.

Ara spent her days working with teams of the most skilled and sought-after designers in Elysian. I'd given her free rein over the entire estate, and thanks to the funds in the royal bank account that belonged to my family—and now to me—a complete redesign was more than affordable. Much to Ara's joy, the palace was busy with constant furniture deliveries, painters, floorers, and the like. The throne room now showcased luxurious red velvet curtains that hung from the clean windows, creating color in a once sunless room. Beautiful, warm light sparkled on the new marble floor, and a red carpet stretched out from the doors to the throne. By the end of the transformation, every room and hall were unrecognizable.

The foyer previously used for entertainment purposes had been done away with entirely, though that one was thanks to Remi. After he'd set Bly safely on the grass, he'd gone straight for the courtyard, barreling into the defense line and wiping out the wulvers in one nosedive. Along with the front wall and the foyer beyond it. He'd then transitioned back onto two legs, tearing through the palace halls until he found his son and queen in the underground dungeon.

I was glad of it, that the room had been destroyed, and didn't ask for it to be rebuilt. No amount of scrubbing would clean what had been done in that room. Instead, the front courtyard was expanded, and a garden was planted in the room's place. A garden that I planted myself in a matter of minutes without using any seeds or gardening spades. Apparently, as High Queen, the soil called to me in all kinds of ways. Sometimes, without meaning to, I summoned a trail of yellow flowers that would sprout each time my foot lifted from the ground to take a step.

Aside from the whirlwind of builders and decorators, there were hundreds of interviews for cooks, cleaning maids, and personal attendants. All of which were overseen by Ara. Most of the palace staff had fled when Xosha took over. Only a small handful had stayed on out of a sense of responsibility to my grandparents, but there was plenty of room to add to the staff now that the Garden wasn't a place to be feared.

The wulvers, however, the ones who had treated me with true evil in their hearts, were banished back into the deepest corners of Empyrean's woodlands, just as quickly as they had lurked out. Back to where their breed had previously hailed from. Far away from me.

Truly, I couldn't have done any of it without Ara and Enzo's help. Without them, I was alone here, with no family or advisors to guide me along the way. It was all still overwhelming. I learned very quickly that no one dared bother the High Queen when she was connecting with her land. It was the only time I could be alone, away from eager competitors hoping to impress Enzo and I with their loyalty and courage to land a spot on the royal guard. Away from the designers with their endless questions. Away from my newest lady-in-waiting, who I liked well enough, but was overly eager to serve and asked if I needed anything every twenty minutes.

I used that knowledge to my advantage, racing out to the nearest field when anything got overwhelming. It was meant to be an escape, but I found that I liked it. I enjoyed being outside under the warm rays of the sun and the cool breeze brushing flowers against my legs. I felt refilled in a way, probably because each moment that I connected with the land was fuel for it. We fueled each other.

But the magic woven in Elysian's soil was needy. After so long without its Core, the land required my attention even when I wasn't able to give it. It had found crafty ways of getting my attention when I was distracted. I'd seen that once already when I couldn't get out of interviews. A newborn lemon tree sprouted rapidly to the second floor, a branch nudging its way into the window and interrupting a conversation with the newest head chef. It refused to retreat until I came outside to coax it down.

Elysian was reborn, but it had been weak for so long that it wanted me now in practically my every waking moment. My presence alone grew ripe tomatoes, plump eggplants, and vibrant squash ready to be plucked from their stems.

Regardless of what my intentions were when returning, despite *loathing* any kind of spotlight, I was now fighting the notion that I was oddly *good* at this. No matter how ridiculous and unbelievable it was to think of myself in a leadership role, I found myself wanting to do it and wanting to do it well.

"You look good up there."

My heart vibrated at the honey-dipped voice. I looked up, and less gracefully than I would have liked, scurried off the throne, embarrassed to have been found there at all. As if it weren't crafted specifically for me. His laugh was deep, a little husky. A little sexy. He leaned against the arch of the entryway with his hands in his pockets and one foot crossed over the other.

Tynan's night eyes were an equal mix of cobalt and amethyst in the lighting of this room, with only the faintest whisper of stars.

"I figured it was time I stop in and say thanks...again. For you know, saving the world and all." The corner of his mouth lifted, and I matched it. He pushed off the archway and met me in the middle of the carpeted runway. He scanned me from top to bottom, taking in the deep-blue, form-fitting dress my lady-in-waiting had put me in for the day. He touched the sleeve at my wrist and rubbed his thumb over the lace once before dropping his arm, as if he hadn't realized he'd reached out at all.

"It's been a week," I said, waiting for an explanation. A part of me was annoyed that I hadn't seen him since the day Elysian claimed me. A part of me was terrified he had abandoned me. "And you just casually pop in now?"

A flash of an apology sparked the stars hiding in his eyes. "The towns in Valhalla that perished at the end needed me. I had things to repair that couldn't wait."

A king, I was reminded. It's not like he was expendable. Not like I was a higher priority than his kingdom.

"And with the way we left things, I figured you'd want a little space. I asked Ara and Enzo to stay and help in my place."

"How we left things?" I didn't want to lose him. Didn't want things to be weird and lose our friendship because of it. Maybe if I ignored what happened, he would too. "I used Xosha's own powers against her and ashed her before she could kill you all. That's how we left things."

He winced, rubbing the back of his neck. "I said thanks." I waited for his dimples to make an appearance, but his smile didn't widen enough this time. I hummed in disappointment.

"Yeah, maybe staying away wasn't the best way to handle things," he added. "But I'm here now. Here to help in whatever way you need me to."

Anything. Anything to make him stay.

"Well," I started, considering all the things that were left to do. All the towns that needed to be fed and repaired, the prisoners still below our feet that awaited a fair trial, this fire in my veins that I desperately needed to learn to control. It occasionally swirled around hotly, waiting to see when I would allow it out of slumber again. "Actually, there is something I could use some help doing. Or finding rather." I chewed on the inside of my cheek, nervous. "I need help with—" I gestured at the room, "all this."

"We'll help you. With all of it."

"No, I mean, Enzo and Ara have been great, but..." I winced. "I need my brother."

Tynan stiffened, and I rushed out the rest before he could react how I knew he would. "I'm not a leader, Ty. I've been thinking about how Darya is in charge of two places, and how she doesn't want anything to do with one of them at the moment. She appointed a regent to deal with the ocean side of things. She's still in control, but her regent handles the communication with the merfolk for her."

"You want a mediator."

It wasn't quite that simple. "Sure."

"We can find you a regent in Elysian."

I repressed a sigh, realizing I'd have to give him the whole truth for him to be on board with this. "It's not just that. My whole life, my true identity has been kept from me. Liam deserves to know the truth about everything. About who he is and where his family comes from. He belongs here just as much as I do. And he would be so good at this. I looked up to him my entire childhood. I know he would be better at speaking to the subjects than I am. He'd be better at making them feel heard and safe."

"Did he make you feel heard and safe?"

I answered with a flat stare. "Don't."

Tynan pressed on, but wisely decided to leave Liam out of it. "Look at what you've done here already. On your first night, instead of getting sleep, you wrote a decree to outlaw slavery in Kalopsia. Do you know how many families have been reunited or given a fresh start because of you? The land has been restored. Elysian has hope for the first time in decades, all by your presence alone." It was true. Even the weeping willow in the back courtyard had regenerated by the time the sun set on that first day. "Elysian needs *you*, not Liam."

"I'll still be High Queen." I lifted my head as I said it. "I'm not running from anything ever again, not even this. I just want him by my side."

He chewed on his lip, considering it. I found it very distracting.

"Just humor me for a moment," I said, cutting into his thoughts. "If I can even figure out where he is, how long can I leave Elysian without hurting the land with my absence?"

His features were tense. "The land is extremely vulnerable right now," he said. "Considering everything, I wouldn't risk more than a day. Half a day even. It can probably hold on without you for a few hours before it realizes you're missing."

"I can do that," I said readily. "Just give me that half a day. Come with me and help me find him. And if we can't, I'll drop it forever."

Tynan watched me intently, debating if he wanted to argue with not just his friend, but now his High Queen.

"I promise," I added.

"You've thought about this a lot, haven't you?"

I nodded. Every night for the past week. "Don't you trust me?"

"Of course, I do."

"Then help me." It came out a half plea and for a moment, he hesitated. I wished he'd open his thoughts to me then, but it was a stone wall when I ventured there.

In truth, I didn't need another to go with me. I could travel there and back on my own just fine. But I didn't want to do this alone. I knew that seeing Liam again for the first time in six years would come with emotions I wasn't ready to unpack alone.

I willed him with my eyes to say yes, and while he thought, the memory of the best kiss I would ever receive in my life weighed on my lips. I pushed it down, along with the fire.

"Okay," he finally agreed. "Let's go find that brother of yours."

# ACKNOWLEDGMENTS

I can't believe I'm actually writing an acknowledgments page. I'm not sure I can even accurately put into words my immense gratitude for everyone involved, but I'll give it my best shot.

Firstly, thank you to every beta reader who cared enough to offer their time and feedback to this story. I'm so sorry you had to see this in its unpolished version, but thank you nonetheless for helping me get it to where it stands today. Jessica Taylor, for pointing out the small (but very important) details I missed. Jessica Papadopoulos and Samantha Barr, for being so immensely kind to me, always being on the ready to give honest feedback, and for hyping me up when I was feeling defeated.

To Dana and Brandon. Ugh. I don't even have to put down words for you to know, but I'm going to anyway. God so strategically placed you both in my life. Brandon, you may never read this book, but you've never doubted me. Your support means the world to me. Thanks for getting my good side in pictures, for always showing up, and for just being you. Dana, there is not another soul that exists in this world that is as pure as yours. God knew exactly what He was doing when He placed you in my dorm room all those years ago. My Anam Cara. I love you forever and ever and ever.

To Sydney Satterwhite (for visual purposes, I am currently climbing onto a rooftop somewhere and literally shouting my thanks for this one). The Wednesday Adams to my Enid Sinclair! The Jenna to my Sabrina. My critique partner and co-founder of #teamromanticize. My twin flame!! I'm so thankful for that first

Instagram message you sent me. It developed into more than I ever could have imagined, and I'm beyond blessed to have you in my corner. My life wouldn't be the same without your insight, your artwork, and your friendship. You're a gem.

I feel like someone giving a speech at the Oscars. Okay, okay... wrapping it up.

A special thanks to my team! Miranda Darrow, who edited this developmentally when it was only a manuscript in the querying process. Without your insight and direction, I don't think this would have ever seen the light of day, and it definitely wouldn't be as strong as the final product is. Thank you, thank you, thank you. To Heidi Shoham, who edited the grammar side of things... Please forgive me for my embarrassingly bad comma misusage. Stefanie Saw, for the brilliant cover. Virginia Allen, for bringing Elysian to life with its incredible map. Belle, for the stunning interior art. And Sydney (again) for the character portraits.

Special shout-out to Storygram Book Tours, Book of Matches Media, MTMC Tours, QP Book Tours, and Jess Taylor at The Reading Chamber for hosting Rise of the Ash Kingdom on their platforms during its debut.

Thank you to my family for your support, and a special thanks to my mom, who believed in me before I believed in myself.

To my children, who bring so much joy to even the most simple days. Everleigh, who was here for all of this journey. I'll never be able to thank you enough for the happiness you've filled my heart with, but I sure will try for the rest of my life. You make me a better person. Nathan, who was here for the publishing portion of this journey. A piece of me I didn't know was missing was filled when you were born. Thank you for being you. You're so special. You are peace and joy and light.

To my husband, Anthony, who has kept me constantly caffeinated with iced coffee throughout this entire process. Who has given me every ounce of time to write and edit and overthink and edit some more until I was satisfied with the day's work. For somehow helping me through countless plot holes and world-building issues, even despite me not letting you read any of it. Who has been supportive of any and every adventure I've taken on in the past eleven years. Thank you. Not many people are as blessed as I am when it comes to their spouse. I will always cherish us.

And the biggest thank you to God. For making me who I am. For making me a storyteller when I was being crafted. For sending me these scenes in bits and pieces of song lyrics and for fueling me with the passion and creativity to fill in the blanks.

# ABOUT THE AUTHOR

Elizabeth R. Olson doesn't remember a time when she wasn't writing stories. Even if most of it was poorly edited and never meant to see the light of day. Now, she gets to write (hopefully much better) stories for a living. Rise of the Ash Kingdom is her debut novel, with more soon to follow.

Currently living in Clayton, North Carolina, she is happiest when immersed in the pages of a heart-pounding book. When not reading or writing, she finds joy in a simple life. A daily raspberry white mocha (iced, of course), seeking out everyday magic with her two children, and an eternal season of autumn are all she asks for.